AN UNLIKELY
BRIDE FOR THE
BILLIONAIRE

BY
MICHELLE DOUGLAS

First Published in Great Britain 2016
By Mills & Boon, an imprint of HarperCollins*Publishers*
1 London Bridge Street, London, SE1 9GF

© 2016 Michelle Douglas

ISBN: 978-0-263-92007-9

23-0816

Our policy is to use papers that are natural, renewable and recyclable products and made from wood grown in sustainable forests. The logging and manufacturing processes conform to the legal environmental regulations of the country of origin.

Printed and bound in Spain
by CPI, Barcelona

Michelle Douglas has been writing for Mills & Boon since 2007, and believes she has the best job in the world. She lives in a leafy suburb of Newcastle, on Australia's east coast, with her own romantic hero, a house full of dust and books and an eclectic collection of sixties and seventies vinyl. She loves to hear from readers and can be contacted via her website: www.michelle-douglas.com.

To Amber and Anthony, and Jessica and Tim,
who are raising the next generation of
heroes and heroines with grace and style…
and a splendid sense of fun!

CHAPTER ONE

'BUT—' MIA STARED, aghast, at Gordon Coulter '—that's not my job!' She was a trainee field officer, not a trainee event manager.

Her stomach performed a slow, sickening somersault at the spiteful smile that touched his lips. Gordon was the council administrator in charge of Newcastle's parks and wildlife—her boss's boss and a petty bureaucrat to boot. Plum Pines Reserve fell under his control. And he'd made no secret of the fact that he'd love to get rid of her—that he was simply waiting for her to mess up so he could do exactly that.

She did her best to moderate her voice. 'I'm in charge of the weed extermination project that's to start on the eastern boundary. Veronica—' the reserve's ranger '—insists it's vital we get that underway as soon as possible. We're supposed to be starting today.'

'Which is why I've handed that project over to Simon.'

Every muscle stiffened in protest, but Mia bit back the objections pressing against the back of her throat. She'd worked ridiculously hard on fine-tuning that project, had gathered together an enthusiastic band of volunteers who didn't care one jot about her background. More exciting still, she and Veronica had planned to take a full botanical inventory of the area—a comprehensive project that had filled Mia with enthusiasm. And now she was to have no part in it.

'This isn't up for debate, Mia.'

Gordon pursed his lips, lifting himself up to his full paunchy height of five feet ten inches. If it was supposed to make him look impressive, it failed. It only drew her attention to the damp half-moons at the armpits of his business shirt.

'You have to understand that teamwork is vital in an area as poorly funded as ours. If you're refusing to assist the administrative team in their hour of need then perhaps this isn't the right organisation for you.'

She wanted to know where Nora was. She wanted to know why Simon hadn't been given *this* job instead of her.

'The Fairweathers will be here at any moment, so if you *are* refusing to assist…'

'Of course I'm not refusing.' She tried to keep her voice level. She couldn't afford to lose this job. 'I'm surprised you'd trust me with such an important assignment, that's all.'

His eyes narrowed. 'If you screw this up, Maydew, you'll be out on your ear.'

She didn't doubt that for a moment.

'Naturally Nora will take over once she returns.' His lips tightened. 'She assures me you're the only one who can possibly deputise in her stead.'

She bit back a sigh. Nora wanted her on the events team, claiming she was wasted as a field officer. Mia had plans, though, and they didn't involve being part of the events team.

Where was Nora?

She didn't ask. She refused to give Gordon the satisfaction of telling her it was none of her business. She'd ring Nora later and make sure she was okay.

The receptionist knocked on the office door. It was Nora's office, but Gordon co-opted it whenever he decided to work from Plum Pines rather than his office at Council Chambers.

'Mr Coulter? Mr Fairweather is here.'

'Send him in.'

Mia moved to the side of the desk—she hadn't been invited to sit—fighting the urge to move to the back of the room, where she'd be able to remain as unobtrusive as possible.

'Mr Fairweather, it's delightful to meet you!' Gordon moved forward, arm outstretched, greasy smile in place.

Mia repressed a shudder.

And then she glanced at Dylan Fairweather—and had to blink, momentarily dazzled by so much golden...*goldenness*. Dear Lord, the papers did Dylan Fairweather no justice whatsoever. Not that Mia spent much time reading the society pages, but even *she*—hermit that she was—knew that Dylan Fairweather was considered one of Australia's bright young things. Earlier in the year he'd been named one of Australia's Top Twenty Eligible Bachelors.

If steal-your-breath sex appeal was one of the criteria then Dylan Fairweather had that in spades! Too-long dark gold hair and sexy designer stubble coupled with a golden tan had Mia's fingers curling into her palms. At six feet two he towered over Gordon, his pale blue business shirt and sand-coloured chinos achieving a casual elegance Gordon had no hope of matching.

Nor did his clothes hide the breadth of his shoulders or the latent strength of powerful thighs. All that power and flaxen golden brilliance should have made him look terrifying—like a prowling lion. But it didn't. He looked...he looked like a prince out of a fairytale.

Mia tried to tear her gaze away, but couldn't. Never, in all of her twenty-five years, had she been in the presence of someone so physically perfect.. She remembered one of the women in prison describing how she'd felt when she'd first laid eyes on Vincent van Gogh's painting *The Starry Night*. That was how Mia felt now.

Swallowing, she shook herself, appalled at the way her heart raced, at the craving that clawed at her belly. Pulling in a breath, she reminded herself that she wasn't some primitive savage, controlled by greed and impetuous impulses. Not any more.

When Gordon had said she'd be taking care of the Fairweathers today, she'd been expecting a blushing bride and her aunt, maybe an attendant or two. She hadn't been expecting the bride's *brother*.

His pleasantries with Gordon exchanged, he turned to her and offered his hand with an easy, 'Dylan Fairweather.'

She took it automatically, appreciating the just-firm-enough grip and almost melting under the unexpected warmth of his smile.

You're not the melting type.

'Mia Maydew. It's nice to meet you. Carla is taking a call. She should only be a moment.'

'That's no problem at all.' Gordon ushered Dylan to a chair, frowning at Mia over his head.

Dear God! Had her paralysing preoccupation been evident for all to see? Heat climbed into her face. Brilliant. Just brilliant.

Gordon took his chair. He still didn't invite Mia to sit. 'Unfortunately Nora can't join us today. She sends her apologies. She was involved in a car accident on her way to work this morning.'

Mia couldn't prevent her involuntary intake of breath, or the way her hand flew to her abdomen, just below her breasts, to counter the way her stomach jumped. Startlingly brilliant blue eyes surveyed her for a moment, and while the brilliant colour might have the ability to distract a mere mortal, Mia sensed the shrewdness behind them.

Dylan Fairweather shifted ever so slightly on his chair. 'I hope she's okay.'

'Yes, yes, she's fine, but her car is apparently a write-off. I insisted she go to the hospital for a thorough examination, though.'

Mia closed her eyes briefly and let out a breath.

'Wise,' agreed Dylan—*Mr Fairweather*.

'In her stead—as a temporary measure, you understand—you'll have Mia here to run you through wedding options.

Anything you'd like to know—ask her. Anything you'd like to see—she'll show it to you. I promise that nothing will be too much trouble.'

Easy for him to say.

She straightened. It wasn't the Fairweathers' fault that Gordon had thrust her into the role of Assistant Events Manager. She'd helped Nora out before with weddings and corporate events. She'd do everything she could to answer the Fairweathers' questions and help Carla plan the wedding of her dreams.

'If you'd like to take it from here, Mia?'

'Certainly.' She forced a noncommittal smile to her face. 'If you'd just hand me the Fairweather file from the top drawer of the desk, I'll take Mr Fairweather through to the meeting room.'

She was tempted to laugh at the disgruntled expression that flitted across Gordon's face. Had he really thought she didn't know about the file? She'd helped Nora compile parts of it earlier in the week. Did he hate her so much that he'd risk a lucrative account, not to mention some seriously good publicity, to undermine her? The thought killed any urge to smile.

She had to counsel herself to take the file calmly, before leading Dylan Fairweather out of the office to the meeting room. Her pulse skittered and perspiration gathered at her nape. She preferred working with animals to people. Better yet, she liked working with plants. With over one hundred and seventy hectares of natural bushland to its name, it should have been relatively easy to avoid human contact at Plum Pines Reserve.

'Can I get you tea or coffee…maybe some water?' She gestured for Dylan to take a chair at the table, doing what she could to stop her fingers from shaking. This account had excited Nora enormously and, Gordon aside, Mia wanted to do her best for her boss.

From across the table Dylan eyed her closely, a frown in

his eyes, although his lips remained curved upwards in a pleasant smile. 'I think a carafe of water and three glasses would be an excellent idea.'

He thought *she* needed a drink of water? Dear Lord. She scurried away to fetch it. Did her nerves show that badly? She usually came across as a difficult study. She took a couple of deep breaths to compose herself before returning to the meeting room.

'Nora is a friend of yours?' he asked when she was seated, taking charge of the carafe and pouring a glass of water before pushing it across the table to her.

It hit her then that he'd misread her nerves as worry for the other woman. She hesitated. Would Nora consider Mia a friend? 'Nora is a close colleague. I like her a lot.'

'The news of her accident was a shock?'

She wasn't used to anyone being interested in her reactions. 'It was. I'm relieved it's not too serious.' When he continued to stare at her—which did nothing to slow her heart-rate—she forced her lips upwards. 'I'll call her later to check if there's anything she needs. It's kind of you to be so concerned. Now, let me show you the material Nora and I have gathered in relation to Ms Fairweather's wedding.'

'Please—you must call us Carla and Dylan.'

Must she? There was a certain protection afforded by the formality of Mr and Ms.

The customer is always right.

She bit back a sigh. If that were the case…

'Dylan.' She tested the name on her tongue. It emerged without any effort at all and tasted like her favourite brand of dark chocolate—flavoured with a bite of sea salt. His smile was her reward, making her forget the rest of her sentence.

'See…it wasn't so hard, was it—Mia?'

He made her name sound like a song.

He smiled. 'I can see why Carla requested you work on her wedding'

She opened her mouth and then closed it, blinking. 'I

think you've mistaken me for someone else. I'm afraid I don't know your sister, Mr Fair—uh... Dylan.'

He stared across at her, but in the end he merely nodded and let it go without challenge. It was as if someone had cut a string and released her.

She glanced down at the folder in an effort to collect herself. 'Do you know...?' She cleared her throat. 'Do you know where Carla would like the ceremony to take place?'

He glanced towards the door, as if hoping his sister would magically appear. 'Beside some lily pond. It's apparently where she and Thierry met.'

Right. Mia jotted a note down on her pad.

Blue eyes twinkled across the table at her when she looked up at him again. 'Aren't you going to gush about how romantic that is?'

Should she? Was gushing part of the job description?

He laughed as if he'd read that thought in her face, pointing a lean tanned finger at her. 'You, Ms Maydew, are *not* a romantic.'

He stared at her as if he knew her. It was utterly disconcerting. She had no intention of letting him know that, though.

She pointed her pen back at him. 'I *am*, however, an excellent worker.'

'Perfect.' His grin widened. 'You'll at least provide a port of sanity amid all the craziness.'

That made her lips twitch. She'd watched TV programs about Bridezillas. Was that what they had on their hands with Carla?

'Hallelujah!' He raised his hands heavenwards.

'What?'

'I finally managed to get a proper smile out of you.'

She stared at him, nonplussed. Why should he care one way or the other whether she smiled or not? Was smiling also part of the job description?

Darn it—it probably was! Give her animals and plants any day.

She forced her lips to curve upwards.

'Oh, dear me, no! On a scale of one to ten, that's not even going to score you a three.' He donned a mock commentator's voice. *'And Mia's smile has only scored a two point one from the Romanian judge!'*

She had to choke back a laugh.

He leant his elbows on the table. There was the whole width of the table between them, but somehow he seemed to bridge that distance without any effort at all. Maybe it was a combination of his height and breadth? She could make out the tiny laughter lines that fanned out from his eyes. She suspected Dylan laughed a lot. She noted the dusky eyelashes...ridiculously long and tipped with gold...and the firm fullness of his bottom lip. She'd bet he kissed a lot too. A pulse started up in the centre of her chest.

'I suspect, Mia Maydew, it'd be really something to make you laugh.'

She couldn't explain why, but she found herself jerking back as if he'd just propositioned her.

To cover her confusion, she folded her arms and narrowed her eyes. 'I have your number, Dylan Fairweather.' She used his full name in the same way he'd used hers. 'You're an incorrigible flirt. I suspect you can't help yourself.'

He raised his hands. 'Guilty as charged! But it's flirting without intent...just a bit of frivolous nonsense.'

His smile made her stomach tumble. 'Then why...?'

'Because it's fun.' His grin widened and she swore he had the devil in his eyes. 'Aren't you going to flirt back?'

She couldn't help it. She laughed.

Thank heavens! The woman *could* laugh.

Dylan sat back and let out a breath when the rather plain and schoolmistressy Mia momentarily transformed from uptight and ordinary-looking to mischievous imp. His gaze lingered on her mouth. He hadn't noticed how wide and generous it was earlier.

Since he'd witnessed her shock at learning of Nora's accident, and sensed her nerves at being thrust into the role of wedding co-ordinator, he'd wanted to put her at ease. Putting people at ease was his stock in trade. Mia might call it flirting, but it was nothing more than a bit of harmless fun designed to make her laugh and loosen up. And it had half worked—she'd laughed.

Having now seen Mia smile for real, though, he could see that she was neither plain nor schoolmistressy. It was just an attitude she cultivated. Interesting…

Nora had been ecstatic yesterday when he'd mentioned that they'd like Mia as part of their wedding team. Nora mightn't have known it, but she'd unwittingly supplied a glowing character reference for Mia. He sat back, resisting the urge to rub his eyes. He wanted everything associated with this wedding to be a joy for Carla. He meant to ensure it went without a hitch.

If only he could be certain the damn wedding should go ahead!

The walls of the glassed-in meeting room pressed in on him. He wanted to be outside and in the fresh air. *Now!* He wanted to be away from the fresh juniper berry scent of the woman opposite. It had his mind turning to black ski runs in St Moritz, with the wind tearing at his hair and the cold making him feel alive. Which was ridiculous. While he might be on leave, this was no holiday. Besides, if there'd been less frivolity in his life recently Carla might never have become embroiled with a man like Thierry.

Carla's happiness—that was what he had to focus on. 'Is the lily pond far? Can you show it to me?'

'You want to see the lily pond *now*?'

'Yes.'

'What about your sister?'

'She's on the phone to her intended. She could be hours. I'll text her so she'll know where to find us.'

Dutifully he pulled out his phone.

Mia taking me to lily pond. Meet there.

He held it out for her to see and then hit 'send'.

Without another word Mia led him out into the warm summer sunshine and he filled his lungs with eucalypt-scented air. The small office block sat on the edge of a rectangle of lush lawn that had to be at least two football fields long. Covered picnic tables marched down each of its sides, shaded by a variety of gum trees, plum pines and bottlebrush trees. The red blossoms of the bottlebrushes had attracted a flock of rainbow lorikeets which descended in a noisy colourful rush.

A peacock strutted through the nearest picnic shelter, checking for crumbs and leftovers, while a bush turkey raked through a nearby pile of leaves. All around the air was filled with birdcalls and the scent of warmed native grasses. Groups of people had gathered around the picnic tables and on blankets on the grass. He could hear children's laughter from the playground he glimpsed through the trees.

'This place is popular.'

She gestured that they should take a path to the left. 'It is.'

Her dark brown hair, pulled back into a severe ponytail, gleamed rich and russet in the bright light. She didn't wear a scrap of make-up. Not that she needed to. She had a perfect peaches and cream complexion that he hadn't appreciated under the strip lighting of the office.

He pulled his mind back to the matter at hand. 'Can we book the entire reserve for the wedding?'

'I'm afraid not. Plum Pines is a public park. What we *can* do, though, is rope off the area where your event is being held to keep the general public out.'

'Hmm...' He'd have to rethink the security firm he'd initially considered hiring. The wedding security would be a bigger job than he'd originally thought.

She glanced up, her gaze sharp. 'Is that going to be a problem?'

'Not if I hire a good security firm.'

'Let me know if you'd like any recommendations.' She led him across a bridge spanning a large pond. 'Officially the park is open from seven a.m. to seven p.m.'

He stared out at the expanse of water, noting several black swans sitting on the edge of the far bank. 'Is this the lily pond?'

'No, it's the duck pond.'

He glanced down into the water and blinked when a tortoise poked its small head out of the water. 'That…' He halted to point. 'That was…'

She glanced over the railing. 'A Common Longneck Tortoise. The pond is full of them.'

Hands on hips, he completed a full circle, taking in the surroundings. Plum Pines was undeniably pretty, and the native forest rising up all around them undeniably grand. He'd visited some of the most exotic places the world had to offer and yet he'd somehow missed experiencing what was in his own backyard.

'I can't believe we're in the middle of the second largest city in New South Wales. It feels as if we're in the middle of the bush.'

'Yes, we're very privileged.'

That was a rote reply if he'd ever heard one—trotted out for the benefit of visitors. What did Mia really think of the place? Did she love it or loathe it? Her lips were pursed into a prim line that had him itching to make her smile again.

'You'll need to apply to the council for an event licence that'll allow the wedding to extend beyond those hours. There shouldn't be any issue with that, though.'

She moved off again, with her no-nonsense stride, and

after another glance at where the tortoise had disappeared he set off after her.

'Have you had any weddings that *haven't* extended beyond seven p.m.?' All of the weddings he'd ever attended had kicked on into the wee small hours.

'There's been a trend for morning weddings with lunchtime receptions. So, yes.'

She was so serious. And literal. He found himself starting to laugh.

She glanced at him, a frown crinkling her forehead. 'What's so funny?'

'You're not so good at small talk, are you?'

Her face fell and she stuttered to a halt. 'You want small talk?'

That made him laugh again. 'How do you enforce the seven p.m. closing time?'

'We close the gates to the car parks. There's a hefty fine involved to have the gates opened. Our people, along with your security firm, will have a list of your guests' number plates so they can come and go as they please.'

'Right.'

'And, as Plum Pines is in the middle of suburbia, we don't get much foot traffic or many homeless people looking for a place to put up for the night.'

That was something, he supposed.

She consulted her notepad. 'Do you know how many guests the bride and groom are planning to invite?'

'Carla informs me that she wants "a small and intimate affair".'

That frown crinkled her brow again. 'Do you happen to know what your sister's idea of "small" might be?'

'I wouldn't have a clue.' He had no idea if Thierry came from a large family or not. The other man had closed up like a clam when Dylan had asked him about them. 'I can't say that I know what she means by "intimate" either.'

Mia nodded. 'I think we can guess that fairly accurately—it probably includes fairy lights strung all around the marquee and surrounding trees, white linen tablecloths with centrepieces involving ivy and candles, vintage china and a string quartet.'

'You don't sound like you approve.'

She swung to face him. 'Mr Fair— Dylan. It's not for me to approve or disapprove. It's Plum Pines' job to help Carla plan the wedding she wants.'

'But—' He broke off.

'What were you going to say?'

He read the thought that flashed through her eyes—*Gordon Coulter promised nothing would be too much trouble.*

'Dylan, I'll do my best to deliver whatever is needed.'

Her moss-green eyes stared back at him, earnest and steady, and he found himself needing to pull a breath of air into cramped lungs. 'I need you to be as committed to this wedding as Carla.'

'I'm committed—I can promise you that.' Her teeth worried at her bottom lip. 'But that's not what you meant, is it? You want me to be exuberant and…and bouncy.'

He winced, realising how absurd that sounded when uttered out loud. He just wanted to see her smile again. *That* was what this was all about—and it was pure nonsense on his part.

He rubbed his hand across his nape. 'I think of weddings and I think of joy and excitement and…and *joy.*'

He wanted Carla's life filled with joy—not just her wedding. A fist tightened about his chest. If Thierry hurt her he'd—

Mia moved into his field of vision, making him blink. 'There's a lot of behind-the-scenes work that needs doing to make a wedding successful.' She pointed her pen at him. 'Joy and excitement are all well and good, but I figure my job is to keep a level head.'

A level head? That was exactly what he needed.

'Don't you believe someone can be quietly enthusiastic?' she asked.

'Of course they can. I'm sorry.' He grimaced. 'It's the bride who's supposed to go loopy, right? Not her brother.'

One of those rare smiles peeped out, making his heart thump.

'You're excited for her.' Too soon she sobered again. 'I'm naturally quiet. It doesn't mean I'm not invested.'

'Whereas I'm naturally gregarious.' It was what made him so good at his job. 'I sometimes forget that not everyone else is.'

'Do you still want to see the lily pond?'

'Yes, please.' He spoke as gravely as she did. 'My seeing the lily pond is not dependent on you being exuberant.'

He could have sworn that her lips twitched—for the briefest of moments. It sent a rush of something warm and sweet surging through his veins. He was glad he'd had a chance to meet her on his own. Carla had spoken of her often enough to make his ears prick up. It had been a long time since Carla had made a new female friend.

The question he needed to answer now, though—was Carla more than just a job to Mia? He'd give his right arm for Carla to have a girlfriend with whom to plan her wedding. And whatever the two of them dreamed up—schemed up—he'd make happen.

When he glanced back he found Mia staring at a point beyond him. He swung around to see an emu enclosure... and an emu sitting on the ground in the dirt. He glanced back to find her chewing her lip. 'Is that emu okay?' They *did* sit down, right?

She hesitated. 'Do you mind...?' She gestured towards the fence.

'Not at all.'

'Hey, Charlie—come on, boy!' Mia rattled the fence and the emu turned to stare, but when he didn't otherwise move she pulled out her phone. 'Janis? It's Mia. Charlie is looking decidedly under the weather. Can you send someone out to check on him?' Her lips pressed together as she listened to the person at the other end. 'He's sitting down and not responding to my calls.' She listened some more. 'But—'

She huffed out a breath and he could see her mentally counting to five.

'Right. If that's the best you can do.' She snapped the phone shut and shoved it back into her pocket.

'You're worried about him?'

One slim shoulder lifted. 'Charlie's been hand-raised. He's a social bird. Normally he'd be over here, begging for a treat. Everyone who works here is fond of him.'

Dylan glanced across at the emu. 'You want to go and give him the once over?'

She glanced around, as if to check that no one had overheard him. 'Would you mind?'

'Not at all.'

'It should only take me a moment. I just want to make sure he doesn't have something caught around his legs. Discarded plastic bags are the bane of our existence—they seem to blow in from everywhere.'

'I don't mind at all.'

Besides, he wanted her full attention once Carla arrived. He wanted her focussed on wedding preparations—not worrying about Charlie the Emu.

She moved towards a gate in the fence and unlocked it with a key she fished out from one of the many pockets of her khaki cargo pants.

She glanced back at him apologetically. 'I have to ask you to remain on this side of the fence. It's actually against the law for me to take you in with me.'

'Believe me, I'm happy to stay on this side of the fence, but…' he glanced across at Charlie '…that emu is huge. What if he attacks you?'

He couldn't in all conscious just stand here and do nothing.

'He won't hurt me. I promise.'

'In that case I promise to stay on this side of the fence.'

Nevertheless, he found his heart pounding a little too hard as she slipped into the enclosure and made her way towards the giant bird. She ran a soothing hand down its neck, not in the least intimidated by its size. He reminded himself that she was trained to deal with these animals, but he didn't take his eyes from her.

Slipping her arms beneath the bird, she lifted it to its knees, and Dylan could see something wrapped tight around its ankles. The poor bird was completely tangled! He watched in admiration as she deftly unwound it, shoving the remnants into her pocket. The entire time she crooned soothingly to the emu, telling him what a good boy he was and how pretty he was. Charlie leaned into her as much as he could, trusting her completely.

Finally she placed her arms beneath him with a cheery, 'Up we come, Charlie.'

The emu gave a kind of strangled *beep* before a stream of something green and vicious-looking shot out of the back of him, splattering all over the front of Mia's shirt. Only then did the bird struggle fully to its feet and race off towards a water trough. Mia stumbled backwards, a comical look of surprise on her face. She turned towards Dylan, utterly crestfallen and…and covered in bird poop.

Dylan clapped a hand over his mouth to hold back a shout of laughter. *Don't laugh*! An awful lot of women he knew would have simply burst into tears. If he laughed and then she cried he'd have to comfort her…and then he'd end up with bird poop all over *him* too.

Mia didn't cry. She pushed her shoulders back and squelched back over to the gate in the fence with as much dignity as she could muster. Still, even *she* had to find it difficult to maintain a sense of dignity when she was covered in bird poop.

She lifted her chin, as if reading that thought in his face. 'As you can see, Charlie left me a little present for my pains.'

He swallowed, schooling his features. 'You did a very good deed, Mia.'

'The thing is, when an emu gets stressed, the stress can result in...' she glanced down at herself, her nose wrinkling '...diarrhoea.'

'God, I'm *so* glad those birds can't fly!'

The heartfelt words shot out of him, and Mia's lips started to twitch as if the funny side of the situation had finally hit her.

Dylan couldn't hold back his laughter any longer. 'I'm sorry, Mia. You deserve better, but the look on your face when it happened... It was priceless!'

She grinned, tentatively touching the front of her shirt. 'That rotten bird! Here I am, supposedly trying to impress you and your sister with our marvellous facilities...and now you're going to live in fear of projectile diarrhoea from the native animals!'

The sudden image that came to his mind made him roar until he was doubled over. Mia threw her head back and laughed right alongside him. She laughed with an uninhibited gusto that transformed her completely. He'd glimpsed the mischievous imp earlier, but now she seemed to come alive—as if her mirth had broken some dam wall—as if she were a desert suddenly blooming with wildflowers.

Dylan's heart surged against his ribs and for a moment all he could do was stare. 'You should do that more often, you know. Laugh. You're beautiful when you laugh.'

She glanced up at him, the laughter dying on her lips. Something in the air shimmered between them, making them both blink. Her gaze lowered momentarily to his lips, before she turned beetroot-red. Swinging away, she stumbled across to the tap that stood by the gate in the fence.

Heat pulsed through him. So...the serious Mia wasn't immune to his charms after all?

The next moment he silently swore. *Damn!* He deserved a giant kick to the seat of his pants. She'd accused him of flirting earlier—but he hadn't meant to give her the wrong impression. He didn't want her thinking anything could happen between them. All flirtation and teasing on his part was entirely without intent.

She knelt at the tap and scrubbed at her shirt with a piece of rag. She must keep a veritable tool shed of handiness in those cargo pants of hers.

He watched in silence as she washed the worst of the mess from her shirt. 'I have a handkerchief if you need it.'

'Thank you, but I think this is the best I'm going to manage until I can change my shirt. Shall we continue on to the lily pond?'

'Yes, please.'

She gestured towards the path. 'Do you mind if I ring the office to give them an update on Charlie?'

'Not at all.'

And just like that they withdrew back into reserved professionalism. But something new pounded through Dylan— a curiosity that hadn't been there before. What an intriguing paradox Mia was proving to be…a fascinating enigma.

Which you don't have time for.

With a sigh, he pushed thoughts of Mia from his mind and forced his attention back to the impending wedding. He had to focus on what really mattered. He couldn't let Carla down—not when she needed him.

CHAPTER TWO

THEY REACHED THE lily pond two minutes later. The moment Dylan clapped eyes on the enchanting glade he understood why Carla had fallen in love with it. True to its name, large green lily pads decorated a small but picturesque body of oval water. Native trees and shrubs curved around three of its sides. The fourth side opened out to a large circle of green lawn.

Mia pointed to that now. 'This area is large enough for our medium-sized marquee, which holds sixty guests comfortably. That leaves the area behind for the caterers to set up their tents and vans for the food.'

Carla chose that moment to come rushing up—which was just as well, as Dylan had found himself suddenly in danger of getting caught up on the way Mia's wet shirt clung to her chest.

Carla grinned at Mia—'Surprise!'—before taking Dylan's arm and jumping from one foot to the other. 'Isn't this just the most perfect spot?'

He glanced down at her—at her smile made radiant with her newfound happiness. 'It's lovely,' he agreed, resolve solidifying in his gut. This wedding had come out of left field, taking him completely by surprise. But if this was what Carla truly wanted, he meant to create the perfect wedding for her. 'Where's Thierry?'

A cloud passed across her face. 'Something's come up. He can't make it.'

That was the problem. Thierry. Dylan didn't like the man.

His sister had suffered enough misery in her life, and Dylan had every intention of protecting her from further heartache.

Carla moved towards Mia. 'Please tell me you're not cross with me.'

'So…you're not really Carly Smith, frequent visitor and keen student of environmentalism?'

Carla shook her head.

Mia glanced down at her notepad. 'With your background, I imagine you need to be careful with your privacy.'

Carla winced. 'Please tell me you don't hate me. You've been so kind. I love shadowing you when you're on duty for the wildlife displays. You never talk down to me or treat me like I'm stupid. Oh!' she added in a rush. 'And just so you know, I really *do* have a keen interest in the environment and conservation.'

Mia smiled. 'Of course I don't hate you.'

That smile made Dylan's skin tighten. When she smiled she wasn't plain. And when she laughed she was beautiful.

He pushed those thoughts away. They had no bearing on anything. Her smile told him what he needed to know—Mia genuinely liked his sister. *That* was what mattered.

'Right.' Mia consulted her notepad. 'I want to hear every tiny detail you have planned for this wedding.'

'Hasn't Dylan told you *anything*?'

Mia glanced at him. 'We didn't want to start without you.'

That was unexpectedly diplomatic.

He stood back while the pair started discussing wedding preparations, jumping from one topic to the next as if it made utterly logical sense to do so. He watched them and then shook his head. Had he really thought Carla needed exuberance from Mia? Thank heaven Mia had seen the wisdom in not trying to fake it. He silently blessed her tact in not asking where Mia's maid of honour or bridesmaids or any female relative might be too.

Carla didn't have anyone but him.

And now Thierry.

And Mia in the short term.

He crossed his fingers and prayed that Thierry would finally give Carla all that she needed…and all that she deserved.

Mia spent two hours with Carla and Dylan, though Dylan rarely spoke now Carla was there. She told herself she was glad. She told herself that she didn't miss his teasing.

Except she did. A little.

Which told her that the way she'd chosen to live her life had a few flaws in it.

Still, even if he had wanted to speak it would have been difficult for him to get a word in, with Carla jumping from topic to topic in a fever of enthusiasm.

She was so different from Carly Smith, the wide-eyed visitor to the park that Mia had taken under her wing. She took in the heightened colour in Carla's cheeks, the way her eyes glittered, how she could barely keep still, and nodded. Love was *exactly* like that and Mia wanted no part of it *ever again*.

Carla spoke at a hundred miles an hour. She cooed about the colour scheme she wanted—pink, of course—and the table decorations she'd seen in a magazine, as well as the cake she'd fallen in love with. She rattled off guest numbers and seating arrangements in one breath and told her about the world-class photographer she was hoping to book in the next. Oh, and then there was the string quartet that was apparently *'divine'*.

She bounced from favours and bouquets to napkins and place settings along with a million other things that Mia hastily jotted down, but the one thing she didn't mention was the bridal party. At one point Mia opened her mouth to ask, but behind his sister's back Dylan surreptitiously shook his head and Mia closed it again.

Maybe Carla hadn't decided on her attendants yet. Mia suspected that the politics surrounding bridesmaid hierarchy could be fraught. Especially for a big society wedding.

Only it wasn't going to be big. It was going to be a very select and exclusive group of fifty guests. Which might mean that Carla didn't want a large bridal party.

Every now and again, though, Carla would falter. She'd glance at her brother and without fail Dylan would step in and smooth whatever wrinkle had brought Carla up short, and then off she would go again.

Beneath Carla's manic excitement Mia sensed a lurking vulnerability, and she couldn't prevent a sense of protectiveness from welling through her. She'd warmed to Carly—Carla—the moment she'd met her. For all her natural warmth and enthusiasm she had seemed a little lost, and it had soothed something inside Mia to chat to her about the programmes Plum Pines ran, to talk to her about the animals and their daily routines.

As a rule, Mia did her best *not* to warm towards people. She did her best not to let them warm towards her either. But to remain coolly professional and aloof with Carla—the way she'd tried to be with Dylan—somehow seemed akin to kicking a puppy.

While many of her work colleagues thought her a cold and unfeeling witch, Mia *didn't* kick puppies. She didn't kick anyone. Except herself—mentally—on a regular basis.

'Can I come back with Thierry tomorrow and go over all this again?'

Why hadn't the groom-to-be been here *today*?

'Yes, of course.'

Hopefully tomorrow Nora would be back to take over and Mia would be safely ensconced on the reserve's eastern boundary, communing with weeds.

Carla glanced at her watch. 'I promised Thierry I'd meet

him for lunch. I have to run.' She turned to her brother. 'Dylan…?' Her voice held a note of warning.

He raised his hands, palms outwards. 'I'll sort everything—I promise. Mia and I will go back to the office and thrash it all out.'

Mia's chest clenched. Thrash what out? She didn't have the authority to thrash *anything* out.

She must have looked crestfallen, because Dylan laughed. 'Buck up, Mia. It'll be fun.' He waggled his eyebrows.

Mia rolled her eyes, but she couldn't crush the anticipation that flitted through her.

'I'll buy you a cup of coffee and a blueberry muffin.'

His grin could melt an ice queen.

Lucky, then, that she was made of sterner stuff than ice.

'You'll do no such thing.' She stowed her notepad in her back pocket as they headed back towards the main concourse. 'Gordon Coulter would be scandalised. All refreshments will be courtesy of Plum Pines.'

During the last two hours they'd moved from the lily pond back to the office, to pore over brochures, and then outside again to a vacant picnic table, where Carla had declared she wanted to drink in the serenity. Now, with many grateful thanks, Carla moved towards the car park while Mia led Dylan to the Pine Plum's café.

He grinned at the cashier, and Mia didn't blame the woman for blinking as if she'd been temporarily blinded.

'We'll have two large cappuccinos and two of those.' He pointed at the cupcakes sitting beneath a large glass dome before Mia had a chance to speak.

'You mean to eat two cupcakes and drink two mugs of coffee?' She tried to keep the acerbity out of her voice.

'No.' He spoke slowly as if to a child. 'One coffee and one cake are yours.'

Mia glanced at the cashier. 'Make that one large cappuccino, one pot of tea and *one* cupcake, thank you. It's to go on Nora's events account.'

Without further ado she led him to a table with an out-
look over the duck pond.

'You're not hungry?' he asked.

She was ravenous, but she'd brought her lunch to work,
expecting to be stranded on the eastern boundary, and she
hated waste. 'I'm not hungry,' she said. It was easier than
explaining that in Gordon Coulter's eyes the events account
didn't extend to buying her any food. 'Besides, I don't have
much of a sweet tooth.'

She frowned, unsure why she'd added that last bit.

For a moment he looked as if he were waging an internal battle with himself, but then he folded his arms on the
table and leaned towards her, his eyes dancing. 'Are you
telling me, Mia...?'

She swallowed at the way he crooned her name, as if it
were the sweetest of sweet things.

'...that you don't like cake?'

He said it with wide eyes, as if the very idea was scandalous. He was teasing her again. She resisted the almost
alien urge to tease him back.

'I didn't say I didn't like it. It's just not something I ever
find myself craving.'

His mouth kinked at one corner. Mia did her best to look
away.

'Now I have to discover what it is you *do* crave.'

How could he make that sound so suggestive?

'Cheesecake? Ice cream?'

She narrowed her eyes. 'Why do I get the feeling you're
trying to find something to use as a bribe?'

'Chocolate?'

Oh. He had her there. 'Chocolate is in a class of its own.'

He laughed, and something inside her shifted. *No shifting!* She had to remain on her guard around this man. He'd
called her beautiful and something in her world had tilted.
She had no intention of letting that happen again.

'You made my sister very happy today. From the bottom of my heart, thank you.'

It was the last thing she'd expected him to say. 'I... I was just doing my job.'

'It was more than that, and we both know it.'

She didn't want it to be more. This was just a job like any other. 'Naturally Carla is excited. I enjoyed discussing her plans with her.'

To her surprise, she realised she was speaking nothing less than the truth.

Their order was set in front of them. When the waitress left Dylan broke off a piece of cupcake, generously topped with frosting, and held it out to her. 'Would you like a taste?'

Unbidden, hunger roared through her. For the briefest of moments she was tempted to open her mouth and let him feed her the morsel. Her throat dried and her stomach churned. On the table, her hands clenched to fists.

She choked out a, 'No, thank you,' before busying herself with her tea.

Why now? Why should a man have such an effect on her *now*? In the last ten months she'd been asked out on dates... the occasional volunteer had tried to flirt with her...but nothing had pierced her armour.

None of them looked like Dylan Fairweather.

True. But was she really so shallow that someone's looks could have such an impact?

When she glanced back up she saw Gordon Coulter, glaring at her from the café's doorway. Had he seen Dylan offer her the bite of cake? *Great. Just great.*

She shuffled her mantel of professionalism back around her. 'Now, you better tell me what it is you promised Carla you'd sort out. It sounded ominous.'

He popped the piece of cake into his mouth and closed his eyes in bliss as he chewed. 'You have no idea what you're missing.'

And she needed to keep it that way.

She tried to stop her gaze lingering on his mouth.

His eyes sprang open, alive with mischief. 'I bet you love honey sandwiches made with the softest of fresh white bread.'

She had to bite her inner lip to stop herself from laughing. 'Honey makes my teeth ache.'

The man was irrepressible, and it occurred to her that it wasn't his startling looks that spoke to her but his childish sense of fun.

'Ha! But I nearly succeeded in making you laugh again.'

She didn't laugh, but she did smile. It was impossible not to.

Mia didn't do fun. Maybe that was a mistake too. Maybe she needed to let a little fun into her life and then someone like Dylan wouldn't rock her foundations so roundly.

He made as if to punch the air in victory. 'You should do that more often. It's not good for you to be so serious all the time.'

His words made her pull back. She knew he was only teasing, but he had no idea what was good for her.

She pulled her notepad from her pocket and flipped it open to a new page. 'Will you *please* tell me what it is you promised Carla you'd take care of?'

He surveyed her as he took a huge bite of cake. She tried not to fidget under that oddly penetrating gaze.

'Don't you ever let your hair down just a little?'

'This is my job. And this—' she gestured around '—is my place of employment. I have a responsibility to my employer to not "let my hair down" on the job.' She tapped her pen against the notepad. 'I think it's probably worth mentioning that you aren't my employer's only wedding account either.'

She spoke gently, but hoped he sensed the thread of steel beneath her words. There also were cages that needed cleaning, animals that needed feeding and logbooks to fill out. They weren't all going to get magically done while Dylan lingered over coffee and cake.

And it didn't matter how much he might temporarily fill her with an insane desire to kick back and take the rest of the day off—that wasn't going to happen.

'Ouch.' He said it with a good-natured grin. 'But you're right. Carla and I have taken up enough of your time for one day. Especially as we'll be back tomorrow.'

He was coming too? She tried to ignore the way her heart hitched.

'Mia, do you know what line of work I'm in?'

Even she, who'd spent most of her adult life living under a rock, knew what Dylan Fairweather did for a living. 'You created and run Fairweather Event Enterprises.' More widely known as Fairweather Events or FWE. Dylan had made his name bringing some of the world's most famous, not to mention *notorious*, rock acts to Australia.

Under his direction, Dylan's company had produced concerts of such spectacular proportions they'd gone down in rock history. His concerts had become a yardstick for all those following.

FWE had been in charge of last year's sensationally successful charity benefit held in Madison Square Garden in New York. He was regularly hired by royalty to oversee national anniversary celebrations, and by celebrities for their private birthday parties and gala events. Dylan Fairweather was a name with a capital N.

'The thing is…' He shuffled towards her, his expression intent now rather than teasing. 'I know that Plum Pines has its own events team, but *I* want to be the person running this particular show.'

Very slowly, she swallowed. 'By *"this particular show"*, I take it you're referring to Carla's wedding?'

He nodded.

Her heart thumped. Nora would be disappointed.

'I want to do this for Carla,' he continued, fully in earnest now. 'The only thing I can give her that's of any worth is my time. You have to understand it's not that I don't trust the Plum Pines staff, it's that I want to give my sister some-thing that'll actually *mean* something to her—something she can cherish forever.'

Mia almost melted on the spot. To have someone who cared about you so much that they'd go to such lengths… That was—

'Mia?'

She started. 'I'm afraid I don't have the kind of clout to authorise an arrangement like that. But I'll present your case to Nora and Mr Coulter. Please be assured they'll do every-thing they can to accommodate your and Carla's wishes.' She bit her lip. 'They may have some additional questions that they'd like to ask you.' Questions *she* lacked the exper-tise and foresight to ask.

He immediately slid his business card across the table to her. 'They can contact me at any time.'

She picked it up. It was a simple card on good-quality bond, with embossed lettering in dark blue—a deeper and less interesting shade than his eyes.

He slid another card across the table to her. 'Would you write down your number for me, Mia?'

She dutifully wrote down the Plum Pines office number, along with Nora's work number.

He glanced at it and his lips pursed. 'I was hoping for *your* number.'

Her hand shook as she reached for her tea. 'Why?'

'Because I think you could be an ally. You, I believe, ap-prove of my plan to be Carla's wedding co-ordinator.'

She hesitated. 'I think it's a lovely idea.' Surely it couldn't hurt to admit that much? 'But I think you ought to know that I have very little influence here.'

'I think you're selling yourself short.'

'If you want to speak to me directly, ring the office and ask them to page me.' She couldn't believe she'd told him to do that, but she couldn't find it in herself to regret the offer either.

For a moment she thought he'd press the matter. Instead he stood and held out his hand. 'Until tomorrow, then, Mia.'

She stood too and shook it, eager to be away from him. 'Goodbye, Dylan.'

She didn't tell him that in all likelihood she wouldn't see him tomorrow. Funny how suddenly the eastern boundary didn't seem as exciting a prospect as it had earlier in the day.

She'd barely settled down in the meeting room with the office laptop, to type up her copious notes for Nora, when the receptionist tapped on the glass door.

'Mr Coulter wants to see you, Mia.'

To grill her about how things had gone with the Fair-weathers, no doubt. She'd have rather discussed it all with Nora first, but she couldn't very well refuse to speak to him.

Taking a deep breath, she knocked on his door, only entering when he bellowed, 'Come in.'

She left the door ajar. She didn't fully trust Gordon Coulter. 'You wanted to see me?'

'Yes.'

He didn't invite her to sit. The smile he sent her chased ice down her spine.

'It's my very great pleasure to inform you, Ms Maydew, that you're fired. Effective immediately.'

The room spun. Mia's chest cramped. She couldn't lose this job. It was all that she had. Her fingers went cold. She *needed* this job!

'You're terminating my contract? But…*why?*'

Dylan stood on the threshold of Gordon Coulter's office, his head rocking back at the words he heard emerging from the other side of the door.

Gordon Coulter was *firing* Mia?

'Your behaviour with Dylan Fairweather today was scandalous and utterly inappropriate. You're not here to make sexual advances towards our clients. You're here to perform your duties as efficiently and as capably as possible—a duty that's obviously beyond you and your bitch-on-heat morals.'

Darkness threatened the edges of Dylan's vision. Mia hadn't made one inappropriate advance towards him—not one! His hands curled into fists. A pity the same couldn't be said for him towards her. He hadn't been able to resist flirting with her in the café—just a little bit. He hadn't been able to resist making her laugh again.

This was *his* fault. How could he have been so careless as to put her in this position?

Gordon continued to wax lyrical on a list of Mia's imaginary faults and Dylan's insides coiled up, tight and lethal. Gordon Coulter was a pompous ass!

'But even if I was prepared to overlook all that,' Gordon continued, his tone clearly saying that he had no intention of doing so, 'I refuse to disregard the fact that when you entered the emu enclosure you put the safety of a member of the public at risk.'

No way, buddy!

Dylan backed up two steps and then propelled himself forward with a cheery, 'Knock-knock!' before bursting into the office.

Two sets of eyes swung to him. Mia's face was ashen. Guilt plunged through him like a serrated-edge knife.

You're nothing but a trust fund baby without substance or significance.

As true as that might be, it meant that he knew how to act entitled and high-handed. He used that to his advantage now, striding into the room as if he owned it and everything inside it.

'You moved very quickly to bring my proposal to the attention of your superiors, Mia. I can't tell you how much I appreciate it.'

He took a seat across from Gordon, making himself completely at home.

'I hope you realise what a gem you have here, Gordon.'

He pulled Mia down to the seat beside him. How *dared* Gordon leave her standing like some recalcitrant child deserving of punishment and castigation? 'Have you finished telling Gordon about my proposal, Mia?'

'Um…no, not yet.'

She swallowed and he saw how valiantly she hauled her composure back into place. *Atta girl*!

'I'm afraid I haven't had a chance.'

'Oh, before I forget—' Dylan turned back to Gordon '—my sister and I will be returning tomorrow with Thierry. If he approves our plans, and if you accept my proposal, then we'll be booking Plum Pines as Carla and Thierry's wedding venue.'

Dollar signs all but flashed in Gordon's eyes. 'That's splendid news!'

'Carla has requested that Mia be available for tomorrow's meeting. I'm sure that won't be a problem.'

'Well, I—'

'Now to my proposal…' he continued, making it obvious that he took Gordon's agreement for granted. He saw Mia bite her lip, as if to hold back a laugh. The tightness in his chest eased a fraction.

'While I understand that Plum Pines has a talented and capable events team, I want to be completely in charge of Carla's wedding preparations—bringing in my own people, et cetera. I understand this isn't how Plum Pines normally operates, but if I promise to acquire all the necessary licenses and, as a show of gratitude, donate…say…a hundred thousand dollars to the Plum Pines Nature Fund, I was hoping you might make an exception.'

Gordon's fleshy mouth dropped open. He hauled it back into place. 'I'm sure we can find a way to accommodate such a reasonable request from such a generous benefactor.'

Dylan rubbed his hands together. 'Excellent.'

Gordon Coulter was ridiculously transparent. Rumour had it he was planning to run for mayor next year. A donation as sizable as Dylan's would be a real feather in his cap. Dylan just hoped the good people of Newcastle were smart enough not to elect such a small-minded bully to office.

He made a note to donate a large sum to Gordon's opponent's campaign.

'If there's any further way we can assist you, don't hesitate to ask. We're here to provide you with the very best service we can.'

'Well, now that you mention it… Carla would like Mia as her official liaison between FWE and Plum Pines.'

Gordon's face darkened. 'Mia doesn't have the necessary training. We can provide you with a far better level of service than that, and—'

'It's non-negotiable, I'm afraid.' He spoke calmly. 'If there's no Mia there'll be no Fairweather wedding at Plum Pines—and, sadly, no hundred-thousand-dollar donation.'

It was as simple as that, and Gordon could take it or leave it. If he refused to let Mia act as liaison then Dylan would whisk her away from Plum Pines and find a position for her in his own organisation. He was always on the lookout for good people.

In fact, poaching her was a damn fine plan.

Gordon wouldn't pass on it, though. Dylan knew his type too well.

'If you're happy with Mia's limited experience…' he began, in that pompous fashion.

'Supremely so.'

'I'll have to insist that she consult with Nora closely,' he blustered, in an attempt to save face.

'Absolutely.'

Gordon swallowed a few times, his jowls quivering. 'In that case I'll raise no objections.'

Dylan leant back in his chair. 'Excellent.'

Mia leaned forward in hers, her dark gaze skewering Gordon to the spot. 'And our earlier conversation…?'

His mouth opened and closed before he shuffled upright

in his seat. 'In the light of these…new developments, any further action will be suspended—pending your on-the-job performance from here on in.'

Very slowly she leaned back. Dylan silently took in the way her fingers opened and closed around each other. Eventually she nodded. 'Very well.'

Dylan stood. 'I understand you're a busy man, Gordon, so I won't take up any more of your valuable time. Mia…' He turned to her and she shot to her feet. 'I forgot to give you Carla's mobile number. You're going to need it. I'm afraid she'll be leaving you messages day and night.'

'That won't be an issue,' Gordon inserted. 'Mia understands that here at Plum Pines our clients are our priority. She'll be at your sister's beck and call twenty-four-seven.'

Dylan barely restrained himself from reciting the 'Maximum Ordinary Hours of Employment' section of the *New South Wales Industrial Relations Act*. Instead he gestured for Mia to precede him out through the door.

'Lead me to your trusty notepad.'

He closed the door behind them and Mia didn't speak until they were safely ensconced in the meeting room.

She swung to him. 'You did that on purpose, didn't you? You overheard him trying to fire me so you jumped in and saved my job.'

His chest expanded at the way she looked at him—as if he'd ridden in and saved the day.

She pressed a hand to her chest. 'I think I just fell a little bit in love with you.'

She was the strangest mix of seriousness and generosity he'd ever come across. And totally adorable to boot.

He leaned towards her, but she took a step backwards.

'Sorry, I shouldn't have said that. It was a stupid thing to say. I only meant I was grateful—*very* grateful—for you coming to my defence like you did.'

'You're welcome. Gordon is a pompous ass.'

'A pompous ass who has the power to terminate my traineeship whenever he sees fit.'

'He'd need to show good cause in the Industrial Relations Court. Don't you forget that. In fact—' he widened his stance '—why don't you forget Gordon and Plum Pines and come and work for *me*?'

The beginnings of a smile touched her lips. It made his pulse beat that little bit harder.

'I don't believe I have enough…*exuberance* for your line of work, Dylan.'

'I was wrong about that. You're perfect.'

'No, I'm not!' Her voice came out tart. Too tart.

He frowned. 'I meant that your work ethic is perfect. Your customer service skills are impeccable.' That was *all* he'd meant.

She swallowed before gesturing for him to take a seat. 'If you want me working so closely with you and Carla then there's something you need to know about me.'

He sat in the chair at the head of the table. 'I know all I need to know.'

She fixed him with that compelling gaze of hers, but for the life of him he couldn't read her expression. She took the chair immediately to his left, gripping her hands together until her knuckles turned white.

'I'd rather be the one to tell you than for you to hear it from other sources.'

He straightened. What on earth…? 'I'm listening.'

He watched the compulsive bob of her throat as she swallowed. Her hands gripped each other so tightly he was sure she'd cut off the blood supply to her fingers if she weren't careful.

'Ten months ago I was released from jail after serving a three-year prison sentence for committing fraud. I think it's only fair that you know I'm an ex-convict.'

CHAPTER THREE

MIA WAITED WITH a growing sense of dread for Dylan's face to close and for him to turn away.

His open-mouthed shock rang through her like a blow, but his face didn't close. He didn't turn away.

His frown did deepen, though, and she could read the thoughts racing behind the vivid blue of his eyes.

'No,' she said, holding his gaze. 'I wasn't wrongfully convicted, there were no mitigating circumstances.' She swallowed. 'Unless you want to count the fact that I was young and stupid.'

And utterly in thrall to Johnnie Peters. So in love she'd have done anything he'd asked of her. So in love she *had* done anything he'd asked of her.

'You're not going to tell me any more than that?'

Curiosity sharpened his gaze, but it wasn't the kind of avid, voyeuristic curiosity that made her want to crawl under a rock. It held a warmth and sympathy that almost undid her.

Swallowing again, she shook her head. 'It's sordid and unpleasant and it's in the past. According to the justice system, I've paid my debt to society. I won't ever steal again. I'll never break the law again. But I understand that in light of these circumstances my word isn't worth much. I'll completely understand if you'd prefer to deal with Nora rather than with me.'

He didn't say anything.

'You don't need to worry about my job. You've done enough to ensure I won't be fired…at least, not this week.' She'd aimed for levity, but it fell flat.

He lifted his chin. 'I meant what I said—come and work for me.'

She realised now what she'd known on a subconscious level after only ten minutes in his company—Dylan Fairweather was a good man.

'I appreciate the offer, I really do, but besides the fact that you don't know me—'

'I know you have a good work ethic. If the way you've treated Carla is anything to go by, where clients are concerned nothing is too much trouble for you. They're valuable assets in an employee.'

'According to Gordon I have a problem with authority.'

He grinned, and leaned in so close she could smell the nutmeg warmth of his skin. 'That's something we have in common, then.'

How was it possible for him to make her laugh when they were having such a serious conversation? She sobered, recalling her earlier impulsive, *I think I just fell a little bit in love with you*. She should never have said it. Instinct warned her that Dylan could wreak havoc on her heart if she let him.

She couldn't let him. She wasn't giving *any* man that kind of power over her again.

She pulled in a breath. 'I was fortunate to be awarded this traineeship. The opportunity was given to me in good faith and I feel honour-bound to make the most of it.'

'Admirable.'

It wasn't admirable at all. She needed a job—a way to earn a living. For the two-year tenure of her traineeship she'd be in paid employment. Maybe at the end of that time she'd have proved herself worthy and someone would take a chance on employing her. She needed a way to support herself. After what she'd done she couldn't ask the welfare system to support her.

'Do you have a passion for conservation?'

'Conservation is an important issue.'

'That's not the same thing,' he pointed out.

Passion was dangerous. She'd done all she could to excise it from her life. Besides, busying herself with weed extermination programmes, soil erosion projects, and koala breeding strategies—plants, dirt and animals—meant she had minimal contact with people.

And as far as she was concerned that was a *very* good thing.

'Here.' He pulled a chocolate bar from his pocket. 'This is the real reason I came back to the office.'

Frowning, she took it, careful not to touch him as she did so.

'You said chocolate belonged in a class of its own and…'

He shrugged, looking a little bit embarrassed, and something inside her started to melt.

No melting!

'I wanted to thank you for your patience with both Carla and me today.'

'It's—'

'I know—it's your job, Mia.'

Dear Lord, the way he said her name…

'But good work should always be acknowledged. And…' An irrepressible smile gathered at the corner of his mouth. 'I fear more of the same will be asked of you tomorrow.'

It took a moment for his words to sink in. 'You mean…?'

'I mean we want *you*, Mia. Not Nora. I want everything associated with this wedding to be a joy for Carla. She likes you. And that's rarer than you might think.' He suddenly frowned. 'How much will taking charge of this affect your traineeship? Will I be creating a problem for you there?'

He was giving her an out. If she wanted one. *If…*

She pulled in a breath. 'The wedding is nine months away, right?'

He nodded.

Being Carla's liaison wouldn't be a full-time job. Very slowly she nodded too. 'That leaves me plenty of time to continue with my fieldwork and studies.'

If it weren't for Dylan she wouldn't have a job right now *or* a chance to finish her traineeship. She owed him. *Big-time.* She made a resolution then and there to do all she could to make Carla's wedding a spectacular success.

Her gaze rested on the chocolate bar he'd handed to her earlier. She suddenly realised how she could tacitly thank him right now. Without giving herself time to think, she ripped off the wrapper and bit into it.

'I'm ravenous. And this is *so* good.'

As she'd known he would, he grinned in delight that his gift had given her pleasure. She closed her eyes to savour the soft milky creaminess, and when she opened them again she found his gaze fastened on her lips, the blue of his eyes deepening and darkening, and her stomach pitched.

She set the chocolate to the table and wiped damp palms down her trousers. 'I… This is probably a stupid thing to raise…'

He folded his arms. 'Out with it.'

'I don't believe you have any interest in me beyond that of any employer, but after what Gordon just accused me of…'

She couldn't meet his eyes. The thing was, Gordon had recognised what she'd so desperately wanted to keep hidden—that she found Dylan attractive. *Very* attractive. He'd woken something inside her that she desperately wanted to put back to sleep.

'I just want to make it clear that I'm not in the market for a relationship. *Any* kind of relationship—hot and heavy or fun and flirty.'

She read derision in his eyes. But before she could dissolve into a puddle of embarrassment at his feet she realised the derision was aimed at himself—not at her.

'No relationships? Noted.' He rolled his shoulders. 'Mia, I have a tendency to flirt—it's a result of the circles I move in—but it doesn't mean anything. It's just supposed to be a bit of harmless fun. My clients like to feel important and, as *they* are important to me, I like to make them feel valued. I plan celebrations, parties, and it's my job to make the entire process as enjoyable as possible. So charm and a sense of fun have become second nature to me. If I've given you the wrong impression...'

'Oh, no, you haven't!'

'For what it's worth, I'm not in the market for a relationship at the moment either.'

She glanced up.

Why not?

That's no concern of yours.

Humour flitted through his eyes. 'But what about friendship? Do you have anything against that?'

That made her smile. People like Dylan didn't become friends with people like her. Once the wedding was over she'd never see him again.

'I have nothing whatsoever against friendship.' She'd sworn never again to steal or cheat. A little white lie, though, didn't count. Did it...?

Thierry Geroux, Carla's fiancé, was as dark and scowling as Carla and Dylan were golden and gregarious. Mia couldn't help but wonder what on earth Carla saw in him.

She pushed that thought away. It was none of her business.

As if he sensed the direction of her thoughts, Thierry turned his scowl on her. She wanted to tell him not to bother—that his scowls didn't frighten *her*...she'd been scowled at by professionals. She didn't, of course. She just sent him one of the bland smiles she'd become so adept at.

'Do you have any questions, Mr Geroux?' He'd barely spoken two words in the last hour.

'No.'

'None?' Dylan double-checked, a frown creasing his brow.

'Stop bouncing,' Thierry said in irritation to Carla, who

clung to his arm, shifting her weight from one leg to the other.

'But, Thierry, it's so *exciting*!'

Nevertheless she stopped bouncing.

Thierry turned to Dylan. 'Carla is to have the wedding she wants. As you're the events expert, I'm sure you have that under control.'

He ignored Mia completely. Which suited Mia just fine.

Dylan turned back to Mia. 'There could be quite a gap between the end of the wedding ceremony and the start of the reception, while Carla and Thierry have photographs taken.'

Mia nodded. 'It;s often the case. With it being late spring there'll still be plenty of light left. I can organise a tour of the wildlife exhibits for those who are interested.'

'Oh!' Carla jumped up and down. 'Could we do that now?'

'Absolutely.'

The exhibits—a system of aviaries and enclosures—were sympathetically set into the natural landscape. A wooden walkway meandered through the arrangement at mid-tree height. This meant visitors could view many of the birds at eye level, practically commune with the rock wallabies sunning themselves on their craggy hillside, and look down on the wombats, echidnas and goannas in their pens.

At the heart of the wildlife walk—and the jewel in its crown—was the koala house. Set up like an enormous tree house, the wooden structure was covered on three sides to weatherproof it for visitors, with an arena opening out below full of native flora and an artfully designed pond.

The entire complex was enclosed in a huge aviary. A visitor could glance up into the trees to view the variety of colourful parrots, or along the rafters of the tree house to see the napping tawny frogmouths. Below were a myriad of walking birds, along with the occasional wallaby and echidna. But at eye-level were the koalas on their specially designed poles, where fresh eucalyptus leaves were placed daily. No wire or special glass separated man from beast—only a wooden railing and a ten-foot drop into the enclosure below.

'I *love* this place,' Carla breathed as they entered.

'This is really something,' Dylan murmured in Mia's ear.

His breath fanned the hair at her temples and awareness skidded up her spine. 'It's a special place,' she agreed, moving away—needing to put some distance between them.

When they'd looked their fill, she led them back outside to a series of small nocturnal houses—the first of which was the snake house.

Carla gave a shudder. 'No matter how much I try, I don't like snakes.'

They didn't bother Mia, but she nodded. 'We don't have to linger. We can move straight on to the amphibian house and then the possum house.'

'C'mon, Thierry.'

Carla tugged on his arm, evidently eager to leave, but he disengaged her hand. 'You go ahead. I find snakes fascinating.'

Finally the man showed some interest—*hallelujah!*

Thierry glanced at her. 'Mia might be kind enough to stay behind with me and answer some questions?'

The snakes might not bother her, but Mia loathed the caged darkness of the nocturnal houses, hating the way they made her feel trapped. She didn't betray any of that by so much of a flicker of her eyelids, though.

'I'd be happy to answer any questions.'

Dylan caught her eye and gestured that he and Carla would move on, and she nodded to let him know that she and Thierry would catch up.

She moved to stand beside Thierry, nodding at the slender green snake with the bright yellow throat that he currently surveyed. 'That's a tree snake. It's—'

'I can read.'

She sucked in a breath. Was he being deliberately rude?

She lifted her chin. He might be hard work, but she was used to hard work.

'They're very common,' she continued, 'but rarely seen as they're so shy. They seldom bite. Their main form of defence is to give off a rather dreadful odour when threatened.'

Mia was convinced there was a metaphor for life trapped in there somewhere.

'*You* give off a bad smell too.'

Thierry moved so quickly that before she knew what he was doing he had her trapped between the wall and a glass display unit—the olive python on the other side didn't stir.

'Dylan told us about your background—that you're nothing but a common little thief with a criminal record.'

The sudden sense of confinement had her heart leaping into her throat before surging back into her chest to thump off the walls of her ribs.

'When I was in jail—' with a supreme effort she kept her voice utterly devoid of emotion '—I learned a lot about self-defence and how to hurt someone. If you don't take two steps back within the next three seconds you're going to find yourself on your back in a screaming mess of pain.'

He waited the full three seconds, but he did move away. Mia tried to stop her shoulders from sagging as she dragged a grateful breath into her lungs.

He stabbed a finger at her. 'I don't like you.'

And that should matter to me because...? She bit the words back. She'd had a lot of practice at swallowing sarcastic rejoinders. She'd made it a policy long ago not to inflame a situation if she could help it.

'Carla and Dylan are too trusting by half—but you won't find *me* so gullible.'

Giving a person the benefit of the doubt did *not* make Dylan gullible.

'You're not a fit person for Carla to know. You stay away from her, you hear? If you don't I'll cause trouble for you... and that's a promise.'

'Is everything okay here?'

A strip of sunlight slashed through the darkness as Dylan came back through the doors. The doors were merely thick flaps of overlapping black rubber that kept the sun out. A few threads of light backlit him, haloing his head and shading his face. Mia didn't need to see his face to sense the tension rippling through him.

Without another word Thierry snapped away and moved through the rubber panels, his footsteps loud on the wooden walkway as he strode off.

'Are you okay?'

Dylan's concern, absurdly, made her want to cry in a way that Thierry's threats hadn't.

'Yes, of course.' She turned and gestured to the snakes. 'Just so you know: a reptile encounter can be arranged for the wedding guests too, if anyone's interested. Though it has to be said it's not to everyone's taste.'

Dylan took Mia's arm and led her back out into the sunshine, wincing at her pallor.

Her colour started to return after a few deep breaths and he found the rapid beat of his heart slowed in direct proportion.

'I heard the last part of what Thierry said to you.'

He hadn't liked the way Thierry had asked Mia to stay behind. It was why he'd doubled back—to make sure everything was okay.

'It's not the first time someone has taken exception to my past, Dylan, and I expect it won't be the last.'

Her revelation yesterday had shocked him—*prison!*—but he'd have had to be blind not to see how much she regretted that part of her life. He'd sensed her sincerity in wanting to create a new, honest life for herself. She'd paid dearly for whatever mistakes lay in her past. As far as he was concerned she should be allowed to get on with things in peace.

Thierry's threat, the utter contempt in his voice...

Dylan's hands clenched. It had been a long time since he'd wanted to knock someone to the ground. He'd wanted to deck Thierry, though. He'd wanted to beat the man black and blue.

He dragged a hand down his face. It had only been the thought of who'd pay for his actions—Mia—that had stopped him.

You didn't even think of Carla!

Mia stared up at him, her gaze steady. 'Don't blame Thierry. He only has Carla's welfare in mind.'

'It doesn't excuse his behaviour.' A scowl scuffed through him. 'The man's a bully and a jerk. What the hell does Carla see in him?'

She gestured that they should continue along the path towards the amphibian house. 'Don't you know?'

He didn't have a single clue.

'Haven't the two of you talked about him?'

Not really. But to say as much would only reveal what a poor excuse for a brother he'd been to Carla these last twelve months.

He glanced across at Mia and found that she'd paled again, but before he could ask her if she was okay she'd plunged into the darkness of the amphibian house. Was she worried about running into Thierry again?

He plunged right in after her.

'Do you want to linger?'

He couldn't have said how he knew, but he sensed the tension coiling through her. 'No.'

She led them back outside and gulped in a couple of breaths. She stilled when she realised how closely he watched her.

He reached out to stop her from moving on. 'What's wrong?'

She glanced away. 'What makes you think anything's wrong?'

When she turned back, he just shrugged.

Her shoulders sagged. 'I'd rather nobody else knew this.'

Silently, he crossed his heart.

She looked away again. 'I don't like the nocturnal houses. They make me feel claustrophobic and closed in.

They were like being in jail!

He had to stiffen his legs to stop himself from pitching over.

'I'm fine out here on the walkways, where we're above or beside the enclosures and aviaries, but the nocturnal houses are necessarily dark…and warm. The air feels too close.'

She finished with a deprecating little shrug that broke his heart a little bit.

In the next moment he was gripped with an avid need to know everything about her—were her parents still alive? How had they treated her when she was a child? What made her happy? What did she really want from life? What frightened her right down to her bones? What did she do in her spare time? What made her purr?

That last thought snapped him back. He had no right to ask such questions. He shouldn't even be considering them. What he should be doing was working out if Carla was about to make the biggest mistake of her life. *That* was what he should be focussed on.

'What about when you're down below?' he found himself asking anyway. 'When you have to go into the cages to clean them out…to feed the animals?'

He saw the answer in her eyes before she drew that damn veil down over them again.

'It's okay. It's just another part of the job.'

Liar. He didn't call her on it. It was none of his business. But it begged the question—why was Mia working in a place like this when enclosed spaces all but made her hyperventilate?

They found Carla and Thierry waiting for them beside the kangaroo enclosure.

The moment she saw Mia, Carla grabbed her arm. 'I want to become a volunteer!'

Mia smiled as if she couldn't help it 'Volunteers are always welcome at Plum Pines.'

Her tone held no awkwardness and Dylan's shoulders unhitched a couple of notches. Thierry's strictures hadn't constrained the warmth she showed to Carla, and he gave silent thanks for it.

Thierry pulled Mia back to his side, gently but inexorably. 'Stop manhandling the staff, Carla.'

Dylan lifted himself up to his full height. 'That's an insufferably snobbish thing to say, Thierry.'

Carla's face fell and he immediately regretted uttering the words within her earshot.

Thierry glared back at him. '*You* might be happy consorting with criminals, Dylan, but you'll have to excuse me for being less enthused.'

'Ex.' Mia's voice cut through the tension, forcing all eyes to turn to her. 'I'm an *ex*-criminal, Mr Geroux. Naturally, I don't expect you to trust me, but you can rest assured that if my employers have no qualms about either my conduct or my ability to perform the tasks required of me, then you need have no worries on that head either.'

'We *don't* have qualms!' Carla jumped in, staring at Thierry as if a simple glare would force him to agree with her.

Thierry merely shrugged. 'Is volunteering such a good idea? You could catch something…get bitten…and didn't you notice the frightful stench coming from the possums?'

'Oh, I hadn't thought about the practicalities…'

She glanced at Mia uncertainly and Dylan wanted to throw his head back and howl.

'You'd need to be up to date with your tetanus shots. All the information is on the Plum Pines website, and I can give you some brochures if you like. You can think about it for a bit, and call the volunteer co-ordinator if you have any questions.'

Thierry scowled at her, but she met his gaze calmly. 'Maybe it's something the two of you could do together.'

Carla clapped her hands, evidently delighted with the idea.

Thierry glanced at his watch with an abrupt, 'We have to go.' He said goodbye to Dylan, ignoring Mia completely, before leading Carla away.

'An absolute charmer,' Dylan muttered under his breath.

Mia had to have heard him, but she didn't say anything, turning instead to a kangaroo waiting on the other side of the fence and feeding it some titbit she'd fished from her pocket. He glanced back at Carla and a sickening cramp stretched through his stomach—along with a growing sense of foreboding.

Mia nudged him, and then held out a handful of what looked like puffed wheat. 'Would you like to feed the kangaroo?'

With a sense of wonder, he took it and fed the kangaroo. He even managed to run his fingers through the fur of the kangaroo's neck. The tightness in him eased.

'Do you have anything pressing you need to attend to in the next couple of hours?'

She shook her head. 'Nora has instructed me to give you all the time and assistance you need. Later this afternoon, if I'm free, she's going to run through some things that I probably need to know—help me create a checklist.'

'Will you meet me at the lily pond in fifteen minutes?'

She blinked, but nodded without hesitation. 'Yes, of course.'

Mia was sitting at the picnic table waiting for him—her notepad at the ready—when he arrived with his bag of goodies.

If he hadn't been so worried about Carla's situation he'd

have laughed at the look on her face when he pulled forth sandwiches, chocolate bars and sodas.

'This is a working lunch, Mia, not some dastardly plot to seduce you.'

Pink flushed her cheeks. 'I never considered anything else for a moment.'

To be fair, she probably hadn't. She'd made it clear where she stood yesterday. When he'd gone back over her words it had struck him that she really *hadn't* thought him interested in her. She'd just been setting boundaries. And if that boundary-setting hadn't been for his benefit, then it had to have been for hers. Which was interesting.

He took the seat beside her rather than the one opposite.

Why was Mia so determined to remain aloof?

He didn't want her aloof.

He wanted her help.

He took her notepad and pen and put them in his pocket. 'You won't need those.' He pushed the stack of sandwiches, a can of soda and a couple of chocolate bars towards her. 'Eat up while I talk.'

She fixed him with those moss-green eyes, but after a moment gave a shrug and reached for the topmost sandwich. She didn't even check to see what it was.

He gestured to the stack. 'I didn't know what you'd like so I got a variety.' He'd grabbed enough to feed a small army, but he'd wanted to make sure he bought something she liked.

She shrugged again. 'I'm not fussy. I'll eat pretty much anything.'

He had a sudden vision of her in prison, eating prison food, and promptly lost his appetite.'

'Dylan?'

He snapped his attention back. 'Sorry, I'm a bit distracted.'

She bit into her sandwich and chewed, simply waiting for him to speak. It occurred to him that if he wanted her help he was going to have to be honest with her.

A weight pressed down on him. Yesterday afternoon she'd looked at him with such gratitude and admiration—as if he were a superhero. Nobody had ever looked at him like that. He didn't want to lose it so quickly.

Not even for Carla's sake?

He straightened. He'd do anything for Carla.

He opened his can of soft drink and took a long swallow before setting it back down. 'I'm ashamed to admit this, but over the last twelve months I've neglected Carla shamefully. She and Thierry have only been dating six months, and the news of their engagement came as a shock. This will probably sound ridiculously big brotherly, but... I'm worried she's making a mistake.'

Mia stared at him for a moment. 'You and Carla seem very close.'

'We are.'

'So why haven't you spent much time together recently?'

How much of the truth did he have to tell her?

He scrubbed a hand through his hair. 'There's an older family member who I have...difficulties with. It's impossible to avoid him when I'm in Australia, and I've wanted to avoid a falling out, so...'

'So you've spent a lot of time overseas instead?'

'Rather than putting up with said family member, I flitted off to organise parties. There was a Turkish sultan's sixtieth birthday party, and then a twenty-fifth wedding anniversary celebration for a couple of members of the British aristocracy. I did some corporate work on the Italian Grand Prix. Oh, and there was a red carpet film premiere that I did just for fun.'

She blinked, as if he'd just spoken in a foreign language. In some ways he supposed he had.

'So there you have it—I'm a coward.'

He lifted his arms and let them drop, waiting for her eyes to darken with scorn. She just stared back at him and waited for him to continue, her gaze not wavering.

He swallowed. 'I came home for Carla's birthday…and for two days over Christmas.' It hadn't been enough! 'That's when she announced her engagement. That's when I realised I'd spent too long away.'

But Carla had finally seemed so settled…so happy. She'd refused to come and work for FWE, preferring to focus on her charity work. Nothing had rung alarm bells for him… until he'd met Thierry.

Mia didn't say anything, but he could tell from her eyes how intently she listened.

'When I heard what he said to you in the reptile house I wanted to knock him to the ground.'

She halted mid-chew, before swallowing. 'I'm very glad you didn't.'

It had only been the thought that Gordon would somehow bring the blame back to her and she'd lose her job that had stilled his hand.

'What he said to you…' His hand clenched and unclenched convulsively around his can of drink. 'I'm sorry you were put into a position where you were forced to listen to that.'

'It's not your responsibility to apologise on behalf of other people, Dylan.'

Maybe not, but it *felt* like his fault. If he'd taken the time to get to know Thierry better before now…

She reached out and placed a sandwich in front of him. 'And you need to remember that just because he dislikes *me*, and my background, it doesn't necessarily make him a bad person.'

Dylan was far from sure about that.

'Even if I didn't have a criminal record, there's no law that says Thierry has to *like* me.'

'Mia, it's not the fact that he doesn't like you or even that he was rude to you that worries me. What disturbs me is the fact that he threatened you.'

'I can take care of myself.'

She said the words quietly and he didn't doubt her. He wished she didn't *have* to take care of herself. He wished she was surrounded by an army of people who'd take care of her. He sensed that wasn't the case, and suddenly he wanted to buy her a hundred chocolate bars… But what good would that do?

No substance, Dylan Fairweather. You don't have an ounce of substance.

The words roared through him. He pulled air in through his nose and let it out through his mouth—once, twice.

'I have less confidence,' he said finally, 'in Carla's ability to take care of herself.' He met Mia's dark-eyed gaze. 'What if he talks to *her* the way he spoke to you? What if he threatens *her* in the same way he threatened you?'

CHAPTER FOUR

DYLAN COULDN'T KNOW it, but each word raised a welt on Mia's soul. The thought of a woman as lovely as Carla, as open and kind as she was, being controlled and manipulated, possibly even abused, by a man claiming to love her...

It made her stomach burn acid.

It made her want to run away at a hundred miles an hour in the other direction.

She recalled how Thierry had trapped her against the wall in the reptile house and her temples started to throb.

She set her sandwich down before she mangled it. 'Have you seen anything to give you cause for concern before now?'

Those laughing lips of his, his shoulders, and even the laughter lines fanning out from his eyes—all drooped. Her heart burned for him. She wanted to reach out and cover his hand, to offer him whatever comfort she could.

Don't be an idiot.

Dylan might be all golden flirtatious charm, but it didn't mean he'd want someone like *her* touching him. She chafed her left forearm, digging her fingers into the muscle to try and loosen the tension that coiled her tight. She wasn't qualified to offer advice about family or relationships, but even *she* could see what he needed to do.

'Can't...?' She swallowed to counter a suddenly dry throat. 'Can't you talk to Carla and share your concerns?'

'And say what? *Carla, I think the man you're about to marry is a complete and utter jerk*?' He gave a harsh laugh. 'She'd translate that as me forcing her to choose between her brother and her fiancé.'

From the look on his face, it was evident he didn't think she'd choose him. She thought back to the way Carla had clung to Thierry's arm and realised Dylan might have a point.

'How about something a little less confrontational?' She reached for a can of soda, needing something to do with her hands. 'Something like… *Carla, Thierry strikes me as a bit moody. Are you sure he treats you well?*'

He gave a frustrated shake of his head. 'She'd still read it as me criticising her choice. I'd have to go to great lengths to make it as clear as possible that I'm not making her choose between me and Thierry, but the fact of the matter is—regardless of what I discover—I have no power to stop this wedding unless it's what Carla wants. And if she *does* marry him and he *is* cruel to her… I want her to feel she's able to turn to me without feeling constrained because I warned her off him.'

His logic made sense, in a roundabout way, but it still left her feeling uneasy. 'You know, you don't have a lot to go on, here. One incident isn't necessarily indicative of the man. Perhaps you need to make a concerted effort to get to know him better.'

'I mean to. I'm already on it.' Her surprise must have shown, because he added. 'It doesn't take fifteen minutes to buy a few sandwiches, Mia. I made a couple of phone calls before meeting you here.'

She frowned, not really knowing what that meant. 'Did you find out anything?'

'Not yet.'

And then she realised exactly what he'd done. 'You hired a private investigator?'

'Yep.'

'Don't you think that's a little extreme?'

'Not when my sister's happiness and perhaps her physical well-being is at stake.'

She recalled Thierry's latent physical threat to her and thought Dylan might have a point. Still…

'I want to ask for your assistance, Mia.'

'Mine?' she squeaked. What on earth did he think *she* could do?

'I want you to befriend Carla. She might confide in you—especially as Thierry has made it clear that he doesn't like you.'

Had he gone mad? 'Dylan, I can be as friendly towards Carla as it's possible to be.' She'd already resolved to do so. 'But when we get right down to it I'm just one of the many people helping to organise her wedding. We don't exactly move in the same social circles.'

'I've thought about that too. And I've come up with a solution.'

She had a premonition that she wasn't going to like what came next.

He leaned towards her. 'If Carla thought that we were dating—'

'*No!*' She shot so far away from him she was in danger of falling off the bench.

He continued to survey her, seeming not put off in the least by her vehemence. He unwrapped a chocolate bar and bit into it. 'Why not?'

She wanted to tell him to eat a sandwich first—put something proper into his stomach—but it wasn't her place…and it was utterly beside the point.

'Because I don't date!'

'It wouldn't be *real* dating,' he said patiently. 'It'd be pretend dating.'

She slapped a hand to her chest. 'I work hard to keep a low profile. I don't need my past coming back and biting me more often than it already does. I have a plan for my life,

Dylan—to finish my field officer training and find work in a national park. Somewhere rural—' *remote* '—and quiet, where I can train towards becoming a ranger. All I want is a quiet life so I can live peacefully and stay out of trouble. Dating you *won't* help me achieve that. You live your life up among the stars. You're high-profile.' She pointed to herself. 'Low-profile. Can you see how that's not going to work?'

He tapped a finger against his mouth. 'It's a valid point.'

He leaned towards her, his lips pressed into a firm, persuasive line. It took an effort not to let her attention become distracted by those lips.

'What if I promise to keep your name out of the papers?'

'How? Australia's golden-boy bachelor slumming it with an ex-jailbird? *That* story's too juicy to keep under wraps.'

Heaven only knew what Gordon Coulter would do with a headline like that.

'I've learned over the years how to be *very* discreet. I swear to you that nobody will suspect a thing.'

'Will Thierry be discreet too?' she asked, unable to hide the scorn threading her voice as she recalled his threat to make trouble for her.

'You leave Thierry to me.'

With pleasure.

Dylan pushed his shoulders back, a steely light gleaming in his eyes, and she had to swallow. The golden charmer had gone—had been replaced by someone bigger, harder…and far more intimidating. Beneath his laughing, charismatic allure, she sensed that Dylan had a warrior's heart.

His nostrils flared. 'I'll make sure he doesn't touch you.'

She couldn't have said why, but she believed him—implicitly. Her heart started to thud too hard, too fast. 'Dylan, surely you'd be better off concocting this kind of scheme with one of Carla's friends? They'd—'

'She doesn't have any. Not close. Not any more.'

Why ever not?

His face turned to stone, but his eyes flashed fire. 'Two years ago Carla's boyfriend ran off with her best friend.'

Mia closed her eyes.

'Carla went into a deep depression and pushed all her friends away. She's never been the sort of person to have a lot of close friends—a large social circle, perhaps, but only one or two people she'd consider close—and...'

'And it was all a mess after such a betrayal,' she finished for him, reading it in his face and wanting to spare him the necessity of having to say it out loud. 'Loyalties were divided and some fences never mended.'

He nodded.

She leapt up, needing to work off the agitation coursing through her. 'Dylan, I...'

'What?'

She swung back to him. 'I don't know how we can pull off something like that—pretending to date—convincingly.'

She sat again, feeling like a goose for striding around and revealing her agitation. When she glanced across at him the expression in his eyes made her stomach flip-flop. In one smooth motion he slid across until they were almost touching. He smelt fresh and clean, like sun-warmed cotton sheets, and her every sense went on high alert.

He touched the backs of his fingers to her cheek and she sucked in a breath, shocked at her need to lean into the contact. Oh, this was madness!

'Dylan, I—'

His thumb pressed against her mouth, halting her words. Then he traced the line of her bottom lip and a pulse thumped to life inside her. She couldn't stop her lip from softening beneath his touch, or her mouth from parting ever so slightly so she could draw the scent of him into her lungs.

'I don't think you realise how lovely you are.'

Somewhere nearby a peacock honked. Something splashed in the lily pond. But all Mia could focus on was the man in front of her, staring down at her as if…as if she were a cream bun he'd like to devour…slowly and deliciously.

It shocked her to realise that in that moment she wanted nothing more than to *be* a cream bun.

Dangerous.

The word whispered through her. Some part of her mind registered it, but she was utterly incapable of moving away and breaking the spell Dylan had woven around them.

'Sweet and lovely Mia.'

The low, warm promise in his voice made her breath catch.

'I think we're going to have exactly the opposite problem. I think if we're not careful we could be in danger of being *too* convincing…we could be in danger of convincing ourselves that a lie should become the truth.'

A fire fanned through her. Yesterday, when he'd flirted with her, hadn't it just been out of habit? Had he meant it? He found her attractive?

'Dylan…' His name whispered from her. She didn't mean it to.

His eyes darkened at whatever he saw in her face. 'I dreamed of you last night.'

Dangerous.

The word whispered through her again.

But it didn't feel dangerous. It felt *right* to be whispering secrets to each other.

His thumb swept along the fullness of her bottom lip again, pulling against it to explore the damp moistness inside, sensitising it almost beyond bearing. Unable to help herself, she flicked out her tongue to taste him.

'Mia…' He groaned out her name as if it came from some deep, hidden place.

His head moved towards her, his lips aiming to replace his thumb, and her soul suddenly soared.

Dangerous.

Dangerous and glorious. This man had mesmerised her from the moment she'd first laid eyes on him and—

Mesmerised...?

Dangerous!

With a half-sob Mia fisted her hands in his shirt, but didn't have the strength to push him away. She dropped her chin, ensuring that his kiss landed on her brow instead of her lips.

She felt rather than heard him sigh.

After three hard beats of her heart she let him go. In another two he slid back along the bench away from her.

'As I said, I don't think being convincing will be a problem. However much you might deny it, something burns between us—something that could be so much more than a spark if we'd let it.'

It would be foolish to deny it now.

'Why do you have a no-dating rule?' he asked.

His words pulled her back. With an effort, she found her voice. 'It keeps me out of trouble.'

He remained silent, as if waiting for more, but Mia refused to add anything else.

'Maybe one day you'll share your reasoning with me, but until then I fully mean to respect your rules, Mia.'

He did? She finally glanced up at him.

The faintest of smiles touched his lips. 'And, unlike you, I'm more than happy to share my reasons. One—' he held up a finger '—if I don't respect your no-dating rule I suspect I have no hope of winning your co-operation where Carla's concerned.'

Self-interest? At least that was honest.

He held up a second finger. 'And, two, it seems to me you already have enough people in your life who don't respect your wishes. I don't mean to become one of their number.'

Despite her best efforts, some of the ice around her heart cracked.

He stared at her for a long moment, his mouth turning

grim. 'I fancied myself in love once, but when things got tough the girl in question couldn't hack it. She left. Next time I fall in love it'll be with a woman who can cope with the rough as well as the smooth.'

His nostrils flared, his eyes darkening, and Mia wondered if he'd gone back to that time when the girl in question had broken his heart. She wanted to reach out and touch his hand, pull him back to the present.

She dragged her hands into her lap. 'I'm sorry, Dylan.'

He shook himself. 'It's true that I'm attracted to you, but you've just pointed out how very differently we want to live our lives—high-profile, low-profile. In the real world, that continual push and pull would make us miserable.'

Mia had to look away, but she nodded to let him know that she agreed. It didn't stop her heart from shrivelling to the size of a gum nut.

'Your no-dating rule obviously rules out a fling?'

'It does.' Anything else would be a disaster.

'So these are our ground rules. With those firmly in place we shouldn't have any misunderstandings or false hopes, right? We just need to remember the reasons why we're not dating at the moment, why we're not looking for a relationship, and that'll keep us safe.'

She guessed so.

He drummed his fingers on the picnic table. 'It occurs to me that I haven't given you much incentive to help me out. I'm a selfish brute.'

His consideration for Carla proved that was a lie.

'I've no intention of taking advantage of you. I'm fully prepared to pay you for your time.'

She flinched at his words, throwing an arm up to ward them off. 'I don't want your *money*, Dylan.'

What kind of person did he think she was?

A thief!

She dragged in a breath. 'I went to jail for fraud. Do you think I'd accept money under dubious circumstances again?'

He swore at whatever he saw in her face. 'I'm sorry—that was incredibly insensitive. I didn't mean I thought you could be bought. I just meant it's perfectly reasonable for you to be financially compensated for your time.'

'No.'

'It doesn't have to be dubious. I'd have a contract drawn up so there wasn't a hint of illegality about it.'

His earnestness made the earlier sting fade, but… 'Tell that to the judge.'

He looked stricken for a moment—until he realised she was joking.

'No money changes hands between us,' she said.

He looked as if he wanted to keep arguing with her, but finally he nodded. 'Okay.'

She let out a pent-up breath.

'So, Mia, what I need to know is…what do *you* want? You help me. I help you.'

He'd already saved her job. She hated to admit it, but that made her beholden to him. She rubbed her forehead. Besides, if Carla was in danger of being controlled, dominated, bullied… She swallowed, remembering Johnnie Peters and all he'd convinced her to do. She remembered how she'd sold her soul to a man who'd used her for his own ends and then thrown her away. If Carla were in danger, this would be a way for Mia to start making amends—finding redemption—for the mistakes of the past.

The thought made her stomach churn. She didn't want to do this.

What? You think redemption is easy? You think it's supposed to be a picnic? It should be hard. You should suffer.

She brushed a hand across her eyes, utterly weary with herself.

'What do you want, Mia.'

She wanted to keep her job. Yesterday she'd have trusted him with that piece of information. Today— She glanced across at him. Today she wasn't convinced that he wouldn't use it against her as a weapon to force her co-operation.

Who are you kidding? You already know you're going to help him. No force necessary.

But it would be unwise of her to forget that beneath the smiling charm Dylan had a warrior's heart. And warriors could be utterly ruthless.

She forced her mind off Dylan and to her own situation. He'd ensured her job was safe for the moment…and for the next nine months until Carla's wedding took place. She'd have less than six months left on her traineeship then. Surely she could avoid Gordon's notice in that time? Hopefully he'd be busy with council elections.

If Carla's wedding takes place.

'There has to be something you want,' Dylan persisted, pushing a chocolate bar across to her.

What *did* she want? One thing came immediately to mind.

She picked up the bar of chocolate and twirled it around. 'Carla's wedding is going to be a big deal, right?'

'A huge deal. If it goes ahead.'

She glanced at him. 'If Thierry does turn out to be your worst nightmare, but Carla still insists on marrying him, will you still go ahead and give her the wedding she's always dreamed of?'

A muscle worked in his jaw. 'Yes.'

She couldn't explain why, but that eased some of the tightness in her shoulders. She stared down at the chocolate bar. 'So—considering this low profile of mine—when you and your people start distributing press releases and giving media interviews about the wedding, I'd like you to give the credit to Plum Pines and Nora and FWE without mentioning my name at all.'

His brows drew down over his eyes. 'But that's unfair! Credit should go where it's due. Being associated with Carla's wedding could open doors for you.'

Or it could bring her past and the scandal to the front pages of the gossip rags. 'You asked me what I wanted. I'm simply telling you.'

He swung back to scowl at the lily pond. 'I don't like it. It goes against the grain. But if it's what you really want, then consider it done.'

She closed her eyes. 'Thank you.'

'But now you have to tell me something else that you want, because I *truly* feel as if I'm taking utter advantage of you.'

She glanced up to find him glaring at her. For some reason his outrage made her want to smile.

'What do I want?' she shrugged. 'I want to be out on the eastern boundary, helping with the weed eradication programme.'

Dylan stared at Mia and his heart thumped at the wistful expression that flitted across her face. He had a feeling that she didn't have a whole lot of fun in her life. Not if weed extermination topped the list of her wants.

If she agreed to his fake dating plan he resolved to make sure she had fun too. It would be the least he could do. There might be a lot of things he wasn't good at, but when it came to fun he was a grandmaster.

He rose. 'Okay, let's go and do that, then.'

'We?' She choked on her surprise.

He sat again, suddenly unsure. 'You'd prefer to go on your own?'

'Oh, it's not that. I… It's just…'

He could almost see the thoughts racing across her face. *It's hard work, dirty work, menial work.* 'You don't think I'm up to it, do you?'

'It's not that either—although it *is* hard work.' She leaned towards him, a frown in her eyes. 'Dylan, you run a world-class entertainment company. I'm quite sure you have better things to do with your time. I expect you're a very busy man.'

He shook his head. 'I'm on leave.' He'd taken it the moment Carla had announced her engagement. 'I have capable staff.'

And he couldn't think of anything he'd rather do at the moment than lighten Mia's load.

Inspiration hit him. 'Listen to this for a plan. If I become a volunteer here that might encourage Carla to become a volunteer too. If you get to work with her and build up a friendship then the fake dating stuff will be easier.'

Her frown cleared. 'There might even be no need for fake dating stuff.'

Maybe. Maybe not. He couldn't explain it, but the thought of fake dating Mia fired him to life in a way nothing else had in a long time. He'd relish the chance to find out what really make her tick.

'We need a cover story.' He rubbed his hands together. 'I can tell Carla that you piqued my interest—hence the reason I became a volunteer—and then we worked together, discovered we liked each other…and things have gone on from there.'

She screwed up her nose. 'I guess that *could* work…'

He grinned at her. 'Of course it'll work.'

She suddenly thrust out her jaw. 'I'm not going to spy on Carla for you.'

'I'm not asking you to. I'm asking you to become her friend.'

'If this works—if Carla decides she wants to be friends—then I mean to be a proper friend to her. And if that clashes with your agenda—'

He reached over and seized her hand, brought her wrist to his lips. Her eyes widened and her pulse jumped beneath his touch. A growing hunger roared through him. He wanted to put his tongue against that pulse point and kiss his way along her arm until he reached her mouth.

As if she'd read that thought in his face she reclaimed

her hand. He forced himself to focus on the conversation, rather than her intriguing scent.

'I'm asking nothing more than that you be Carla's friend.'

The way her gaze darted away betrayed her assumed composure. 'That's okay, then. As long as we're on the same page.'

'The same page' meant no fling, no relationship…no kissing. He had to keep things simple between them. There was too much at stake.

'Definitely on the same page,' he assured her.

Starting something with Mia was out of the question. She wouldn't last the distance any more than Caitlin had. His whole way of life was anathema to her.

A fist reached inside his gut and squeezed. Caitlin had left him at the absolute lowest point in his life. The devastation of losing his parents *and* her had… It had almost annihilated him. The shock of it still rebounded in his soul. The only thing that had kept him going was Carla, and the knowledge that she'd needed him. He'd found his feet. Eventually. He wasn't going to have them cut out from under him again by repeating the same mistakes.

He turned to find Mia halfway through a sentence.

'… I mean, we can give you overalls, but that's not going to really help, is it?'

She was worried he'd ruin his *clothes*? 'I have my workout gear in the car.'

She folded her arms. 'Along with a four-hundred-dollar pair of trainers, no doubt? I don't want to be held responsible for wrecking *those*.'

He had no idea how much his trainers had cost. But she was probably right. 'Couldn't you rustle me up a pair of boots?'

She gave a reluctant shrug. 'Maybe. Are you sure you want to do this?'

'Absolutely.'

'We'll need to register you as a volunteer. There'll be

forms to fill out and signatures required to ensure you're covered by the Plum Pines insurance.'

The more she tried to put him off, the more determined he became.

He rose with a decisive clap of his hands. 'Then let's get to it.'

She rose too, shaking her head. 'Don't say you weren't warned.

'What's going on here?' Gordon boomed, coming into the office just as Dylan emerged from the change room wearing the overalls and boots that Mia had found for him.

She sat nearby, already dressed for an afternoon of hard work.

She shot to her feet. 'Dylan—'

'Mr Fairweather,' Gordon corrected with a pointed glare.

'Dylan,' Dylan confirmed, deciding it would be just as satisfying to punch Gordon on the end of his bulbous nose as it would Thierry. He glanced at Mia and wondered when he'd become so bloodthirsty. 'I've decided to register as a volunteer.' He shoved his shoulders back. 'I want to see first-hand what my hundred-thousand-dollar donation will be subsidising.'

Gordon's jowls worked for a moment. 'It's very generous of you to give both your money *and* your time to Plum Pines...'

Behind Gordon's back, Mia gestured that they should leave. Dylan shrugged himself into full supercilious mode and deigned to nod in the other man's direction.

'Good afternoon, Gordon.'

'Good afternoon, Mr Fairweather.'

Dylan didn't invite Gordon to call him by his Christian name—just strode out through the door that Mia held open for him.

Behind him he heard Gordon mutter to the receptionist, 'Bloody trust fund babies,' before the door closed behind them.

Mia grinned as she strode along beside him. 'I think he likes you.'

He glanced at her grin and then threw his head back and roared.

'What on earth…?'

The moment Dylan rounded the side of their family home—affectionately dubbed 'The Palace'—Carla shot to her feet. Behind her a vista of blue sea and blue sky stretched to the horizon. It was a view he never tired of.

'Dylan, what on *earth* have you been doing? You're so… dirty! Filthy dirty. *Obscenely* dirty.'

He grinned. 'I signed up as a volunteer at Plum Pines. That was an inspired idea of yours, by the way. The place is amazing.'

She started to laugh, settling back into the plump cushions of the outdoor sofa. 'I have a feeling it's a certain Plum Pines employee rather than a newfound enthusiasm for conservation that has you *truly* inspired.'

He sobered. *What on earth…?* That was supposed to come as a surprise.

He managed a shrug. 'I like her.'

'I can tell.'

How could she tell?

She couldn't tell!

Romance had addled Carla's brain, that was all. She wanted everyone travelling on the same delirious cloud as she. It made her see romance where none existed. But he could work that to his advantage.

'I'm not sure she likes me.'

'And you think by becoming a volunteer it'll make her look upon you with a friendlier eye?'

'Along with my newfound enthusiasm for weed eradication.'

Carla laughed—a delightful sound that gladdened his heart. There'd been a time when he'd wondered if he'd ever hear her laugh again.

'She won't take any of your nonsense, you know.'

He eyed his sister carefully. 'Would it bug you if I asked her out?'

'Not at all.' She studied her fingernails. 'If you'll promise me one thing.'

'Name it.'

'That you won't judge Thierry too harshly based on today's events. He wasn't at his best. He's very different from us, Dylan, but I love him.' She turned a pleading gaze on him. 'Please?'

He bit back a sigh. 'Okay.'

'Thank you!'

He widened his stance. 'But I want to get to know him better before you two tie the knot.'

'That can be arranged.' Her smile widened. 'We can double date!'

Perfect.

'Perhaps,' he said, not wanting to appear too eager to share Mia with anyone else. 'Are you going to let him talk you out of volunteering?'

'Not a chance.' She laughed. 'I'm signing up first thing tomorrow.'

CHAPTER FIVE

MIA STARED INTO the mirror and rubbed a hand across her chest in an effort to soothe her racing heart.

You look fine.

Dylan had assured her that tonight's date—*fake*date—was casual, not dressy. They were meeting Carla and Thierry at some trendy burger joint for dinner and then going on to a movie.

She really needed to go shopping for some new clothes. She'd not bothered much with her appearance since getting out of jail. She'd avoided pretty things, bright colours, shunning anything that might draw attention.

She glanced back at the mirror. Her jeans and pale blue linen shirt were appropriately casual, if somewhat bland. The outfit wouldn't embarrass her. More to the point, it wouldn't embarrass Dylan. On impulse she threaded a pair of silver hoops through her ears.

For the last five days Dylan had spent every morning at Plum Pines, helping her dig out weeds. And for the entire time he'd remained unfailingly cheerful and good-natured. He'd never once made her feel as if he was counting down the hours until he'd met his side of the bargain.

He continued to flirt outrageously—not just with her but with all the other female volunteers too. It made her feel safe.

She shook her head at that thought. She had to remain vigilant, make sure she didn't become too comfortable around him.

She swung away from the mirror, tired of her reflection. The fact remained that she had limited wardrobe options and this was the best that she could muster. Brooding about it was pointless. Besides, she had more important things to worry about.

Like what on earth was she going to add to the conversation tonight?

She strode into her tiny living room and dropped to the sofa. She needed to come up with five topics of conversation. She glanced at the clock. *Fast!* Dylan would be here to collect her in fifteen minutes. She chewed on her bottom lip. No matter how much she might want to, she couldn't sit through dinner without saying anything. That wouldn't be keeping her end of the deal.

Dear God! What to talk about, though? *Think!*

A knock sounded on the door.

Her gaze flew to the clock. He was early. And she hadn't come up with even one topic of conversation!

Dylan hated to admit it, but he couldn't wait to catch a glimpse of Mia out of uniform. Not that he had anything against her uniform, but there was only so much khaki cotton twill a man could take.

In some deep hidden part of himself lurked a male fantasy he should no doubt be ashamed of, but… He'd love for Mia to answer the door in a short skirt and sky-high heels. *So predictable*! He had a feeling, though, that Mia probably didn't own either.

Still, he'd make do with jeans and a nice pair of ballet flats. That would be nice. Normal. And maybe away from work she'd start to relax some of that fierce guard of hers.

He knocked again and the door flew open. He smiled. *Bingo!* She wore jeans and ballet flats. With the added bonus of surprisingly jaunty earrings that drew attention to the dark glossiness of her hair. He'd not seen her with her hair down before. He had an insane urge to reach out and run his hand through it, to see if it were as soft and silky as it promised.

He curved his hand into a fist and kept it by his side. He'd meant to greet her with his typical over-the-top gallantry—kiss her hand, twirl her around and tell her she looked good enough to eat—except the expression in her eyes stopped him.

He made no move to open the screen door, just met her gaze through its mesh. 'What's wrong?'

Puffing out a sigh, she pushed the door open and gestured him in. 'You're early.'

'If you haven't finished getting ready I'm happy to wait. You look great, by the way.' He didn't want her thinking that he thought she didn't *look* ready. He didn't want her stressing about her appearance at all.

'No, I'm ready. I just… I don't do this, you know?'

'Date? Yes, so you said. It's not a date, Mia.'

Her living room was small. In fact the whole cottage was tiny. She'd told him earlier in the week that she rented one of the Plum Pines workers' cottages. There was a row of three of them on the south side of the reserve. From what he could tell, she ate, breathed and slept Plum Pines. He glanced around. Which seemed odd when she'd clearly taken few pains to make her cottage cosy and comfortable.

'Are you sure about this plan, Dylan?'

He turned back, frowning at her unease. 'What are you worried about?'

One slim shoulder lifted. 'That I'll embarrass you.' She gestured for him to take a seat on the sofa. She planted herself on a hard wooden chair at the little dining table pressed hard up against one wall.

She moistened her lips and he realised she wore a pale mocha-coloured lipstick. Desire arrowed straight to his groin. Gritting his teeth, he did his best to ignore it. For pity's sake, he'd warned himself off her—that should have been that!

He gritted his teeth harder. Apparently not. But, while he might find her attractive, he didn't have to act like a teenager. He needed to put her at her ease—not crank up the tension further.

'I can't imagine how you think you'll embarrass me.'

'I'm… I'm not much of a talker, but I know I need to keep up my share of the conversation tonight.'

His heart stilled before surging against the walls of his ribs.

She lifted her hands, only to let them drop back to her lap. 'I've been trying to come up with five fool-proof topics of conversation so that…' She shrugged again. 'So that I'm pulling my weight.'

In that moment he wanted nothing more than to tug her into his arms and hug her. He had a feeling that would be the last thing she'd want. He contented himself with leaning towards her instead. She wore a soft floral scent and he pulled it as far into his lungs as he could.

'I don't expect you to become a sudden chatterbox. It's not who you are. I don't want you to change. I like you just the way you are. So does Carla.'

Was she worried that the better they got to know her the less they'd like her? The thought disturbed him.

'It's just…you and Carla are so bubbly and fun. I should hate to put a dampener on that.'

She thought he was *fun*? A smile tugged through him. 'You mean Carla and I are noisy chatterboxes who dominate the conversation and won't let anyone else get a word in edgewise.'

Her eyes widened. 'I did *not* say that!'

He burst out laughing. After a moment she rolled her eyes, resting back in her seat.

'You must've worked out by now that Carla and I love an audience.'

She gave a non-committal, 'Hmm…'

'And you have to remember Thierry will be there, and no one could accuse call *him* of liveliness.'

'I'm not sure I want to be compared to Thierry.'

He tried a different tack. 'How did the school group go this afternoon?'

Her face lit up. 'They had a great time. It's so funny to watch them the first time they touch a snake or a lizard.'

He picked up the book sitting on her coffee table—a recent autobiography of a famous comedian. 'Good?'

'Yes, very. She's as funny on the page as she is on the television.'

He set the book back down. 'Did you hear about that prank the engineering students at the university pulled with the garden gnomes?'

She sent him an odd look. 'I saw the photos in the paper. It was rather cheeky…but funny.'

'What's a dish you've always meant to cook but never have?'

Her frown deepened. 'Um…veal scaloppini.'

'I couldn't help noticing that these cottages don't have any off-street parking.'

Her eyes narrowed. 'And…?'

'And I didn't see a car parked out the front, which leads me to conclude that you don't have a car.'

She folded her arms. 'That's correct.'

'Are you planning to get one?'

'Maybe.'

'When?'

Her forehead creased. 'What is this, Dylan? Twenty Questions?'

'There you go. There's your five topics of conversation, should you need them—a funny incident at work, a book recommendation, a local news story, does anyone have a recipe for veal scaloppini they'd recommend, and I'm thinking of getting a small to medium-sized hatchback—what should I get?'

She pushed her hair back behind her ears, all but glaring at him, before folding her arms again. 'How do you know I want a hatchback?'

'You're young and you don't have kids, which means you don't have to settle for a station wagon yet.'

She unfolded her arms, but then didn't seem to know what to do with them. She settled on clasping them in her lap. And then she smiled—*really* smiled—and it lit her up from the inside out. Her dark eyes danced and he felt a kick inside that should have felled him.

'Five topics of conversation—just like that.' She snapped her fingers. 'You managed it effortlessly. How can you make it so easy?'

'Probably the same way you can identify the difference between a bush orchid and a noxious weed.' He grinned, referencing an incident earlier in the week when he'd set about eradicating the wrong plant.

She continued to stare at him as if he were amazing, and he had the disconcerting feeling that he could bask in that admiration forever. He shrugged. 'Practice. In my line of work I have to talk to a lot of people. Though, if the truth be told, the sad fact is that I have a talent for frivolity and nonsense.'

'Good conversation is neither frivolous nor nonsensical.'

He waggled his eyebrows. 'It should be if you're doing it right.'

She didn't laugh. She met his gaze, her face sober. 'It's not nonsense to put someone at ease.'

His gut clenched up all over again. If he continued to put her at her ease would she eventually let him kiss her?

He stiffened. He and Mia were *not* going to kiss. They weren't going to do anything except find out if Thierry deserved Carla. Full stop.

This was nothing more than a case of opposites attracting. He and Mia were too different—too mismatched—to make things work in the long term. And he refused to do anything to hurt her in the short term. She'd been through enough.

By the end of dinner Dylan could cheerfully have strangled Thierry. The only contributions he'd made to the conversation had been negative, except when Carla had won a grudging concession that his gourmet burger was *'okay'*.

Mia, for all her worry, had been a delightful dinner companion. And nobody had needed to ask her if *her* burger was good. The expression on her face after she'd taken her first bite had made him grin.

Thierry had scowled.

From what Dylan could tell, scowling was Thierry's default setting.

When a lull had occurred in the conversation Mia had mentioned the book she was reading and asked if anyone else had read it.

Thierry had ignored the question.

Carla had invited Mia to join her book group.

Mia had kept her expression interested, but in her lap her fingernails had dug into her palms, creating half-moons in her flesh that he'd wanted to massage away.

She'd swallowed. 'Are you sure I'd be welcome?'

'All are welcome! We meet at the library on the first Wednesday of the month.'

'Well…thank you. It sounds like fun.' And she'd promised to read the following month's book.

Dylan had wanted to hug her. He hadn't known that asking her to befriend Carla, and the specific details involved, would be so difficult for her. The thing was, friendship didn't seem to be an issue at all. He sensed that both women genuinely liked each other. But going out and mixing with people was obviously a challenge for Mia.

He couldn't help thinking, though, that locking herself away and hiding from the world wasn't the right thing to do.

He'd taken his cue from her, however, and gone out of

his way to invite Thierry for a game of golf. Thierry had declined, saying he didn't play the game. Dylan had then tried inviting him out on his yacht, but Thierry had declined that too, saying he was too busy with work at the moment.

His heart had sunk when Carla had avoided his gaze. What on earth did she *see* in the man?

Now dinner was over, and they were finally seated in the cinema—Mia on one side of him and Carla and then Thierry on the other—Dylan let out a sigh of relief, no longer obligated to attempt small talk with his sister's fiancé.

It wasn't until the cinema darkened, though, that he suddenly remembered Mia's thin-lipped, pale-faced reaction to the nocturnal houses. *Damn it!* Did the cinema have the same effect?

He touched her arm and she started.

'Is being here uncomfortable for you? Is it like the nocturnal houses?' He kept his voice low so no one could overhear.

'No, it's fine. High ceiling…and it's cool. Those things make a difference.' Her eyes gleamed in the dim light. 'Actually, I'm really looking forward to the film.'

It made him wonder when had been the last time *he'd* relished an outing as simple as this one. Reaching over, he took her hand. When she stiffened, he leaned closer to whisper, 'It's just for show.'

It wasn't, though. He held her hand because he wanted to. He leaned in closer because he wanted to breathe in that subtle floral scent she wore.

When the movie started her hand finally relaxed in his as if she'd forgotten it was there. For the next ninety minutes Dylan experienced the romantic comedy tactilely— entirely through Mia's reactions. They weren't reactions visible in her face, but evident only via her hand in his— in the twitches, squeezes, sudden letting go, in her hand's tension and relief. He sat there spellbound as Mia worried for and cheered on the romantic leads. All of it rendered for him through her fingers.

What miracle allowed him to read the language of her hand so fluently? His heart surged against his ribs. He had to be careful not to let his fascination with this woman grow. *Very* careful. Nothing good could come of it.

When Dylan pulled up outside the front of Mia's cottage at the end of the evening she didn't invite him in.

She shook her head when he reached for his door handle. 'You don't need to walk me to my door.'

But what if he wanted to?

This isn't a real date.

He nodded. 'Right.'

She undid her seat belt. 'I just wanted to say…' She swung back, and even in the dark he could see the wariness in her eyes. 'I did have a nice time tonight, Dylan. Thank you.'

'I'm not after thanks. I want to apologise. For Thierry. Again.'

She shook her head. 'Not your place.'

He clocked the exact moment when she gave in to her curiosity.

'But why in particular this time?'

There'd been an excruciatingly awkward moment at dinner. Carla had asked Mia what the last film she'd been to see had been, and Mia had paled. Thierry had pounced with a narrow-eyed sneer.

'It might be more pertinent to ask, *When was the last time you went to the movies?*'

Dylan's gut had churned and an ugly heat had flushed through him.

Mia had answered with a quiet, 'It'll be over four years since I've been to see a movie.'

And the reason why—the fact she'd been in jail—had pulsed in all the spaces between them.

Dylan couldn't imagine Mia in prison—he couldn't make it make sense. But then he recalled her Spartan cottage and wondered if she'd actually left prison at all.

He rubbed a hand across his chest, trying to dislodge the hard ball that had settled there. 'Thierry went out of his way to make sure everyone remembered *why* you'd not been to see a film in so long.'

She glanced down at her hands. 'Dylan—'

'It wasn't only rude, it was unkind.' How could Carla marry someone like that?

Mia rubbed her hands down the front of her jeans. Finally she glanced at him. 'No matter how much you try to ignore it or justify it, the fact I've been in prison is not a small issue.'

He reached out to cup her face. 'Mia, you're more than your past. You're more than the mistakes that landed you in jail.'

Her bottom lip trembled. The pain that flashed through her eyes speared straight into his gut.

She reached up and with a squeeze removed his hand. 'It's kind of you to say that, but it's not what it feels like. It feels huge. It was a defining moment in my life. I completely understand why other people take issue with it.'

With that she slipped out of the car and strode up to her front door.

Dylan waited until she was safely ensconced inside and the veranda light was switched off with an unambiguous 'the night is over' conviction. With a sigh he didn't understand, he turned the car towards home.

Mia set her sandwich down and unclipped her ringing phone. 'Mia Maydew.'

'Mia, it's Dylan and I have brilliant news.'

The sound of his voice made her pulse gallop. She swallowed and did her best to sound cool and professional. 'Which is…?'

'I have an appointment with Felipe Fellini—the photographer Carla's been so hot for.'

That made her brows lift. She hadn't thought the guy did

weddings or celebrity functions any more. Still, the Fair-weathers had a lot of clout.

'She must be over the moon.'

'I haven't mentioned it to her yet. He's agreed to a meeting—nothing more. I don't want to get her hopes up until it's official.'

Dylan was certainly going above and beyond where Carla's wedding was concerned. Especially when he wasn't even convinced that it would go ahead.

Correction—he wasn't convinced that the groom was worthy of the bride. That was an entirely different matter.

'Mia, are you still there?"

'Yes. I… That's great news.' She tried to gush, but she wasn't much of a one for gushing. 'I'm very impressed.'

'Liar.' He laughed. 'You couldn't care less.'

'I want Carla's wedding to be perfect.' And she didn't care how surly, bad-tempered or humourless Thierry happened to be. With her whole heart she hoped he treated Carla with respect, that he made her happy…that he did indeed deserve her.

'That I *do* believe. The thing is, Felipe wants to meet at Plum Pines this afternoon—two o'clock, if possible. He's only in Newcastle for a couple of days, and his decision on whether or not to take the job apparently depends on the potential locations Plum Pines offers for wedding shots. He wants to start with the lily pond.'

In other words he wanted *her* to be available at two this afternoon to take Felipe around.

'That won't be a problem.'

She'd finished supervising the weed eradication programme last week. She was in the process of helping Veronica create an action plan for a particularly inaccessible area on the northern boundary. That, along with path maintenance, was what her week consisted of.

'Are you on your lunchbreak?'

She traced a finger along the wooden edge of the picnic table. 'I am.'

'Excellent! That means we can chat.'

She stared up into the eucalypt canopy above and shook her head. Dylan *always* wanted to chat. The sooner he got back to FWE and his usual work the better. He wasn't the kind of guy who liked sitting around and twiddling his thumbs, and she had a feeling Carla's wedding wouldn't have his full attention until he'd passed judgement on Thierry.

She suspected he rang her just to 'chat' in an effort to remove the sting of Thierry's incivility. Which was totally unnecessary. Only she didn't know how to say so without sounding ungracious.

'What are you having for lunch?'

She was having what she always had. 'A sandwich.'

'What's in it?'

She lifted the top slice of bread. 'Egg and lettuce. Why is this important?' Nevertheless, she found herself suppressing a smile.

'Are you having chocolate once you finish your *delicious* sandwich?'

She choked back a laugh. 'I refuse to have chocolate with *every* meal. I have a banana.'

'But you're missing a food group! You have carbohydrate, protein, a fruit and a vegetable, but no dairy. Chocolate is dairy. It makes for a rounded meal, Mia.'

She couldn't help but laugh. 'I'll see you at two, Dylan.'

She hung her phone back on her belt, a frown building through her. In the last fortnight Dylan had developed the habit of calling her a couple of times a week—always during her lunchbreak. Some days he didn't mention the wedding at all. She sometimes thought his sole reason for calling was simply to make her laugh. But why would he do that?

Was it really all for Carla's benefit?

Do you think he's doing it for your benefit? Do you really think he could be interested in you?

It was a ludicrous notion—utter wishful thinking. They'd set their ground rules. Dylan wasn't any more interested in a relationship than she was, and a fling was out of the question. But the wisdom of that reasoning didn't dissipate the heat building between them. It didn't quash the thrill that raced through her whenever she heard his voice. It didn't stop her from looking forward to seeing him this afternoon.

She bit into her sandwich. Since when had the prospect of a meeting become more attractive than tromping along solitary paths with loppers and a pair of secateurs?

She had to be careful around Dylan. *Very* careful. She couldn't go falling for his charm. Never again would she be a man's sap, his puppet. Not even one as alluring and attractive as Dylan. She'd sworn never to travel that particular path again.

Couldn't you just kiss him once anyway? Just to see?

The illicit thought came out of left field. She stiffened. No, she could not!

No *way* was she kissing Dylan. Any kissing was absolutely and utterly out of the question. That way led to the slippery slope of lost good intentions and foolish, deceitful dreams. She wasn't descending that slope again. She had no intention of falling into the pit that crouched at its bottom.

So...that's a no, then?

A definite no!

She wrapped up what was left of her sandwich and tossed it into a nearby bin. A glance at her watch told her she could manage an hour's worth of path maintenance before she had to get back to meet with Dylan and his photographer. Wrestling with overgrown native flora sounded exactly what she needed.

Neither the exercise nor Mia's resolution to resist Dylan's appeal stopped her every sense from firing to life the moment she clapped eyes on him that afternoon. It made her want to groan in despair.

No despair! She'd only need despair if she gave in to her attraction—if she handed her heart to him on a platter and became his willing slave. The attraction part of the equation was utterly normal. She'd defy *any* woman to look at Dylan and not appreciate him as the handsomest beast she'd ever laid eyes on.

Not that he *was* a beast. Not when he moved towards her, hand outstretched, a smile of delight on his face at seeing her. Then he was an utter sweetheart.

She couldn't stop herself from smiling back.

It's polite to smile.

Polite or not, she couldn't help it.

He kissed her cheek, his warm male scent raising gooseflesh on her arms.

'Mia…' He ushered her towards the other man. 'I'd like you to meet Felipe Fellini.'

She shook the photographer's hand. 'I've heard a lot about you, Mr Fellini.'

'Yes, yes, it is inevitable. Now *this*…' He gestured to encompass the lily pond and its surrounds. 'You must tell me that you have something better, something more original for me to work with than this.'

He strutted through the area in a coat embroidered with wild, colourful poppies, flinging his arms out in exaggerated disappointment while speaking in an affected American-Italian accent.

Mia stared at him, utterly flummoxed. Never, in all of her twenty-five years, had she ever come across someone like Felipe Fellini!

She moistened her lips. 'I…uh…you don't like it?'

'Ugh, darling! You *do*? I mean, *look* at it!' He pointed at the pond, the grass, a tree.

Behind Felipe's back, Dylan started to laugh silently. Mia had to choke back her answering mirth. 'I… I can't say as I've ever really thought about it.'

He swatted a hand in her direction. 'That's because you're

not an *artiste*. My sensitivities are honed to within an inch of their lives, darling.'

It should have been dismissive, but the words held a friendly edge and she suddenly realised he was having the time of his life.

She planted her hands on her hips. 'What's wrong with it?'

'It's a cliché. An utter cliché.'

'But isn't that what a wedding is all about?'

The question slipped out before she could censor it. She wished it back the moment both men spun to face her—Felipe with his hands up to cover his mouth as if utterly scandalised, Dylan contemplating her with those deep blue eyes, his delectable lips pursed.

'Dylan, *darling*, it appears I've met a creature I never thought existed—a truly unromantic woman.'

Dylan folded his arms, nudging the other man with his shoulder. 'I saw her first.'

Felipe spluttered with laughter. 'Darling, I'm not a ladies' man—but if I were…you'd be in trouble. I'd have her eating out of my hand in no time.'

Mia started to laugh. She couldn't help it. Felipe, it appeared, enjoyed flirting and games every bit as much as Dylan.

'Come along, you unromantic girl.' Felipe draped an arm across her shoulders with a smirk in Dylan's direction. 'Show me something worthy of my talents.'

Dylan fell in behind them with a good-natured grin. Mia led them to the utility she'd parked further down the track. One hundred and eighty hectares was a lot of ground to cover. They wouldn't manage it all on foot before dark.

Felipe discounted the first two spots Mia showed him—a forest glade of wattle, with low overhanging branches, and a pocket of rainforest complete with a tiny trickling stream.

'Clichéd?' she asked.

'Totally.'

'You don't know what you want, but you'll know it when you see it, right?'

Dylan's chuckle from the back seat filled the interior of the car, warming Mia's fingers and toes.

'I'll have none of your cheek, thank you, Dylan Fairweather. You, sir, are an uncultured and coarse Philistine.' He sniffed. 'I understand you have a *Gilmore* on your wall.'

For a moment Dylan's eyes met Mia's in the rear-vision mirror. 'You're welcome to come and admire it any time you like, Felipe.'

'Pah!'

At Mia's raised eyebrow, Dylan added, 'Jason Gilmore—like Felipe, here—is a world-class photographer.'

Felipe gave a disbelieving snort and Mia found herself grinning, Dylan and Felipe's high spirits momentarily rubbing off onto her.

'I've never heard of Jason Gilmore, but I've heard of Felipe. So I'm not sure this Mr Gilmore can be all that good. He certainly can't be in the same class as Felipe.'

Felipe reached out and clasped the hand she had on the steering wheel, pressing his other to his heart. 'I *love* this girl.'

In the next instant he almost gave her a heart attack.

'Stop!' he screeched.

She slammed on the brakes, and even though they weren't going fast gravel still kicked up around them from the unsealed road. Before she could ask Felipe what was wrong, he was out of the car and moving with remarkable agility through the neighbouring strip of bush.

She glanced at Dylan in wordless enquiry.

He shook his head. 'I have no idea. But I suspect we should follow him.'

'This!' Felipe declared when they reached him.

Mia stared. 'It's a fallen tree.'

He seized her by the shoulders and propelled her to the tree, ordered her to straddle it. Next he forced Dylan to straddle it as well, facing her. Mia straightened and folded her arms, frowning at the photographer.

'Why do you frown at me?' He glared at Dylan. 'Why does she frown at me? Make her stop.'

'Uh… Mia…?'

'I can see that *you*—' she pointed a finger at Felipe '—will have no regard for Carla's dress.'

'*Pah!* This is art. If Carla wants art then she will need to make sacrifices. Now, do as I say and lean in towards each other.'

Whipping out his camera, he motioned with his hands for them to move closer together.

He heaved an exaggerated sigh. 'As if you're about to kiss. Mia, darling, I know you don't have a romantic bone in your delightful body, but you have a pulse, and you have to admit that your fellow model is very pretty. I need to capture the light and the landscape. Art is *work*.'

She glanced at Dylan to see if he'd taken Felipe's 'pretty' remark as a slight on his masculinity. She found him grinning.

He winked at her. 'You heard what the man said.' And then he puckered up in such an exaggerated way that any threat inherent in the situation was immediately removed. She puckered up too.

With the odd, 'Tsk!' as if in disapproval of their antics, Felipe set about taking photographs.

The flash made Mia wince.

'Headache?' Dylan asked.

'I just don't like having my photo taken.' The last time a flash had gone off in her face had been when she'd been led from the courthouse…in handcuffs. It wasn't a memory she relished.

As if he could sense her ambivalence, Dylan leapt to his feet.

'Darling!' Felipe spluttered. 'I—'

'You'll have to make do with just me as a model, Master Fellini. Run!' he muttered out of the corner of his mouth to Mia.

So she did. She shot to her feet and all but sprinted away, to stand behind and to one side of Felipe, in amongst the bracken fern.

She watched the two men's antics with growing enjoyment. Felipe barked out orders and Dylan promptly, if somewhat exaggeratedly, carried them out. He flirted with the camera without a scrap of self-consciousness. Felipe, in turn, flirted outrageously back.

Double entendres flew through the air until Mia found herself doubled up with laughter. It was just so much *fun* watching Dylan!

Without warning, Felipe turned and snapped a shot of her.

She blinked, sobering in an instant.

Dylan was immediately puffed up, all protective.

Felipe beamed as he stared down at his camera. 'Perfect!'

CHAPTER SIX

MIA SWALLOWED. 'WHAT do you mean, *perfect*?'

He gestured her over. 'Come and see.'

She didn't want to see. She wanted to run away to hack and slash hiking trails, to fill in potholes and be away from people with their unspoken questions and flashing cameras.

Dylan's not like that.

Dylan was the worst of the lot!

She forced reluctant feet over to where Felipe stood with his camera held out to her. Dylan moved across too, and she sensed the tension in his shoulders, in the set of his spine.

'You said you just wanted to test the light—to get a sense of scale and a feel for the locations, figure out how to make them work for you.'

'Darling, I'm an *artiste*. My mind, my eyes, my brain… they're always searching for the perfect shot.'

She went to take the camera from him, but he shook his head.

'Just look.'

She leaned in to look at the display on the screen. Her gut clenched up tight at what she saw.

Dylan leaned over her right shoulder. 'Holy cow…'

In the photograph, Mia stood knee-high in bracken fern, bent at the waist with her head thrown back, her mouth wide with laughter and her eyes crinkled and dancing. The entire picture rippled with laughter. She didn't know how Felipe had managed it, but when she stared at the photo she could feel delight wrap around her and lift her up.

He'd made her look beautiful.

She swallowed and straightened, bumping into Dylan. She moved away with a murmured apology.

'You see what I mean?' Felipe demanded. 'The picture is perfect.'

Her temples started to throb. 'It's a lie.'

'Art doesn't lie, darling.'

She was aware of how closely Dylan watched her, of how darkly his eyes throbbed as they moved between the image of her on the camera and the flesh and blood her. She found him just as disturbing as Felipe's photograph.

'Will you sign a release form, darling, allowing me to use that photograph in my next exhibition? This is *precisely* what I need.'

Her mouth dried. She had a plan. That plan was to remain in the background. *This* wasn't remaining in the background.

Her hands curled into fists. 'No.'

Felipe switched the cameral off with a sniff. 'That photograph could be the centrepiece of my next exhibition. And, darling, I don't actually *need* your permission. I was only being polite. This is a public place. As such, I'm free to take photographs of anything I please.'

Instinct told her that pleading with him would do no good. Her stomach started to churn.

'How much would a photograph like that sell for?'

She'd been aware of Dylan growing taller and sterner beside her. She glanced up and realised he'd transformed into full warrior mode. A pulse started up in her throat, and a vicarious thrill took hold of her veins even as she bit back a groan.

Felipe waved him away. 'It's impossible to put a price on a photograph like that. I have no intention of selling it.'

'Sell it to me *now*.'

Dylan named a sum that had her stomach lurching.

'No!' She swung round to him and shook her head. 'Don't even think about it. That's a ludicrous amount of money for a stupid photograph.'

He planted his hands on his hips. 'It's obvious you don't want it shown in a public exhibition. Let me buy it.'

She folded her arms to hide how much her hands shook. 'I don't want it hanging on your wall either.'

Why would he pay such a huge sum for a photograph of her anyway?

Because he cares?

She pushed that thought away. She didn't want him to care. She hadn't asked him to care!

As if he'd read that thought in her face, Dylan thrust out his jaw, his eyes glittering. 'Felipe, sell me the photo.'

She stabbed a finger at the photographer. 'You'll do nothing of the sort.'

Felipe turned to Dylan, hands raised. 'You heard what the lady said, darling.'

Dylan glowered—first at her and then at the photographer. 'Okay, let me make myself crystal-clear. If that photograph is ever displayed publicly I'll bring the biggest lawsuit you've ever seen crashing down on your head.'

Felipe merely smiled. 'The publicity will be delicious!'

Mia grabbed Dylan's arm and shook it, but her agitation barely seemed to register. It was as useless as rattling iron bars.

'You will do absolutely nothing of the sort!' she said.

His brows drew down low over his eyes, his entire mien darkening. 'Why not?'

'Because you don't own me. You don't get to make decisions for me.' She swung to Felipe. '*You* don't own me either. In a just world you wouldn't get to make such a decision either.'

Nobody said anything for a moment.

'Mia, darling…'

She didn't want to hear Felipe's excuses and justifications.

She turned towards the car. 'I thought art was supposed to make the world a better place, not a worse one. I think it's time we headed back.'

'Darling!'

She turned to find Felipe removing the memory card from the camera. He took her hand and closed her fingers over it. 'It's yours. I'm sorry.'

Relief almost made her stagger. 'Thank you,' she whispered, slipping it into her top pocket and fastening the button. She tried to lighten the mood. 'I expect for an *artiste* like yourself great photos are a dime a dozen.'

'No, darling, they're not,' he said, climbing into the car.

All the while she was aware of the brooding way Dylan watched her, of the stiff movements of his body, betraying...*anger*? It made her heart drum hard against her ribs.

'That photograph is truly unique, but I could not exhibit it without your blessing. I do not wish anyone to feel diminished by my art.'

She nodded. Felipe was a good man. So was Dylan. She was surrounded by people she didn't deserve.

'But if you should have a change of heart...ever change your mind...' He slipped a business card into her hand.

She nodded. 'You'll be the first to know.'

She didn't add that a change of heart was highly unlikely. She had a feeling he already knew that.

She glanced in the rear-vision mirror to find Dylan staring at her, his gaze dark and brooding. She had no idea what he was thinking...or what he must think of *her*. Her pulse sped up again. Did he hate her after what she'd said?

She didn't want him to hate her.

She had a feeling, though, that it would be better for both of them if he did.

Dylan showed up at her cottage that night.

Without a word she ushered him in, wondering at her own lack of surprise at seeing him.

'I wanted to discuss what happened this afternoon,' he said without preamble.

'I don't see that there's much to discuss.' She turned towards the kitchen. 'Can I get you something to drink—tea or coffee? I have some light beer if you'd rather.'

'No, thank you.'

Good. They could keep this quick, then. She grabbed some water for herself and motioned him to the sofa, taking a seat at the table.

Dylan didn't sit. He stood in the middle of the room, arms folded, and glared at her.

She heaved a sigh. 'I'm sorry, Dylan, but I'm not a mind-reader. What exactly did you want to discuss?'

'I didn't appreciate your implication this afternoon that I was trying to own you. I simply felt responsible for putting you in a situation that had obviously made you uncomfortable. I set about fixing the situation. I don't see how that can be seen as trying to control you.'

She stared into her glass of water. 'I appreciate your intentions were good, but it doesn't change the fact that you didn't ask me my opinion first.'

'There wasn't time!' He flung an arm out. 'Where people like Felipe are concerned it's best to come at them hard and fast.'

'And what if I told you that your solutions were more horrifying to me than the initial problem?'

'Were they?'

'Yes.'

He widened his stance. 'Why?'

She stood then too, pressing her hands to her stomach. 'Ever since I got out of jail I've had one objective—to keep a low profile, to keep out of trouble. A lawsuit would create a hundred times more furore than an anonymous photograph in some exhibition.'

He straightened, his height almost intimidating. Not that

it frightened her. She sensed that frightening her was the last thing he wanted.

'Are you concerned that someone from your past will track you down?'

'No.' And she wasn't. That was all done with.

His hands went to his hips. 'Look, I understand your dismay at the thought of publicity, but what on earth was wrong with *me* buying the photograph?'

'I'm already beholden enough to you!'

'It's my money. I can do as I please with it.'

'Not on my watch, you can't. Not when you're spending that money solely for my benefit.'

He stared at her with unflinching eyes. 'You'd rather have let that picture go public then be beholden to me?'

She met his gaze. 'Yes.'

He wheeled away from her. When he swung back his eyes were blazing.

Before he could rail at her about ingratitude and stubbornness, she fired a question back at him. 'If Felipe had sold you that photograph, would you have given it to me?'

He stilled. His chin lowered several notches. 'I'd have promised to keep it safe.'

They both knew it wasn't the same thing. She could feel her lips twist. 'So, in the end, it was Felipe who did what I truly wanted after all.'

A tic started up in his jaw. 'This is the thanks I get for trying to help you?'

She refused to wither under his glare. 'You weren't trying to help me. What you're angry about is missing your chance to buy that picture.'

He moved in closer. 'And that scares the pants off of you, doesn't it?'

Bullseye.

She refused to let her fear show. 'I've told you where I stand on relationships and romance. I don't know how I can make it any plainer, but offering such a ludicrous sum for a photo of me leads me to suspect that you haven't heard me.'

'Some women would've found the gesture romantic.'

Exactly.

'Not me.'

He shoved his hands in his pockets and strode around the room. Mia did her absolute best not to notice the way the muscles of his shoulders rippled beneath the thin cotton of his business shirt, or how his powerful strides ate up the space in her tiny living room. He quivered like a big cat, agitated and undecided whether to pounce or not.

She knew exactly how to soothe him. If she went to him, put her arms around his neck and pressed her length against his, he'd gather her in his arms and they'd lose themselves to the pleasure they could bring each other.

The pulse at her throat pounded. She gripped her hands together. It wouldn't help. It might be possible to do 'uncomplicated' when it came to a fling, but refused to risk it.

If only that knowledge could cool the stampede of her blood!

He swung around. 'You might have your heart under lock and key, Mia, but you have no right to command mine.'

He wasn't promising her his heart. Heat gathered behind her eyes. He wasn't promising anything more than a quick roll in the hay, and they both knew it.

'You're forgetting the ground rules. We promised!'

'Just because I wanted that photo it doesn't mean I want *you.*'

But they both knew he desired her in the most primitive way a man could want a woman. And they both knew she desired him back. They were balancing too narrowly on a knife-edge here, and she couldn't let them fall.

She clamped her hands to her elbows. Wrapped up in his attraction for her were feelings of pity, a desire to make things better, and perhaps a little anger. It was an explosive combination in a man like Dylan—a nurturer with the heart of a warrior. He knew as well as she did that they could never fit into each other's lives. But hard experience had taught her that the heart didn't always choose what was good for it.

He leaned in so close his breath fanned her cheek. 'Did you destroy the photo?'

She wanted to say that she had.

No lying. No stealing.

She pulled in a ragged breath. 'No.'

'You *will* give it to me, you know.'

She shook her head. 'I have no need of your money.'

He ran the backs of his fingers down her cheek, making her shiver. 'I didn't say anything about buying it from you, Mia. I meant that eventually you'll give it to me as a gift.'

She wanted to tell him to go to hell, but his hand snaked behind her head and he pulled her mouth close to his own and the words dried in her throat.

Dear Lord, he was going to kiss her!

'The girl in that photograph is the woman you're meant to be. I know it and you know it.'

He was wrong! She didn't deserve to be that girl. She deserved nothing more than the chance to live her life in peace.

His breath fanned across her lips, addling her brain. She should step away, but she remained, quivering beneath his touch, hardly knowing what she wished for.

He pressed a kiss to the corner of her mouth. Her eyes fluttered closed as she turned towards him…

And then she found herself released.

'You want me as much as I want you.'

Her heart thudded in her ears. She had to reach out and steady herself against a chair.

'I don't know why the thought of being happy scares you.'

Disappointment and confusion battled with relief and her common sense, and it took a moment for his words to sink in. She pushed her shoulders back, but didn't lift her chin in challenge. She didn't want him to take chin-lifting as an invitation to kiss her.

'I am happy.'

Easing back from him, she seized her glass of water and took several steps away.

'Liar.'

He said the word softly, almost like a caress. He had a point. The thing was, she didn't need happiness. She just needed to stay on track.

She kept her back to him. 'I don't mean this to sound harsh, Dylan, but my happiness is not dependent on my sleeping with you.'

'I'm not talking about myself, here, Mia, or my ability to make you happy. I'm removing myself from the equation.'

'How convenient.'

'I think you're just as imprisoned now as you were when you were in jail.'

She spun around at that, water sloshing over the side of her glass. 'If you believe that, then it just goes to show how naïve you are.'

He blinked and then nodded. 'I'm sorry, I didn't mean that to sound glib.'

She didn't say anything. She just wanted him gone.

'Was it really so awful?'

She closed her eyes at the soft question. 'Yes.' She forced her eyes open again. 'I am *never* going back. And happiness is a small price to pay.'

His eyes throbbed at her words.

'I think it's time you left, Dylan.'

He stared at her for a long moment, but finally he nodded. 'Are you still okay for Saturday?'

For reasons known only to himself, Dylan had booked her and Carla in for a day of beauty treatments at a local spa. In the evening Mia, and presumably Thierry, were to dine with the Fairweathers at their coastal mansion.

Despite her curiosity about Dylan's home, she wasn't looking forward to either event. But she'd promised.

'Yes, of course.'

'Carla and I will collect you at ten.'

'I'll be ready.'

She'd need to go shopping before then. She had a feeling that she owned nothing appropriate for dinner at the Fair-weather estate.

'You're very tense.'

Mia did her best to relax beneath the masseuse's hands, but found it almost impossible. She'd been poked and prod-ded, scrubbed and wrapped, and waxed and tweezed to within an inch of her life.

People did this for *fun*?

What she'd really like was to ask the masseuse to hand her a bathrobe, find her a cup of tea and leave her alone to soak up the glorious view on the other side of the picture window.

The spa was located on the sixth floor of an upmarket beachside hotel that boasted a sweeping view of Newcastle beach. It would be a relief and a joy to spend half an hour contemplating gold sands and blue seas.

'It's probably because of all the hard physical work she does,' Carla said from the massage table beside Mia's, her voice sounding like nothing more than a blissed-out sigh. 'Isn't this a gorgeous treat, Mia?'

'Gorgeous,' she murmured back. She might have made a no-lying promise, but in this instance the lie was lily-white. She had no intention of dampening Carla's enjoyment. That had been the one good thing about all this—spending time with Carla.

So Mia didn't ask for a bathrobe and a cup of tea. She gritted her teeth instead and endured a further forty minutes of kneading, pummelling and rubbing down.

'Change of plan,' Carla announced, waving her phone in the air as she and Mia moved towards Dylan in the hotel bar.

Mia swallowed and nodded in his direction, not able to meet his eye, glad to have Carla there as a buffer.

He turned on his bar stool. 'Change of plan?'

Mia glance up to find him staring straight at ʰ
could do was shrug. She had no idea what Carḷ.
of plan entailed.

Meeting his gaze made her mouth go dry. Lookinᵍ
had the oddest effect on her. She should look ᶜ
could, perhaps she would. Instead, she gazed at ᵢ
grily. He wore a pair of sand-coloured cargo shorts ᵢ
and a Hawaiian shirt that should have made him lᵣ
but didn't.

It made him look… She swallowed again. He looᵤ
a Hollywood heartthrob, and as he raised the beer he ᵣ
to his lips, a searing hunger burned a trail throuᵍʰ

'Yes.' Carla finished texting before popping
into her handbag. 'Thierry's coming to collect me.ʳ

He was? Carla was leaving her alone with Dylanᵖ
Ooh…*horrible* plan!

'I've talked Mia into spending not just the eveniₙₖ
us, but the rest of the afternoon as well. So you'll ·
take her home to collect her things. Thierry and ᵗ
you by the pool at four.'

With a perfumed air-kiss, Carla dashed out. Mia ᵤ,
know where to look. She glanced at her feet, at tʰ
dow, at the bar.

'Would you like a drink?'

She glanced at his glass, still three-quarters full.
with a sigh slid onto the bar stool beside his. 'Do yᵣ
they'd make me a cup of tea?'

'I'm sure of it. English Breakfast, Earl Grey or Chamoₙ.

'Earl Grey, please.'

He ordered the tea and without further ado asked ´
wrong?'

Straight to the heart of the matter. It shouldn't surₚ.
her.

'Are you feeling awkward after the words we eᵉ
on Tuesday evening?'

She wished she could say no, but that lie *wouldn't* be lily-white.

'Aren't you?'

She doubted she'd ever have the power to hurt him, but she *had* disappointed him. She suspected women rarely turned Dylan down.

For heaven's sake, why would they? You must be crazy!

'Mia, you've every right to speak your mind. I might not like what you have to say, but there's no law that says you have to say things with the sole purpose of pleasing me. The only person you need to please is yourself.'

Did he mean that?

'I came on unnecessarily strong. I was upset…and I was prepared to throw our agreed ground rules out of the window.' He dragged a hand down his face. 'I'm sorry. You were right to hold firm.'

Her heart had no right to grow so heavy at his words.

'I know a relationship between us wouldn't work. And you've made it clear that a fling is out of the question.' He wrapped both hands around his beer. 'The thing is, I like you. It's as simple and as complicated as that.'

Her eyes burned.

'I'm sorry.' He grimaced. 'Can we be friends again?'

She managed a nod.

They were quiet while the barmen slid her tea in front of her. When she glanced back to him he sent her a half-grin. 'How did you enjoy the treatments?'

'Oh, I…' She hesitated too long. 'It was lovely.' She scrambled. 'Thank you.'

'You're lying!'

She debated with herself for a moment and then nodded. 'I hated it.'

His brows drew down low over his eyes, fire sparking in their depths. 'Was anybody rude or unpleasant…or worse?'

'No!' Before she could stop herself she reached out and touched his arm, wanting to dispel his dark suspicions. 'Ev-

eryone was attentive and professional. I couldn't fault any-one. It was me—not them. I just… I just don't like being touched by people I don't know.'

She closed her eyes and pulled in a breath. He must think her a freak.

When she opened them she found him staring down at her, his lips rueful. 'I'm sorry. It seems I'm constantly forc-ing you to do things you hate.'

She waved that away. 'It's not important. It's all in a good cause.'

'It does matter.'

'Let's talk about Carla and—'

'No.'

Mia blinked.

'Let me apologise. I'm sorry I took it for granted that you'd enjoy a spa day.'

'The majority of women would.'

'You're not the majority of women.'

That was true, but if she dwelled on that fact for too long she might throw up.

'Apology accepted.'

He sat back and she found she could breathe again. He had the oddest effect on her—she simultaneously wanted to push him away and pull him closer.

Maybe this time it wouldn't be like it was with Johnnie.

Maybe. Maybe not. But even if Dylan were willing she had no intention of finding out. She couldn't risk it.

She pushed those thoughts firmly out of her mind. 'Now, can we talk about Carla?'

He grinned. 'Absolutely.'

Despite her confusion she found herself smiling back. 'That was the one good thing about today. I enjoy spending time with her. She's good company.'

'Did she confide anything in you?'

Mia poured herself some tea and stared down into the dark liquid. 'She's totally in love with Thierry. Even if he *is* all your worst fears rolled into one, I can't see how you'll be able to stop this wedding.'

He dragged a hand down his face and her heart went out to him.

'But on the plus side…'

He glanced up, his eyes keen. 'Yes?'

How to put this delicately…? 'I've had some close experience with women who've been in emotionally and physically abusive relationships.'

His eyes went dark. 'How close?'

She knew what he wanted to know—if *she'd* ever been in an abusive relationship. She sidestepped the unspoken question. 'My father was abusive to my mother.'

'Physically?'

'Not quite.' Though that latent threat had hung over every fraught confrontation. 'But he was emotionally abusive until I don't think she had any sense of self left.'

'I'm sorry.'

'I'm not telling you this so you'll feel sorry for me. I'm telling you because I don't see any of the same signs in Carla that I saw in my mother. Carla is neither meek nor diffident. She's kind and easy-going, and I suspect she's peace-loving, but I wouldn't describe her as submissive or compliant. I don't think she's afraid of Thierry's displeasure.'

'Changes like the ones you describe in your mother— they don't happen overnight. They're the result of years of abuse.'

He had a point.

'There are men out there who prey on emotionally vulnerable women.'

He didn't need to tell *her* that. 'You think Carla is emotionally vulnerable because of what happened between her boyfriend and her best friend?'

He ran a finger through the condensation on his glass of beer. 'It's one of the reasons. She was only sixteen when our parents died. It was a very difficult time for her.'

'I expect it was a difficult time for you too. How old were *you*?'

'Twenty-one.'

Twenty-one and alone with a sixteen-year-old sister. Mia swallowed. 'It must've been devastating for you both. I'm sorry.'

He looked haggard for a moment. 'It was tough for a while.'

Understatement, much?

'And then there's the Fairweather name…'

She shook her head, not knowing what he meant.

'It's hard to know if the people we meet like us for ourselves or whether what they see is the money, the tradition, and the power behind the name.'

'But… That's awful!' To have to go through life like that… 'So that's why Carla didn't tell me who she really was when we first met.'

He nodded. 'I've not been sure of any woman since Caitlin.'

Her mouth went dry. 'The girl who broke your heart?'

'The very one.' He lifted his beer and drank deeply.

Leave it alone!

'You said she couldn't handle it when things got rough. Did she…?' She frowned. 'Did she dump you when you were in the middle of your grief for your parents?'

Pain briefly flashed in his eyes, and she went cold all over when he gave one curt nod.

She had to swallow before she could speak. 'I'm sorry.'

He sent her a self-deprecating half-smile that made her want to cry. 'I was head over heels for her. We'd been dating for two years. I had our lives all mapped out—finish uni, get married, see the world. I thought she was my rock. I wanted to be hers. I thought we were…not perfect—never that—but special.' He shrugged. 'I was a fool.'

The grief in his eyes caught at her. 'You were so young,

Dylan. You couldn't possibly have known she wouldn't last the distance. She probably didn't know either.'

He turned his head, his gaze sharpening. 'The thing is, I know you haven't the slightest interest in my money or my name. Funny, isn't it?'

'Hilarious.' She swallowed, understanding now, in a way she hadn't earlier, how serious he was about not pursuing a relationship. The realisation should have been comforting. 'But we both know we wouldn't fit.'

He stared into his glass. 'Building something worthwhile with someone is more than just being attracted to them.'

'Very true.' She wished her voice would emerge with more strength. 'You need to have shared values...to want the same things from life.'

That wasn't them.

He drained his beer. 'Luckily for us we have our ground rules to keep us on the straight and narrow.'

Her heart thudded hard. 'Amen.'

'Are you ready to go?'

She started to nod and then broke off to fiddle with the collar of her shirt. 'I have a problem.'

'Tell me,' he ordered. 'Fixing problems is my specialty.'

'Carla mentioned swimming and lounging by the pool. But the thing is... I don't have a swimsuit.'

He stared at her, and then he smiled—really smiled. 'That's a problem that's easily remedied.'

CHAPTER SEVEN

WHEN DYLAN PARKED the car at the shopping centre Mia removed her seat belt and turned fully to face him. 'We're not going to do the *Pretty Woman* thing in here, Dylan.'

He knew exactly what she meant and a secret fantasy—or not so secret, in this case—died a quick death.

He didn't argue with her. He'd already forced her into too many situations that she hadn't wanted this week.

He wanted to make her smile. Not frown.

He wanted to make her life a little bit easier. Not harder. And he had been making it harder. He couldn't deny that.

Then walk away now. Leave her be.

The look on her face when Felipe had snapped that photograph of her… It burned through his soul now. He'd wanted to make it up to her. He'd wanted to make things right. Nothing before had ever stung him the way her rejection of his aid had done.

She heaved out a sigh. 'Are we going to have to argue about this?'

He shook his head. 'Tell me exactly what you want to have happen in there.' He nodded towards the shops.

'I want to walk into a budget chain store, select a pair of board shorts and a swim-shirt, and pay for them with my own money. I then want to leave.'

Precise and exact.

'Can I make one small suggestion?'

She stared at him as if she didn't trust him and it occurred to him that he didn't blame her. His heavy-handed attempts to come to her defence last Tuesday hadn't been entirely unselfish. He'd wanted that photo.

He'd taken one look at it and he'd wanted it for himself.

He couldn't even explain why!

It was pointless denying his attraction to her, but he had no intention of falling for Mia. It would be a replay of his relationship with Caitlin all over again, and he'd learned his lesson the first time around.

It was just… Mia had got under his skin. He hated the way Thierry treated her. He hated the way Gordon treated her. He chafed at how hard her life was—at the unfairness of it. He wanted her to feel free to laugh the way she had in Felipe's photograph.

It's not your job to make her laugh.

Maybe not, but what harm would it do?

He shook himself, realising the pause in their conversation was in danger of becoming too charged.

'It's just a small suggestion.'

She pursed her lips. He did his best not to focus on their lushness, or the need that surged into his blood, clenching hard and tight about his groin. If he stared at them too long she'd know exactly where his thoughts had strayed, and that would be a disaster. For whatever reason, she was determined to ignore the attraction between them. Today he didn't want to force her to face anything she didn't want to face or do anything she didn't want to do.

'Okay.' She hitched up her chin. 'What's this *small* suggestion?'

Her tone told him it had better be small. Or else. Her *'or else'* might be interesting, but he resisted the temptation. Today was about making things easier for her.

'I have it on pretty good authority that swim-shirts can chafe.'

She folded her arms, her lips twisting as if she thought he was spinning her a story.

'So you might want to buy a one-piece suit to wear underneath. And, while shirts are great for avoiding sunburn, they don't protect your face, arms and legs, so you might consider adding sunscreen to your shopping list too. And a hat.'

She smiled, and the noose that had started to tighten about his neck eased. 'I have sunscreen at home. I use it for work. But a new hat might be nice.'

He stared at that smile and then fumbled for the door handle. He needed to get out of the car now or he'd be in danger of kissing her.

'Let's go shopping.'

Mia looked cute in her board shorts and swim-shirt—a combination of blue and pink that set off the warmth of her skin and provided a perfect foil for the dark lustre of her hair. She'd look cute in the modest one-piece that he knew she wore beneath too, and while he'd be lying if he said he didn't care about seeing her in a bikini, a large part of him simply didn't care what she wore. That large part of him just wanted her to relax and be happy.

He glanced across. She reclined on a banana lounger, staring at her toes and smiling.

He moved to the lounger beside hers. 'What are you smiling at?'

Her cheeks went a delicious pink. 'Oh, I...'

He leaned closer, intrigued. ''Fess up.'

Her eyes danced. Not long ago they'd all enjoyed a rousing game of water volleyball in the pool, and it had improved everyone's mood—even Thierry's.

'This is going to sound utterly frivolous, but... I'm admiring my toes.'

He glanced at her toes and she wiggled them at him.

'I haven't had painted toenails since I was fifteen or sixteen...and the pedicurist has made them look so pretty.'

They were a shiny fairy-floss pink…and totally kissable.

'I think I'll sit here and admire them too. They're too cute for words.'

She laughed, and something inside him soared.

'I've had a really nice afternoon, Dylan. I just wanted to say thank you.'

'You're welcome. I'm hoping the fun continues well into the evening.'

She glanced across at Carla and Thierry, sitting at a table on the other side of the pool, a giant umbrella casting them in shade. 'Thierry seems a bit more relaxed today. Maybe pool volleyball is the secret to his soul.'

He found himself strangely reluctant to focus on the other couple's real or imagined issues at the moment. 'Would you like to see the Jason Gilmore?' At her frown he added, 'You remember. The photographer Felipe scoffed at?'

She hesitated, and then gestured out in front of her. 'Can it compete with this?'

He stared out at the view spread before them and then rested his hands back behind his head. 'Nothing can compete with this view.'

And it was all the better too for having Mia's toes in the foreground.

'You have a pool that looks like it belongs in a resort.'

The pool was long enough for laps, curving at one end to form a lagoon, with an island in the middle—a handy spot for resting drinks and nibbles. There was an infinity edge that had utterly bewitched Mia when she'd first seen it.

He nodded. The pool *was* amazing. 'But even better is the view beyond it.'

The Fairweather mansion sat on a headland, and the forest leading down the cliff obscured the beach below, but the Pacific Ocean was spread out before them in all its sapphire glory. Waves crashed against rocky outcrops and the spray lifted up into the air in a spectacular display of the ocean's power. It was elemental, primal and magnificent.

'We're incredibly lucky to live here.'

'You are,' she said, but her voice lacked any resentment. She glanced across at him. 'I suspect you work very hard for your luck.'

He gestured to the pool and the house. 'We inherited this from our parents.'

She gazed at him, her eyes moss-dark. 'And yet I bet you'd give it all up to spend just one more day with them.'

Her words hit him squarely in the secret, private part of himself that he let no one but Carla see. If only he could see his father again and ask his advice about how best to deal with his uncle. If only he could sit down with his mother and ask her how he could best support Carla. To have the chance to simply hug them one more time…share a meal with them…laugh with them. His chest burned with the ache of their absence.

'I'm sorry. I didn't mean to make you sad.'

He pushed himself out of his grief. 'Not sad.'

She shot him a tiny smile. 'You're a dreadful liar, Dylan.'

For some reason that made him laugh. 'I miss them. I don't know what else to say.'

'You don't have to say anything.'

With Mia he felt that might indeed be true.

'Is this photograph of yours in your bedroom?'

He stared at her, and a grin built through him. 'Did you think I was trying to whisk you away under false pretences?'

She pointed a finger at him, her lips twitching. 'I'm on to your tricks. You are *not* to be trusted.'

'Ah, but do you *want* me to be trustworthy?' He seized her finger and kissed it.

She sucked in a breath, her eyes widening, and it was all he could do not to lean across and kiss her for real.

If he kissed her now, she'd run.

And he was starting to realise that he'd do just about anything to make her stay. He had no idea what that meant.

'However, in this instance, madam, I'm being eminently trustworthy. The photo hangs in the formal lounge.'

She glanced at her toes, the view, and then at him. 'In that case I should like to see it.'

He rose, holding out his hand to her. She hesitated for a beat before putting her hand in his and letting him help her to her feet. He laced his fingers through hers, intent on holding on for as long as she'd let him.

'Why do you keep it in the formal lounge rather than the living area?'

'You'll understand when you see it.'

She left her hand in his and it felt like a victory.

The moment Mia clapped eyes on the photograph she understood why Dylan didn't keep it in the more informal living areas. Even distracted as she was by Dylan's touch, his fingers laced casually through hers as if he was used to holding hands with a woman, the power of the photograph beat at her.

In her entire life she'd only ever held hands with three men—her father, when she'd been very small, Johnnie, when she'd been very stupid, and now Dylan.

You're no longer either very young or very stupid.

She wasn't convinced about the latter.

She tugged her hand from his to take a step closer to the picture and he let her go—easily and smoothly.

'It's…awe-inspiring.'

She wasn't sure she'd be able to live with it every day. It was so powerful. She wasn't even sure where the power came from…

On the surface it seemed a simple landscape—a preternaturally still ocean with not a single wave ruffling its surface. In the foreground crouched a grassy headland, with every blade of grass as still as the water—unruffled by even the tiniest of breezes. But storm clouds hung low over the ocean, turning the water a menacing monochrome. Behind the photographer, though, the sun shone fierce, piercing the

picture with a powerful light, making each blade of grass stand out in brilliant green relief. The contrast—so odd and so true—held her captive.

'What do you think?'

She had to swallow before she could speak. 'Your Mr Gilmore has caught that exact moment before a storm hits—before the wind rushes through and the clouds cover the sun. It's…it's the deep breath. It's like a duel between light and dark, good and evil.'

He moved to stand beside her. 'I feel that too.'

'And you know that in this instance the dark is going to win…'

'But?'

'But I can't help feeling it's not going to prevail—the dark is only temporary. Once the storm has worn itself out the sun will reign supreme again.'

They stood in silence and stared at it. Mia stiffened.

'It's about grief and hope,' she blurted out, unable to stop herself. 'It makes me feel sad and hopeful, and happy…and incredibly grateful, all at the same time.'

She turned to him and found all her emotions reflected in his face.

He nodded. 'I know.'

'It's the most amazing picture I've ever seen.'

'It's the second most amazing one *I've* seen.'

She'd started to turn towards the photo again, but at his words she turned back with a raised eyebrow. 'You've seen something to top this?'

'That photo Felipe took of you—it made me feel all of that and more.'

It was as if a hand reached out to squeeze her chest, making breathing all but impossible. 'Oh, I…'

She didn't know what to say, and the spell was broken when Carla burst into the room.

'Oh, Dylan!'

It seemed to her that he turned reluctantly. 'What's wrong?'

Carla wrung her hands, making odd noises in her throat, and Dylan's gaze sharpened.

Mia stepped forward to take her hand. 'What is it, Carla?'

Carla grasped her hand in a death grip. 'Oh, Mia, there aren't enough apologies in the world.' Turning to Dylan, she said, 'Uncle Andrew has just arrived.'

Her words seemed to age Dylan by ten years. It didn't take a rocket scientist to work out that there was no love lost between them and their uncle. He must be an utter ogre if his arrival could cause such an expression to darken Carla's eyes. As if…as if she might be *afraid* of the man.

Mia glanced at the photograph that dominated the wall and then pushed her shoulders back, aching to see Carla and Dylan smiling and laughing again.

'So…your uncle is a storm?'

Dylan's gaze speared hers. She sent him a small smile.

'I have a relative like that. I guess we'll just have to weather him.' She winked at Carla. 'Who knows? Maybe Thierry will charm him.'

Carla choked back a laugh.

Dylan glanced at the photo and something in his shoulders unhitched. He reached out and gave Mia a one-armed hug, pressing his lips to her hair. It was friendly and affectionate, not seductive, but it heated her blood all the same.

'Come on, then,' he said. 'Let's go and face the dragon.'

Over dinner Mia discovered that the elder Fairweather was everything she most feared—an intimidating authoritarian with views that were as narrow as they were strong. He was the kind of man who took his privilege for granted, but considered it his God-given duty to ensure that no one else in his family did.

Add to that the fact that Andrew Robert Fairweather was a Federal Court judge—he sent people to jail for a living—and Mia could feel her legs start to shake.

This was the person who'd replaced Carla and Dylan's

parents as role model and guardian? Her stomach rolled in a slow, sickening somersault. For all their trust fund money and fancy education, Mia didn't envy Dylan and Carla one jot. She found her heart going out to them in sympathy.

'It's past time I was introduced to this man you mean to marry, Carla. As you won't bring him to meet me, I've had to resort to descending on you unannounced.'

'You're welcome here any time, Uncle Andrew.' Dylan's smile didn't reach his eyes. 'Your room is always kept ready for you.'

'Humph!' He fixed his gaze on Mia. 'Who are *you*?' he barked.

Three years in prison had taught Mia to hide all visual evidence of fear. It had also taught her to fly beneath the radar. 'I'm Mia. Just a friend of Carla and Dylan's.'

He immediately passed over her to start grilling Thierry.

Thierry, it appeared, ticked every box on the elder Fairweather's list of what was desirable. As a self-made man in the world of finance, Thierry had power, position, and money of his own. They even knew some of the same people.

If Andrew Fairweather had expected Thierry to fawn he'd be sadly disappointed, but for the moment at least he didn't seem to hold that against the younger man.

Their exchange took the heat off the rest of them for a good fifteen minutes. Three sets of shoulders lowered a fraction. Dylan, Carla and Mia even dared to nibble at their thin slices of smoked salmon.

It wasn't until the entrée had been cleared away and a delicious risotto served that Fairweather Senior turned his attention back to his niece and nephew.

'Pray tell, Carla Ann, what are *you* doing with the education you've been so fortunate to have had? Frittering it away like your brother, no doubt?'

Carla glanced at Dylan. The older man had to be joking, right?

'Carla has no need to work for a living,' Thierry inserted

smoothly. 'She's in the fortunate position of being able to help others—a role she takes seriously and one I'm happy to support. Recently she's been busy working on charitable projects, including some important conservation work. I couldn't be more proud of her.'

Wow! Go, Thierry. Mia didn't blame Carla in the least for the look of unabashed adoration that she sent him.

Dylan glanced at Mia and raised an eyebrow. She could only shrug in answer.

'Well, what about *you*?'

His uncle fixed Dylan with a glare that made Mia quail internally. Silence stretched and she searched for something that would help ease the tension that had wrapped around the table.

She forced a forkful of food to her mouth and made an appreciative noise. 'This meal is really lovely. I'd... I'd like to become a better cook.'

Everyone stared at her. Her stomach curdled. She loathed being the centre of attention. She grasped the lifeline Dylan had given her on a previous occasion.

'I've always wanted to make veal scaloppini. I don't suppose anyone has a good recipe for that particular dish, do they?'

It was Thierry, of all people, who answered. 'I have a fool-proof recipe.'

Thierry *cooked*? She shook off her surprise. 'Would you be willing to share it?'

'Yes.'

Andrew Fairweather's face darkened. 'Dylan, I—'

'Maybe I could make it and you could all come to dinner at my place to try it?'

Carla finally got with the programme. 'What a lovely idea, Mia.'

From the corner of her eye Mia could see Mr Fairweather opening his mouth again, his hard gaze burning in Dylan's direction. She set her fork down.

'Maybe we should set a date?'

She couldn't seem to help herself, but she had a feeling she'd say anything to halt the malice she could see sitting on the end of the older man's tongue.

'What about Saturday two weeks from now?' Carla suggested.

'I'm free.' She had no social plans slotted into her calendar at all.

When she glanced at Dylan she found him smiling at her.

'Sounds great. If you're sure?'

Her stomach started to churn. She was very far from sure, but she couldn't back out now. 'If it's a disaster we'll just call out for pizza.'

She'd aimed for light, but even though both Dylan and Carla laughed it occurred to Mia then that nothing could lighten the mood around the table.

'Back to business!' Mr Fairweather boomed. 'Dylan, I want to know what you're working on at the moment.'

All her offer of dinner had done was delay the inevitable. His uncle fired question after question at Dylan—all of them designed to put him on the defensive, all of them designed to make him look small.

A frown built through her. But...*why*?

She glanced from Dylan to his uncle, trying to understand the animosity that crackled between them. Carla said nothing, just stared down at her plate of untouched food. Thierry met her gaze, but there was no help to be had there. His curled lip was directed at *her*, not at Fairweather Senior.

'You were given all of the tools to make something of yourself and you've wasted them,' Andrew Fairweather was saying.

No, he hadn't!

'I'm sorry I've disappointed you, sir.'

No! A hundred times no! Dylan shouldn't apologise to this man. In whose world could Dylan ever be construed as a failure? How could anyone conceivably interpret Dylan's achievements as worthless or lacking in value?

Would *no one* stick up for him?

Fairweather Senior slammed his knife and fork down. 'You could've done something *important*! Instead you've wasted the opportunities presented to you on trivial nonsense. You should be ashamed of yourself. You lack backbone and brains and you're—'

'You are *so* wrong!' Mia shot to her feet, quailing inside but unable to sit and listen to Dylan being run down like that any longer. 'What Dylan does is neither shallow nor trivial. He brings people's dreams to life. Don't you realise how important that is?'

'Important? He throws *parties* for a living. It's disgraceful!'

'You really mean to tell me you can't see the merit in what Dylan does?' Her daring and defiance made her stomach churn, but she couldn't stop herself. She turned to Dylan. 'How long have you had to put up with this?'

'Mia, I—'

She swung back to his uncle. 'Your nephew provides people with memories they can treasure for a lifetime. Dylan doesn't just "throw parties"—he doesn't just light sparklers and eat cake. He creates events that mark milestones in people's lives. He creates events that honour their accomplishments. He provides an opportunity for people to celebrate their achievements with their families, their friends and their peers. That's what life is about. It's not trivial or shallow. It's *important*!'

'*Duty* is what's important!'

Mia swallowed and reminded herself that she wasn't on trial here. Regardless of how much she displeased him, Fairweather Senior couldn't send her to jail simply for disagreeing with him.

'I agree that working hard and being a useful member of society is important—it's what we should all strive for.

And Dylan does both those things.' She lifted her hands skywards. 'Can't you *see* how hard he works? Can't you *see* how talented he is? He has a gift—he's a creator of dreams. And if you can't see the value in that then I pity you.'

She dropped her crisp linen napkin to the table. 'If you'll all excuse me for a moment…?'

She turned and walked out of the dining room. Everything started to shake—her hands, her knees…her breath. Letting herself out of a side door, she stumbled down a series of steps and collapsed onto a low retaining wall that stood just beyond the light of the house. Dropping her head to her knees, she felt her shoulders shaking with the sobs she couldn't hold back.

'Shh…'

She found herself lifted and planted in Dylan's lap. His arms moved about her, holding her securely against him. His warm scent surrounded her.

'Why are you crying, Mia? You were magnificent.'

'I scared myself.' She hiccupped through her sobs. 'I… Men like your uncle scare me.'

'Men like that scare everyone. But at the moment I think he's more afraid of you.'

He said it to make her laugh, but she was still too shaken. She lifted her head and scrubbed her fists across her face. Dylan slapped her hands away and dried her face gently with the softest of cotton handkerchiefs.

'Look at me,' he urged gently.

'No.' She stared instead at her hands, but she couldn't prevent herself from leaning into him and taking comfort from his strength and his warmth.

'Why not?'

She pulled in a shaky breath. 'Because I know what I'll see in your face, Dylan, and I don't deserve it.'

'You don't think you deserve admiration and gratitude?'

'I don't.'

'Mia, you—'

'It was a man like your uncle who sentenced me to three years in jail. And he was right to do so. I'd broken the law. I'd taken money that didn't belong to me.'

She hadn't kept it, but that was neither here nor there.

'That's why my uncle scares you?'

She met his gaze then. 'I meant everything I said at the table. Every single word.'

His eyes throbbed into hers. 'I know.'

'But, Dylan, don't you see? All it would've taken was for Thierry to tell your uncle that I'm an ex-convict and that would've instantly negated everything I'd said.'

'Not in my eyes.'

No, not in Dylan's eyes. She reached up and touched his cheek. 'But it would in your uncle's…and most other people's too.'

He turned his head to press a kiss to her hand. She went to pull it away but he pressed his hand on top of it, trapping it between the heat of his hand and the warmth of his face.

'Does it matter what people like my uncle think?'

'Yes.'

'Why?'

'Because it means that whenever I stand up against some injustice, as soon as my background is known my protests have no effect, no impact. In fact it usually makes things worse—as if their association with me taints them. I might as well have kept my mouth shut.'

'You're wrong.'

The intensity of his gaze held her trapped. She couldn't look away.

'After you left just then, Carla announced to the table at large that she was proud of me. It's the very first time she's ever stood up to him.'

Her heart pounded against the walls of her chest. 'Have *you* ever stood up to him?'

'On Carla's account—but never my own.'

She couldn't stop herself from brushing his cheek with her thumb. It turned his eyes dark and slumberous.

Dangerous.

The word whispered through her, but she didn't move away. She liked being this close to Dylan.

'You shouldn't let him treat you the way he does.'

'I realised that tonight for the first time. I've made a lot of excuses for him over the years. He lost his brother, and he and my aunt provided a home for Carla when our parents died.' He shrugged. 'The family tradition of law and politics is important to him, but I had no intention of ever following that path. Letting him rant and rave at me seemed a small price to pay, but…'

'But?' she urged, wanting him to break free from all the belittling and bullying.

'But I hadn't realised until tonight how much I'd let his voice get inside my head. Somewhere over the years I'd unknowingly started to agree with him—started to define myself by his standards. But tonight you stood up and reminded me of why I do what I do. And I felt proud of it.'

She smiled. It came from way down deep inside her.

Dylan stared at her. His gaze lowered to her lips and the colour of his eyes darkened to a deep sapphire. A pulse started up in the centre of her.

'I want to kiss you, Mia.'

Her heart fluttered up into her throat. 'Oh, that would be a very, *very* bad idea.'

'Why?'

A part of her wished he'd just seize her lips with his and be done with talking.

Crazy thought!

'Because…' It was hard to talk with her heart hammering in her throat. 'Because I've made it clear where I stand in relation to romance and relationships.'

'And you think I want more?'

They'd set their ground rules, but…

'Do you?'

'Things change.' He spoke slowly, frowning.

His reply frightened her, and yet she didn't move away.

'I haven't changed.' She'd meant the declaration to sound defiant, but it came out whisper-soft and full of yearning. She couldn't drag her gaze from the firm promise of his lips.

'If you really don't want me to kiss you, I won't.' He trailed his fingers down her throat and along her collarbone. 'I meant to say earlier that I love your dress.'

The change of topic should have thrown her, but she grasped it like a lifeline. 'It's new. I bought it especially.' She hadn't been able to resist the raspberry-coloured linen dress once she'd tried it on.

'For tonight? For me?'

Her eyes met his.

No lying.

'Yes.'

His fingers continued to trail delicious paths of sensation across her skin. 'Are you sure your stance on romance hasn't changed?'

She couldn't look away. 'Positive.'

Liar.

'I still want to kiss you.'

She should move away, put an end to this insanity.

'And I think you want that too.'

Her heart beat so loud she thought he must hear it.

'Would you like me to kiss you, Mia?'

Her pulse thumped. 'I'll own to some curiosity,' she managed.

'Is that a yes?'

She met his gaze and nodded. 'Yes.'

CHAPTER EIGHT

MIA REALISED HER mistake the moment Dylan's mouth claimed hers.

She'd thought his first touch would be gentle, but it wasn't. It was sure and firm and a complete assault on her senses.

Dylan wanted to overwhelm her with sensation—perhaps in punishment for her 'my stance on romance hasn't changed' comment. He wanted to thank her for sticking up for him at the dinner table... And somehow both of those impulses cancelled out the underlying threat in the other and dragged Mia under as if she'd been picked up by a giant wave.

She wound her arms around his neck and held on, waiting for the crash to come as the wave barrelled her along... But it didn't slam her down as she'd feared. Dylan's arms cradled her, holding her safe, and in the end all Mia could do was sink into them.

He nibbled her bottom lip, coaxing her to open to him. And she did. She wanted to hesitate, to hold back, but she couldn't. His tongue laved her inner lips and something inside her unfurled. His tongue coaxed hers to dance and something inside her sparked to life, filling her veins with heat and her soul with joy.

Dylan deepened the kiss, kissing her so thoroughly and with such intensity that his name was wrenched from her throat.

He lifted his head for a moment, his eyes glittering, and she suddenly realised that the flirtatious charmer had been stripped away to reveal the warrior beneath. And every potent ruthless sinew of his being was focussed wholly on *her*.

It should have made her afraid.

But she wasn't afraid of him. All she had to do was tell him to stop. And she knew that he would.

One corner of his mouth lifted, as if he'd read that thought in her face. 'You think I'm going to give you a chance to *think*, Mia?'

Her heart thumped. 'Dylan, sex won't make a scrap of difference. I—'

The force of his kiss pushed her head back. One of his hands traced the length of her—slowly, lazily—and Mia couldn't help but kiss him back with just as much force, hunger ravaging her body.

She wanted this man.

If she couldn't have him she thought she might die.

And then his hand was beneath the skirt of her dress… and her hands were where they shouldn't be…

And somewhere nearby a door slammed.

Mia stiffened and pulled her hands to her lap. Dylan tugged her skirt down and put his arms around her, holding her close, just as Carla came around the side of the house.

She pulled up short when she saw them. 'I hope I'm not interrupting anything.'

Dylan laughed, the rumble vibrating through Mia's body in a delicious wave of sensation. 'Of course you're interrupting something.'

Carla waved that away. 'I wanted to let you know that Uncle Andrew has left. He's decided to stay at his club in town before heading back to Sydney tomorrow.'

Mia gripped her hands together. 'I'm sorry. I had no right to cause such a scene—'

'You were wonderful! I wish…' Carla hauled in a breath.

'I wish I'd had the gumption to say something like that to him years ago.'

'Carla,' Dylan began, 'you—'

'No.' She fixed him with a glare. 'You've always stuck up for me. I should've done the same for you.'

She turned to Mia. Mia tried to remove herself from Dylan's lap, but he held her there fast.

'The thing is,' Carla said, thankfully unaware of Mia's agitation, 'I've always been so terribly afraid of him. But tonight when you said you pitied him I realised you were right. And…' she shrugged '…now I find I'm not as afraid.'

Dylan frowned. Mia had to fight the urge to smooth his brow.

'I don't want you to be afraid of anyone,' he said.

Mia knew he meant Thierry.

Carla waved that away. 'I just wanted to make sure the two of you were okay. And to let you know the coast is clear.'

'We're fine.'

'And you, Mia?' Carla checked despite her brother's assurance.

'I'm fine too.'

'Carmen—' she was the Fairweathers' housekeeper '—is making ice cream sundaes.'

'We'll be along in five minutes.'

'Don't let him sweet-talk you into anything you're not ready for, Mia.'

'Cross my heart,' Mia promised, but that reminded her that Carla knew her brother's reputation. It reminded her that Dylan had a lot of experience with women while she had very little experience with men.'

Carla sent them a cheeky grin. 'But I *will* say the two of you do look cute together.'

Mia had to fight the urge to drop her face to her hands and weep. How could she have let things go this far?

Carla disappeared and Mia tried once again to rise from Dylan's lap, but his arms tightened about her.

'Do you really mean to ignore that kiss?'

His hand splayed against her hip, as if to urge her to feel what he was feeling.

'That kiss was amazing...intense.' His face darkened. 'It was a whole lot more than just a kiss and you know it.'

Her heart thumped. If she let them, his words could weave a spell about her. She couldn't let that happen.

'Yes,' she said. And then, so he knew what she was referring to, she added, 'Yes, I *do* mean to ignore that kiss.'

Her words made him flinch. Heat gathered behind her eyes and her throat started to ache.

'To punish yourself?' The question was scratched out of him—a raw rasp.

'No.' She refused to let the tears building behind her eyes to fall. 'To save myself.'

'I don't understand.'

The throb in his voice had her closing her eyes. 'And I hope to God you never do.'

This time when she tried to get up he let her.

Dylan watched Mia walk away and his heart pounded against the walls of his ribs. He wanted her with a savagery that frightened him.

He couldn't recall wanting Caitlin like this.

He couldn't recall wanting any woman with this kind of hunger!

He wanted to shred their ground rules to pieces—tear them up and burn them. He wanted Mia in his bed.

But do you want her in your heart?

The roaring inside him screeched to a halt. He swallowed. *No.*

But you're prepared to seduce her? To make things harder for her.

He shot to his feet. He wouldn't make them harder! He'd make sure she enjoyed every moment of their time together.

He'd make her laugh and he'd lavish her with gifts. He'd give her anything she wanted.

Except the quiet life she craves.

He whirled around, hands fisted. She was wrong about that. She should be living life to the full—not hiding herself in the shadows. She should be living her life like the woman in Felipe's photograph—full of joy and laughter. If only he could get her to see that.

If only…

He stilled. If he managed that, then maybe she'd rip up those ground rules herself and welcome some fun—some pleasure—into her life. It was worth a shot.

Thrusting out his jaw, he moved towards the house.

Mia sat at a picnic table, listlessly feeding a peacock what looked to be part of her usual lunchtime sandwich, and something in Dylan's chest tightened. It was four days since their kiss and she looked pale and tired. She looked the way he felt. It didn't give him the slightest sense of satisfaction or triumph.

He wanted her. His lips tightened. And she wanted him.

She had another think coming if she thought he'd give up. He wanted to know what she'd meant by saving herself, and he had every intention of finding out. Once he knew, he'd be able to develop a game plan for knocking down those walls of hers.

She half turned, as if she'd sensed his presence, dropping her sandwich when their gazes collided. The peacock immediately pounced on it.

Dylan forced his legs forward. 'It's just as well I brought these or you'd go hungry.' He dropped a couple of chocolate bars to the table before taking the seat opposite. 'How are you, Mia?'

'I'm okay.' She reached for one of the chocolate bars but didn't unwrap it, worry lurking in the depths of her eyes. 'How are *you*?'

He'd meant to tell her that he couldn't sleep at night for thinking of her. Instead he shot her a grin and winked. 'I'll be a whole lot better once I've eaten this.'

He seized the second chocolate bar and was rewarded when her shoulders unhitched a fraction.

'I'm glad you dropped by today,' she said.

He stared at her. For a moment he felt like punching the air. He didn't push her, though. He'd let her tell him why in her own time.

'Carla asked me to give you this.' He pulled a piece of paper from his pocket. 'It's Thierry's veal scaloppini recipe.'

'Why didn't she give it to me herself?'

He shrugged, hoping he hadn't given himself away. 'She said she was busy.' And he'd latched on to any excuse to see Mia. 'Maybe she thought I'd see you first.'

'Are you busy? There's something I'd like you to see.'

'I'm free as a bird.' Even if he hadn't been he'd have cancelled any appointment for her.

'Good. Come with me.'

She led him along a narrow track through dense native forest. Everything was hushed and serene. He marvelled anew that such a place existed in the middle of the city. Mia didn't talk and he was content to follow behind, admiring the dark lustre of her hair and the innate grace of her hips.

After ten minutes she slowed. Turning to him, she put a finger to her lips and then held down the branch of a Bottlebrush tree, gesturing for him to look.

He glanced at her, wondering what on earth she'd brought him here to see. He turned to survey the view and sucked in a breath. Moving closer, he held the branch for himself while Mia moved off to one side.

She'd brought him via a circuitous route to the far side of the lily pond. Just in front of him—no more than twenty yards away—stretched out on a picnic blanket, were Carla and Thierry. Carla's head was in Thierry's lap and he was idly combing his fingers through her hair. She laughed up at him at something he'd said.

Dylan's heart started to thump. He stared from his sister's face to her fiancé's face and back again. Eventually Mia's fingers wrapped about the top of his arm and she pulled him away. Pressing her finger to her lips again, she led him along a different path until they emerged into a rocky clearing. She sat on a boulder and stared at him with pursed lips.

He fell down onto a neighbouring rock, his mind racing. Finally he glanced across at her. 'I have *never* seen Carla that happy.'

She nodded, as if the sight of that much happiness had awed her.

'How did you know they were there?'

'I accidentally stumbled across them on Monday. I noticed Thierry's car in the car park a little while ago and figured they'd be there again today.'

'She's totally in love with him…and…and completely *happy*.'

'Did you notice the way he looked at her?'

He had. An ache stretched behind his eyes. 'He looked at her as if she were the most precious person on earth.' His shot to his feet and paced up and down for a bit before swinging back to Mia. 'A man who looks at a woman like that is never going to hurt her. He's going to do everything in his power to protect her, to cherish her…to make her happy.'

Mia nodded.

He started to pace again. Seeing Carla and Thierry together like that, so unguarded, it should put his mind at rest…

He collapsed back on his rock and Mia reached out to clasp his hand briefly. 'Dylan, you're not losing Carla. You're gaining a brother-in-law.'

'But he's such an unpleasant man!'

She sat back. 'I suspect the more you get to know him, the better you'll come to like him.'

Could she be right?

'I also think…'

He glanced up, suddenly on guard. There was something too tight in her voice, which was at odds with the casual way she ran her fingers along a tall spike of native grass.

'You also think…?' he prompted.

She rubbed her hand across her throat, not looking at him. 'I think our dating pretence is no longer necessary.'

She told you kissing her would be a bad idea.

He hadn't known it would have her bringing their relationship to such an abrupt halt!

There is no relationship.

But he wanted there to be. Not a relationship, *exactly*, but a relationship of sorts.

He was careful to keep his thoughts hidden. He didn't want to scare her off more than he already had—didn't want her retreating further. He hadn't got where he was today by revealing his hand too soon.

'You're probably right,' he said instead.

She seemed to tense up and then relax in equal measure. He ducked his head to hide his smile. Mia Maydew was one conflicted lady. If she'd just let him help solve that conflict…

'Please tell me you're not going to dump Carla as abruptly?'

Her head shot up. 'Of course I'm not going to dump Carla. Carla and I will be friends for as long as she wants us to be friends.' She folded her arms and glared at him. 'And, Dylan, I hate to point this out, but I'm not dumping *you* either. We were never going out to begin with. We were only pretending.'

'I wasn't pretending when I kissed you. And I don't care how good an actress you are, Mia, I don't think you were pretending either.'

She moistened her lips and swallowed. The pulse at the base of her throat fluttered like a caged thing. A ravaging hunger swept through him. If he kissed her now, here in this quiet, private place where they wouldn't be interrupted...

'Don't even think about it!'

Her eyes flashed fire. So much for not showing his hand. He stared at the ground and pulled in a breath, nodding. 'Sorry, I lost my head for a moment—let it drift to where it shouldn't have gone.'

He shoved his shoulders back and lifted his chin.

'Though if I'm ever fortunate enough to make love with you, Mia, it'll be in place where I'll have the opportunity to show you in every way I know how just how beautiful and desirable I find you. There'll be no rush. And your comfort will be paramount.'

Her eyes grew round.

He leaned in close. 'I've no inclination for a quick roll on spiky grass, where we'd be half eaten by ants and mosquitos or happened upon by unsuspecting hikers. When I make love to you, Mia, I mean for you to be fully focussed on me.'

She swallowed.

He brushed his lips across her ear. 'And when it happens I promise that you will be.'

She leapt away from him, glancing at her watch. 'My lunchbreak is almost up. I have to get back to work.'

He followed her to the main picnic area. It was awash with people enjoying the afternoon sun.

A question pressed against the back of his throat, but he held it in until they were fully surrounded by people. 'Will you give me one more fake date?'

Her hands went to her hips. 'Why?'

It would give him something to work towards. It would give him time to come up with a plan to overcome her objections to an affair.

'I want a chance to grill Thierry in a non-confrontational way, in a place that's not intimidating...and you *did* invite us all to dinner.'

Her shoulders suddenly sagged. 'I did, didn't I?'

She'd only done it to try and keep the peace, to try and head off his uncle's vitriol.

'You can cry off if you want. I can make your excuses easily enough. Nobody will mind.' He didn't want her looking so careworn—not on his account. 'Cooking for guests can be stressful if you haven't done it in a while.' He gave an exaggerated eye-roll. 'And I suspect I've stressed you out enough already.'

Her lips twitched. 'The cooking doesn't worry me. It's only for four—not fourteen.'

'What *does* worry you, then?'

She hesitated. 'My house.'

He couldn't gauge what she meant, but the way her hands twisted together caught at him. 'What's wrong with your house? I know it's small, but none of us are going to care about that.'

'It looks like a prison cell.'

He winced at her bluntness.

'It's bare and uninviting and…and I'm ashamed of it.'

'You've no reason to be ashamed of it. It's clean and functional. Neither Carla nor I care about things like that. And if Thierry does then he's an idiot.'

One slim shoulder lifted. 'I know it shouldn't matter. It's just… I have no talent for making things look nice.' She stared at a copse of trees. 'Maybe I could get a magazine or two, for tips on how to make it look a bit better.'

'I can help you with that.'

She raised an eyebrow, but he waved her scepticism away. 'You don't want a complete makeover. You just want it to look a little cheerier…a bit warmer, right?'

She nodded, but the wariness didn't leave her eyes.

'Look, I'm not an interior designer, but I've had to consult on set designs for concerts and themes for parties. Seriously, we could spruce up your little cottage with nothing more than a few accessories. I swear you'll be amazed at how easy it is.'

She didn't say anything.

'What's your budget?' he asked, so she'd know he wasn't offering to pay for anything, that he wasn't trying to bribe her.

She named a sum that, while small, would easily cover what she needed.

He rubbed his hands together. 'We can work with that.'

Her eyes narrowed. She folded her arms, her fingers drumming against her upper arms. 'What on earth do *you* know about budgets?'

It was a fair question. 'I had a crash course when I started up my company. And I'm given a budget from my clients for every event I take on. If I want to make money I have to stick to it.'

She glanced down at her hands. 'I'm sorry—that was ungracious. Of course you—'

'I'm a trust fund baby, Mia. If I chose I could live in the lap of luxury for the rest of my life without having to lift a finger. You're not the first person to question my credentials.'

She stared up at him, a frown in her eyes. 'You *haven't* chosen to live that way, though.'

He shrugged. 'I wanted something more. I wanted to create something of my own. Besides, the family tradition is not to sit idly back and rest on one's laurels. And as neither law nor politics interested me…'

'You decided to forge your own path?'

'And—as you so succinctly reminded me last Saturday night—I should be proud of that. And I am.'

She nodded.

'So, in return, will you let me help you decorate your cottage? We might not be dating for real, but there's no rule that says we can't be friends, is there?'

She chewed her lip.

Dylan's heart dipped. '*Is* there?'

'I…'

She moistened her lips and a sudden thirst welled inside him.

'I've largely kept to myself since…over the last eleven months.'

Would she *ever* confide the hows and the whys that had landed her in prison? He could search out police reports, court records—and he had no doubt that Thierry had done exactly that—but he didn't want to. He wanted Mia to tell him herself. It was obvious she regretted her crime. And she'd paid her debt to society. But her past still haunted her.

His heart surged against his ribs. 'Do you resent my and Carla's intrusion into your life?'

'No. I… I'd forgotten how nice it is to have friends.'

As those words sank in his mouth dried. 'I'm honoured to be your friend, Mia.' He swallowed. 'Carla would say the same if she were here. Neither of us take our friends for granted.'

'I know. It seems strange, when we're from such different backgrounds, that we can have so much in common.'

He rolled his shoulders in an effort to loosen the tension in them. 'Shall we go shopping, then? On Saturday? To spruce up your cottage?'

'I'm working till midday.'

'I'll call for you at one.'

'Um…'

She hesitated, and he knew it was a big step for her.

'Okay.'

He gave in to the temptation of kissing her cheek. 'I'll see you on Saturday.'

When he reached the end of the path he looked back to find her still watching him. He lifted his hand in farewell. With a visible start she waved back, before disappearing along a path between the office and a picnic table.

His hands clenched. Had anyone ever put her first? Fought for her? Put everything on the line for her?

He knew the answer in his bones—no, they hadn't.

Do you want to be the next person to let her down?

He *wasn't* going to let her down! He was going to show her how to live. When they parted company, she'd be glad they'd met. *That* was his objective.

Mia gazed around her tiny living room and could barely credit the difference a few knick-knacks made. She'd never had a chance to try her hand at decorating before. Her father had maintained a rigid view on what was and wasn't respectable—a line her mother had never crossed—and Mia hadn't even been allowed to put up posters in her room. She'd learned early on that it was easier to submit and keep the peace than to rebel.

When she'd met Johnnie his home had already been beautifully furnished. She'd been in awe of his taste. And in the two years between leaving home and moving in with Johnnie she'd lived such a hand-to-mouth existence there'd been no money left over for decorating the mean little rooms she'd rented.

And then there'd been prison. She'd learned to make do with as little as possible there. She'd left the place with the same attitude, but for the first time she questioned that wisdom. It was true that she didn't want to get too attached to material things—like Johnnie had. But it wasn't a crime to make her living space comfortable. It wasn't a crime to make it welcoming for visitors.

'Earth to Mia?'

She snapped back when a hand was waved in front of her face.

'You were miles away,' Dylan teased. He gestured to the room. 'Do you like it?'

'I love it.'

Shopping with Dylan today had been...*fun*. It had also been a revelation. She'd thought he'd walk through the shops and select the things she needed—like her father and Johnnie would have done. He hadn't, though. He'd asked her opinion every step of the way.

'I love the colour scheme you've chosen.' He planted his hands on his hips and glanced around. 'It makes everything so much lighter in here.'

'The colour scheme was a joint effort. I'd never have known where to start.'

He'd taken her shopping and asked her what colours she liked. She'd eventually settled on a china-blue and a sandy taupe. She now had scatter cushions and throw rugs in those colours on the couch, as well as a tablecloth on the table. New jars in a jaunty blue lined the kitchen counter, a vase and some knick-knacks sat on the mantel, and two beach prints in funky faded frames hung on the walls. A jute rug with a chocolate-coloured border rested beneath the coffee table and a welcome mat sat at the door.

Mia turned a full circle. 'It's made such a difference.' She clasped her hands beneath her chin and let out a long pent-up breath. A breath she felt she'd been holding ever since she'd proffered the dinner invitation. 'I no longer need to feel embarrassed.'

'A vase of fresh flowers here.' Dylan touched a spot on the kitchen counter. 'Maybe a plant on the coffee table or the hall table there, and the room will be perfect.'

Yellow-headed daisies in the kitchen and an African violet on the coffee table. 'I'll get them through the week.'

He grinned at her. 'Even better—it all came in under-budget!'

His delight with himself made her laugh. She watched his face light up with pleasure as he studied the room he'd helped her to transform and her heart started to thud against her ribs.

Friends? She didn't believe in promises and words, but Dylan's actions today had spoken volumes. He'd given her his friendship willingly and generously. He'd treated her like a friend.

Now it was her turn.

CHAPTER NINE

'WITH US COMING in under-budget and all...' Mia's mouth started to dry. 'Well, I was thinking...how about I buy you dinner as a thank-you?'

Dylan swung to her, his eyes alert and watchful...hopeful.

'As a friend,' she added. She didn't want him getting the wrong impression.

'When?'

She strove for a shrug. 'This evening, if you're free.'

'I'm free.' He glanced down at himself. He wore a pair of cargo shorts and a button-down cotton shirt. So did she. 'Can we go somewhere casual?'

'Casual sounds good.' Casual sounded perfect!

'I know—gorgeous evening...end of summer and all that... There's this great pizza place down near the beach. It does takeaway.'

His face lit up and all she could do was stare. When—how?—had he learned to milk enjoyment from every moment?

'When was the last time you had pizza on the beach?'

'I... Never.'

'C'mon, then.' He took her hand and led her to the front door. 'That's an oversight that should be corrected immediately.'

* * *

'See? Didn't I tell you this was an inspired idea?' Dylan claimed a patch of pristine white sand and grinned at her.

Mia bit back a laugh and spread out a towel so he could place the pizza boxes onto it. 'I'll reserve judgement until I've tried the pizza.' She dropped two bottles of water to the towel too, and then turned to survey the view spread out in front of them.

They had another half an hour of light—possibly longer. The water reflected the last of the sun's brilliance in tones of pink, gold and mauve. Barely a breath of breeze ruffled her hair, and the only sounds were the whoosh of the waves rushing up onshore, the cries of the seagulls wheeling overhead and the laughter of a family group picnicking further along the sand. To her left, Newcastle's famous Nobby's Lighthouse sat atop the headland. Straight out in front of her was the Pacific Ocean.

So much space. So much room to breathe.

She pulled in a deep breath before turning to find Dylan watching her. With a self-conscious shrug she sat beside him. But not too close. She kept the pizza boxes between them. 'You couldn't have chosen a better spot. It's wonderful down here.'

'A perfect night for a picnic. Now, try a piece of this pizza.'

She took a piece from the proffered box and bit into it. The flavours melted on her tongue and it was all she could do not to groan in appreciation. 'Good…' she murmured. 'Seriously good.'

They munched pizza in silence for a bit. The longer they sat there, the lighter Mia started to feel. Dylan reminded her of all the pleasures—big and small—that the world held. Even after almost eleven months she was still afraid of giving herself over to enjoyment.

'A penny for them.'

His voice broke into her thoughts.

'One moment you were enjoying all of this and the next moment you weren't.'

'Oh!' She swung to him. 'I'm having a lovely time. Truly.'

Her stomach clenched. She'd come here to tell him the truth.

So tell him the truth.

She finished off her piece of pizza and reached for a paper napkin. 'If you want to know the truth, I'm afraid of enjoying it too much.'

'Why?'

She couldn't look at him. 'In case I do something stupid and it's taken away from me again.'

He was silent for a couple of beats. 'You're talking about prison?'

She nodded.

'Is there any reason to believe you'll end up back there?'

Not if she remained vigilant.

'I find it hard to take my liberty for granted.' She grimaced. 'You don't understand how much you take it for granted until it's taken away. Prison is a punishment—it's supposed to be unpleasant. The thought of messing up and ending up back in there...' She shivered. 'So sometimes I find myself lost in a moment of enjoyment and then I remember jail and I wonder... I wonder how I could cope if I found myself back there again.'

He leaned towards her, drenching the air with a hint of smoky nutmeg. It mingled with the scents of ocean and pizza and she couldn't recall relishing anything more in her life. She wanted to close her eyes and memorise that scent, so she could pull it out and appreciate it whenever she needed to.

'Mia, you're a different person now. You won't make the same mistakes again.'

She wasn't convinced—especially on that last point. 'I think you need to know my story.'

'I'd like to know it very much.'

'It's sordid,' she warned.

She couldn't make this pretty for him, no matter how much she might want to. He just shrugged, his eyes not leaving her face. It made her mouth dry.

'Have you really not looked me up?' There'd be newspaper articles and court reports he could access.

'I wanted to hear the story from you—not from some so-called factual report that leaves out the truly relevant facts.'

She had a feeling that should have surprised her, but it didn't. She glanced down at her hands. 'I think I mentioned that my father was a…a difficult man.'

'Emotionally abusive to your mother?'

She nodded, fighting the weariness that wanted to claim her. 'When I was sixteen I finally stood up to him.'

'What happened?'

'He gave me a black eye and kicked me out.'

Dylan's hands fisted.

'I found temporary shelter in a homeless refuge and got work waitressing.'

'School?'

'I couldn't manage school *and* work.' She blew out a breath. 'That's something prison *did* give me—the opportunity to finish my high school education. It's my high school diploma that made me eligible for the traineeship at Plum Pines.'

'Right.'

She couldn't tell what he was thinking so she simply pushed on. 'When I was eighteen I met a man—Johnnie Peters. He was twenty-five and I thought him so worldly. I'd had a couple of boyfriends, you understand, but nothing serious.'

'Until Johnnie?'

'Until Johnnie…' She swallowed the lump that threatened her throat. It settled in her chest to ache with a dull throb. 'He swept me off my feet. I fell hopelessly in love with him.'

A muscle in Dylan's jaw worked. 'Would I be right in suspecting he didn't deserve you?'

She could feel her lips twist. It took all her strength to maintain eye contact with Dylan. 'The key word in my previous sentence was *hopelessly*.' She stared back out to sea. 'I had a lot of counselling when I was in jail. I understand now that there are men out there who target foolish, naïve girls. Which is exactly what I was.'

He reached out to squeeze her hand. 'You were young.'

She pulled her hand from his. 'When something looks too good to be true, it usually is. I knew that then, but I ignored it. He made me feel special, and I wanted to be special.' She gripped her hands together. 'He organised a new job for me—nine to five—where I was trained in office administration. It seemed like a step up. I was ridiculously grateful not to be on my feet all day, like I had been when waitressing.'

When she'd been in prison she'd longed for that waitressing job—aching legs and all. She should have been grateful for what she'd had. Content.

'He moved me into his lovely house and bought me beautiful clothes. He was a stockbroker, and I thought he could have his pick of women. I felt I was the luckiest girl alive.'

'He cut you off from your family and friends…controlled your finances?'

'My family had already cut me off, but…yes.' That was something she'd come to realise during sessions with her counsellor. 'Things seemed perfect for a couple of years. What I didn't realise was that he had a gambling problem.'

'What happened?' he prompted when she remained silent.

'He started asking me to deposit cheques into accounts that weren't in my name and then to withdraw the funds.'

'You gave all the money to him?'

'I gave him everything.' She'd been an idiot. 'Of course it was only a matter of time before I was traced on CCTV.'

'And Johnnie?'

'He was cleverer than I. He was never seen in the vicinity of any of the banks at the time, and he denied all knowledge.'

His mouth grew taut. 'The scumbag fed you to the wolves.'

She turned to him, the ache in her chest growing fierce. 'He was even smarter than that, Dylan. He convinced me to feed *myself* to the wolves. I told the police he was innocent.'

Anger flared in his eyes. 'How long did it take you to realise what he was?'

Her stomach churned. She'd told herself it would be better for Dylan to despise her than it would be for him to love her. A part of her died inside anyway.

'About four months into my sentence…when he hadn't been to see me…when he stopped answering my letters.'

'Then you turned him in to the authorities?'

She shook her head.

'You continued to let him walk all over you?'

She stiffened at the censure in his voice. 'Three things, Dylan. One—I had no proof. Especially not after the testimony I'd given in his favour. Any testimony to the contrary would've simply been written off as the ravings of a disaffected lover. Two—I needed to draw a line under that part of my life and move forward. And three—I deserved my punishment. Nothing was ever going to change that.'

'He *manipulated* you!'

'And I let him. I *knew* what I was doing was wrong. The first time I cashed a cheque he told me it was for his elderly aunt. The second time he said it was a favour for a work colleague. The third time he just asked me to do it for him, said that he was in trouble. I knew then that I was breaking the law, but I did it anyway. He never physically threatened me. I just did it.'

'But I bet the emotional threat of him breaking up with you hung over every request?'

It had. And she hadn't been able to face the thought of losing him. Talk about pathetic! 'I told you it was sordid.'

'Three years seems a long sentence for a first offender.'

She moistened her lips. 'I stole a *lot* of money.'

He stared out to sea and her heart burned at the conflict

reflected in his face. 'You made a bad choice and you've paid for it.' He turned, spearing her with his gaze. 'Would you make the same decision again, given what you know now?'

'Of course not. But we don't get the chance to live our lives over. We just have to find ways to live with our mistakes.'

'Shunning the simple pleasures in life won't help you do that.'

He had a point.

His brows drew down low over his eyes. 'Don't you worry about other young women he might have targeted?'

Her heart started to thump. Trust Dylan to worry about vulnerable women he didn't even know. She glanced down at her hands. 'Fourteen months into my sentence Johnnie attempted an armed hold-up on a security van. He wasn't successful. He was sentenced to fifteen years. I think the foolish young women of the world are safe from him for the moment.'

'Good.'

Neither one of them went back to eating pizza.

'Is that why you let men walk all over you?'

She stiffened. 'I don't let *you* walk all over me.'

His lips twisted, though his eyes remained hard. 'There's hope for me yet, then.'

'No, there's not! I—'

'You've let Gordon, Thierry and Felipe all treat you like you're worthless. Your father and Johnnie both treated you badly. Do you *really* hold yourself so cheaply?'

Her heart surged against her ribs. 'Neither my father nor Johnnie are in my life any more. Thierry doesn't matter to me one jot! Felipe *didn't* take advantage of me. And as for Gordon...'

Dylan folded his arms and raised his eyebrows.

'He has the power to fire me. Keeping my head beneath the parapet where he's concerned is the smartest course of action. It won't be forever.'

'There'll always be Gordons in your life in one form or another. Are you going to turn yourself into a doormat for all of them?'

'If I do it'll be none of your business!'

'Why tell me all of this, then?'

'Because if we're going to be *friends*—' she ground the word out '—eventually the press will find out who I am and my story will come out. And it wouldn't be fair to have the press spring something like that on you without preparing you first.'

He dragged a hand down his face.

'And…'

He stilled. 'And…?'

She didn't want to continue, but she had to. It was the reason she'd started this conversation. 'And I wanted you to understand why I have no intention of ever pursuing another romantic relationship.'

He stared at her, but she couldn't read the expression in his eyes.

'Because you were burned once?'

'Because I don't like who I am when I'm in love. I refuse to become that person again.'

He shot to his feet. 'Are you likening me to this Johnnie Peters?'

She shot to her feet too. 'Of course not!'

He stabbed a finger at her. 'That's *exactly* what you're doing. You're saying that if you let yourself be vulnerable to me, I'll take advantage of you.'

She could feel herself start to shake. 'This is about me, not you!'

'Garbage. I—'

He broke off when a bright flash momentarily blinded both of them. Mia realised two things then—night had fallen…and someone had just snapped their photo.

Without another word, Dylan charged off into the darkness.

Biting back a groan, Mia set off after him.

* * *

Dylan hurled himself at the shape that had emerged in the darkness, bringing the anonymous photographer down.

He tried to clamp down on the rage that had him wanting to tear things apart with his bare hands. He wanted to tear apart the men who'd let Mia down—her father, the despicable Johnnie Peters. He wanted to tear apart her mistaken view of herself as some kind of spineless push-over. He wanted to tear apart her view of *him*! Most of all he wanted to tear himself apart, and he didn't know why.

Don't tear the photographer apart. He's just doing his job.

'Fair go, Fairweather!'

Dylan pushed himself upright as Mia came running up. She shone the torch on her phone on the photographer, confirming Dylan's suspicions. A hard ball lodged in his belly.

'Percy Struthers. What the hell do you think you're doing, sneaking up on me again *now*?'

Percy had created a PR firestorm last year, when Dylan had been in charge of a Turkish sultan's sixtieth birthday celebrations. Percy had released a photo of Dylan and the Sultan's very beautiful youngest daughter, linking them romantically. It had been a lie, of course, but try telling *that* to an enraged Turkish sultan...

Percy Struthers was the grubbiest of the gutter press, and trouble with a capital T.

Mia had broken the law—she'd done wrong and she'd paid the price—but the world was full of immoral, unethical people who lied and cheated. Were *they* sent to jail? Hardly! Some of them were applauded and clapped on the back for it—like tabloid journalists and politicians.

'It's news whenever a new woman turns up in your life—you know that.'

'Give me the camera.'

With a sigh, Percy handed it over.

Dylan stood and indicated for Mia to shine her torch

on the camera. With a flick of his fingers he removed the memory stick.

Percy clambered to his feet, caught the camera when Dylan tossed it back to him. 'It won't stop the story, you know.'

'Without a photograph the story won't gain traction.'

They both knew that.

The photographer gave an ugly laugh. 'But one of us will eventually get a photo—you can't remain on your guard twenty-four-seven.'

Beside him, Mia stiffened. Dylan wanted to throw his head back and howl. This was her worst nightmare, and it was he who'd dragged her into it.

'I know who she is,' Percy continued. 'And I know what she's done.'

Her *absolute* worst nightmare.

'Aren't you afraid she's on the make? That you're simply her latest target?'

He felt rather than saw Mia flinch. A ball of fury lodged in his gut.

Don't rise to the bait. Don't give the pond scum anything. Don't feed the frenzy.

It hit him suddenly how much his name, his position, were black marks against him in Mia's book.

Percy gave another of those ugly laughs. 'An ex-con? *Really*, Dylan? What are you trying to prove? Or have you developed a taste for a bit of rough?'

Dylan reached out and took Mia's hand. 'I think we're done here.'

'Run along, darlin'.' The photographer smirked. 'We all know what you're after.'

And then he called her a name that no man should ever call a woman.

Dylan whirled around, his right hand fisted, and smashed him square on the nose. Blood burst from it as the man reeled backwards to sprawl on the ground. Pain shot up Dylan's arm.

Mia sucked in a breath, and even in the darkness he could see the way her eyes flashed.

Percy cursed. 'You'll pay for that, Fairweather.

Mia tried to tug her hand from Dylan's but he refused to relinquish it. He towed her in the direction of the car instead. He had to get out of here before he did something truly despicable—like beat Percy Struthers to a pulp.

Mia sat in tight-lipped silence all the way home, only unfolding her arms to push herself out of the car once he'd pulled up at the front of her cottage. She slammed it with a force that made him wince.

He had to jog to catch up with her. She didn't hold the front door open for him, letting it fall behind her, meaning he had to catch it. But at least she hadn't slammed it in his face. He told himself that was something.

'You're…uh…cross with me?'

She turned on him, and her eyes flashed with so much anger the hair at her temples seemed to shake with it.

She seized his right hand and glanced down at it. 'Does it hurt?'

'Yes.'

'Good.'

She dropped it as if it burned her. Moving to the freezer, she took out a packet of frozen peas. Grabbing his hand, she slammed it on top of his grazed knuckles. It didn't really hurt any more, but he winced anyway, hoping it would give her more bloodthirsty impulses a measure of satisfaction. And he submitted when she pushed him towards one of her hard wooden chairs—not so hard now they sported pale blue chair pads.

She lifted his left hand and dropped it on top of the peas to hold them in place, then retreated to sit on the sofa and glower at him.

The silence started to saw on his nerves. 'You think I'm an idiot?'

'Totally.'

'He had no right to call you what he did.'

'You are *utterly* infuriating!' Her hands balled into fists. 'What he called me was despicable, but the best thing you could've done was walk away without giving him the satisfaction of reacting.' She shot to her feet and started to pace. 'Oh, but, *no*—you couldn't manage that, could you? No! Your honour demanded reparation for the lady—regardless of how much more difficult you'd be making it for said lady!'

He shifted on the chair. 'I…uh…'

'The story will break in the tabloids, the ugliest accusations will be made, and I'll be hounded by reporters and photographers at work. *Hell!*' She flung her arms out. 'Just wait until Gordon catches wind of this. I'll be out on my ear.' She swung to him, thumping a hand to her chest. 'I *need* to finish this traineeship. I need a decent qualification so I can get a job.'

'I've already told you—come and work for me.'

'I don't *want* to work for you!'

Her rejection stung. He shot to his feet then too. 'That's right—you'd rather bury yourself in some godforsaken place where you can sentence yourself to a life of solitary confinement.'

'That's *my* decision to make.'

He wanted to hurl the peas across the room. Except he didn't want to ruin the pretty new furnishings. He had to settle for dropping them in the sink instead.

He moved back into the middle of the room. 'I have no intention of making light of your experiences with the criminal justice system, but you're letting one experience colour your entire life.' That hard lump of anger in his chest rose up into his throat. 'And I am *not* Johnnie Peters.'

Her entire frame shook. 'I told you—this is about *me*. Not *you*.' She didn't yell, but her words speared through him as if they'd come at him at great volume. 'You *punched* a man tonight, Dylan. That photographer can have you charged with assault. He'd be within his rights.'

It was true. It had been foolish to react. He couldn't find it in himself to regret it, though.

'And you made *me* an eye witness to the event.'

He swung back to meet her gaze. What he saw there made his heart burn.

'If I were in love with you, and you asked me to lie to the police about what had happened tonight...'

She didn't finish the sentence, but her pallor made his stomach churn.

'You're afraid you'd perjure yourself for me?'

'If I fell in love with you, Dylan, I'm afraid I'd risk everything again.'

He reached out to curl his fingers around her shoulders. 'I would *never* ask that of you.'

She moved away until his hands dropped back to his sides. 'The best way for me to avoid that kind of temptation is to avoid romantic attachments altogether. All I want is a quiet life. It doesn't seem too much to ask. It doesn't seem like such a big sacrifice to make.'

Ice sped through his veins. 'You're mistaken if you think living a half-life isn't a sacrifice. It'll keep you out of jail, it'll keep you out of trouble, but there are worse things than jail.'

She blinked, as if that wasn't a thought that had ever occurred to her.

'Living a life without love is one of them. And here's another thing for you to think about. If I fell in love with *you*—' he pointed a finger at her '—who's to say you wouldn't have the same power over me that Johnnie had over you? Who's to say you wouldn't force me to turn my back on my principles?'

The words spilled from him with an uncanny truth that left him reeling.

Her mouth dropped open.

He forged on, not understanding what was happening to him. 'Do you think I'd lie, steal or perjure myself for you?'

Her hands twisted together. 'You might lie for me…if it wasn't a big lie.'

He widened his stance. 'But the rest?'

She bit her lip and finally shook her head. 'No.'

'What makes you think *you* would, then?'

'My past tells me I'm weak.'

'Do you really think three years in prison—with all the education and counselling you received—hasn't made you stronger?'

She still labelled herself as weak-willed and easy to manipulate. He understood her fear of prison, and her determination never to find herself back behind bars, but she was wrong. She might let people like Gordon push her around, but she was as strong as one of the Plum Pines the reserve was named after.

Behind the dark moss of her eyes he could see her mind racing. He mightn't have convinced her. *Yet.* But he'd given her something to think about.

He snaked his hand behind her head and drew her face close to his.

'What are you doing?' she squeaked.

'I'm giving you something else to think about. Do you *really* want to live without this, Mia?'

He wanted to slam his lips to hers and kiss her with all the pent-up frustration tearing at his soul. He didn't. She'd tensed, ready to resist such an assault. And he didn't want to hurt her. If she'd let him he'd do everything he could to make her happy.

He touched his lips to hers gently, slowly exploring the lush lines of her mouth—savouring her. He poured all of himself into the kiss, wanting to give her as much pleasure as he could.

With a shiver and a sigh she sank against him, her hands fisting in his shirt. At his gentle demand she opened up to him and he felt as if he was home. Murmuring her name, he moved to gather her close—only to find a hand planted on his chest, pushing him away.

'Stop.'

He released her immediately.

Her chest rose and fell as if she'd been running. 'You shouldn't be kissing me.'

He couldn't think of anything he'd rather do.

'What you should be doing is readying yourself for the PR disaster that's about to hit.'

He remained silent until she lifted her gaze to his. 'I promise you won't lose your job.'

She snorted her disbelief. 'Will you please warn Carla too? I think it'd be a good idea if you told her all that I told you tonight.'

'You want Carla to know?'

'It seems only fair.'

'No.' He refused to be a party to her shutting herself off from people. 'If you're truly her friend, Mia, then *you* tell her.'

With that, he spun on his heel and left.

Dylan stumbled down Mia's front steps, feeling as if he'd descended a drop of a thousand feet. He put out a hand to steady himself, but there was nothing to grab on to. He stood there swaying, praying he'd find his balance soon.

What had just happened?

Idiot!

The word screamed over and over in his mind, but he didn't know why.

What was so idiotic about anything he'd done tonight? Mia might think him an idiot for punching Percy Struthers, but the man had deserved it. Given the chance, he'd do it again! And he wasn't an idiot for refusing to be labelled as another Johnnie Peters either.

Pain shot into his jaw from clenching his teeth too hard. He was *nothing* like Johnnie Peters!

He lurched over to his car and flung the door open, but he didn't get in.

He wasn't an idiot for fighting against Mia's mistaken view of herself. She wasn't weak! She was one of the strongest women he knew.

Stronger than Caitlin.

He froze. Where had *that* come from?

But… Mia *was* stronger than Caitlin.

His mouth dried, and his heart was pounding so hard it sent nausea swirling through him. Mia was *exactly* the kind of woman who'd go the distance with a man—who'd take the good times with the bad, who'd weather the storms. Mia wouldn't turn tail and run at the first sign of trouble. If things got tough she'd dig her heels in and wait it out.

Idiot!

It finally hit him why that word kept going round and round in his mind. He collapsed on to the car seat. He'd been telling himself all this time that what he wanted with Mia was an affair, but that was a lie.

He wanted it all. *He loved her.* He wanted a chance to build a life with her.

His vision darkened. He raked his hands through his hair. All this time he'd thought he'd been keeping his heart safe… and yet the whole time he'd been falling in love with her.

His hands clenched about the steering wheel. He would *not* give up! Mia had told his uncle that he, Dylan, made dreams come true. Was there the slightest chance on earth that he could make *her* dreams come true?

If he wanted to win her heart he had to find out.

CHAPTER TEN

THE STORY DIDN'T break on Monday or Tuesday. It didn't break on Wednesday or Thursday either. There wasn't a single item in the newspapers about Dylan, let alone any shady ex-convict women he might be dating.

Not that they *were* dating.

Even if he'd made it clear that he'd like to be.

Mia's wilful heart leapt at the thought, avoiding all her attempts to squash its exuberance.

She'd finally gathered up the courage to ring Carla on Tuesday night. Carla had claimed she didn't care about Mia's history—that she only cared about the kind of person Mia was now. Mia had even believed her.

She hadn't seen Dylan all week. He hadn't dropped by Plum Pines during her lunchbreak. He hadn't rung her for no reason at all other than to talk nonsense until she started to laugh in spite of herself. He hadn't even rung to talk about the wedding.

Despite her best intentions, she missed him.

She didn't just miss him—she *ached* for him.

On Friday morning, when it was barely light, she rushed the one and a half kilometres to the nearest newsagent's to buy a newspaper. Again, nothing.

Saturday dawned—the day of her dinner party—and still no scandal broke. She could hardly imagine what strings

Dylan had pulled to hush up the story. Could she start to breathe more easily?

It didn't make the memory of their encounter with the photographer fade, though. She physically flinched whenever she recalled the moment Dylan had punched the other man. Was he *crazy*? He could have been hauled off in a paddy wagon and thrown in a cell overnight! All because someone had called her a bad name.

Couldn't he see that for the rest of her life there'd be people who'd be happy to call her bad names? What would he do—punch them *all* on the nose?

Dylan deserved better than that.

So do you.

The thought whispered through her and she had to sink down into the nearest chair. Her heart thumped, the pulse in her throat pounded and her temples throbbed.

There are worse things than prison.

Dylan was right.

Shame, sharp and hot, engulfed her. She'd stolen money from people—people who hadn't deserved it. Knowing she was capable of that—living with that knowledge—was the worst thing of all. She'd willingly spend another three years in prison if it would rid her of the taint. But it wouldn't. Nothing would. Saying sorry to the people she'd hurt, doing her jail time, being a model prisoner, having the counselling—none of that had helped.

The only way she could ensure she never did something like that again was to stay away from people as much as she could.

Heat burned the backs of her eyes. She pressed a fist to her mouth. She wanted to believe Dylan—believe that she'd changed, become stronger, that no one could manipulate her now. His face rose up in her mind…a beautiful dream she'd kept telling herself was out of reach. Her every atom yearned towards him.

With a half-sob, she closed her eyes. She couldn't reach for that dream until she was certain she'd changed.

But how could she ever be certain of that?

Mia glanced at the plate of nibbles she'd set on the coffee table—some nice cheese and fancy crackers, along with some fat feta-stuffed olives. Should she add some grapes to the platter?

She clasped and unclasped her hands. She wasn't serving an entrée—just a main and a dessert…and these pre-dinner nibbles.

She peered into the refrigerator to check on the individual crème-brûlées she'd prepared earlier. What if they'd spoiled?

They hadn't.

She glanced at the wine. What if she'd chosen the wrong sort? She knew nothing about wine. The man at the liquor store had been helpful, but still…

What if nobody wanted wine? What if they wanted something she didn't have? She'd stocked up on mineral water and cola. She'd filled umpteen ice cube trays, so there'd be plenty of ice, but… She hadn't thought to buy port. What if someone wanted an after-dinner port? Or sherry!

She twisted her hands together. What if she ruined the veal scaloppini?

We'll call out for pizza.

What if she spilled a whole bottle of wine?

We'll mop it up.

What if—?

Relax.

The voice in her head sounded suspiciously like Dylan's. Funnily enough, it *did* help calm her panic.

It's just a dinner for friends. Nothing to get het up about.

A knock sounded at the front door and her heart immediately leapt into her throat.

They were twenty minutes early!

Does it matter?

Yes. No. She didn't know.

She wiped her palms down her pretty pink summer dress—another extravagant spur-of-the-moment purchase. She'd been making a few of those since she'd met Dylan—not that she could find it in herself to regret them.

Pulling in a breath, she went to answer it. Dylan stared at her from behind the screen. He held a bottle of wine and a bunch of flowers, but she barely noticed them against the intensity of his burning blue eyes.

Swallowing, she unlatched the screen and pushed it open. 'Come in.'

He kissed her cheek—all formality—and handed her the wine and flowers. 'Gifts for the hostess.'

She swallowed again, her senses drenched with the nutmeg scent of him. 'Thank you.'

While he might be physically close, his reserve made him seem a million miles away. Her fingers tightened around the stems of the flowers. She had no idea how to breach that distance. She wasn't even sure she should attempt it.

'I didn't know if you'd come.' She moved behind the kitchen counter to find a vase for the flowers—yellow-headed daisies.

'I'd have let you know if I couldn't make it.'

Of course he would. He had impeccable manners.

She glanced up to find him scrutinising her living room, a frown—small but unmistakable—settling over his features.

She set the vase of flowers on the kitchen bench and walked across. 'What's wrong?' Maybe he hated cheese and olives. She could have sworn he'd eaten them the night she'd dined at the Fairweather mansion.

He gestured to the room. 'Do you mind if I make a few adjustments?'

'Knock yourself out.'

He immediately shifted the cushions out of their perfect alignment and shook out her throw rug before casually draping it across the sofa. He took a decorative rock from the mantel and placed it on the coffee table, pushed the platter of cheese and olives from the centre further towards one end. He moved the vase of fresh flowers she'd bought that morning to the end of the mantel, rather than dead centre, and then pulled a magazine and a book from the magazine rack, all but hidden by the sofa, and placed them on the little table by the door.

'There!' He dusted off his hands. 'Now the place looks lived in.'

Mia blinked. His few simple changes had made a big difference. The room now radiated warmth rather than stiff awkwardness.

Her hands went to her hips. 'How do you even know how to do that?'

He shrugged. 'You just need to relax a bit more, Mia.'

Relaxing around Dylan… Was that even possible?

She swallowed. 'I spoke to Carla through the week.'

'I know. She's talked of little else.'

Mia couldn't work out whether he was pleased about that or not.

'Carla's the reason I'm early. She seemed to think you might need a hand, and that I should be the one to offer it.'

He didn't smile.

She gestured to the room, trying to lighten the mood. 'Obviously she was right.'

He just stared at her, his eyes blue and brooding.

She pressed a hand to her stomach. 'I…uh… I think I have everything under control.' She kicked into hostess mode. 'Can I get you a drink? Beer, wine…soft drink?'

He chose wine. She poured wine for both of them and invited him to help himself to the cheese and olives. They sat there barely talking, barely looking at each other. Mia excused herself and pretended to do something in the kitchen.

They were rescued from their excruciating awkwardness when Carla and Thierry arrived fifteen minutes later.

'Oh, look at your cottage!' Carla gushed, hugging her. 'It's so quaint and pretty.'

Carla's kindness eased some of the burning in Mia's soul, and she could only give thanks that his sister's presence made Dylan a little more sociable. Thierry neither hugged her nor kissed her cheek. Not that she'd expected him to do either. He barely said hello.

The veal scaloppini was a melt-in-the-mouth success. The dinner, however, wasn't. Dylan complimented her on the food, made small talk about nothing of note, and every time Mia glanced at him a knife twisted into her heart. His despondency—his *unhappiness*—was her fault.

She hated it that she'd hurt him. And she didn't know how to make it right. More to the point, she didn't know if she *should* make it right.

Carla's eyes grew increasingly narrow as she glanced from Mia to Dylan. Thierry just continued to survey Mia with his usual and by now familiar suspicion.

She told a funny story about a wombat at Plum Pines but only Carla laughed.

She mentioned that she was considering getting a car and asked if they had any opinions on what she should buy. Thierry said he wasn't interested in cars.

Carla gaped at him. 'Liar!'

'I'm interested in *sports* cars. Mia can't afford one of those.'

'Don't be so rude!'

'No, Thierry's right,' Mia jumped in. 'I'm just after something reliable and economical.'

Dylan then subjected them all to a long, monotonous monologue about the pros and cons of a particular model of hatchback that had their eyes glazing over and Mia wishing she'd never asked the question in the first place.

'What is *wrong* with you two?' Carla finally burst out at the two men. 'I think it's brave of Mia to tell us the full story of her past. I don't care what the two of you think—it doesn't change the way *I* feel about her. She's been a lovely friend to me.'

'Carla, that's really nice of you.' Mia's heart hammered up into her throat. 'But I think you ought to know that Dylan doesn't have an issue with my past either.'

Carla folded her arms, her eyes flashing. 'Then what's the problem? What's wrong with the pair of you?'

'That's none of your business,' Thierry bit out.

'Dylan is my brother. Mia is my friend. Of *course* it's my business.' She turned to Mia. 'Is it because of that incident with the photographer?'

Dylan's hands clenched about his knife and fork. 'Why the hell did you have to tell Carla about that anyway?' he shot at Mia.

An answering anger snapped through her. 'I didn't know it was a state secret. Besides, I thought it only fair that Carla be prepared for the story to break.'

'I told you I'd take care of it!'

'You'll have to excuse my scepticism. I didn't know your reach was both long and powerful enough to stop a story that juicy from making the headlines.'

'There's a lot you don't know about me!'

He glared at her.

She glared back.

'Why did you wait until Tuesday night to tell Carla?'

The question ground out of Thierry, cutting through everything else.

Mia moistened her lips. 'Because I was afraid that once she knew the whole truth she'd despise me.'

Thierry leaned towards her. On her other side she felt Dylan tense.

'She *should* despise you.'

'Thierry!'

Carla's pallor caught at Mia's heart.

'Ignore him. He has a giant chip on his shoulder because his father was in and out of prison all through his childhood.'

Mia's jaw dropped as Thierry's animosity made sudden and perfect sense.

Thierry shot to his feet. 'I told you that in the strictest confidence!'

They all stared after him as he slammed out of the house.

Carla leapt up too, grabbing her handbag. 'I'll call you tomorrow,' she said to Mia, before racing after him.

Mia glanced at Dylan. Did *he* mean to slam out of her cottage as well?

He stared back, his mouth a hard straight line, and she realised he meant to do no such thing.

She swallowed. 'Dessert?'

'Please.'

Before Mia could retrieve the crème-brûlées the cottage phone rang. That phone hardly ever rang.

She lifted the receiver. 'Hello?'

'This is Andrew Fairweather, Ms Maydew—Dylan and Carla's uncle. Perhaps you remember me?'

His tone of voice said, *Of course you remember me.*

'Yes, sir, I do.'

'A disturbing report has reached me claiming that you and my nephew are romantically involved. Well?'

His tone reminded her of her father. Her hands trembled. *You stood up to your father.*

She pushed her shoulders back. 'No comment.'

'I know about your background, young lady!'

Her fingers tightened about the receiver. 'I can't say as I'm surprised.' She glanced at Dylan to find him watching her closely.

'I'm giving you a friendly warning.'

Oh, yes—very friendly.

'Stay away from my nephew and niece or you *will* be sorry.'

'I'll keep that in mind.'

The line went dead. She dropped the receiver to the cradle and made for the kitchen.

'Was that the press?' Dylan demanded.

She set a crème-brûlée in front of him and slid into her seat. 'Have a taste.'

He looked as if he wanted to argue, but he spooned some of the dessert into his mouth and an expression of bliss spread across his face. He swore—just a little swear word—in an expression of wonder, not of alarm or anger. 'This is *amazing.*'

She stared at him, her chest clenching and unclenching, her skin going hot and cold, and something inside her melted so fast she wanted to cry out loud at the shock of it.

She loved him.

She loved him utterly, but she couldn't see how things between them could ever work out.

'Mia?'

She straightened. 'It wasn't the press on the phone, Dylan. It was your uncle.'

Dylan swore—one of the rudest words he knew.

Mia flinched. For all that she'd been to jail, she was no hardened criminal.

'I'm sorry. I shouldn't have said that.'

She waved his apology away. 'It doesn't matter.'

It *did* matter. She deserved better. 'He warned you off?'

'Yes.'

He set his spoon down. 'What did he threaten you with?'

Her lips lifted a fraction. 'It wasn't a threat, but a "friendly warning".'

As if that were somehow different! He wished to God he could smile with her, but his sense of humour had deserted him. It had abandoned him when he'd walked away from her last week.

Fear had taken its place. Fear that he would never find a way to win her love.

'And it wasn't specific—just a general warning to stay away from you and Carla or I'd be sorry.'

'Are you going to heed him?'

She picked up her spoon and pressed it gently to the crust of her crème-brûlée until it cracked. 'Surely you and Carla have some say in the matter?'

He stilled. That felt like progress. 'You're not going to buckle under to his bullying?'

'Your uncle reminds me of my father. I stood up to my father and the world didn't come crashing down. Mind you—' her sigh arrowed into his chest '—it didn't do me any good either.'

The smile she sent him made his eyes burn.

'I suspect that if he chooses, your uncle could cause trouble for me.'

'And all you want is a quiet life?'

She lifted her eyes heavenward. 'I *crave* a quiet life.'

Life with him would never be quiet.

She brought her spoon down on top of her dessert again, shattering the toffee crust further. 'But me standing up to your uncle isn't going to be enough for you, Dylan, is it?' She met his gaze, her eyes troubled. 'You want more from me, and I don't know if I can give it to you.'

He straightened *I don't know* was a monumental improvement on *No chance at all*.

'You want our relationship to become physical, and you assure me you can keep that news under wraps from the press. I'm even starting to believe you. But can you promise me—?'

He leaned across and pressed a finger to her lips. 'First things first.' He needed to remove a significant problem before focusing on the reasons behind her softening. 'You think my uncle can cause problems for you at work with Gordon?'

'The thought has crossed my mind.' She stabbed the spoon into her dessert. 'I liked my plan—gain a useful qualification that'll keep me in employment—but I think it's time to say goodbye to it.'

He removed the crème-brûlée from her grasp and placed

it out of reach before she totally mangled it. 'You have a new plan?' Even though he knew it was a long shot, he couldn't help hoping he featured in this Plan B of hers.

'I think I'd better start looking for unskilled work—factory work or waitressing. At a pinch I suppose I could join the fruit-picking circuit.'

A hand reached out and wrung his heart. *No!*

Her raised eyebrow told him he had no say in the matter. 'I *won't* leave you worse off than I found you. I *won't* be responsible for that.'

Too late.

The words whispered through him, leaving a bitter aftertaste. 'I promise to do everything in my power to ensure you keep your job at Plum Pines.'

He could see that while she believed the sincerity of his intention she didn't think he'd be able to achieve the desired outcome. She had a point. His uncle held a lot of sway.

He drummed his fingers on the table. 'Right. If that doesn't work… Look, I know you don't want to work for FWE, but you could still do a traineeship with the company.' He drummed his fingers harder as his mind raced. 'I'd put you under one of my managers. You'd hardly see me. Our paths would barely cross.' He'd make sure they didn't if it would help her accept his offer. 'After two years of working for FWE, you could get a job anywhere in the industry. Job security would never be an issue for you again.'

'Dylan, I—'

He held up his hand. 'This is only a fall-back plan, in case you're fired from Plum Pines. I don't want to be responsible for you losing your job. Ever since I've met you, all I've done is cause you trouble.' He started to tick off the list on his fingers. 'Gordon tried to fire you for flirting with me, when I was the one doing the flirting. I introduced you to Thierry, who tried to play the heavy with you. Felipe put you in an untenable position when he snapped that photograph. The press have tried to go to town on you. And now my uncle has threatened you. It's not a list to be proud of.'

She glanced away. When she turned back, her eyes were dark and troubled. 'I fear you're paying for it too, though,' she said.

She was worth any price he had to pay. Which would be fine if he were the one paying the piper and not her. When he looked at the facts baldly, he'd done nothing but cause her trouble.

'That really is quite a list.' For the briefest of moments her eyes twinkled. 'It hasn't been all bad. You've bought me chocolate, and I've had my toenails painted. And I got the opportunity to see some amazing art.'

It was a paltry list in comparison.

She pressed her hands together. 'Most importantly, though, we now know Thierry isn't mistreating Carla.'

That *was* something. He'd never have found that out if it weren't for Mia.

'I've also learned some decorating tips and had the opportunity to cook veal scaloppini. What more could a girl want?'

A whole lot more!

He dragged a hand back through his hair. 'Dinner tonight was truly awful. Not the food,' he added quickly. 'The atmosphere.' And that had mostly been his fault too.

Mia pleated the tablecloth. 'I thought you were sulking.'

He couldn't seem to find any middle ground where she was concerned. 'I've been trying to give you some space, but the effort is killing me.'

As soon as he said it he knew the admission was too much. Mia sat further back in her seat. Further away from him. He had to swallow a groan at the pain that cramped his chest.

Pulling in a breath, he forced himself to focus on the important topic of their conversation. 'Please tell me that if you do lose your job you'll allow FWE to employ you. I can't stand the thought of bringing that much trouble to your door.

I know it means working in events management, rather than in conservation, but once you've gained the qualification you can arrange your working hours so you can study at night for a different qualification if you want. If I'm reading you correctly, it's job security that's really important to you.'

She was silent for several long moments, but eventually something in her shoulders unhitched. 'Okay.'

He stared at her. 'You mean it?'

'I'm really, *really* hoping I don't lose my position at Plum Pines.'

'We'll call that Plan A.'

'But if I do lose it, then, yes… I'd like to accept your offer of a position at FWE. We can call that Plan B'

'You'll trust that I won't try and take advantage of the situation?'

She nodded, and he found that he could smile. If she trusted him that far…

He rubbed his hands together. 'I feel we're making progress.'

'Progress?' The word squeaked out of her. 'How?'

He leaned towards her. 'I want to throw our ground rules out the window, Mia. I thought I only wanted an affair with you—fun, pleasure, satisfaction.'

At each word her eyes widened.

'But I was wrong. I want a whole lot more than that. I want—'

She pressed her fingers to his lips before he could tell her he loved her. Her throat bobbed convulsively. 'You're moving too fast for me.'

He pressed a kiss to her fingers before wrapping her hand in his. 'I'll slow down.'

'Do you even know how to do that?'

'I'll learn.'

Her brow creased. 'Dylan, I can't promise you anything.'

'I know. I might have hope, but I don't have any expectations. I have no right to expect anything from you.'

Dark eyes stared into his. 'You have so much faith in me, and I have so little in myself.'

She had to find that faith or there'd be no chance for them. They both knew that.

Her gaze drifted down to his mouth. Her eyes darkened and her lips parted, as if she couldn't get enough air into her lungs.

'And yet your beauty continues to addle my brain,' she murmured, almost to herself. 'That can't be good.'

An answering desire took hold of him, his stomach muscles tightening and his skin tingling. 'I think it's excellent.'

She moistened her lips, her chest rising and falling. 'Would you like to stay the night?'

For a moment he couldn't breathe. His free hand clenched and then unclenched, before clenching again. 'I would *love* to stay the night, but you told me sex wouldn't make a difference.'

Her mouth opened, but no sound came out.

'Can you promise me that it *will* make a difference, Mia?'

Her gaze slid away and she shook her head.

He pulled in a breath and held strong. 'I want more than crumbs from you. I want everything.'

She looked as if she wanted to run away. 'I'm sorry. That was stupid of me. Especially when I just asked you to slow down.' She rubbed her brow. 'We should bring this evening to a close and you should say goodnight.'

He rose, forcing her to rise too. If he didn't leave soon he'd be in danger of settling for anything, however small. 'It's a hostess's duty to escort her guests to the door.'

She bit back a smile as he pulled her along in his wake. 'You're just angling for a kiss.'

He backed her up against the wall. 'It excites me to know you're burning for me.'

Her breath hitched. 'You promised slow.'

'It's just a kiss, Mia.'

'Nothing is *just* anything with you, Dylan. We both know that.'

'Then tell me to stop.'

Her gaze moved from his eyes to his mouth. 'Just a kiss?'

He grinned down at her and shook his head. 'I mean to leave you *really* burning, Mia.'

Her eyes widened. 'I—'

He covered her mouth with his own, keeping the caress gentle until she relaxed beneath his touch, her lips moving against his, her mouth opening to him... And then, without warning, he deepened the kiss, intensifying it using his lips, tongue, teeth. His hands pressed into the small of her back until her full length was against his. He used every weapon in his armoury to assault her senses.

'*Dylan...*'

His name was a groan of need on her lips, and it nearly drove him mad. She tangled her hands in his hair, drawing him closer as she tried to crawl into his skin, inflaming him beyond endurance. He pressed her back against the wall, his hands sliding down over her backside, his fingers digging into her buttocks, pulling her up and into him, his need for her a fire in his blood.

She wanted him too. They could have each other and...

He eased away from her. Their eyes locked. He wanted so much more than this from her, but he knew that if she asked him to stay now, he would.

She pulled in a breath, as if reading that thought in his face. With something that sounded like a sob, she planted a hand to his chest and gently pushed him away.

'Go.'

CHAPTER ELEVEN

MIA BARELY SLEPT that night. She gave up trying just before dawn. So when Carla pulled up at the front of the cottage just after six a.m. Mia happened to be sitting on her front step, nursing a mug of coffee.

She stood and opened the front gate, ushered Carla through. Carla trudged up the path and collapsed on to the step, and Mia's heart clenched at the sight of her friend's red-rimmed eyes.

Then she noted the faint blue bruise on Carla's right cheekbone and a hot pit of anger burned in her belly.

She brushed her fingers beneath it, unable to stop her eyes from filling. 'Not Thierry?'

Carla's eyes filled too. 'No. He's a jerk, but not that much of a jerk.'

'Not Dylan.'

It was a statement rather than a question. Dylan would never strike a woman.

Carla gave a short laugh. 'I think he'd rather throw himself off a cliff than hurt a woman.' She glanced at Mia and rolled her eyes. 'I mean *physically* hurt a woman. From what I can tell he's broken his fair share of hearts. The fact you're up so early leads me to believe he's given *you* a sleepless night.'

Mia felt her lips twist. 'In this instance I believe it's safe to say I've returned the favour.'

Carla's attempt at a smile almost broke Mia's heart. She sat down and put her arm around Carla's shoulders. 'Your uncle?'

Carla rested her head against Mia's. 'Yes…' she whispered.

The swine!

They sat like that for a while, letting the early-morning peace seep into their souls.

A sigh eventually shuddered out of Mia. 'He hit you because of me, didn't he? Because you refused to end our friendship. I'm sorry I've caused trouble for you, Carla. You don't deserve it.'

Carla lifted her head. 'He hit me because I refused to obey him—because I'm choosing to live my life the way I see fit. And it's not the first time it's happened.'

Mia called him one of the worst names she could think of.

A giggle shot out of Carla, but she nodded in agreement.

'C'mon.' Mia hauled her to her feet. 'Have you had an *ounce* of sleep?'

Carla shook her head.

She led her inside and pushed her in the direction of the bathroom. 'Go wash your face.' She pulled a soft cotton nightie from a drawer and ordered her to put it on, then pulled the covers back from her bed. 'In.'

'Oh, but…'

'We'll make a game plan after you've had some sleep.'

Carla glanced at the bed. 'A couple of hours *would* be good.' She glanced back at Mia, biting her lip. 'I really, *really* don't want to see either Thierry or Dylan at the moment. I know it's asking a lot of you, Mia, but I just…'

'You want to sort through things at your own pace. That's understandable.'

'I'm tired of men thinking they know what's best for me, telling me what to do.'

'I'll take care of Thierry and Dylan if they show up.'

Carla climbed into the bed.

Mia pulled the covers up to her chin, squeezed her hand briefly. 'Sleep well.'

She fortified herself with more coffee and went to sit back out on the front step to keep guard.

Dylan showed up at nine o'clock.

He looked tired and haggard and her heart went out to him. She forgave him—a little—for her own sleepless night.

He collapsed onto the step beside her. 'I've been looking for her for a couple of hours.' He gestured to Carla's car. 'Thierry rang at seven. I thought she was with him. That's when I realised she was missing. I'm glad she's here.'

Thierry chose that moment to pull up behind Dylan's car.

'She's a grown woman, Dylan. If she chooses to spend the night elsewhere, surely that's her business? Not to mention her prerogative. I'm sure *you* wouldn't appreciate it if she sent out a search party whenever *you* didn't come home.'

He thrust out his jaw. 'She's not answering her phone.'

'Likewise.'

She said it as gently as she could, but Dylan's eyes narrowed, the irises going a deep sapphire.

Thierry charged up the path. 'I want to see her!'

'I'm sure you do.' She kept her voice calm. 'But the fact of the matter is she doesn't want to see either of you at the moment.'

'Me?' Dylan shot to his feet. 'Why doesn't she want to see *me*?'

'I believe the phrase was, "I'm tired of men thinking they know what's best for me."'

Both men's jaws dropped.

Dylan paced.

Thierry just stood there with his hands clenched. He glanced at the door.

'It's locked,' Mia said. 'And if either one of you has the slightest interest in her well-being you won't start banging on the door. She's asleep.'

Dylan halted his pacing. 'You put her to *bed*?'

'I did.'

Thierry rested his hands on his knees, his face grey. 'I don't know what to do. I've been such an idiot.'

Dylan leapt forward and grabbed him by his shirtfront and shook him. 'What the *hell* have you done to her?'

'If I have to get the hose out to cool the pair of you off, I will.'

Those blue eyes swung to her. She read the anger in them—and the indecision.

'Let him go, Dylan. Carla is perfectly aware that the two of you have her best interests at heart, but she's entitled to a time out whenever she needs one. She doesn't have to consult with either of you beforehand.'

Dylan stared into her eyes so intently it felt as if he was scouring her soul. Finally, with a nod, he released Thierry. 'Sorry.'

Thierry straightened his shirt. 'No problem.'

She glanced back at Thierry. 'I don't know what your argument was about last night, but if you're truly sorry—'

'I am!'

'Then I suggest you come up with an honest explanation for why you behaved the way you did, promise to do better in the future, and have a heartfelt and grovelling apology ready.'

His fists opened and closed several times. He nodded hard. 'Right.'

His earnestness almost made her smile. 'Flowers might help too.'

His chin lifted. 'I can come back?'

She knew she wouldn't be able to keep him away indefinitely.

'You can come back at four. I'm not making any promises. It's up to Carla to decide if she wants to see you or not.'

'Right.' He swung away and made for the gate. He halted when he reached it and turned back. 'Thanks.'

With a nod, he was gone.

Had Thierry just *thanked* her? Wow!

Both she and Dylan watched him drive away—Mia from her spot on the step, Dylan from where he stood in wide-legged masculine magnificence on her pocket of front lawn.

As soon as Thierry's car had disappeared, he swung back to face her. 'Okay, you can let me see her now.'

'I'm sorry, Dylan, but the same holds true for you too.'

'You have to be joking!' He stalked across to loom over her. 'You *know* I only have Carla's best interests at heart.'

She stood, using the step to give her a height advantage. 'Has it never occurred to you that all your big brotherly protectiveness—some might call it *over*-protectiveness—could be a *little* stifling?' She uttered 'little' in such a way that he couldn't miss the fact that she meant *a lot*.

He gaped at her. 'It's my job to look out for her.'

'She's an adult. She can look out for herself.'

'Just because your family let you down, it doesn't mean that's the way every family works.'

He spoke the words in a voice so low and controlled it sent ice tiptoeing down her spine.

He held out his hand, palm flat, eyes glittering. 'Give me the key.'

Her heart quailed, because she suddenly realised what a betrayal he would see this as—her keeping him from his sister. She wanted to weep. She'd finally found the one sure way to distance him, and now that she had she didn't want to use it.

Give him the key.

She lifted her chin and forced steel to her spine. 'No.' Planting her hands on her hips, she leaned towards him. 'Carla doesn't want to see you at the moment. Go home, Dylan. Stop being a bully.'

His hands fisted and his entire body started to shake. 'I could take it from you by force.'

She folded her arms and raised an eyebrow. They both knew he wouldn't.

He swore and she flinched. He didn't apologise, but she didn't expect him to.

'A *bully*?' The word ground out of him. 'I can't believe you're lumping me in the same class as Thierry.'

The pain in his words cut at her. 'I *do* put you in the same class as Thierry. Thierry loves Carla—adores her. He'd lay his life down for her. I know you would too. It doesn't change the fact that Carla doesn't want to see either of you for the time being.'

His eyes blazed, but his face turned to stone. He turned and stormed down the path, leaving as she'd ordered him to.

The backs of her eyes burned and her vision blurred. A lump lodged in her throat. Whatever fragile link had bound them together had been severed, and she felt the pain of it deep down inside her. It tore at something she thought might never be fixed.

At the gate, he halted. His shoulders sagged. She hated it that she'd hurt him, but she readied herself for a different form of attack.

He came back, his face sombre, his eyes throbbing. 'I owe you an apology. I just acted like a two-year-old throwing a tantrum because he's been denied what he wants. But I'm worried about Carla.'

'I know.'

He clasped her shoulders. 'Is she okay?'

He stared into her eyes and she realised he meant to trust whatever she told him. Her mouth went dry.

'Mia?'

Her heart thudded, though she couldn't explain why. 'She's upset.'

'With Thierry?'

'I suspect so. But mostly with your uncle.'

Dylan's lips pressed together in a tight line. 'His car was at the house when I got back last night. It was late, so he was already in bed. He left after breakfast. We shared a few home truths. I don't think he'll be back. I told him that if he caused trouble for you at your place of employment you'd come and work for FWE. I don't think your job will be in jeopardy from *that* region, Mia.'

'I... Thank you.'

'I didn't know he'd spoken to Carla.'

It wasn't her place to tell him about his uncle's violence. 'I think that after some sleep, and some lunch and some talking, Carla will be fine. She just needs time to clear her head.'

He squeezed her shoulders and then released her. 'Okay.'

He really meant to trust her?

'Thank you for looking after her.'

'She's my friend. Of course I'm going to look out for her.'

His eyes throbbed into her. 'I don't mean to be a bully.'

It took all the strength she had not to reach out and touch his face. 'I know that too.' And he wasn't—not really. 'If you were really a bully you'd have taken the key from me by force.'

'You don't see it, do you?' he said.

A desolation that made her heart catch stretched through his eyes. Her mouth went dry. 'What don't I see?'

'I just harangued you, bullied you, all but emotionally blackmailed you, but you held firm. You chose to do what you thought was right rather than submit to my will. Do you still believe you're weak and easy to manipulate?'

She froze. 'I...'

The yard spun.

'I can't keep doing this, Mia.'

Her gaze speared back to his. 'What do you mean?'

'I love you.'

Her heart stuttered in her chest.

'You *know* I love you. With everything that's inside me. I'd do anything to win your love. But it's not enough, is it? You're still so far away. I lose myself and I get so frustrated... I start to yell and then I turn into a bully.'

'Dylan, I—'

He pressed his fingers to her lips. 'I love you, Mia. I want to have a life with you. But I won't bully you into that. If you ever come to me, I want it to be because you love me too.'

She did love him, but…

Confusion swirled through her and she couldn't make sense of the riot raging through her. The smile he sent her made her want to cry.

He leaned forward and pressed a kiss to her brow. 'Tell Carla if she needs anything to call me.'

She nodded.

He held her gaze for a moment. 'I mean to give you all the space you want, Mia. If you change your mind, you know where to find me.'

Fear clutched at her heart.

With a nod, he turned and strode away. This time he didn't stop at the gate.

Every step that he took away from her increased the ache in her chest tenfold.

Carla slept until noon.

'Did Thierry show up?'

'He did. So did Dylan.'

'What did he say?'

'Dylan said you're to call him if you need anything.'

'What did *Thierry* say?'

Oh. 'The man is half out of his wits with worry for you… and fear that you're going to dump him.'

'Good!'

'I told him to come back at four. I didn't guarantee that you'd see him. But if you really don't want to see him again he'll need to hear it from you.'

Carla bit her lip.

'Can things not be fixed?' Mia asked.

Carla folded her arms. 'I guess that depends on him. He wants to be all strong and solitary and untouchable—but that's *not* how relationships work. It's not how *marriage* works.'

Each and every one of those darts found their mark, although they hadn't been aimed at her.

Mia rubbed a hand across her chest, trying to ease the ache there. 'I believe he's sincere in wanting to make amends.'

'You think I should see him?'

She recalled the absolute happiness on Carla's face when she and Thierry had picnicked. 'I think you should give him a hearing. I think things can be patched up.'

The other woman tried to hide it, but she brightened at Mia's words. 'What about Dylan?'

'I think you should call him.'

'I meant what about *you* and Dylan?'

Oh. She glanced down at her hands. 'I don't know. I need to go somewhere quiet and think.'

'So there's hope?'

She met Carla's gaze. 'I *hope* there's hope.'

After a moment Carla said, 'I'm going to ring Dylan. I want Uncle Andrew charged with assault.'

Mia's head shot up, a fierce gladness gripping her. 'Good for you. Women shouldn't have to put up with violence at the hands of men.'

Carla twisted her hands together. 'It'll create a media circus, though.' She eyed Mia uncertainly. 'And the reason for our argument will come out—which means you'll be spotlighted in the media too.'

'Me?'

Carla reached out and took Mia's hand. 'I know how much you've dreaded the media getting hold of the story that you and Dylan are dating. If the thought of publicity freaks you out that much, I won't go ahead with it.'

Her heart thumped. She waited for dread and fear to fill her, but they didn't. *Why* wasn't she crippled with fear?

The answer came to her in an instant. Ever since she'd

been released from jail she'd thought that scandal and losing her job, losing the chance of the quiet life she craved, were the worst things that could happen to her. She'd been wrong. Watching Dylan walk away this morning—that had been the worst thing.

Very slowly she shook her head. 'It doesn't freak me out. At least, not much.' She met her friend's gaze. 'You have every right to slay your dragons. I'll help in any way I can.'

Carla wrapped her in a hug. 'Thank you.'

At four o'clock Mia let herself into the Plum Pines office. Sunday was one of the busiest days as far as the general public were concerned—lots of barbecues, picnics and viewing of the exhibits. It was a busy day for the volunteers who helped to run the wildlife displays too, but the administration of the reserve was a strictly Monday-to-Friday enterprise. Which meant she'd have the office to herself.

With a heart that pounded too fast, she switched on one of the computers and then pulled Felipe's memory card from her pocket. Swallowing hard, she retrieved the image he'd snapped of her.

It filled the screen. She flinched and had to look away.

It's only a photograph!

She glanced back and tried to study the picture objectively, but after only a few seconds she had to look away again.

Muttering something rude under her breath, she pushed out of her chair and paced across to the far wall. Hauling in a breath, she turned back to the image once more.

Her heart squeezed tight and her eyes filled. Felipe had captured something that attracted and repelled her at the same time. He'd captured something that both soothed and frightened her.

What was it?

In that photo her expression was so unguarded it made her head spin. Was it hope?

She moved back towards the computer monitor to study the image more minutely, biting down on her thumbnail.

Hope was part of it, but…

She reached out and touched the face on the screen.

That smile…

The emotion pulsing through the photograph was *joy*. It was so present she could almost feel the laughter wrap around her.

Joy? She'd spent so long feeling ashamed of herself, so determined not to repeat her mistakes, she'd forgotten. She'd forgotten she had a lot of good inside her too.

Her hands clenched and unclenched. She'd told herself that she couldn't have fun and hope and joy in her life because she didn't deserve them—not after the things she'd done.

But…

She'd made a mistake—a big one—but that mistake didn't have to define the rest of her life unless she let it. Her heart hammered against her ribs. She didn't need to shut herself away. She just needed to choose the right path… the right life.

She fell back into the chair, her cheeks wet. There wasn't a tissue in sight, so she dried her cheeks on the sleeves of her shirt and sniffed rather inelegantly.

'Right, then.'

She might as well start living that life right away.

She seized the phone and punched in a number.

'Felipe Fellini.'

'Felipe, it's Mia.'

'Mia, darling—what can I do for you?'

She told him.

After she'd hung up she pulled in a breath and rang Dylan. He answered immediately. 'Mia! Is everything okay?'

His caller ID must have given her away.

The sound of his voice made her throat dry and she had to clear it before she could speak. 'Yes.'

'I've spoken to Carla. Are you sure you're all right with the publicity that a suit against Andrew will involve?'

She nodded, and then realised he couldn't see her. 'I'm sure.'

There was a pause. 'That's a surprise.'

She nodded again, more to herself this time. 'Yes.'

'What can I do for you?'

'I was wondering…' She wiped a damp palm down her jeans. 'I was wondering if I could invite you on a date next Saturday night. There's something I want you to see.'

'Has this anything to do with Carla and Thierry?'

'No. It's to do with me.'

'What time would you like me to pick you up?'

Dylan's heart thumped when he knocked on Mia's door. All week he'd alternated between hope and despair. Hope that this was the new beginning with Mia that he craved. Despair that this would be her way of bringing things between them to an end once and for all.

She opened the door. For a moment all he could do was stare. 'You look stunning!'

She wore a scarlet dress with a shimmering satin bodice, fitted beneath her breasts. The skirt fell to her knees in a cloud of chiffon that moved as she walked.

She pushed a strand of hair behind her ear. 'You look very nice yourself.'

He was glad he'd worn a dinner jacket. Especially when her hand fluttered up to her throat, as if the sight of him made it hard for her to breathe. The smile she sent him, though, held a hint of shyness—like a girl on her first date.

This probably *was* her first real date in nearly four years. Tenderness washed over him.

After she'd locked the front door he held out his arm, ridiculously pleased when she placed her hand in the crook of his elbow. 'Your chariot awaits.'

For good or for ill, he had a feeling he'd remember to-night for the rest of his life.

'Where are we going?'

She gave him an inner-city address. He had no idea what was there, but he didn't ask any further questions. He'd let the evening unfold at the pace she chose for it.

Dylan glanced out of the car window. Light spilled from the industrial-sized windows of a warehouse. He opened his mouth to ask Mia if she was sure she had the address right, but closed it again when she lowered her window and waved a card at an attendant standing on the footpath. The attendant directed them to a parking spot in front of the warehouse's huge double doors—the doors were closed except for a smaller door inset into one of them.

He switched off the ignition and turned to her. 'What *is* this?'

'I—' She broke off and hauled in a breath.

That wave of tenderness washed over him again, threatening to crush him. He reached for her hand. 'Are you nervous?'

'A little.'

'Of me?'

'Yes.'

The word whispered out of her and something blossomed in his chest. *Hope.* And it took firm root. 'You don't need to be nervous about me, Mia.'

He was hers. All hers. He didn't tell her out loud that he loved her, but he pressed a kiss to her palm, knowing that if she wanted to see it his love for her would be written all over his face.

Her gaze travelled over him and her breath snagged, her gaze catching on his mouth. Hunger and need chased themselves across her face. An answering hunger roared through him.

'Oh!' Her hand tightened in his. 'You can distract me *so* easily!'

The grin inside him built. 'Excellent.'

'Before you distract me further, I want to show you something. And then I want to talk.'

'And *then* can I distract you?' He waggled his eyebrows.

She gurgled back a laugh. 'Perhaps. If you still want to.'

He'd definitely still want to.

Without another word, he pushed himself out of the car and went around to open her door. She took his arm.

'This—' she gestured to the building in front of them '—is something of a first. Felipe has been prevailed upon to give the people of Newcastle a preview of his up-and-coming Sydney show.'

Dylan's stared at her. 'Who prevailed upon him?'

She moistened her lips. 'Me.'

She had?

Before he could ask what that meant, Felipe came towards them, arms outstretched.

'Darlings!' He kissed them on both cheeks in flamboyant greeting. 'I'm honoured to have you as my guests. Come!'

Dylan's head whirled as Felipe gave them a personal tour of some of the most amazing photographs Dylan had ever seen—his commentary both entertaining and revelatory.

Dylan glanced at Mia. She'd contrived this for *him*? Because she knew he appreciated art and photography? His heart gave a giant kick. Nobody had ever arranged anything so perfect for him in all his life. It had to mean *something*.

'And this, darlings, is the *pièce de résistance*! The jewel in my crown.'

Felipe led them around a screen to an enormous photograph positioned on one of the warehouse's end walls.

Mia!

He took a step towards it and Mia's hand slipped from his arm. It was the photograph of Mia! Her joy, her laughter and her love greeted him from the wall and he almost stopped breathing.

His every muscle tightened. He swung back to her, hands fisted at his sides. He'd lost the ability to be charming. Everything had been stripped away except raw need. 'What does this mean?'

Mia glanced at Felipe, who put a key into her hand.

'Lock up when you're done.'

She nodded her thanks.

It was only then that Dylan realised they were alone in this magnificent space. The show had been for him alone.

Mia didn't speak until the clang of a door informed them that Felipe had left. She moistened her lips. 'Are you cross that I gave Felipe permission to use the photograph in his exhibition?'

'Cross? No.' He glanced at the photo again and searched himself. He didn't feel disappointment either. Only wonder. 'I just want to know what all this means.'

'It means I've finally realised you were right.'

She moved to stand beside him and gestured up at the picture, though he could only look at *her*—the flesh and blood woman.

'That *is* the person I should become. It's…' She met his gaze. 'It's the real me.'

Her admission stunned him.

'I've realised that I deserve to be happy. More to the point, I've realised I *want* to be happy. And I've realised that being a field officer and leading a quiet life *won't* make me happy.'

She glanced at the photo and then at him.

'*You* make me happy, Dylan.'

He stared at her, humbled by the vulnerability in her eyes.

'I… I couldn't be happy until I forgave myself for my past.' Her hands twisted together. 'I know I've hurt you, and I'm so sorry for that. Truly. I'm hoping I haven't hurt you so badly that you can't forgive me. I'm hoping—'

He didn't let her finish. He kissed her instead.

The shock of his assault made her wobble on her heels, but he wrapped an arm about her waist and pulled her close, steadying her. She wrapped her arms around his neck and kissed him back.

When he lifted his head her eyes glittered and her chest rose and fell. And then she smiled, and it was just like the smile in the frame behind her—full of joy and love.

'That felt an awful lot like a you-still-love-me-too kiss.'

He stroked his fingers down her face. 'I will *always* love you.'

She took his face in her hands. 'I promise I will look after your heart and be the best person I can for you.'

He stared into her eyes, humbled all over again. 'Nobody has ever made a more meaningful vow to me. I'll cherish it forever.'

A cheeky smile peeped out. 'Good, because I'm also going to ask you to give me a job. I quit Plum Pines yesterday.'

He gaped. She just grinned back at him, so delighted with herself that he had to laugh.

'I don't want to be a field officer, and I don't want to be an events manager either. I just want you to give me a regular office job so I can put myself through a psychology major at university. I want to be a counsellor.' She lifted her chin. 'I think I have something of value I could offer to people.'

He ran his hands up and down her back, revelling in the way it made her shiver. 'How about I gift you the opportunity for full-time study as a wedding present?'

She went very still and Dylan held his breath.

'You want to *marry* me?' she whispered.

Very gently he took his arms from around her and, gripping both her hands, went down on one knee. 'Beautiful Mia, will you do me the very great honour of becoming my wife?'

Tears shone in her eyes. When she nodded, they spilled onto her cheeks.

He rose and she threw her arms around his neck. 'I can't

think of anything I want more than to spend the rest of my life with you, Dylan.'

He laughed for the sheer joy of it, swinging her around. 'How does November sound? We have a wedding going begging. We might as well use it.'

She eased back. 'What on earth are you talking about? Carla and Thierry have made up and—'

'They flew out to Vegas yesterday.'

She gaped. 'No!'

'So… November is ours if we want it.'

An enormous smile spread across her face. 'It's…perfect!'

He glanced at the photo on the wall and then down at her. 'No, Mia, *you're* perfect.'

She touched his face, her smile radiant. '*We're* perfect. Together.'

He couldn't top that, so he kissed her instead.

EPILOGUE

CARLA AND THIERRY bundled Mia out of the limousine and whisked her straight inside the small marquee that had been set up especially for her benefit—to shield her from the press and allow her a chance to freshen up.

As they'd only driven from her suite at an inner-city hotel with glorious views of the harbour to Plum Pines Reserve—a drive of less than fifteen minutes—she didn't really see what kind of freshening up was required. Unless she was supposed to try and quieten the excited dervishes whirling in her stomach. She had no chance of stilling *those*. She wasn't sure she wanted to.

Perhaps she should try and tame the grin that made her face ache? But she had no hope—nor desire—to do that either.

Carla, stunning in her hot-pink bridesmaid's dress, crouched down to adjust Mia's skirts.

Mia laughed ruefully. 'I went overboard, didn't I? I look like an oversized meringue.'

'You look *gorgeous*.' Carla continued to fluff up the skirts. 'Your dress is *beautiful*.'

The moment Mia had clapped eyes on the confection of raw silk and pearl beading she'd fallen in love with it. Apparently when she had said that she meant to live life to the full rather than hide in the shadows she'd meant it.

She hugged herself. 'It *is* beautiful.'

'I can't wait to see Dylan's face when he sees you.'

Today, nobody could mistake Mia for anything other than what she was—the bride, the centre of attention, the belle of the ball marrying her prince.

Those dervishes whirled faster and faster. Her cheeks ached from smiling. She lifted her chin. She wasn't ashamed of her joy. She wanted to share it with everyone.

She turned to find Thierry surveying her with his now familiar unsmiling gaze.

He nodded. 'You look stunning.'

She wriggled with excitement. 'I *feel* stunning. I'm so happy I think I could float off into the atmosphere.'

For the briefest of moments Thierry smiled, and it tempered the severe lines of his face. When he smiled, she could see why Carla had fallen for him.

She touched his arm. 'Thank you for agreeing to give me away.' He hadn't hesitated when she'd asked. He'd agreed immediately.

'I'm honoured.' One shoulder lifted. 'I'm starting to think I'd do anything you asked of me.'

From behind him, Carla sent her a wink.

Thierry frowned. 'You're sure we're okay?'

She rolled her eyes. 'I swear to God, Thierry, if you apologise to me one more time we're going to fall out.'

He shuffled his feet. 'It's just… I'm really sorry I misjudged you.'

Given his background, and the hardships his father's choices had forced on his family, Mia couldn't blame him for his reservations where she'd been concerned.

'As I misjudged myself, I can hardly blame you for doing the same. But it's all in the past now, and that's where it'll remain. It's time to move on.'

That was her new motto and she'd embraced it with gusto.

She reached out to take Carla and Thierry's hands. 'You're my family now—my sister and brother. I can't tell you how fortunate that makes me feel.'

Carla's eyes filled. Thierry cleared his throat a couple of times.

Mia blinked hard. She would *not* ruin her eye make-up. She wanted to look perfect for Dylan. 'So that's a yes—we're *very* okay.'

On impulse, they all hugged—before Carla tut-tutted and said something about crushing Mia's dress.

Mia laughed at her fussing, but a wave of excitement somersaulted through her. 'Oh, is it time yet? I can't wait—'

The flap of the marquee flew open and Felipe appeared. He clasped his hands beneath his chin when he saw her.

'Radiant!' he pronounced, before whisking a compact from somewhere and touching a powder puff lightly to her nose. He kissed the air above her cheeks. 'Perfect!'

He pulled out his camera and snapped a couple of pictures.

She waggled a finger at him. 'Don't forget—those photos are mine and Dylan's. None are to mysteriously appear in an exhibition.'

'Cross my heart, darling. Besides, your dishy intended is paying me enough to make it worth my while.' He pouted. 'Also, he made me sign some awful form full of lawyer-speak.'

Mia laughed.

'I've been sent to tell you everything is ready.'

'Oh!' She clasped her hands together.

'Nervous, darling?'

'Excited.'

He squeezed her hands. 'I wouldn't have missed this for the world.'

And then he was gone.

Carla handed her a bouquet of pink and white peonies. 'Ready?'

A lump lodged in her throat. All she could do was nod.

Thierry held the flap of the marquee open to reveal the red carpet that would lead her to Dylan. Carla set off down the carpet first. Thierry made Mia wait until Carla was half-way down the makeshift aisle before stepping after her.

Mia was vaguely aware of the beautiful music playing, of the murmurs of appreciation from their wedding guests, but her focus was wholly centred on the man standing at the other end.

His blond hair gleamed golden in the sunlight. His broad shoulders and strong thighs were outlined to perfection in his tuxedo. His heart was in his eyes. He didn't try to hide it from anyone, and she wasn't sure she'd ever seen anything more beautiful in her life.

Awe rose up through her...and more happiness than her body could contain. It spilled from her eyes and onto her cheeks.

He took her hand. His throat bobbed with emotion as he swallowed.

'You're so beautiful you make my eyes water,' she whispered, not caring about her make-up.

He smiled down at her. 'You're so beautiful you make my heart sing.'

The celebrant cleared her throat. 'Ready?'

Mia smiled up at Dylan. 'Yes.'

The service was simple but heartfelt. The reception was the epitome of joy and elegance. Mia felt like a fairytale princess.

After the meal had been eaten, toasts made, the cake cut and the bridal waltz completed, Dylan took her hand and they sneaked outside to stand at the wooden railing overlooking the lily pond. Lights twinkled in the trees, glimmering across the water's surface.

Dylan took her face in his hands and kissed her. A sweet, gentle kiss that promised a lifetime of kisses.

'Happy?' he murmured, easing back.

'More than I ever thought possible.' She smiled up at him before glancing back towards the marquee. 'Has anyone ever told you that you know how to throw a fabulous party?'

'What can I say? I'm gifted.'

She gurgled back a laugh. 'Look.' She pointed to Carla and Thierry dancing. 'They look gorgeous together.'

Dylan snorted. 'Carla should've had a wedding like this! *Elopement?*' He snorted again.

Mia leaned back against him. 'You just love any excuse to throw a party.'

'What's wrong with a party?'

'Absolutely nothing. I adore parties. I'm especially loving this one.'

She bit her lip then, and glanced up at him again.

'Are you sorry your Uncle Andrew isn't here?' The man might be a miserable excuse for a human being but he was still Dylan's uncle.

'Not a bit. I'll be happy if I never clap eyes on him again.'

There hadn't been enough evidence to charge Andrew with assault against Carla, but the scandal hadn't done the older man any favours. Especially since a young intern who worked in his office had made similar allegations against him. He'd been suspended pending an internal inquiry. If found guilty he'd lose his job. His political ambitions would be nothing more than dust.

Mia glanced up into her new husband's face and knew Andrew wouldn't be making trouble for any of them ever again.

Dylan smiled down at her. 'The day I won your heart was the luckiest day of my life.'

She turned in his arms, resting her hands against the warm hard contours of his chest. 'I'm the real winner, Dylan. You made me believe in love again. You showed me the power it had to do good. Whatever happens in the future, I'll never forget that lesson.' She touched her fingers to his face. 'I love you. I'm going to spend the rest of my life making you very, *very* happy.'

She wondered if her face reflected as much love as his did. She hoped so.

'Want to know what would make me happy right now?' he murmured, a wicked light flitting through his eyes. 'A kiss.'

Laughing, she reached up on tiptoe and pressed her lips to his, telling him in a language that needed no words how much she loved him.

* * * * *

On a scale of one to ten, with ten being the worst, the reality of sharing a bed with Jon was a fifteen.

It pushed twenty when she felt the mattress dip from his weight. And the masculine scent of his skin drifted to her, firing up her hormones even more.

"Good night."

"'Night." His voice was ragged, rough.

Dawn couldn't speak for him, but she was as tense as a bowstring and ready to snap. "Jon, I—"

He threw back the covers. "This isn't going to work."

She rolled over to face him. "What's wrong?"

"I want you." There was no mistaking the need in his voice this time. It was honest and raw. "I can't help it. I can't make it stop. If I touch you—" He swore under his breath. "I'm going in the other room."

This time he didn't say anything about sleeping. And there was no mistaking the way her heart soared in response to his declaration. *He wanted her.*

Before he could get out of bed she moved closer and reached for him. It was automatic, instinctive. Her hand touched his arm, the warm skin. And this time she said the word. "Stay."

* * *

**Montana Mavericks:
The Baby Bonanza**
Meet Rust Creek Falls' newest bundles of joy!

HER MAVERICK
M.D.

BY
TERESA SOUTHWICK

First Published in Great Britain 2016
By Mills & Boon, an imprint of HarperCollins*Publishers*
1 London Bridge Street, London, SE1 9GF

© 2016 Harlequin Books S.A.

Special thanks and acknowledgement are given to Teresa Southwick for her contribution to the Montana Mavericks: The Baby Bonanza continuity.

ISBN: 978-0-263-92007-9

23-0816

Teresa Southwick lives with her husband in Las Vegas, the city that reinvents itself every day. An avid fan of romance novels, she is delighted to be living out her dream of writing for Mills & Boon.

To editor Susan Litman,
who guides us through this Montana Mavericks
maze with a combination of grace and humor.
It's always a pleasure working with you.

Chapter One

Dr. Jonathan Clifton had never understood what it meant to be stopped dead in your tracks. That changed when he walked into the Rust Creek Falls Medical Clinic and saw the woman behind the reception desk. She stopped him cold—or maybe hot—with long blond hair falling past her shoulders and bluebonnet-colored eyes that could tempt a man to kiss her. Or bring him to his knees. Since he had no intention of letting that happen to him again it was strictly an observation about the very pretty receptionist he would be working with.

Moving to the open window separating her from the crowded waiting room, Jon patiently waited for her to hang up the phone. That was when he noticed her blue scrubs decorated with cartoon animals. The stethoscope draped around her neck was a clue that she probably wasn't the receptionist. But she sounded a little frazzled, possibly fatigued and even prettier up close than she'd appeared from across the room.

When she hung up the phone, he smiled at her. "Hi. Is it always this busy in here?"

"Pretty much. But today is more crazy than usual."

Say something brilliant, he told himself. *And funny.* "It's still summer. Not even flu season yet."

"Tell me about it," she agreed. "Things should get really interesting in a couple months."

"Flu shots would help. Might want to think about having a flu shot fair. Kind of like a health fair but with the focus on prevention." When she smiled at him he nearly broke his promise to not let a woman bring him to his knees. "Just a thought."

"It's a good one. There are few things Rust Creek Falls likes more than a reason for a community get-together."

"Folks here do like a gathering."

"So you know our little slice of Montana paradise," she said.

"Yeah."

The woman tilted her head, studying him. "Have we met? You look familiar."

"I've been here before. My brother lives just outside of town."

"Ah, a visitor. And you're here to see the doctor. I'm sorry you're not feeling well. Have you signed in?"

He looked at the lined sheet attached to a clipboard. Each line was a sticky strip. When patients arrived, they signed in then the name was removed for privacy purposes. "I'm not a patient."

"Oh?" Her expression turned appraising and a little wary. "Are you selling something?"

He was trying to sell himself—his personality, at least—because he would be working with this woman. But he'd always been more interested in doctoring than witty repartee.

And Jon could feel it coming on. The persona his brothers referenced when they'd nicknamed him Professor. The one where he turned a little formal, a little stiff and standoffish. Too analytical. But trying not to be left him a lot tongue-tied. "I'm here— The kids—"

"So you have an appointment for your child?" She glanced past him, looking for one.

"No." That sounded abrupt. He smiled. "I don't have kids. That I know of."

She looked a little surprised at the lame remark. "You're a visitor and may not know this, but thanks to Homer Gilmore's wedding moonshine prank more than one man became a father this year without knowing. It's not something to be cavalier about."

"That was a bad joke," he acknowledged.

"No problem." Her tension eased. "Guess we're still a little sensitive about the incident."

"I understand. In fact my brother was a victim of the punch. He'd just closed escrow on his ranch—"

"So, you're a cowboy." She looked interested.

At least he thought so and really hated to tell her the truth. "I'm not a cowboy."

"Oh." She sounded disappointed. "The snap-front shirt and worn jeans threw me off. Sorry."

"No problem."

She glanced over her shoulder and smiled apologetically. "I really have to get back to work."

And Jon wanted just a little bit longer with her. So he started talking. "A lot of people dress like this who don't herd cows on a ranch. In fact, you're wearing scrubs, but I didn't jump to the conclusion that you're a doctor. But I feel pretty confident that you're not the receptionist."

"Really?" The corners of her mouth curved up. "What makes you so sure?"

"You have a stethoscope around your neck. Someone who answers the phone wouldn't need one handy." He smiled and leaned his forearms on the wall separating them. "And this is just the process of elimination, but my next guess would be that you're a nurse. If I'm right, it's a waste of your education, training and experience to have you answering phones."

"We have a receptionist. Brandy. Somewhere." She glanced around the front office area looking a little irritated with the missing receptionist. "But since she's not here at the moment, my job description has spontaneously been expanded to include security checkpoint because I have to ask. Since you're not a patient, or accompanying someone who is, do you have business here?"

"Technically the clinic *is* my business." Good God, he sounded like a pompous idiot. This was not the first time he'd met and talked to a pretty girl, so what was his problem? Plastering a smile on his face, he held out his hand. "I'm Jon Clifton, MD. That is—Dr. Jonathan Clifton. I met with Emmet DePaulo about joining the staff here at the clinic—"

"The new doctor." Suddenly her tone completely lacked warmth, as if he'd revealed his alter ego was Jack the Ripper.

"Pediatrician, technically."

"Emmet told us the new doctor would be here in a couple of days. Wow, and I just jumped to the conclusion that you were a cowboy." As comprehension slid into her eyes her cheeks turned pink.

The color in her face made her even prettier, if possible. "You should do that more often."

"What? Humiliate myself?"

"No. Of course not. It's just that blushing looks good on you."

The brief bit of vulnerability in her expression disappeared and her blue eyes darkened with what appeared to be suspicion. "Really?"

Uh-oh. Apparently he'd stepped in it there. Note to self: they'd just met. She didn't know his sense of humor yet. There was no way to accelerate the process of learning it. Only putting in one day after another, working together in the trenches during traumas and emergencies could do that. But maybe a little information about himself could speed things up.

"I actually live in Thunder Canyon. I've been working at the resort there with Dr. Marshall Cates. They added a pediatric specialist to the staff because a lot of families vacation there."

"Is that so?"

"Yes. And when the word spread that Rust Creek Falls could use my specialty I decided to lend a hand. I signed a contract for a year."

"Ah."

Hmm. One syllable, technically not even a word. It was a signal but he wasn't certain whether or not the meaning was an invitation for him to continue with information. As a physician he'd been trained that the more facts you obtained in order to make a diagnosis, the better.

"It's possible you know my brother. Will Clifton. Like I said, he owns a ranch and I'm staying in his guesthouse— well, it used to be the foreman's house but... Anyway, I was at the wedding last summer when he accidentally married Jordyn Leigh."

Her full lips pulled tight for a moment. "You say that as if it wasn't really an accident on her part."

"Don't get me wrong. I understand that alcohol lowers one's inhibitions. But it seems unlikely that punch— even a spiked one—can make someone do anything they don't really want to." Some part of his brain registered that based on the way her eyes were practically shooting fire he should stop talking, but the words continued to come out of his mouth. "There were a lot of babies conceived, which means there was quite a bit of ill-advised behavior. Should people have known better?" He shrugged at the question.

"Have you ever heard the saying 'Never judge anyone unless you've walked a mile in their shoes'?" she asked sweetly.

"Are you suggesting that I should try the punch?"

"If the shoe fits…" She stared at him. "And for the record, *spiked* punch means something was added without the knowledge of those drinking it."

"True, but—"

"Sometimes things are more complicated than they appear."

He didn't just sound like a pompous idiot, he decided, he actually was one. In his defense— Who was he kidding? There was no defense.

"Let me explain—"

"No need. I have to go find Brandy and get back to work."

There was a definite coolness in her tone now. "Look, I feel as if—"

"I'll let Emmet know the new doctor is here."

Before Jon could come up with anything to keep her there—like letting her know he wasn't always such a jerk—she walked away. Clearly something he'd said had hit her the wrong way, so it was a good thing she couldn't read his mind. Because he was thinking that she filled out those unflattering scrubs in a fairly spectacular way. She—

And that's when he realized that he forgot to ask her name.

It was customary when you introduced yourself to get that important information from the person you were introducing yourself to. But he'd kept talking about himself. It was probably just as well that she'd left before he said more to tick her off. After that fairly spectacular crash and burn he was anxious to get to work. Kids were a much easier crowd.

Moments after the nurse disappeared the door beside the reception window opened and Emmet DePaulo stood there. The man was tall and lean, somewhere in his sixties. When Jon had heard from family who lived here that there was a need in this town for healthcare professionals, he'd contacted Emmet, who was a nurse-practitioner. They'd met for dinner and Jon had found out the older man was a Vietnam-era veteran in addition to being easygoing and bighearted. He had a neatly trimmed beard that was more silver than brown and a wide, warm smile on his weathered face.

He'd explained that Rust Creek Falls was a rural area and his advanced nursing degree and certification allowed him to see and treat patients. He'd started this small clinic some years ago and kept it going through skill and sheer guts. That deserved respect. The fact was Emmet had the trust of the people in this town and Jon was the new doctor who would do his best to earn the same. In his book that made Emmet the boss.

He held out his hand. "Welcome to Rust Creek Falls, Jon. Follow me and we can talk in my office."

Behind the other man he walked down a long hallway with exam rooms on either side. Corridors branched off and he figured soon enough he would get a tour of the place. And somewhere here in the back office was the pretty nurse he'd somehow offended, although there was no sign of her now.

The last door on the left opened to a room with a big flat-topped desk stacked with a computer and enough charts to bring on carpal tunnel. Framed degrees and cer-tifications lined the walls along with a couple of photos. One showed a younger Emmet DePaulo in camouflage with several other people dressed the same way and a tent with a big red cross behind them. His army days.

"Have a seat, Jon." When Emmet sat in the cushy black leather chair behind the desk Jon took one in front of it. "I didn't expect you until next week."

"I got here yesterday and decided to stop by. Get a jump on orientation."

"Bored?"

"Maybe." Jon had been on automatic pilot at his job for a while now and was looking for a change.

"You saw the standing-room-only in the waiting area. We could sure use your help seeing patients if you're up for starting work early."

"Happy to help." He sincerely meant that. "Patient over-load would explain why the young woman at the front desk was so—"

"Uptight?" Emmet's brown eyes sparkled with amuse-ment.

"I wasn't going to say it." Especially since he'd just been taken to task for being judgmental. "But she did seem sort of on edge."

"Dawn—"

"That's her name?"

"Yes. Dawn Laramie."

"Ah." One syllable to hide the fact that, in his opinion, the name suited her. She was as lovely as the morning sun coming up over the mountains. That thought stopped him. He was a science and medicine guy, not a poet. Where had that come from?

"The clinic is very lucky to have her. She's a pediatric

nurse. Came from the PICU at Mountain's Edge Hospital, the closest Level One trauma center."

Jon whistled. "That's quite the commute from Rust Creek Falls."

"Over an hour," the other man confirmed. "That's why I was able to lure her to the clinic. And along with Callie Crawford, my other nurse-practitioner, and Brandy Walters, who handles the front office, she's overworked."

"I see."

"Like I told you when we talked, Rust Creek Falls is experiencing population growth and we're really feeling it here at the clinic. Folks don't abuse our walk-in policy so if they show up it's because they really need medical attention." The older man met his gaze. "And we make it a point to see everyone who shows up."

"Are you trying to scare me off?"

"Heaven forbid. Just want you to know what you're getting into."

The job at Thunder Canyon Resort was occasionally challenging, but mostly not. It was cushy and predictable. But that's exactly what Jon had been looking for when the position was offered to him—time and space to assess his career. The call for help here had come at a point when he was restless and looking for more.

"I'm ready for whatever you've got."

"Good." Emmet leaned forward and rested his forearms on the desk. "And when you're ready to tear your hair out, you should know that more help is on the way. Another doctor and nurse will be here shortly."

"Okay."

Emmet stood. "I'll show you around and introduce you to the staff. Although you've already met Dawn."

About her... Jon wished he could have a second chance at making a good first impression. But he was sure that when she got to know him, she'd put that initial skirmish behind her.

The two of them were going to get along just fine.

The new doctor.

That's how it started when Dawn's life had fallen apart.

She hadn't thought this day could get any worse when Dr. Jon Clifton had shown up, but she'd been wrong. Apparently the slightest exposure to him deactivated brain function, because she had failed to process the fact that Jamie Stockton was bringing his triplets in for their monthly checkup on Dr. Dreamboat's first day. Clifton was a pediatrician. As a nurse-practitioner Callie saw patients so Dawn was technically the clinic's only nurse. Hence, she was going to have to be intimately involved in said checkup.

An office visit for three babies born prematurely almost six months ago was throwing the new doctor into the deep end of the pool on his first day. She could almost feel sorry for him if she didn't already feel sorry for herself. Most nurses would be ecstatic at the opportunity to be in an exam room with the good-looking pediatrician. But most nurses hadn't once upon a time been used and lied to by a new staff doctor. So when the guy had told her she should blush more, warning signals had gone off like a heart monitor during cardiac arrest.

But he was Emmet's golden boy and they needed his kind of help here at the clinic. Her job was to assist him and she was all about doing a good job.

Dawn got a text on her cell phone that Jamie had just pulled into the clinic parking lot on South Lodgepole Lane. She pushed open the back exit door and headed for the rancher's familiar vehicle. The cowboy slid out of the driver's side and opened the rear passenger door. He was tall, a blue-eyed blond, although it was hard to tell the color of his hair because of the Stetson he always wore. There was an air of sadness about the tanned, muscular man. His wife had died in childbirth in February, nearly six months ago, and now he was working his ranch and raising triplets by himself.

He couldn't manage three infant carriers alone so she always waited for his text, then helped bring the babies inside.

"Hi, Jamie. How are you?"

"Tired." He sighed, looking into the backseat full of babies.

"I bet." She reminded herself never again to whine about being exhausted. This single working father of triplets was the walking definition of *exhaustion*. He hadn't had a good night's sleep in months and had little prospect of one in the near future.

She grabbed one of the carriers and the bulging diaper bag, while Jamie took the other two and followed her into the building. All of the infants were sleeping soundly, probably soothed by the movement of the car during the drive.

"We're going into exam room four, as always." It was the biggest and had an infant scale. "The doctor will meet us there. Dr. Clifton is new, a pediatrician."

"Okay."

As it happened, the doctor didn't meet them there—he was waiting for them. "Mr. Stockton, I'm Jonathan Clifton."

"Nice to meet you, Doc." Jamie put down one of the carriers to shake the other man's hand. "Everyone calls me Jamie."

"Okay. Please, call me Jon." He glanced at the babies. "That's a good-looking bunch you've got there. Cute kids."

"Yeah." That got a rare smile from the new father. "Henry, Jared and Kate. Just wait until they start crying all at once."

"Doesn't scare me. It means they're healthy and that's a good thing." Dr. Clifton looked confident, cheerful and incredibly competent. Friendly and approachable.

Dawn thought the white lab coat over his shirt and jeans could have been sexier, but she wasn't sure how. She'd been through this triple checkup scenario before and could have taken the lead, but decided to see how he'd deal with it. "Let me know what you want me to do, Doctor."

He looked sincerely conflicted when he said, "It's a shame to wake them, especially because they're not going to like being undressed. But…" His gaze met hers. "Let's do this assembly line style. We'll put them on the exam table. Jamie, you ride herd and make sure no one rolls off. Dawn, you undress them down to the diaper and hand them to me. I'll weigh and measure them."

In the past they'd dealt with one baby at a time. This process, she had to admit, was faster and more efficient, over before the babies were fully awake and notations were made in their charts. Then came the part where things usually deteriorated even more. Dr. Clifton warmed the cold metal stethoscope between his hands before placing it on each small chest and back.

Dawn always did her best to be a health care professional, emphasis on *professional*. So when the sight of the doctor's big hands handling each infant with such capable gentleness made her heart skip a beat, it was cause for alarm. On top of that, he smelled amazing—some spicy scent mixed with his particular brand of masculinity. All that and he was gorgeous. Darn it. Why couldn't he look like a hobbit?

After examining the last baby he straightened and

smiled at each of them. "Henry, Jared and Kate are perfectly healthy."

"Good to hear." Jamie seemed to relax a little.

"I'm sure when they were born someone explained to you that preemies begin life just a little behind the curve compared to full-term babies. But most children born early catch up and reach normal size for their age in a year or two."

"They did tell me," Jamie said.

"But right now we're dealing with their adjusted age as opposed to gestational age, which would be how long they were in the womb. They're almost six months old, but because they were eight weeks early, their adjusted age means they have the physical development of a four-month-old."

There was the barest hint of panic in the single father's eyes. "Is that a problem?"

"Not at all. The only reason I mention it is that a flu shot is recommended for infants at six months old."

Clifton glanced at her, obviously remembering their friendly, almost flirty flu conversation. If she'd known then that he was the new doctor, she wouldn't have given him a chance to be charming. And it was annoying to admit that she had been charmed by his lack of smoothness. Refreshing. But she'd learned the hard way not to trust new doctors.

"I'm not sure I understand," Jamie said.

"For these three," Clifton continued, "we need to wait another couple of months until their growth and development catch up. It's not a big deal."

"Whatever you say, Doc."

"Something else you should be aware of…" The doctor hesitated a moment, obviously thinking about what he was going to say. "Sometimes with preemies, the lungs aren't fully developed and a virus can be problematic. There's a medication that can protect them from RSV—"

"What's that?" Panic was back in Jamie's eyes.

"It's a very common infection that makes the rounds during flu season and presents with all the symptoms of the common cold. It isn't a problem unless an infant is severely premature—which yours are not. Or if there's a weakened immune system for some reason."

"Should I be worried?" Jamie asked.

The baby closest to the doctor started to fuss and the pink elastic headband clued them in that it was Kate. Without hesitation Clifton picked her up and cuddled her close.

"It's okay, kiddo. You and your brothers are just fine."

At the sound of his smooth, deep voice the little girl stopped crying and just stared at him with big, wide blue eyes. Dawn wondered if all females were like that—putty in his hands. Susceptible to a handsome face that hid the heart of a self-indulgent, narcissistic snake.

He smiled reassuringly. "There's nothing to worry about. Their lungs sound great, completely normal. New parents sometimes are critiqued for being overprotective but in your case that isn't a bad thing. I always recommend taking steps to keep them as healthy as possible. It's just basic common sense." He leaned a hip against the exam table, apparently in no hurry to put the baby girl down. "Anyone who's sick should keep their distance from the triplets. Stay away from places where people and germs tend to gather—churches, malls."

That got another smile out of the single dad. "Not a problem there. Shopping isn't high on my list."

"Didn't think so." Clifton grinned but the amusement disappeared as quickly as it had come. "Day care centers, too."

"Thanks to the baby chain I don't need day care."

"The what?" The doctor absently rubbed baby Kate's back as he listened intently.

"It's a group of volunteers. They've set up a schedule and folks come out to my place to take care of the triplets while I'm working the ranch." He had a firm hand on each of his boys, preventing them from rolling away. His eyes had a faraway look before filling with shadows. "I always wanted a family, but I never thought it would happen like this."

"Losing your wife must have been difficult." When Jamie looked up he explained, "It was in the babies' charts." His eyes held a man-to-man expression of sympathy.

"It was hard. For a lot of reasons. And now there are three little lives depending on me. Hasn't been an easy adjustment." The grieving father shook his head and started to dress one of the boys. "The baby chain is a lifesaver. I honestly don't know what I'd do without them."

"You'll never have to find out." Dawn moved beside him and began dressing the other boy. "This is Rust Creek Falls and people here take care of each other."

"It's a lot of work now, but that will get better," Clifton assured him. "Granted, there will be new challenges. When they're mobile it will be like roping calves."

"That's something I have experience with." Jamie secured the boys in the carrier, then looked up and grinned.

Dawn was shocked. She didn't think she'd seen this guy ever smile and the new doctor had gotten three out of him, the last one practically a laugh, for goodness' sake. Clifton was charming everyone around him and still holding that little girl. Kate seemed completely happy in his strong arms and Dawn felt herself melting. It was like déjà vu. She'd been taken in once by a handsome doctor, only to find out the hard way that he played fast and loose with the truth. She knew better than to go soft on Dr. Dreamboat.

The dreamboat in question handed Kate over to her father. "Right now the mission is to keep these three healthy. And I can't stress enough the importance of hand washing. It's a simple thing but very effective."

"Got it, Doc." Jamie dressed his daughter, then secured her in her carrier. "Appreciate it."

From the desk beside him Clifton grabbed a scratch pad with a pharmaceutical logo at the top and scribbled something on it. Then he handed the paper to the other man. "This is my cell number. Call me anytime, day or night, about anything. About the babies. Or if you just want to talk."

Jamie glanced at it, then stuck the paper in his pocket before shaking the doctor's hand. "Thanks. See you next time."

"I look forward to it." He sounded very sincere.

Dawn went outside with Jamie and helped secure the triplets for the ride home. As she watched him drive out of the parking lot, she sighed. Raising three babies would be a challenge for a husband and wife together but he didn't have a wife. What he had was the baby chain. And thank goodness for that.

Walking to the clinic door she braced herself to go inside. If only she could get the sight of the new doctor holding that sweet baby girl out of her mind. It was enough to make the average female heart beat a little too fast and Dawn's was no exception.

She reminded herself that she had an immunity to his type, the kind of man who was shallow as a cookie sheet. Never again would she allow a man to use her. And now she was in a similar situation, but this time she knew what to do.

Be professional at work.

Ignore his charm.

And most important, never see him outside the clinic. That was nothing but trouble. But her free time was her own and keeping her distance from him away from the job should be easy.

Chapter Two

Dawn parked her hybrid compact car behind her mom's in front of the house on South Main Street, not far from the elementary school. She'd bought the fuel-efficient vehicle for her long commute to the hospital but now her job was located two streets away. A tank of gas would last her months.

Unless she had to change jobs because of the new doctor.

She hated to be a whiner, but things had been going so well at her new job until he sashayed through the door.

But that was a problem for tomorrow. She grabbed her purse and headed up the walk that bisected the lush, neatly trimmed front grass lined with colorful flowers. Dawn didn't know the names of the plants; her mom was the gardener.

She walked inside. "Mom?"

"In here."

Dawn passed the unfurnished living and dining rooms

on her way to the kitchen where the voice had come from. "Hey."

Glory Laramie was sitting at the small, inexpensive dinette set in the breakfast nook. She was in her forties but looked at least ten years younger. Her strawberry blond hair was cut in a pixie style that highlighted her high cheekbones and pretty blue eyes. Folks said Dawn had her mom's eyes and she hoped so. They were the window to the soul and Glory's was honest, hardworking and loyal.

"There's a plate for you in the fridge. I can microwave it."

"I'll do it in a little while. Right now I just want to get off my feet for a few minutes." She sat across from her mother and noticed there were sample paint chips on the table. Glory always picked them up when she was frustrated about the length of time it was taking to accumulate enough money to do a fixer-upper project.

"You look tired. More than usual."

Dawn chalked that up to the strain Clifton created, but she didn't want to talk about it. "I have a rent check for you."

Glory heaved a sigh. "It doesn't seem right to take your money. I love having you here with me."

"That's what you say every month. And my response is always the same."

"I know." Her mom went into the shtick. "You're a grown woman and should have your own place but there's not a lot to choose from in this small town and the money will help me fix this place up."

"That's right." Dawn glanced around the room at the new drywall that had yet to be painted. "The extra money will speed up your timetable."

Glory nodded and smiled when she looked around. "I

only feel a little guilty that someone's misfortune made it possible for me to buy a home of my own."

"You're not responsible for that awful flood a couple years ago that damaged so much of the town."

"I know." Glory sighed. "But I hope the family who walked away from this house has a nice place to live again."

"I'm sure they're fine. And it's not like this place was move-in ready when you bought it from the bank. You've already got a lot of sweat equity in it."

"It had to be livable. Appliances, flooring, window coverings."

"That you made yourself. And don't forget the yard," Dawn reminded her.

"You helped."

"Oh, please. I fetched and carried while you worked magic. If I even look at a plant it threatens to shrivel up and die."

Glory laughed, and then amusement faded. "There's so much I want to do. But—"

"One step at a time. Right now we have a roof over our heads and walls around us. I know there's a lot of work ahead, but it will happen. Your house-cleaning business is thriving, what with the new contract at the medical clinic. You're a successful businesswoman."

"Which no one thought would happen when I was eighteen, married and pregnant—not necessarily in that order."

Dawn smiled for her mom's benefit but she could remember her parents fighting and the night when Glory dragged Dawn and Marina, her older sister, into the local bar to confront Hank. He was drinking and flirting with a woman who worked there. After Glory divorced him he wasn't around much but he hadn't been even before that. He'd stood the girls up for scheduled visitations, rarely paid child support and hardly ever showed up for holidays or birthdays. Her mom had nothing but a high school diploma and two little girls to support. She was the one who nursed them, helped with homework, taught them about being a family and encouraged them to have a career and not rely on a man for money.

Glory had no marketable skill except cleaning a house until it gleamed from top to bottom. But it was always someone else's house. For years she'd dreamed of having a home of her own. Now she did.

Dawn reached across the table and squeezed her mother's hand. "You should be incredibly proud of yourself and what you've accomplished."

"I am." Glory scooped her daughter's hand into her own. "But more than that, I'm proud of my girls. Marina is a teacher. You're a nurse. It's so rewarding to see both of you successful."

In her mother's blue eyes Dawn could see maternal delight and pleasure. She never wanted to see disappointment take its place. And that's what would happen if Glory knew the main reason she'd quit her job at the hospital and taken the one at the clinic was because of the scandal. It hadn't been her fault but that didn't matter. He was a doctor and she was just a nurse.

"Is everything okay, sweetie?"

"Hmm?" Dawn blinked away the painful memories and put a fake smile on her face. "Yeah. Why?"

"You look like something's bothering you."

"Busy day."

"Anything exciting happen?"

Glory asked her this almost every day when she came home from work. Mostly Dawn gave a generic answer. Even if there had been something medically electrifying, privacy laws prevented her from discussing it.

But today something exciting had happened and not in a good way. It was the last thing she wanted to talk about but if she tried to dodge the question her mom would suspect something. She and Marina could never put anything over on this woman.

Dawn took a deep, cleansing breath. "The new doctor showed up today."

"Didn't you tell me he's a pediatrician?"

"That's right," she confirmed. "Emmet seems really impressed with him."

"What's he like?"

Gorgeous. Cheerful. Gorgeous. Good-natured. Did she mention gorgeous? And empathetic. The babies seemed to like him, but Dawn wanted to hide in the break room. She didn't particularly want to discuss any of that, though.

"It's hard to know what he's like yet."

"What does he look like?" Glory persisted.

A movie star. A male model. He could play a doctor on TV. "He's nice looking, I guess. Average. Probably wouldn't have to walk down the street with a bag over his head."

"There's high praise." Her mother laughed. "Is he single?"

A knot twisted in Dawn's stomach. It was as if her mother could read her mind. She forced a nonchalance into her voice that she didn't feel. "I don't know. The subject didn't come up."

"It really must have been busy." Glory's tone was wry.

"Yeah." Her mom was implying that the women of Rust Creek Falls Medical Clinic pried personal information out of people. That was probably true, but not today.

"Is something wrong, sweetie?"

Hopefully not; she wouldn't let there be. "No. Like you said. I'm just tired."

"It seems like more. As if something's bothering you."

She must look bad. That was the third time her mother mentioned it. "It was just a long day." A change of subject would be good. "And an interesting first day for Dr. Clifton since Jamie Stockton came in with the triplets."

And he'd handled it brilliantly, she thought.

"Those poor little motherless angels." Glory smiled sadly. "The volunteers who help him out say that the babies are getting big and are totally adorable."

"All true." Dawn was relieved that her mom was distracted, as she'd intended. "Jamie is very grateful for the help."

"It's hard to imagine dealing with three needy infants at the same time." Glory shook her head sympathetically. "I know how hard it is to be alone with one baby."

"You said Hank wasn't around much." Dawn didn't call him dad. He hadn't earned it.

"That's why I know about caring for a baby without help. But he and I were awfully young to be parents." Suddenly her mother wouldn't make eye contact.

"Mom?" Glory wasn't any better at hiding things than Dawn.

"I heard from your father."

"When?"

"I'm not sure exactly."

"That means it's been a while and you just didn't say anything." The knot in her stomach tightened. "Does Marina know?"

"Maybe."

"Okay." There was no need to get upset. "So based on his track record it will be months, maybe years until he surfaces again to bug you. So, no problem."

Her mom looked up. "He's got a handyman business in Kalispell. It's doing really well."

The town was about a twenty-five-minute drive south of Rust Creek Falls. That didn't matter too much, but the building-a-business part was different. "Did he want something from you?"

"No. Only to help." Glory tapped the paint chips on the table. "He dropped these off for me."

"A prince of a guy."

"I think he's changed, Dawn."

"Please tell me you're not going to make the mistake of counting on him, Mom."

"People make mistakes."

For some men that mistake was humiliating a woman by using her to cheat on a fiancée. Dawn's experiences with men had left an impression—a bad one. Dr. Jonathan Clifton probably had some good qualities, but she didn't plan to take a chance on finding out for sure.

This time if she was forced to leave a job it wouldn't mean commuting to another one. To find work in her field, she'd have to move away and leave behind everything and everyone she loved. And that was something she was not prepared to do.

Jon lowered himself into the chair behind his desk and let out a long sigh. It felt good to get off his feet. He loved being a doctor, couldn't imagine doing anything else. But he was glad his second day was over. There'd barely been time to choke down a sandwich at lunch. How had the clinic staff managed to keep up with the patient load before he took over Pediatrics? Emmet, Callie and Dawn had been running all day, too.

Dawn.

Without her he couldn't have done it today, but it was clear that she could do without him. And that was more than a little annoying. After his less than positive first impression, he'd made an effort to be nice to her, friendly, charming and that had made her even more standoffish.

Even though he had a bunch of sisters, no one would ever accuse him of understanding women. But this one baffled him. She'd been very friendly at first, right up until finding out he was the new doctor. Then she backed off as if he was radioactive and he didn't know why. More often than not he got flirted with so it was possible this acute curiosity about Dawn was the result of a banged up ego. But he didn't think so.

Maybe the time he'd worked at Thunder Canyon Resort had rusted out his ability to interact with coworkers. Although no one else at the clinic seemed to have a problem with him. It wasn't as if he was looking for a life partner, just a work one. Friendly. Pleasant. Was that too much to ask?

He heaved another sigh and turned on his laptop, preparing to work. Before he could start there was a knock on his door.

"Come in."

A moment later Dawn stood there. Since he'd been expecting to see anyone but her, he did a double take, closely followed by a hitch in his breathing. There was a wholesome prettiness about her that suddenly made him feel like a gawky teenager. Then the frosty expression on her face checked it. Courtesy dictated he should greet her, but all day she'd given him the "back off" vibe and he was irritated enough to let this move into the awkward zone and force her to initiate a conversation. That would be a first today.

"I'm sorry to interrupt," she finally said. She had pieces of paper and a notepad in her hands.

"I haven't started anything yet so technically you're

not interrupting." He indicated the chairs in front of his desk. "Have a seat."

"That's okay," she answered. "I'll stand."

"Okay." That ticked him off just a little more and he waited for her to state the purpose of this unexpected visit.

"I have to return phone calls from patients. All of them involve questions about new babies from first-time mothers and Emmet said since we have a pediatrician on staff now we should ask him—I mean you. It's all ordinary stuff but Emmet says we—I—need to know where you stand on these issues."

So, she'd tried to get her answers in a way that didn't involve interacting with him. Okay, then. Battle lines drawn. "Right. Ready when you are."

She looked at one of the notes. "Chloe Thornton's baby has a runny nose. He's four months old and she has questions about fever."

New parents were understandably worried and overprotective. This wasn't his first rodeo. "She wants facts because that will make her feel more in control. Tell her if his temp is ninety-nine degrees she can give him acetaminophen to keep it stable. A hundred and one or more, she should call me. Anytime of the day or night. The clinic has an answering service, right?"

"Yes."

He met her gaze. "Next."

"Chelsea Dolan has red bumps on her face. She's barely four months old and her mom read on the internet that it should be gone by now." Dawn met his gaze.

"Of course we know that if it's on the internet it must be true," he said wryly. "The pimples are perfectly normal and can last longer than three months, especially in breastfed infants. She should baby the skin, no pun intended."

For just an instant the tension in Dawn's expression disappeared and her lips twitched, as if she wanted to smile. "Anything else?"

"She should keep it clean and dry. No cream or lotion. Next question."

She continued writing then looked up. "Alice Weber says her friend's baby is sleeping through the night and has been since he was born. Her Finn is still waking up every couple hours and she wants to know if there's something wrong or maybe she's doing something incorrectly."

"She's not. It's hard enough being a new mother without comparing your baby to someone else's." He sighed and rested his forearms on the desk. "Some babies wake because they're hungry. If she feeds the baby before she goes to bed everyone gets more uninterrupted sleep."

"Okay."

"There's also the pacifier." He gave her tips for using it more successfully and watched her taking notes, trying to keep up.

Dawn flipped the page on her tablet. "Anything else?"

He couldn't resist giving her more information than necessary, only to mess with her a little because she refused to come any closer to him. "There are a lot of quirky fixes for restless babies from putting them in a swing all night to dad driving around the block or mom sitting on the dryer and cradling her infant."

She stopped writing and looked up, a little startled. "My sister did that with Sydney, my niece—"

He held up a hand. "I'm not judging. Next question."

"There aren't any more."

"Okay. It would be nice if all the questions were this easy to answer."

"I probably should have known this but most of my experience is in acute care. And the volume of questions seems higher but that's probably because your specialty is children." Her tone had a tinge of grudging respect.

"Makes sense." Maybe that was a break in the ice. Jon stood and walked around the desk, then rested his hip on the corner. "This place was rockin'. and rollin' today. How did you do it?"

"Do what?"

"Handle the patient load with one less person?"

She backed up a step into the open doorway. "We managed."

"Obviously. But it can't have been easy."

"No." She glanced over her shoulder. "I should go—"

"That kind of pace makes downtime even more important." He wanted to talk to her. About something other than work. "What do people in Rust Creek Falls do for fun?"

"Fun?" Her eyes flashed just before the deep freeze set in again. "If you'll excuse me, I have to return these phone calls, Dr. Clifton."

"That's so formal. Please call me Jon."

"That's all right. Formal works for me. Have a good evening, Dr. Clifton."

One second she was standing there, the next she was gone. She hadn't wanted to talk to him at all and wouldn't have if the questions were about adults instead of kids. Apparently with her, friendly and pleasant *was* too much to ask. What was her deal?

Admittedly he'd always been more studious than social. He could talk to people; after all he had to communicate with his patients and their caregivers. But talking to a woman was different. Of course they were people, but there was often an undercurrent or subtext to the conversation that he didn't get.

Jon wasn't sure how long he'd been contemplating the

mystery of Dawn Laramie but he snapped out of it when Emmet walked into his office.

Without invitation or conversation the other man sat in one of the chairs facing the desk. Why couldn't a woman be more like a man?

"You're just standing here, Jon. Something wrong?"

That's what he'd been trying to figure out. "How long have you known Dawn?"

"Let me think." The older man contemplated the question. "She lives with her mom and is a native of Rust Creek Falls so I've seen her from time to time. But I didn't really get to know her until she came to work here."

"After leaving Mountain's Edge Hospital."

Emmet nodded. "Like I said, the commute must have been bad because she took a cut in pay leaving that job."

"Sometimes it's not about the money." If it was, Jon could have had his pick of lucrative career opportunities. Thunder Canyon Resort was what he'd needed at the time.

"Care to elaborate?"

"No. Guess my Zen just slipped out." Jon straightened and moved behind the desk. "How well do you know her?"

Emmet thought for a moment. "We work closely together. She's conscientious and good-natured. Her previous job was in the pediatric ICU at the hospital. Parents relate to her. Kids seem to love her. She's efficient and knowledgeable. An invaluable asset to this place."

"So if adults and children like her she must be pretty easygoing?"

"Real friendly. Callie and Brandy took to her right away." Emmet studied him for a long moment. "Why?"

Jon started to say no reason but knew that wouldn't fly, what with his interrogation. He wasn't sure how to answer. It would sound like a complaint and that wasn't the case.

Her interaction with him had been completely professional, but all the friendliness had been surgically removed.

Finally he said, "I like to get to know my coworkers."

"Makes sense." Emmet nodded thoughtfully as he stood. "And it occurs to me that when the rest of the reinforcements arrive, I should get everyone on staff together socially."

"To get to know each other better?" Jon asked.

"Yes. In a relaxed setting where we can let our hair down. A friendly office is a happy office and everything runs more smoothly."

"Very forward looking of you, Doctor. Sounds like you're open to suggestion."

"Yeah," Emmet agreed. "Why?"

Jon figured he had nothing to lose and this had been on his mind since yesterday when he walked into the clinic. "What do you think about setting up a separate waiting room for kids?"

The other man met his gaze. "Because of the wedding babies?"

"What?"

"All the infants who were born as a result of the spiked punch from the wedding last summer." Emmet's eyes twinkled.

Obviously he didn't hold the adults' behavior responsible for the population explosion. Jon wasn't touching that topic, not after his run-in with Dawn.

"Yeah, the wedding babies," he said. "Infectious disease control would say that a waiting room full of sick people is a breeding ground for germs and it's especially bad when folks' immune systems are already compromised by illness."

"A catch-22. If they weren't sick, they wouldn't be there in the first place," Emmet agreed.

"And infants shouldn't be exposed to all of that," Jon said.

"It's a good idea and would probably mean some re-modeling. There's still grant money left from rebuilding this place after the flood. I'll look into it."

"Good."

"Now, I'm going home. And you need to get out of here, too, Jon. Don't want you to burn out."

"Right."

The other man nodded and left. When he was alone Jon thought about burnout and figured in his case it felt more like a flameout when he considered Dawn. It sure sounded as if she was friendly and easygoing with everyone but him. If that was the case, the logical assumption was that he'd said or done something to upset her.

But, for the life of him, he didn't know how he'd man-aged to alienate her. Mentally he reviewed every conver-sation, all of it up to his innocent question about what people did for fun in this town. From her reaction, you'd have thought he'd hit on her...

Jon winced.

That hadn't been his intention, but he could see how she might have jumped to that conclusion. Truthfully, he wouldn't mind getting to know her. She was an attractive woman and, as much as she'd tried to hide it, they shared a similar sense of humor. But none of that meant a tinker's damn if the workplace was hostile. Doctors were trained to take symptoms and form a diagnosis. That's what he was going to do with Dawn.

If he didn't find out what he was doing to put her scrubs in a twist, it was going to be a very long year.

Chapter Three

After a second day of working with Dr. Jonathan Clifton, Dawn needed to vent to someone who knew all the skeletons in her closet. Her sister, Marina, had talked her through the personal crisis that was so much of the reason she'd quit her hospital job. For two shifts now Dawn had watched the new doctor charm everyone within a two-mile radius of the clinic. Except her. Was she just being overly cautious and seeing problems where there weren't any? Talking to Marina might give her a better perspective.

Dawn knocked on her sister's front door and waited. It could take a while sometimes to get an answer if Marina was busy with the baby. But not tonight.

The door opened and there she was with baby Sydney in her arms. "Hi, little sister."

Dawn was four inches taller than her petite, red-haired sibling but Marina was three years older. The tease was a running joke between them.

"Hi." She smiled at her niece. "Hello, sweet girl. Come to Auntie Dawn?"

Sydney grinned and that was all the encouragement necessary for grabbing her up and squeezing her close. "Ooh, you feel so warm and soft and good. And you smell like a baby."

"She is a baby."

"Trust me. They don't always smell like flowers."

"Tell me about it. She got a quick bath after you called. I figured that would give us more time to visit." With her index fingers, Marina added air quotes to the last word. Clearly she knew there was something out of the ordinary going on. "Let's talk in the other room. Are you hungry? I can throw something together."

"No. Thanks, though." She carried the baby through the kitchen and into the adjacent family room where a baby gym was set up on the carpet.

"You can put her down there and let her play. She likes that toy, don't you, sweet Sydney?"

Of course the baby didn't answer but Dawn put her down where directed. The two women sat on the rug, watching Syd bat at all the bright-colored things that dangled and rattled.

Marina met her gaze. "So, what's up?"

Instead of answering Dawn asked, "Do you ever think about that night?"

"The wedding and reception last July Fourth." Her sister wasn't asking a question. The two of them were close and somehow always on the same wavelength. "I do think about it. But I'm not sure where you're going with this."

"Syd was conceived that night. Along with a lot of other babies." She met Marina's gaze. "It seems crazy what happened."

"It is crazy. Whatever was in that punch made a lot of people behave in ways they never would have otherwise."

"Irresponsibly?" Dawn asked, remembering what Clifton had said.

"I suppose so. But Homer Gilmore is the one at fault for spiking the punch in the first place." Marina's blue eyes darkened. "They say crisis reveals character and I found that to be true. When I told Gary I was pregnant he dropped me like a hot rock. In his defense our relationship was still new when we went to the wedding together."

"Don't defend him. Everything he did before that night telegraphed to you that he was serious. If you hadn't believed that you never would have slept with him, punch or no punch. He has the character of a toad and that's an insult to toads. I'd like to punch him for not being a man and supporting you."

Marina took her daughter's tiny, flailing foot in her hand and smiled lovingly. "I can't regret what happened because now I have this beautiful, precious little girl."

"She is precious." Dawn studied the blue-eyed, red-haired baby who was going to be a clone of her mom. "And she's healthy."

"I'm so thankful for it. Sometimes I forget that you see a lot of children who are sick." Marina's eyes filled with empathy. "That must be hard for you."

"I just focus on what will help them get better." She recalled how Clifton had explained the timing for the triplets' flu shots. And how he patiently answered new parent questions, no matter how routine. There was no way she could say he wasn't good at what he did. "And we see a lot of kids for regular checkups to chart their growth and prevent them from getting sick."

"True."

"In fact Jamie Stockton brought the triplets in to see Dr. Clifton yesterday."

"The new doctor?" Her sister's eyes grew bright with curiosity.

"Yeah. He told him—"

"What's he like?"

That was what their mother had asked. But unlike Glory, her sibling knew the unfortunate, the bad and the ugly about the last new doctor Dawn had worked with. That was why she was here, to confide in someone who had all the facts.

"He's really good-looking." Gorgeous, in fact.

"Yeah. And?"

"Everyone likes him. Patients. Parents. Clinic personnel. They're all singing his praises."

Marina turned serious. "What do you think of him?"

"Do you want the good list or the bad?"

"You just did the good."

Dawn shook her head. "That was general. There are specifics. Just to be fair…"

"Okay. Do specific good," her sister encouraged.

Dawn tapped her lip as she thought over the last two days. There was a sizable amount of good specific, she realized. "He made Jamie Stockton smile."

"Wow. Sounds like a miracle. That man doesn't have a lot to smile about."

"I know, right? He actually got two smiles and a full-on grin when he'd warned Jamie that it was going to get better and worse when he was wrangling three toddlers."

Marina frowned as she looked at her little angel. "I didn't want to know that. What's to smile about?"

"I guess you had to be there."

"If you say so."

"Then there was his tips for new moms. Sensible and helpful. Like the pacifier."

"For or against?" her sister asked.

"Neutral, but with information for the 'for' group."

Marina studied her. "And? Throw me a bone here. A new mom needs all the free professional advice she can get."

She smiled, remembering his wry comment about all things on the internet being true. During that conversation he'd made her want to smile or laugh at least three times. But she held back. "He listed pointers to promote sleep, like sitting on the dryer—"

"I did that!" Marina exclaimed.

"So I told him."

"You didn't." Her sister groaned. "He probably thinks I'm a lunatic."

"*I* think you're a lunatic," Dawn clarified. "He apparently doesn't judge."

"Wow." Her sister looked awed. "Where was he when Sydney was little?"

"She's still little. Aren't you, sweetie pie?" Smiling at her niece, Dawn laughed when the baby smiled back and kicked her chubby legs in response. "But I know what you meant."

"After that it's impossible for me to believe there's anything bad about him."

"He made a comment about irresponsible behavior during the wedding reception."

Marina shrugged. "It sounds that way if you weren't there."

"Actually he was. He's Will Clifton's brother and we all know Will accidentally married Jordyn Leigh."

"And, as you said," her sister reminded her, "if it wasn't

right for them deep down, they wouldn't have done it. And those two are ridiculously in love."

"Still—"

"Obviously the doctor didn't have any punch." The words were said in that tone a big sister used to shut the door on a disagreement.

"Why are you defending him?"

"Why are you so critical?" Marina shot back. "Could it have anything to do with the fact that he's handsome and new? And the last time someone handsome and new walked into your life your world fell apart? Because he sweet-talked you out of your knickers after specifically telling you he was single and then his fiancée showed up and all the people you worked with treated you like a home wrecker? Could that be what's going on with you?"

"No." Dawn folded her arms over her chest.

Marina laughed but instantly stopped when she got the glare. "No offense."

"None taken."

"But seriously, I think you've got a thing for Dr. Clifton and because you were burned so badly, you're making up reasons to peg him as a jerk."

"But seriously," Dawn said, imitating her sister's tone. "I still think you're a lunatic."

"One man's lunatic is another man's genius." It was annoying how unfazed this woman was. "I completely understand your instinct to protect yourself. Our father split and left mom alone to raise us, then only showed up when it was convenient for him. My baby's father ran screaming from the room when I told him I was pregnant and never showed up again. And the new doctor you took a chance on was a lying, cheating snake who made your life a living hell."

"Don't sugarcoat it." Dawn sighed. "We are pathetic.

Really. The curse of the Laramie women to hook up with the wrong kind of man."

"And by focusing on the perceived faults of the handsome new Dr. Clifton, you're trying to break the curse."

There was a little too much truth in those words for Dawn's peace of mind. Time to shift the focus of this conversation. "What would you do?"

"Fortunately, I won't ever have to find out. Sydney is the best thing that has ever happened to me and we don't need a man to take care of us." She picked up the little girl who'd started to fuss.

That was an interesting response because it completely didn't answer the question. "I'm probably wrong and you're the teacher, but I think that was a non sequitur."

"Well, I'm not the one with the man problem." She pointed at Dawn. "You will have to find a way to deal with the situation—because you are wildly attracted to the new doctor."

"You're wrong."

At least Dawn hoped so. But she couldn't swear to it because her sister knew her better than anyone. It was a bad sign that a conversation which should have relieved her anxiety just made her more conflicted.

"Okay, Tucker, I'm going to take a look at your knee." Jon saw fear bordering on panic in the kid's blue eyes.

The eleven-year-old looked at his mom, then back to Jon. "Don't touch it."

"I'm not going to do anything. Right now I just need to look."

"Promise?"

Jon knew stitches would be necessary, but he needed to work up to that revelation with a skittish kid. "I'll put my hands behind my back."

He glanced at Dawn who was standing by. For just a moment her mouth curved into a smile, but when she noticed him looking it disappeared, and she wouldn't glance his way again. What had put that guarded look in her eyes and, more important, how could he get her to drop it? If anything, she grew more reserved every day. She hardly spoke to him unless it was about work and walked out of any room he entered if she didn't need to be there for a patient.

"Okay," Tucker said.

Distracted, Jon met the boy's gaze. "Hmm?"

"You can look, but you have to put your hands behind your back first." His dirty, freckled face was streaked with tears and his shaggy brown hair in need of a trim fell into his eyes.

Jon held up his hands, then clasped them behind his back. "Just looking."

"How did you get that nasty gash?" Dawn moved beside the exam table where the boy had his legs stretched out in front of him.

Jon knew that it was strictly professional because of the way she deliberately didn't look at him. She was distracting the boy, using her pediatric nursing skill.

"Me and my friends were playing by the creek." He shrugged. "I fell on a sharp rock."

"Looks like it hurt."

The laceration was about five centimeters long and deep, down to the fat, but fortunately he couldn't see bone. Sutures were definitely necessary.

Jon straightened and folded his arms over his chest. "Okay, kid, I'm going to give it to you straight. This needs stitches."

"No way." Tucker folded his arms over his chest, too, as stubbornness settled on his young face.

"Well, you could choose to do nothing, but your knee will keep bleeding."

"I don't care."

"I do." Molly Hendrickson had the same freckles and brown hair as her son.

Jon met the boy's mistrustful gaze. "I could leave it alone if that's what you want, but before deciding there are some things you should take into consideration."

"Like what?"

"It's deep and will take a long time to heal. And it's in a bad spot because you bend it and all that movement keeps the wound from closing up. On top of that, until it closes you can't get dirt in it or you risk an infection."

Doubt cut through the kid's stubborn expression. "Would that hurt?"

"Yeah it would." Jon shrugged. "Bottom line is you'll spend what's left of your summer in the house with your leg propped up."

"Mom—"

"He's the doctor, Tuck." Molly looked sympathetic but resigned.

"How bad will stitches hurt?"

"A little. But probably not as much as when you fell." In his experience treating children, it helped not to talk down to them. Jon believed in telling the patient exactly what was going to happen. "I'll swab some medicine around the cut so when I give you the shot to numb the area it won't hurt as bad. I promise you won't feel any pain when I close up that laceration."

"You'll still have to keep it clean," Dawn said. "But it won't take as long to heal and you'll have a little summer left to get as dirty as you want."

"He probably appreciates permission to be grubby, but trust me, he doesn't need it." Molly tenderly brushed the hair off his forehead. "It is what it is. A little summer left is better than nothing. Man up, buddy."

"Okay." He glared. "But I'm not going to look."

"Me, either," Jon said.

"You have to." Tucker saw his grin and looked sheepish. "Oh. You're messing with me."

"I am." Jon saw Dawn smile, then shut it down when she glanced at him.

Jon tamped down his irritation. The way she always did that was really starting to bug him. But he couldn't deal with it now. Soon, though.

"I'll go get a suture kit." She left the room.

He washed his hands at the exam room sink and in a few minutes when Dawn returned he was ready.

"Okay, Tuck, here we go. When you're all patched up you can get your mom to take you for ice cream."

"But it's almost dinnertime."

"I bet she'll make an exception this one time," Dawn said.

"That can be arranged." Molly put her arm across her son's shoulders. "Be brave, kiddo."

"What if I cry?"

Jon took the syringe of lidocaine and prepared to inject it. "From my perspective, as long as you hold still, you can cry, scream and swear."

"I can say bad words?" Apparently using bad language without punishment was more exciting than ice cream.

His mom was squirming now. "Do you even know any curse words?"

"I've heard dad say some stuff—"

"Here we go. A little pinch," Jon said. He gently pricked the skin with the needle. "How you doing, Tuck?" Jon quickly glanced up.

"Okay. It hurt at first. But now it just feels like you're pushing on my leg."

"Good. That's what should happen. It's going to take a little time for the medicine to work, but that was the worst of it. Now we're going to clean out the cut so it doesn't get infected. Then I'll do the stitches and put a big Band-Aid on it so the girls will be impressed."

The kid made a face and looked as if he was in real pain. "I don't like girls."

"You don't have to." *Give it a couple years*, Jon thought. Then you might get to work with a girl who hated your guts and you had no clue why. When they were finished here he was going to find out what was going on with her.

Jon finished quickly then bandaged the knee. "You'll need to change the dressing every day. Bring him back in a week and I'll check to see if the stitches are ready to come out."

"Does it hurt when you take out stitches?" Tucker wanted to know.

"Nah. And you know I would tell you if it did."

"I know." Tucker looked relieved.

"Thank you," his mom said, helping her son off the exam table.

"You're welcome. See you, buddy."

Tucker looked up at him. "You're a pretty good doctor."

"You're a pretty good patient."

Dawn opened the door and said to the mom, "When you check out up front, Brandy will make a follow-up appointment. Remind her to give you the sheet with instructions on how to deal with the stitches."

"Will do."

After mother and son walked out Dawn started cleaning up the room, though she still wouldn't look at him. This was as good a time as any to say what was on his mind.

"Dawn, I'd like to talk to you." He slid his hands into the pockets of his white lab coat.

"All right."

That was the appropriate response but the stubborn look in her eyes and the step back she took clearly reflected her attitude.

There was no point in beating around the bush. "You obviously have a problem with me."

"What makes you say that?"

At least she didn't flat out deny it. "You're exhibiting all the symptoms. Refusing to call me by my first name. Avoiding me when possible. Remaining professional but cool."

"I don't see anything wrong with that."

"Technically there's not. But with Emmet and everyone else on staff here at the clinic you're warm and friendly. I'm the only one you treat differently."

"Do you have a problem with my work?" she asked.

"No. You're an excellent nurse."

"Then I'm not sure what to say."

That she liked him. Thought he wasn't bad looking. Maybe she was even a little bit attracted to him. Anything but this robotic Stepford-nurse routine.

"Look, you and I both know that working as closely together as we do, things flow more smoothly if staff gets along and has each other's back."

"I couldn't agree more," she said emphatically.

That was the first time she'd shown any real spirit to him since the day he'd walked into the clinic. "Okay, then. Let's fix this. We're finished for the day. Join me for a drink at the Ace in the Hole."

"No. I don't think that's a very good idea."

"I disagree." He dragged his fingers through his hair. "Whether you admit it or not, we have a problem. And it's like I told Tucker. You can choose to ignore it, but that will just make the situation worse. Let's clear the air."

"Why don't we clear it right here?" Reluctance mixed with the obstinate expression in her eyes. "No need to go for a drink."

"I think this conversation would be more effective on neutral ground." He looked around the exam room. "And, I don't know about you, but I'd like to get out of here and relax a little bit. What do you say?"

Dawn caught her bottom lip between her teeth as she studied him. "You're not going to drop this, are you?"

"No." He sensed her weakening and wanted to smile, but held back. A victory lap now would make her dig in and that's the last thing he needed.

"Okay." She nodded reluctantly. "One drink."

She didn't look happy, but then again she hadn't slammed the door in his face, either. Finally, the opportunity he'd been waiting for.

Chapter Four

Dawn insisted on driving herself to the Ace in the Hole. Jon followed her. And when the heck had she started thinking of him by his first name instead of simply Clifton? Maybe she should let that go. It felt weird and unnatural anyway. She was basically a friendly person and calling him Dr. Clifton when everyone else used his first name made her look as if she had a stick up her butt. Which, of course, she did.

He parked beside her and they walked side by side to the bar's entrance.

"Nice night," he said.

She stared up at the dark sky awash in stars that looked like gold dust. A light breeze brushed over her skin. Perfect. "A Goldilocks night."

"I'm sorry. What?"

Their arms bumped and she met his puzzled gaze as a sliver of awareness sliced through her. He was very cute and she should never have agreed to this drink. But he'd just asked her a question and it would be rude not to answer.

"Remember Goldilocks and the three bears? Porridge was too hot, too cold, then she found the perfect one. Same for the beds." She looked up and sighed. "This night is—"

"Not too hot or cold."

"Just right," they both said together.

Dawn smiled at him and it took a couple seconds to realize she wasn't supposed to do that. She shut the feeling down, then fixed her attention on the Ace in the Hole. Considering it was impossible to count the number of times she'd been here, the place felt like an old friend. She was going to need one.

There was a hitching post where a cowboy could tie up his horse if he was out for a ride and wanted to stop in for a cold one before heading back to the ranch. The front window had a neon beer sign that blinked on and off along with a lighted, oversize ace of hearts playing card. It was rustic and full of character.

They stepped up on the wooden porch and before she could reach for it Jon grabbed the handle on the screen door, pulling it open for her. A loud screech sounded, clearly showing that the rusty hinges could use some TLC.

Inside, across from the door, a bar ran the entire length of the wall. The mirror behind it reflected the lined up bottles of hard liquor. Circular tables big enough for six ringed a wood plank dance floor. Booths with a more intimate feel lined the room's perimeter.

Jon pointed to an empty one and put his other hand to the small of her back. "Let's sit over there."

Dawn would have preferred a bar stool and less intimacy, especially because the heat of his fingers fried the rational thought circuits of her brain. By the time connections reestablished, any protest would have required an explanation and she didn't want to go there. Besides, it was only for one drink and then she was gone.

"Okay," she said.

It was a weeknight in early August and the place was only half-full—mostly cowboys, a few couples and ladies who hung out in groups. No one noticed them cross to the booth but Dawn couldn't help noticing Jon behind her. And hated that she did.

After they'd barely settled in the booth, the owner of the bar walked over. Rosey Shaw Traven was somewhere in her sixties and quite a character in her own right. In her customary peasant blouse, leather vest with wide belt, jeans and boots, she could have been the captain of a pirate ship. Only her short dark hair pegged her as a contemporary heroine and her brown eyes snapped with humor and worldly wisdom. No one messed with Rosey and if they were stupid enough to try, Sam Traven, her retired navy SEAL husband, made them regret it.

"Hi, Dawn. Good to see you." Rosey's assessing gaze rested on her companion. "I know you've been in here before, but I can't place you."

"Jon Clifton. Will's brother."

"Right." She nodded at the scrubs he still wore. "The new doctor."

Dawn's stomach twisted at the words that still haunted her. That was bad enough, but the way he smiled and looked so boyishly handsome added an element of heat that tipped into temptation. No matter how sternly she warned herself not to, this was the way she'd felt just before the rug was pulled out from under her. This idea was getting worse by the second.

Rosey put a hand on her curvy hip. "What can I get you two?"

"A couple of beers." Jon looked across the table, a question in his eyes.

"I don't really like beer."

"What would you like?" he asked.

To run for the exit, she thought. A little bit of panic was starting to set in. She wanted to tell him he really didn't care what she wanted, but Rosey was standing right there. "White wine, please. Chardonnay."

"Okay. Beer, white wine. Any appetizers?"

Jon looked at her again, then made an executive decision. "Chips and salsa. I'm starving."

"Coming right up." The bar owner walked away, her full hips swaying.

Jon looked around. "How long has this place been around?"

She shrugged. "No idea."

"It's got a lot of local color. Could have been here a hundred years ago."

"Yup."

"Do you come here often?" he asked.

"Girls night out once in a while. With my sister, Marina, now and then." She looked everywhere but at him.

The awkward silence was getting more awkward when Rosey arrived carrying a tray with their drinks, a basket of tortilla chips and a bowl of salsa.

"If you want to order dinner, just let me know." She smiled at them. "I'm probably not the first one to say this, but you two make a cute couple."

The comment shocked the words right out of Dawn, and Rosey was gone before she could set the woman straight. The new doctor didn't seem at all bothered and held up his beer bottle.

"Let's drink to—"

"Don't you dare say to us," she warned.

"Why would I?"

"It's what guys do."

He frowned. "Not this guy. But I get the feeling some other guy did a number on you."

Bingo. But she had to ask, "Why do you say that?"

"Evasive answer. Interesting," he observed.

"Not to me." She took a sip of the cold, crisp wine and made a silent toast. *Here's to never being a fool again,* she thought.

"Look, Dawn, you've been hostile since the day we met. And just now you made a disparaging comment about men in general." He sipped his beer but never took his eyes off her. "This is pretty far out there, but I doubt there's much I could say to make things any worse. So, here goes. I get along pretty well with people, try not to tick them off and it works. I've bent over backward to be friendly with you but every time I crash and burn. The only thing I can come up with is that I remind you of a guy who dumped you. Feel free to point and laugh at my theory."

Dawn wasn't laughing. Mostly she was amazed at his insight. "That's pretty close."

"Seriously?" He looked astonished. "I got it right? That's what's been bugging you?"

"Either you think I'm a psychotic victim or you're surprised at yourself."

"The latter. No one would peg me as someone who could figure out what a woman is thinking." The doctor looked decidedly pleased with himself.

Dawn was not pleased and couldn't resist a dig. "It took you long enough."

"In my defense, you didn't give very many clues, what with not talking to me." He snagged a chip and dipped it in the salsa, then took a bite. After chewing he said, "So what happened?"

The cat was out of the bag so she might as well tell him. "Technically I dumped him after finding out he was a weasel dog toad boy."

One corner of Jon's mouth curved up. "That clears everything up."

"Why are you so cheerful?"

"I'm just glad you're not mad at me."

The comment made her want to smile and she realized he did that to her a lot. "I suppose you deserve a more detailed explanation."

"You don't owe me anything. But I'd like to understand."

"A man willing to listen."

"Actually, I mean I really would like to understand women in general. You'd think since I have sisters it wouldn't be a challenge, but you'd be wrong." He shrugged. "Every time I think I've figured women out they change the rules."

Dawn didn't trust this self-effacing man but she'd gone too far not to explain now. "When I was working at Mountain's Edge Hospital they hired a very good-looking pediatric specialist."

"Let me guess. Weasel dog toad boy?"

"Yes." She did laugh then, but humor faded fast when she recalled the humiliation. "All the female employees had a crush on him, but the unattached ones flirted. Including me. When he singled me out, everyone noticed. I couldn't believe he'd picked me. But even then I was careful. He didn't wear a ring, but a man in his thirties was bound to have a romantic past and I asked him. He assured me he was free and I believed him or I never would have—"

"Yeah. I get it."

Hmm. She realized he was sparing her the humiliation of saying it out loud. "Not long after we...did the deed, his fiancée showed up at the hospital to have lunch with him. Hospitals are like a small town and everyone knows what's going on. The people I worked with looked at me like I was a home wrecker. The workplace became embarrassing and uncomfortable. I worried about getting fired."

"Is that why you took the job at the clinic?"

She nodded. "But I told everyone—including my mom—that the commute was getting to me."

"Your mother doesn't know what happened?"

"No. It was so humiliating, I couldn't tell her." Only Marina knew the truth. And now him.

"Fast-forward to me showing up at the clinic. The new doctor."

And so good-looking that she could hardly stand it. "Yeah."

"I'm not him, Dawn."

"I know. But it's not just that." She met his gaze. "My father is a flake who got my mother pregnant, twice, then walked away and left her to raise two little girls. Oh, he showed up every once in a while. When it was convenient for him."

"I'm not him, either," he said gently.

"You think I'm crazy. I would think so, too, if I hadn't lived the curse of the Laramie women." She took a chip and started breaking it into little pieces, dropping them on her cocktail napkin. "My sister and her date drank that spiked punch at the wedding. They...you know—"

"Did the wild thing?"

Dawn nodded. "Before you judge, you should know she's super responsible. A teacher. If there wasn't something about that punch..."

"She got pregnant."

"Yes. But she's not a flake."

"Not judging," he assured her.

"But you did. That first day when you walked into the clinic. You implied that the increase in the town birth rate was because of irresponsibility. That's not my sister. When she told Gary about the baby, he freaked out and left her to raise my niece alone."

He looked really angry. "Rat weasel dog toad boy."

"I couldn't have said it better." She took a deep breath. "Sydney is four months old now. Beautiful. Healthy. And Marina is the best mother."

Jon took a long drink of beer, then met her gaze. "I can see why you reacted to me the way you did. And since we're clearing the air, I need to apologize for what I said that day. I was far too offhanded about the increase in births and I formed an opinion without all the facts."

Dawn thought he looked sincere, but she couldn't help being skeptical. "Okay."

"In my defense, I have to say that I saw a lot during my pediatric residency. Children abused and abandoned by irresponsible adults who simply had reckless sex."

She saw the shadows in his eyes. "That must have been hard. I can't even imagine."

"Kids often are innocent victims of the very adults who should protect them. So, I may have jumped to conclusions."

His obvious regret over his comments and caring concern for children was so darn appealing Dawn didn't have the heart to hold the remarks against him. "I can see how it could look that way to an outsider."

"How about that." A smile sliced through his intensity. "We're really starting to communicate."

He was right, she thought. Even weirder was the fact that he was still there and actually smiling. After explaining the curse of the Laramie women she'd expected him to run as far and fast as he could.

Dawn took a corn chip and this time dipped it in the salsa and ate it. She was hungry, too, now that her dark secret had been revealed. Points to him for figuring it out. "These are good."

He watched her scarf down a few more in rapid succession. "Maybe we should get something more substantial to eat."

"Oh, boy." She blushed and hoped the subdued lighting hid it from him. "I guess that wasn't very ladylike."

"Not judging." He held up his hands in a surrender gesture. "And you're obviously starved. So am I. Let's get some burgers."

"That sounds so good. With cheese." She thought for a moment. "And onions. Mushrooms, too."

Jon signaled Rosey back over and put in the order. Ten minutes later they were biting into juicy, messy cheeseburgers. In silence she put away nearly half of it before pulling a napkin from the dispenser on the table to wipe her mouth. She shouldn't care whether or not this guy thought she was a slob but couldn't seem to help it.

With the worst of her hunger pains taken care of, she thought about something he'd said that piqued her curiosity. "So you have sisters." His blank look told her that statement needed more context. "A little while ago you said you should understand women because you have sisters."

"Right." He practically inhaled the last bite of his food, then reached for a napkin. The man hadn't been kidding about being hungry. "I have four. Catherine, Cecelia, Calista and baby Celeste. She's twenty."

"And there's your brother Will."

"Rob and Craig, too. We grew up on a ranch in Thunder Canyon."

She did the math. "Wow, your parents have eight children. Where do you fit in the lineup?"

"I'm the second oldest."

"That explains a lot."

"Oh?" One of his dark eyebrows rose questioningly.

"Why you specialized in pediatrics." She studied him while he thought that over. Clearly he didn't usually make off-the-cuff remarks but reflected on his answers.

"It wasn't quite so neat and tidy, Dr. Freud," he teased. "I did help out with the younger kids, but it's what you do in a big family. Not only that, my mom said I doctored the animals. If one of them stood still long enough I would bandage it."

She got an entirely too adorable image of him as a little boy with a toy stethoscope and blood pressure cuff. "Now that you've been turned loose with needles and sharp medical instruments, do the animals run from you?"

"No." He grinned. "The critters on my brother's ranch wave every morning when I drive by. And my dog seems quite taken with me."

"You have a dog?"

He took a drink of his beer. "Don't sound so surprised."

"Really?" She stared at him. "Guess I just can't picture you with a pet."

"Rerun isn't just a pet. He's family."

She made a scoffing sound. "All parents and pet owners think their dependent is gifted."

"Would you like to meet my dependent?" he offered cheerfully, as if he had nothing to hide.

It was half request, half challenge and all bad idea as it required going to his place.

"I don't think so." Dawn shook her head. "You see one, you've seen them all."

There was something wicked about the grin that spread across his handsome face. "Rerun is a miracle."

"Right," she said skeptically.

"He has three legs."

"No way."

"You're really challenging my veracity?" One dark eyebrow rose. "Call my bluff. Come and meet him."

An invitation to see his three-legged dog was a teaser that Dawn couldn't resist. She just hoped she didn't regret the decision.

"You're on, Doctor."

Jon pulled his truck to a stop in front of the guesthouse located on his brother Will's ranch, a short distance from the main compound of buildings. Dawn had followed him from the Ace in the Hole and parked beside him.

He couldn't believe she'd agreed to have a drink with him, let alone tagged along to his place. Maybe he'd missed his calling and should be in the diplomatic corps working on world peace.

He walked over to her, then glanced at his front door. The paint was brick red, cracked and peeling. He knew the space behind it was more cabin than house with a living room/kitchen combination, one bedroom and a small bathroom.

Looking down at her he said, "Be it ever so humble…"

"I have to ask you." She caught her top lip between her teeth. "Is this whole three-legged dog thing the equivalent of 'would you like to come over and see my etchings?'"

"Are you asking if I'm hitting on you?" He wasn't always sure about subtext and figured it was better to ask straight out rather than assume.

"Well… That's a definite maybe."

"Then the answer is no. This is not a come-on. And I should be offended that you're questioning my motive and integrity."

And he would be if the thought of kissing her had never

crossed his mind. The urge to see if her lips were as soft
as they looked had occurred to him the first time he saw
her. It had grown more acute tonight at the Ace in the Hole,
when she'd stopped looking as if she'd eaten a lemon every
time she glanced at him.

"I asked you here," he explained, "because you seemed
open to the idea of meeting my dog."

"I am. I love animals. When I was a little girl I begged
my mom for a dog, but she was a single mom and food,
clothes and a roof over our heads were always more important." She shrugged. "Go figure."

"Look, Dawn, I have no ulterior motive." In the moonlight he could see the conflict in her eyes. Damn the part
of him that wanted to fix it, because not pulling her into
his arms was taking every ounce of willpower he had. That
was a bad idea. She'd said that a man in his thirties was
bound to have a romantic past and Jon was no exception.
He had so much baggage it got in the way of his ulterior
motives. "The only way to find out if I'm telling the truth
is to take a leap of faith."

A high-pitched whining came from just inside the door
and she grinned. "Sounds like a three-legged dog who
knows his human is home."

"At least you know that I'm not making it up. And, for
the record, there are no etchings."

She laughed. "Darn."

He turned the knob. "Out here on the ranch with Will
and Jordyn Leigh coming and going there's no need for
locks. The only thing in here I care about anyway is
Rerun." When he pushed the door wide, Rerun's welcoming whine escalated to an ear-piercing pitch.

"Rerun," he said sternly.

Instantly the happy dog sound changed to a friendly

yipping. He sat down and put his only front paw on Jon's leg by way of greeting.

"Hey, fella. You've got a visitor." He bent and petted the dog. "Put your hand out so he can scent you," he said to Dawn.

She did, and laughed when the animal licked her fingers. "He's adorable," she said. "What kind of dog is he?"

Jon saw skepticism give way to tenderness and wished the look was for him. An involuntary reaction, he knew, because there was about as much chance of that happening as him negotiating world peace. "A poodle–Shih Tzu mix."

"He moves pretty well without that leg."

"He adapted. Of course, he was wobbly at first but there was no keeping him down."

"At first?" She knelt on the wood floor just inside the door and the dog practically crawled into her lap as she rubbed his back. "Is he an animal who you actually needed to bandage?"

"I was coming home late at night after a hospital shift during my residency. How I even spotted him in the dark by the side of the road is truly amazing. He'd obviously been hit by a car."

"Oh, no—"

"Let's just say that there's a special place in hell for someone who would hit an animal and not stop to help." Jon would never forget the screams of pain the dog made when he was moved, no matter that it was to get him help. "I took him to a veterinary urgent care. He had internal injuries in addition to his leg trauma and needed surgery."

"You paid for it?" she guessed.

He nodded. "The vet couldn't save his leg but the rest was fixable."

"What about his owner?"

"No one came forward and he didn't have a collar or an identification chip."

"And you still have him." She stated the obvious. "That means you—"

"Adopted him. Yeah." He was glad she'd stopped looking at him as if she thought he was the kind of guy who'd pull the wings off flies. "Animals with disabilities are harder to find homes for and if they don't…" He shook his head. "I just couldn't—"

"Let that happen," she finished.

"Something like that."

There was no reason to explain that it had been a low point in his life. A kid he'd grown close to at the hospital had died unexpectedly and the woman he'd been planning to propose to had walked out on him. Also unexpectedly.

He was a man in his thirties with emotional baggage, just like Dawn had said. Choosing not to talk about it didn't mean he would lie to her like weasel dog toad boy. He had no ulterior motives because he had no intention of getting involved. Staying alone was best.

Dawn stood and smiled at him as if he had wings, a halo and walked on water. "You are—"

Just then the dog barked twice and ran out the still-open door. Jon called after him. "Rerun!"

He stepped outside in time to see the animal head toward the brush in his awkward half hop, half-run. "Rerun, come." The dog paid no attention and disappeared into the bushes a short distance away. "Damn it."

"What's wrong?"

"He likes to chase rabbits even though there's not a chance he'll ever catch one and wouldn't know what to do with it if he did." He looked at her. "Out here I don't have to worry about cars and traffic but there are predators, and if he wanders too far away, he'd be pretty vulnerable. I've tried to break him of it but you can see how much success I've had so far."

"We should go after him," she urged.

Just as they started in the direction the dog had disappeared, Rerun ran out of the bushes straight to Jon. He went down on one knee. "You're going to turn my hair white, you disobedient scoundrel."

"Spoken like a devoted pet parent." Dawn laughed. "You are really something, Dr. Clifton."

This time the use of his full name didn't bother Jon. It was because of the tone in her voice, the respect. Maybe a little admiration. It was a good bet he'd been elevated from weasel dog toad boy status to a level that remained to be determined.

Still, when you made it out of the basement there was nowhere to go but up.

Chapter Five

Dawn stood just outside the clinic front office and watched Jon walk down the long hallway toward her. He was graceful and lean, like a runner. And so good-looking that resistance by the average woman would be futile. She was average and had successfully resisted him—until last night. Her heart had begun to thaw when she'd observed him interact so well with the boy who'd needed stiches in his knee. Then they'd had drinks, and it melted even more when she got a firsthand look at his devotion to a three-legged dog.

Once you saw that, there was no unseeing it, no going back. The warming process had begun and continued as he got closer and smiled at her.

"Hi." He leaned a broad shoulder against the wall by the doorway. "Busy morning. Couldn't have gotten through it without you."

"Just doing my job."

The last morning patient had left and there was a break until the afternoon. More often than not this didn't happen because of walk-ins or an appointment going longer than anticipated. But today the schedule had purred along like a fine-tuned Ferrari. She wondered if part of it had to do with her attitude shift and the fact that she was now working with him in a spirit of cooperation. All because she'd seen for herself that he wasn't a jerk.

She met his gaze. "I have a confession to make."

"Uh-oh. Should I be afraid?"

"Maybe." She glanced into the room beside them and through the reception window to the empty waiting area. "This place is a little creepy when it's so quiet."

"Ah." He nodded knowingly. "Fortunately it's not quiet very often from what I've seen so far. That means the potential for being weirded out is limited."

"And I should enjoy it while I can."

"That's my medical opinion. And worth the price you paid for it," he added.

Dawn knew that was her cue to say she needed to take advantage of this break in the action and grab some lunch. That would be the smart play. But being smart took a backseat because she was thinking of some topic to prolong this conversation.

"How's Rerun?" That was the best she could come up with. "Chasing any poor, unsuspecting jackrabbits?"

"No. He's grounded." His look was wry. "And I think word is out and the local rabbit population has headed to greener, safer pastures away from the crazy Shih Tzu who thinks he's a mighty, three-legged hunter."

She remembered the dog barking before he ran out. Now, she was no expert on animal behavior, but it had sure seemed like he knew something was out there. "If not rabbits, what was he chasing last night outside your house?"

"Could have been anything." He shoved his hands into the pockets of his white lab coat. "A snake. Gopher. Prairie dog."

"So he's not selective about his prey?" she teased.

"No. Not really. It's the thrill of the chase he's after."

And what about the dog's owner? she wondered. He didn't wear a wedding ring and there was no white mark interrupting the tan on his left ring finger indicating he'd taken one off recently. He hadn't told her last night that he was single or had a fiancée, but she hadn't asked. It hadn't been relevant to their discussion. For reasons she refused to examine closely it seemed awfully darn relevant right now. If the new doctor *was* single, the question was—why? Did he only like the chase?

"Rerun sure is a cutie." Just like his human. "With you gone all day, who lets him out for—"

"Bathroom breaks?" he teased.

"Yeah. That."

"Will mostly, or his wife, Jordyn Leigh. She's busy with work and school but the ranch is my brother's job and he's there most of the time to check on Rerun." He frowned a little. "In Thunder Canyon my house has a fenced-in yard so there was a doggy door and he could come and go. It concerned me, long days at the clinic and leaving my dog alone. But having family around helps."

Last night she saw that he really loved a dog that someone left for dead and no one wanted. He'd even said Rerun was family.

The outside clinic door opened and a young man walked over to the reception window, then looked around and spotted them. "Hi. I'm picking up for Medical Diagnostics. Do you have anything to go to the lab?"

Once a day someone from the medical lab located in

Kalispell came by for blood samples and anything else the doctors wanted analyzed.

"We have some. I'll get them for you." Dawn took a step away, but Jon stopped her with a hand on her arm, and the heat from his fingers could have started a forest fire. It was instinctive to avoid the heat and she jerked away, not very gracefully judging by the question in his eyes.

"I'll take care of this," he said. "Why don't you grab some lunch while you can?"

"Are you sure? I don't mind—"

"Yeah," he said. "I've got this."

"Okay. Thanks."

He nodded, then walked over to the window. As much as Dawn wanted to stick around, just to look at him, she headed down the hall in the direction of the break room. Callie Crawford, the clinic's other nurse-practitioner, exited the first exam room and intercepted her.

"Hi, there." The brown-eyed brunette smiled as if she knew a juicy secret, then fell into step. "What's up?"

"I'm headed to the break room for lunch. Have you eaten yet?"

"No."

"Wow, the earth, moon and stars have aligned and we're really getting a break where we can chat. I feel as if I've gone through a portal to an alternate universe."

"Don't think it too hard. Everything could collapse in a heartbeat." Callie grinned.

Dawn had liked this woman right away and hadn't changed her mind in the five months she'd worked here at the clinic. Callie Kennedy Crawford was a former corporate executive from Chicago who'd traveled all over the world and shopped at exclusive boutiques. But she gave it all up for tiny Rust Creek Falls, Montana, and a job where she wore scrubs and could help people.

Her medical certification/license was limited but her training allowed her to see the less seriously ill patients and take some of the burden off the MDs. A good NP knew what and what not to handle and Callie was excellent at making those calls.

The two of them grabbed their respective lunches and took seats across from each other at the small table in the break room which doubled as a storage area. Upper and lower cupboards held office and medical supplies. Next to the sink was a coffeepot which was usually half-full of some sludge-like substance.

Dawn took a bite of her tuna sandwich and studied her friend while she chewed. "How's Nate?"

"My husband is awesome. And busy with Maverick Manor."

That was the rustic but upscale hotel Nate Crawford had opened just outside of town after coming into some money. Callie was an original member of The Newcomer's Club, a group of women who'd come to Rust Creek Falls for various personal reasons, most of which were about finding husbands.

Callie met Nate and it hadn't been love at first sight, but they did eventually fall for each other. Though Dawn was skeptical of love herself, no one liked a love-conquers-all story more than her. The Crawfords were a stable couple and had been together for a while now. Next step for them?

Dawn had to ask. "So, I have a job here in Rust Creek Falls thanks to the recent spike in births. It begs the question—and feel free to tell me if I'm prying—when are you and Nate going to have a little bundle of joy?"

"When they come out of vending machines." Callie said it with a straight face but couldn't hold back a grin. She shrugged and said, "It will happen when it happens."

Dawn thought about her sister and how it happened

when her situation couldn't have been more wrong. Somehow a mother's unconditional love made Marina's unexpected surprise work.

"So what's new?" she asked her friend.

"That's my line. What's going on with you?"

Dawn shrugged. "Same old, same old."

"That's not what I heard."

She brought her tuna sandwich to her mouth for a bite, then stopped and blinked at her friend. "Excuse me?"

"I heard from someone who swears the rumor is reliable that you were at the Ace in the Hole last night. With Dr. Clifton."

"Oh, that." Why in the world would that statement make her blush? It shouldn't. Nothing happened. But her face was hot anyway.

"So," Callie persisted. "What's going on?"

"Nothing." That was true, but more heat climbed up Dawn's neck.

"Really. Just now I saw you talking, in a friendly way, with our new doctor. So what gives?"

"Really, not a darn thing." *Please don't push it*, Dawn silently begged.

"Hey, this is me," Callie said. "Nothing goes on in this clinic that I don't know about."

"Okay, good. Then I don't have to say anything." She almost laughed at the expression on the other woman's face, as if someone had taken away her chocolate.

"Wrong. There's something. Silly you to think I would give up." Callie tsked. "Since that handsome hunk of baby doctor got here you've been like the ice queen around him. Very out of character for you, I might add. Then the two of you have a drink together and get chummy in the hall."

"You shouldn't put too much faith in rumors—"

Callie held up a finger to stop her. "There's no rumor

involved. I saw that for myself. And I heard you say something about being at his place last night."

"So you were eavesdropping."

The other woman looked smug. "I can't help it if sound carries in this place."

Oh, boy. "It was totally innocent."

"Hmm." Callie's tone clearly said she didn't believe that for a second. "But there is something going on."

Throw her a bone, Dawn decided. "I didn't warm up to him when he first got here."

"Tell me something I don't know." Her friend picked up the other half of her ham sandwich.

"He asked me to have a drink and discuss the situation. It seems I've misjudged him."

"So this conversation started at the Ace in the Hole and continued at his house."

Rather than address that directly, Dawn said, "Did you know he has a three-legged dog?"

"Rerun. So you met him."

"Yes. Then I left. End of story."

"That's what I first thought after meeting Nate." Callie chewed a bite of her sandwich. "But after repeated exposure something between us shifted. I think there's romance in the air between you and Jon."

"No. Absolutely not."

"You can't be sure, Dawn."

"I can." When her friend started to say something she held up her hand. "I know it because I refuse to be the doctor/nurse affair cliché."

The other woman didn't know because Dawn wouldn't share the information, but she'd been there, done that. The whole awful situation was hurtful and humiliating. Worst of all it jeopardized her career. Lesson learned.

"You could do worse," Callie said. "Jon's a nice guy."

"He is. But all he wants is a peaceful work environment. He won't push for more and neither will I. And speaking of prying..." She said the words teasingly, but there was no way she would make a drink, a hamburger and meeting his dog into something more than it was.

"Okay," Callie conceded. "But never say never. Look what happened to Nate and me. Attraction is all about chemistry."

Dawn took a bite of her sandwich, using the couldn't-talk-with-her-mouth-full defense. There was too much truth in the statement and denying it would be a falsehood. She needed to have a stern talk with her mother about teaching her to be honest. There were times it was darned inconvenient not to be able to lie and get away with it.

So the luxury of lunching with a girlfriend didn't come without a price. Now she knew she was the subject of juicy town gossip and she also knew from firsthand experience how destructive it could be when people at work made your business their business. And here in Rust Creek Falls everyone did that.

So, there would be no more socializing with the new doctor for her.

After a couple days of détente with Dawn, Jon was really hitting his stride at the clinic. He was getting into the work flow of the busy medical facility as opposed to the Thunder Canyon Resort, where there'd been a lot of downtime. And, more important, he lapsed into a routine of glimpsing the pretty nurse going in and out of patient rooms and wondering what cartoon character would be on her scrub top when she came in to work each morning. He liked that routine. A lot.

And then Emmet called the staff into his office. The patients had all been seen and the clinic was closed for the day. Brandy had plans and had already left so it was Callie, Dawn and Jon standing in front of their boss's desk along with two strangers. The good part for Jon was that Dawn stood next to him. There wasn't a lot of room so she had to stand very close. He could feel the heat from her skin, and need curled like a fist in his gut.

"Everyone," Emmet said, "I'd like to introduce you to Dr. Steve Shepard and nurse Lorajean Quinn. I promised you more help and here they are. Don't ever say I don't keep my word."

"Reinforcements," Callie said. "Yay!"

Emmet introduced each member of the staff and everyone shook hands. The nurse looked somewhere in her late fifties, possibly sixty. She was tall, about five foot nine, with blond hair and brown eyes that had a don't-get-on-my-bad-side look in them. The new doctor was a little taller than Jon. Jon was no expert, but was pretty sure women would think the new guy was nice looking. He had dark brown hair, blue eyes and a square jaw to go along with that rugged build.

Jon met the other MD's gaze. "What's your specialty, Dr. Shepard?"

"Internal medicine. And a rotation in trauma surgery."

He waited for more and they stared at each other for several moments before it became clear that no more information would be forthcoming. Jon glanced at Emmet sitting in the leather chair behind his desk. It wasn't obvious, but he swore the other man shrugged in a you-got-me gesture. Maybe he'd have more luck with the nurse.

"Where are you from, Lorajean?"

"Dallas."

"I thought I heard the South in your voice," Callie said.

The other nurse grinned. "Just FYI, the 'Don't mess with Texas' slogan is about littering the roads not Lone

Star State attitude. Although I don't recommend testing that out on me."

"Understood," Dawn said.

Everyone else in the room laughed but the new doctor didn't seem to have a sense of humor.

"What brings you to Rust Creek Falls besides a job here at the clinic?" Dawn looked from one newcomer to the other, putting the question out to both.

Lorajean fielded it. "I retired from the army. Been around the world. I'm ready to put down roots and this little town seemed like a real nice place to do that."

"Dr. Shepard?" Dawn asked. "How did you find us?"

"Emmet still has contacts in the army medical corps." Lorajean fielded this one, too. "He reached out. Steve and I reached back."

"These two come highly recommended," Emmet chimed in. "Performing surgery under combat conditions is a unique qualification."

"One we hope you don't need here at the clinic," Callie interjected.

"So, you're a trauma surgeon?" Jon asked.

"That's the rumor." Shepard's tone was almost a challenge and there was something guarded in his eyes.

"Emmet said a lot of babies have been born here since March," the nurse said.

"Did he tell you why?" Dawn glanced up and Jon resisted the urge to look at her.

Emmet chuckled. "You mean did I tell them about the legend of Homer Gilmore and the spiked wedding punch?"

"That would be the one, yes," Dawn answered.

"Sounds like a good party," Shepard commented.

"It was." Dawn smiled at him. "Unfortunately most of the people who drank that punch can't remember very much about what happened."

"Shame."

Jon waited for Dawn to get all icy and clipped with the guy and when she shrugged it off, he was a tad miffed.

She merely nodded. "What do you think of Rust Creek Falls, Dr. Shepard?"

"It's Steve."

"Okay. Steve. This town must seem awfully small to you," she persisted.

"Small isn't bad."

So Nurse Laramie obviously didn't have a problem with this new doctor. Huh. John had had to buy her a drink and introduce her to his dog to earn the privilege of being on a first name basis with her.

This was more than a little irritating.

Emmet cleared his throat. "I asked Steve and Lorajean to come in after hours to get acclimated now so tomorrow they can hit the ground running."

"I'll orient them," Callie offered.

"Me, too." Dawn raised her hand. "I'll show them where all the supplies are kept."

Emmet looked grateful. "If you ladies don't mind staying a bit longer this evening, that would be awesome sauce."

"What?" Dawn stared at him as if his beard had just caught fire.

"Aren't you the man going all cultural reference on us." Callie made a fist and when she held it out, Emmet bumped it with his.

"Just trying to be current," he explained. "Saw it on a commercial. Been waiting for a chance to drop it into casual conversation."

Everyone laughed. Well, not Steve, but he did crack a smile. And this wasn't casual, Jon thought. Adding personnel was going to change the dynamic just when everything had fallen into place.

"Come with me, Lorajean," Callie offered. "I'll show you around."

"Right behind you, Callie."

"Steve, I'll give you the guided tour." Dawn smiled and headed for the door.

"Roger that." Steve was wearing jeans and a T-shirt but the clipped response was all military. It wasn't hard to picture him in camouflage saluting his commanding officer.

Jon watched the four of them file out of the office, feeling uneasy about all of this and not sure why. He could see Dawn in the room across the hall pointing out instruments and supplies in the cupboard above the sink. But it was the look on her face that grabbed his attention. She was smiling at the new doctor as if they'd known each other for ten years instead of ten minutes. It had taken Jon almost a week to get a smile out of her. What the—

"Jon?"

"Hmm?" He turned to Emmet. "What?"

"Something bothering you?" The older man leaned back in his chair and linked his fingers over his flat stomach.

"No. Why?"

"You look like someone tied a knot in your favorite stethoscope. And it has something to do with Steve Shepard."

That was an opening and Jon figured he should run with it. "Are you sure he's the right fit for the clinic?"

Emmet's expression was wry. "When I started looking for help there wasn't a lot of positive response so I had to get creative. And hope any takers would work out."

"Okay. Fair point." Jon moved closer and leaned a hip on the desk. "But what do you know about him?"

"Not much," the older man admitted. "I got his name from an army buddy. I contacted Steve and he was receptive to the offer. His credentials checked out and his references were impeccable." Emmet raised a brow and chuckled. "And he's not wanted by the law as far as I could tell."

Jon didn't think it was funny. "I see."

"Those are the right words but they don't match the expression on your face. If you've got a beef, I'd like to hear it."

"He doesn't say much," was the best he could come up with.

"He's a hotshot doctor who lets his skill do the talking. That's good enough for me."

Not good enough for Jon, not when he heard voices in the hall followed by Dawn's laughter. The new doctor might not be wanted by the law, but Jon wanted something—to get him the hell away from her.

He wanted something else, too. *Dawn.*

The thought had been there since he'd met her. It was vague and distant because in the beginning she was barely speaking to him. But the moment she walked away with Steve Shepard the urge turned white hot.

From a physical perspective this reaction made perfect sense. He hadn't had sex for a long time, and Dawn was pretty and fun. He liked her. But he sure as hell didn't like seeing her smile at another man.

He gave these feelings some more thought and realized the only explanation that made sense was jealousy. He'd never believed in it before. Attraction was chemistry— hormones, pheromones—not emotion. But now he had to admit it. He was jealous as hell.

Suddenly everything was complicated and he hated complications. Especially when they involved feelings. Because feelings were nothing but a confusing pain in the ass.

Chapter Six

Dawn left the clinic even later than usual after orienting the new doctor. Not for the first time since leaving her job at the hospital she was relieved that the drive home was so short. Dr. Shepard seemed nice enough, although he mostly listened and didn't say much. He was good-looking, in a rugged, loner sort of way. Since Steve Shepard had the don't-violate-my-space thing down to a science, she didn't feel the need to distance herself from him like she had with Jon when he was new. And now she'd warmed up to Clifton after getting to know him more and—well—meeting his dog.

That made her smile. But the warm feeling disappeared when she turned the corner and saw a Ford F-150 truck with Hank the Handyman printed on it parked at the curb in front of the house.

"Great," she muttered. "When I needed a father he was hardly ever around and now he shows up like a bad rash."

Walking into the house she'd always thought of as a cute little place, she couldn't help wishing it was a McMansion with thirty-five rooms and multiple places to hide. But there was nowhere to go, so she'd best get it over with.

"I'm home," she called out.

"In here," her mom answered. "Hank is here."

"I noticed." Under her breath she added, "Pretty hard to miss Hank the Handyman's truck."

In the family room she found her mother with the man Dawn had come to think of as hardly more than a sperm donor. Glory and Hank were standing together looking at the far wall, just in front of the fireplace.

"You're late tonight, honey," her mom said without turning. "How was your day?"

"I had to show the new doctor around," she explained.

"Hi, Dawn." Hank half turned and smiled at her.

He was about the same age as her mother and still handsome. He looked a lot like a younger James Brolin. Hank was fit and trim, probably from the handyman stuff. Grudgingly she admitted, if only to herself, that she could see why her mom might possibly still be attracted to him. If Glory was smart she wouldn't pursue that, but who was Dawn to judge after her disaster. Curse of the Laramie women strikes again.

"Why are you here?" she asked him.

Her mother turned then and gave her the stink eye. "I'm trying to decide what color to paint the walls. Come and look."

If this wasn't so important to her mom, Dawn would have made a snarky remark and voluntarily gone to her room for a time-out. But she wasn't nine years old and her mom meant everything to her. She would be supportive if it killed her.

She dropped her purse on the sofa and walked over,

standing on the other side of her mom. There were several paint chips taped on the wall. "Okay."

"Which one do you like?" Glory asked.

"They're all beige."

"There are subtle differences," Hank said. "Sahara has more yellow and Sun-kissed Wheat more brown. Honey's got a little pink."

Dawn stared at the man and wondered if he was an alien visitor from *Better Homes and Gardens.* "All three look the same to me."

Glory tapped her lip. "She might be right. Are they too boring?"

"You could do an accent wall in a bold color to make it more interesting," he suggested.

"Isn't that more work?"

"Not much." He shrugged. "Some folks are having me paint the walls a lighter color, something neutral, then a darker coordinating shade for the baseboards and doors."

"Hmm." Her mother intently studied the colors as if trying to picture what he was describing. "I'd have to see that in person to know if I liked it."

"I could arrange for you to take a look at some of the jobs I've done," Hank offered. "The Swensons were really accommodating and pretty happy with the results. They'd probably be open to showing it off. If you want I'll give them a call and you could come to Kalispell. Take a look."

The thought of Glory driving all the way there only to find out he was full of hot air put a knot in Dawn's stomach. "You don't have time to waste, Mom."

"We're all busy, sweetie." There was a warning tone in her mother's voice. She looked up at Hank. "Aren't there some projects in this house that I need to do before paint? Should that be the last step?"

"Depends on the project," he said. "In that back bathroom there's a dark spot on the wall and my guess is it's a leaky pipe behind the wallboard. That needs fixing and patching before paint. But I could do the rest of the house first."

"I'll consider that."

Dawn made a scoffing sound because it seemed to her that he was promising to paint her mother's house. Memories scrolled through her mind, all of them bad. "Don't go there, Mom."

"I'm not going anywhere. All I'm doing is thinking it over," Glory said.

"It's not the thinking that I'm concerned about. It's the part where he doesn't follow through and hurts you." She looked at her father. "That's what he does."

"Sweetie, let's just—"

"Forget?" she interrupted. "It's hard to do that when his pattern was to not show up because something else was more important than his wife or daughters."

"Dawn—"

"Remember the time he swore he would come to my birthday party? He said a kid only turns eight once and he would be there. No-show." She saw shadows in Hank's eyes and knew he remembered. "Or the father-daughter dance when I was twelve. You scraped up the money to buy me a new dress and did my hair. I waited for hours but he didn't call, didn't come."

"This isn't helpful," Glory said.

"It is to me. Then there was that apple pie I baked for him. I cried myself to sleep because he couldn't be bothered to fit me into his busy schedule. On Christmas."

"Dawn, you're being rude," her mother scolded.

"You're right. I'm being a brat. But you can't tell me I'm lying."

"Dawn Debra—"

"She's right, Glory." Hank's mouth pulled tight for a moment but he never looked away. There was sadness in his eyes. "I was a lousy husband to you and an even worse father to the girls."

"At least we can agree on that." Something twisted inside Dawn as he winced, telling her the verbal arrow struck and drew blood. Good. She told herself she wasn't being mean. Trusting someone who had constantly disappointed you was just plain stupid. Reminding her mother not to trust him again was a public service.

"What I did cost me big-time because I'm not Glory's husband anymore."

"No, you're not." Dawn stared him down.

"I'd like to be her friend, if possible. I'm ashamed about what I did to her and you girls. You'll never know how sorry I am and I plan to do my best to make it up to you. Because, the thing is, I'll always be your father."

Unfortunately he had a point there. But her mom gave her another stern look so she kept the thought to herself.

"I haven't done very much to make you believe this, but if you or Marina ever need me, I'll be there for you."

"So I should put you on speed dial in case I need a kidney?" Where was this nasty sarcasm coming from? Good golly, she needed therapy. This had been bottled up for a long time and it wasn't as if she hadn't seen him here and there. Why let him have it now? All she could think of was that using her father's past behavior as a horrible warning to explain to Jon why she'd pushed him away had churned things up. And, apparently, she couldn't keep it inside any longer.

"I deserve that." There was no anger or defensiveness in Hank's voice. Just acceptance. "And there's nothing I can say to make you believe I'm being straight with you now."

"Right again."

"But I made a promise to your mother and I intend to honor it."

"And what would that be?" Dawn just heard him imply that he was going to help paint the house but wanted to hear him say it.

"I'm going to fix this place up for her. Paint, plumbing, a rack in the kitchen for her pots and pans. Lights under the cupboards like she's always wanted. I'm going to keep my word to her."

"Well, I sure hope she doesn't hold her breath. But, then, we all have to live with disappointment. And after being married to you she's had a lot of practice."

"Not this time." He looked at his ex-wife. "I'm not nineteen anymore and overwhelmed at being a teenage father. Or feeling like a failure because I couldn't support my family. It took a while for me to grow up, but I did. I can't undo what I've already done. All I can do is try to be a better man. Do the right thing from now on."

Dawn wasn't falling for it. "That was a good speech."

"Everyone deserves a second chance," Glory said.

"I stopped counting the chances I gave him a long time ago." Dawn looked at her mother. "How can you be so gullible? Even more than Marina and me, you had to deal with the messes he always left behind."

"Don't make me the saint and him the sinner, Dawn. We were hardly more than babies ourselves when we had babies." She glanced at Hank. "Mistakes were made on both sides."

He smiled at her. "As far as I'm concerned it's all water under the bridge. Now is a new start. Like a fresh coat of paint."

"Friends," Glory said, smiling at him.

"Works for me."

Apparently Dawn didn't inherit the forgiveness gene

from her mom. "Have you ever heard the expression that leopards don't change their spots?"

"Yeah, I have," he said. "All I can say is watch me."

"I don't have to—"

"Dawn—" Glory's tone allowed no argument. "Before anything else comes out of your mouth that you might regret, you should know that I've invited Hank to stay for dinner."

After that bombshell there was no danger of saying anything she'd regret because she couldn't say anything at all. The three of them stared at each other while tension crackled in the air. The adrenaline pounding through her was so loud that she almost didn't hear the doorbell.

Thank God she did. Saved by the bell. "I'll get that."

She hurried to the door, fully prepared to buy whatever they were selling or kiss whoever had rescued her. But that was before she opened the door and saw Jon Clifton standing there.

"Hi." He lifted his hand in a wave.

"Hi?"

Jon had no trouble at all reading the expression on her face and could tell what she was thinking. Not that he was very intuitive with women, but his stopping by was unexpected. "I'm the last person you expected to see."

"Yeah. Pretty much." She looked puzzled. "How did you get my address?"

"I called Emmet."

"Why did you need it? Or, more to the point, why are you here?"

He held up a cell phone in its neon green case. More than once he'd seen her pull it out of her scrubs pocket and knew right away who it belonged to. "When I was turning off lights and locking up, I noticed your phone in the break room. I thought you might need it. Probably you set it down in there when you were showing Dr. Shepard around the clinic."

"Probably. Thanks for bringing it by." Dawn took it and put it in her pocket, then leaned a shoulder against the doorjamb and studied him. "You don't like Steve."

"I didn't say that." Apparently he wasn't the only one who was intuitive. But his reaction to Shepard was a ridiculous and completely irrational, emotional response which he wouldn't dignify by admitting she was right. "What makes you think I don't like him?"

"It was the tone of your voice—"

"Ah."

"I'm not finished yet," she said. "Your mouth got all pinchy and tight. And your eyes turned sort of flinty and dark." She folded her arms over her chest. "What's your problem with him?"

"I don't have a problem. I don't know him." All Jon knew was that Dawn had smiled at the guy and that got his juices flowing, none of them good. "It doesn't make sense that I could judge him so quickly as someone not to like."

"Doesn't mean you didn't. So, what gives, Jon?"

No way he would admit to being jealous because then he'd have to explain why. He and Dawn had just gotten past his negative first impression and he enjoyed getting along with her. Talking. Teasing. Seeing her look at him like a hero who'd adopted a three-legged dog. He didn't want to go back to cold looks and clipped tones.

"Let's chalk it up to a long day and hunger. So, on that note, I'll leave and you can get on with your evening. Good night, Dawn." He turned and started down the path to his truck parked at the curb behind her compact.

"Wait—"

When he stopped and turned back she was twisting her

fingers together, looking uncertain about something. Then she seemed to make up her mind.

"Would you like to stay for dinner?" she asked.

The thought of not going back to the empty guesthouse and slapping together ham and stale bread for a sandwich was so appealing he nearly jumped at the request. Then his manners kicked in. "That hunger remark wasn't me hinting for a dinner invitation."

"I didn't think it was."

"I wouldn't want to put you out," he said.

"If it was an imposition, I wouldn't have said anything in the first place. And I don't feel obligated because you dropped off my cell phone. Thanks again for that, by the way."

"You're welcome."

"It's just—" She caught her bottom lip between her teeth.

"What?"

"My father is here," she said.

"The flaky weasel dog toad boy?"

She smiled. "Yes."

"Way to make the invitation irresistible," he teased. The uneasy expression on her face said something was up but he had no idea what. He'd taken a lot of classes in medical school but understanding women wasn't one of them. "Want to tell me what's going on?"

"He was here when I got home from the clinic. Looking at paint chips with my mom. She bought this place after the flood a couple years ago and is fixing it up. He swears he's changed and is going to paint the house for her."

"So, your father is Hank the Handyman." He shrugged at her look. "It was hard to miss on the side of the truck."

"Yeah. The thing is, I think he's cozying up to her because he wants something. He's trying to worm his way into her good graces. Then he'll disappear like he always does and she's going to get hurt. So—" She slid her hands into the pockets of her scrubs. "I said some things. Told him how I felt."

"It's healthy to get your feelings out." Jon didn't see agreement in her expression. "No?"

"It might have been if I hadn't said it before Mom told me he was staying for dinner. Now it's just awkward."

"Aha. You want me to take the heat off you."

"Kind of. My mother actually sent me to answer the door with the words 'before anything else comes out of your mouth that you might regret.'"

"Hmm." He pretended to think about it, partly to mess with her and partly because he didn't want to seem too eager. "I've never been the rose between two thorns before. What's in it for me?"

"My everlasting gratitude?" There was a pleading note in her voice. "I would seriously owe you one. Big-time."

Owing him wasn't the reason he was going to accept but it definitely was not a bad thing. No, the deciding factor was that he wanted to fix this for her. And it was best not to examine too closely why that was. "Okay. If you're sure it's no bother—"

"Let that go, Clifton." She swung the door wide. "Come on in."

A muffled female voice carried from another room. "Dawn, who's at the door?"

"Coming, Mom." She looked up at him and said, "Follow me."

He did and was mesmerized by the way her very fine rear end gave a sexy shape to the shapeless scrubs. In the kitchen he saw an older, strawberry blonde woman stirring a pot of spaghetti sauce on the stove. A man about her age lowered the oven door to look inside and the smell of garlic was a clue that there was bread in there. Jon's mouth watered and hunger twisted in his stomach.

Then it hit him that these were her parents and suddenly he felt a little pressure. If he had to guess, he'd say it was because he wanted them to like him, but that didn't make sense. He had no emotional investment. He was there to take the heat off Dawn. That was all. It didn't matter what they thought of him.

"Mom, Hank—" Dawn hesitated for just a moment, as if she was feeling pressure, too, but for her it was tension with the man she'd obviously refused to refer to as "father." "This is Jon Clifton. Dr. Clifton. We work together at the clinic. I forgot my cell phone and he brought it by. I invited him to stay for dinner."

"Happy to have you." Her mother put down the wooden spoon and wiped her hands before moving closer. "Dr. Clifton, it's nice to meet you. I'm Glory."

"A pleasure," he said, shaking hands with both of them. Then he looked down at the scrubs he was still wearing. "Sorry. I came right from work and didn't expect a dinner invitation."

"No problem." Glory waved her hand dismissively. "We're not formal."

"I hope it's no trouble for me to stay for dinner."

"Of course not," Glory said. "We're having spaghetti and meatballs so there's plenty. Would you like a beer?"

"Beer would be great."

After grabbing two bottles from the refrigerator, Hank walked over and handed one to Jon. "How do you like Rust Creek Falls, Doctor?"

"It's a lot like Thunder Canyon. That's where I'm from," he said. "But smaller."

"It's growing fast." Glory glanced over her shoulder,

then stirred the pasta. "Folks are lucky to have you and Dawn here."

"I heard about the population explosion," he said.

Dawn looked up from making the salad and there was a wry expression on her face. "I guess that's our claim to fame."

"Dawn tells me you're a pediatrician. Hank and I have a granddaughter."

"Dawn told me about Sydney. I look forward to meeting her and her mom. For her regular checkups," he added.

Glory nodded but it was Hank who spoke. "You're in for a treat." There was obvious pride in his voice and expression. "She's a beauty."

Jon saw the surprised look on Dawn's face, as if she hadn't known that her father had seen the little girl. She didn't comment, just finished making the salad and then set the table, but there was tension in her shoulders. Before he could think of something to say that would make her relax, Glory announced dinner was ready.

She put everything on the table while Dawn poured two glasses of red wine for her mom and herself. He noticed that she grabbed the one with noticeably more in it and sipped.

When the four of them took their seats Hank lifted his beer bottle, obviously preparing to make a toast. Jon recalled that night not long ago when Dawn had ordered him not to drink "to us." He met her gaze and the wry expression on her face told him she was remembering it, too.

"Let's drink to beginnings," Hank said, looking at Glory.

He noticed that when everyone clinked glasses Dawn managed to avoid touching her father's. *Time to be the rose between two thorns*, he thought.

"So, Glory," he said, "you're fixing up the house."

"Yes." She explained about purchasing it at a super discounted price from the bank and her impatience at the slow pace of the improvement projects. "Thanks to Dawn insisting on paying rent, I can afford to do things a little faster."

"Up in Thunder Canyon we heard about that flood," he said. "A lot of folks came to help."

"I remember. It was really bad." Dawn's eyes were full of shadows as she twisted her fork in the spaghetti. "You can still see the effects of it here and there."

"Those reminders are disappearing slowly but surely," Hank said. "Thanks to people like Glory who are willing to put in hard work."

Jon took another piece of garlic bread. "There's nothing like small town spirit, the way neighbors pull together."

"Emmet received grants to rebuild the clinic and now we're expanding personnel." Dawn took a bite of pasta. "Another new doctor is starting. We met him today." Her eyes sparkled when she met Jon's gaze.

"I talk to a lot of people." Glory explained to Jon about her cleaning business and the contract she'd just signed to take care of the clinic. "Folks are really glad that more health care professionals are settling here. Me included. When Dawn was little she had an allergic reaction to peanuts. Do you remember, Hank?"

"Do I?" The older man shook his head. "Scared me to death. And I had to drive you two all the way to Kalispell so the doc there could take a look at her."

Dawn's eyes blazed with antagonism. "Funny. I don't remember—"

"Allergic reactions are pretty scary," Jon said. "And peanut allergies are common in children."

Mission accomplished. Jon had earned his dinner by successfully refereeing the conversation. Her mother and father reminisced about being young parents and how

they'd matured. He knew some of the bad stuff from the little bit Dawn had told him but Glory seemed to have made
peace with the past. There was a fondness and friendly
banter between her and Hank, but Dawn looked more hostile the longer the meal went on. Every time she started
to open her mouth, Jon said something to interrupt her.

"I'll do the dishes, Glory," Hank said when they had
all finished eating.

"Bless you." She stood and picked up a bowl with the
remaining pasta. "I'll take care of the leftovers."

"Can I help?" Jon asked.

"No, you're our guest. Dawn, why don't you take him
out back and show him what you did with the yard."

"You mean what you did," she said. "I could kill a cac-
tus."

"Me, too." That was something they had in common,
he thought. "But I'd enjoy seeing the fruits of someone
else's green thumb."

"Right this way." Dawn turned her back to her parents
and mouthed "thank you."

There was a French door leading outside and he followed her through it. He stepped onto a small patio that
had lush grass surrounding it. Flower beds against the
wooden fence added color around the perimeter.

"I hope that wasn't too awful for you," she said.

"You're not going to want to hear this, but your father
doesn't seem like such a bad guy."

"You're right."

"I am?" He'd expected pushback.

"I don't want to hear that." But she smiled. "I just don't
want my mother to count on him and be disappointed when
he lets her down."

"Time will tell."

"Well, thanks, Jon, for bringing my phone back. And bailing me out."

"I had a good time. Your mom is really something. You look a lot like her." *And you're really something, too.* Fortunately that thought stayed in his head. He folded his arms over his chest because of how badly he wanted to pull her against him and kiss her.

"It actually wasn't bad," she admitted. "Pleasant even, because of you."

She was looking at him that way again, like she had when she met Rerun. As if he was a hero. It was an expression he could get used to. The problem was he knew how fast a guy could go from hero to has-been. He wasn't willing to open himself up to that again.

And the regret rolling through him was how he learned the hard way that détente had its downside. In a way it would have been easier if she was still mad at him. His attraction to her was so strong, trying to stay just friends was the very definition of *trouble*.

Chapter Seven

"I hardly recognize everyone in civilian clothes. Thank you all for coming." Emmet DePaulo looked at the clinic employees gathered in his living room. "Dawn, I appreciate your help in organizing this soiree."

"It was nothing."

All she'd done was put a sheet of paper up in the break room for everyone to write down what they were bringing to the party. Their boss wanted a barbecue/potluck at his house so the staff could get better acquainted on neutral territory and away from the busy office.

"Does everyone have a drink?" he asked.

"Yes, sir. I made sure of it." She'd also assumed unofficial hostess duties, even though they were at Emmet's place.

His living room still looked a lot like the waiting room it had once been when his home had doubled as the town's temporary medical facility after the flood. There was a sofa against the wall, but card table chairs were scattered around the open area. The matching table sat in the center of the room with chips, guacamole dip, nuts and cut-up fresh vegetables which so far remained untouched.

"Okay, listen up," he said. "I have a good reason for bringing you all here. I did a couple tours of duty in a war zone and saw firsthand how soldiers under fire band together and have each other's back. They took bullets for their buddies or fell on a grenade to protect soldiers who were closer to them than brothers. Just because we're stateside and not taking enemy fire, it doesn't mean we can't connect in a similar way.

"There are days in the clinic when it feels as if we're under fire and I can't stress enough the importance of teamwork." There was a hushed silence in the room as he looked at each of them in turn. "It starts at the top, which is why we're at my house. Now that our merry little band of health care professionals is complete, I'd like to make everyone feel at home. Especially, Steve Shepard and Lorajean Quinn." He held up his water bottle. "Welcome."

Jon and Dawn as well as old-timers Callie Crawford and Brandy Walters echoed his greeting. The nurse-practitioner was the only married staff member but Emmet had requested her to come alone as it was a bonding experience.

"So," Emmet continued, "I'd like to thank everyone for their food and beverage contributions and for giving up a Saturday night to be here. Your unquestioning cooperation illustrates the spirit of pulling together that is the hallmark of Rust Creek Falls. And—" there was a twinkle in his eyes "—you'd all go hungry if you hadn't brought stuff."

Dawn watched the others teasingly harass him for that but her gaze settled on Jon. It was a good thing no one was doing a blood pressure reading on her because her heart literally skipped a beat and would have thrown the numbers completely off.

The other night he'd made the uncomfortable situation with her father...well, comfortable. She hadn't been lying when she'd told him it was actually a good time. Thanks to him running interference between her and Hank. Now, the irony wasn't lost on her. Jon wouldn't admit it, but she'd gotten the impression he had an issue with Steve. She would give almost anything to know why.

The staff was teasing Emmet unmercifully, all but Steve. Even Lorajean was in the thick of it but the new doctor was holding back. She walked over to the snack table and filled a plate with guacamole, corn chips and, out of guilt, some carrot and celery sticks.

"Come on, you guys," she said, "someone worked their fingers to the bone on these veggies."

"And I didn't cut myself," Brandy said. The brown-eyed brunette was dedicated to healthy eating and exercise. It showed.

"And we're all grateful to you for that." Dawn looked at the group. "Come on, you guys, eat up."

No one needed permission but something about giving it started a stampede. Again, everyone but Steve. He hung back. This party was to get to know each other and bond. That happened when personal information was shared. She decided to start the ball rolling.

"So, Steve," she said, "where are you from?"

"Here and there." He took a drink from his beer bottle. "Military brat."

"Do you have family in Montana?" Callie asked. It was a question designed to find out just why he'd taken this job in a small town like Rust Creek Falls.

"No," he said.

"Is there a Mrs. Shepard?" Although most women would

be smitten and flirty with the macho doc, Brandy only looked curious. She was in her early twenties, too young for him and sensible enough to know it.

"No."

Apparently the new doctor wasn't familiar with the sharing of personal information rule in the bonding ritual. And he didn't look the least bit uncomfortable about holding back.

"Let me fill you a plate, Steve." Lorajean set down her white wine and put a variety of snacks together before handing it to him.

"Thanks."

Dawn got the feeling the nurse was running interference, protecting him, and she was a little surprised that Jon hadn't taken the lead on that. Usually guys stuck together, but he showed no inclination to jump in and do any wingmanning for the other doctor. Too bad because he was good at it. He'd sure bailed her out when her father had stayed for dinner. She still owed him one for that.

Dawn wasn't ready to give up yet on bonding with Steve Shepard. "Are you seeing anyone? And before you say you see patients every day, let me put a finer point on it. When I say 'seeing' I mean dating."

"No," he answered. "Are you?"

Involuntarily her gaze shifted to Jon. "No."

"I'm not, either," Lorajean chimed in. She didn't look annoyed as much as perceptive about the fact that if you put women in the room with a man they were going to pepper him with questions. Do their best to pry information out of him.

Dawn got the message, which was twofold. The new guy was private and the nurse was new, too. "Are you married, Lorajean?"

"Widow." Murmured sounds of sympathy followed the revelation. "Cancer. About ten years ago."

"Do you have any children?" Callie asked.

"It never happened for us." Instead of sadness there was resignation in her eyes. Clearly she'd come to terms with that disappointment long ago.

"How do you like Rust Creek Falls so far?" Brandy bit into a guacamole-loaded chip.

"I like it a lot. Everyone is friendly and I'm getting to know people quickly."

Because Dawn had done the same thing with Jon a few minutes ago, she noticed when the older woman's gaze settled on Emmet. It took a lot of willpower to resist asking about a spark between them. Lorajean would handle it fine, in Dawn's opinion, but she wasn't so sure about Emmet. Come to think of it, she didn't know all that much about her boss.

Dawn looked at him. "How long have you lived in Rust Creek Falls, Emmet?"

"I think it's time to light the barbecue for those burgers." Her boss's expression turned coy and cagey just before he walked away.

"He might need help," Steve said and followed the older man out of the room.

"Wow," Callie marveled. "Did you see that? Steve actually said four words."

"He doesn't waste them, that's for sure," Dawn agreed. "The only thing we found out about him is he's not particularly chatty. Why use three words when one will do?"

There was mumbled agreement from the other women.

"I don't know what the big deal is with that guy." Jon took a long drink from his beer, then noticed four females staring at him. "What?"

"That's what I'd like to know," Callie said. "What's bugging you?"

"Nothing."

"That's not going to fly, Doctor." Lorajean shrugged. "There's a wrinkle in your boxers and don't even think about going to help Emmet with the fire. I'm pretty sure the other two can handle it."

"I have to agree with Lorajean. Something is on your mind. And, just so you know," Dawn said, "resistance is futile. Four against one."

Jon blew out a long breath. "Okay. I'm not proud but this is the truth. I haven't been here in town all that long and suddenly I'm old hat. No one asked me how I like it here in Rust Creek Falls. Or if I'm settling in."

Brandy scoffed. "Your brother lives here and you're not a complete stranger."

"She's right. You have a dog and live in a cabin on your brother's ranch. You are an open book." Callie grinned wickedly. "I think you're jealous of Steve."

"What?" Jon's tone was a little too sharp.

"He's mysterious, that's for sure." Brandy finished her wine, then set her glass on the card table. "Monosyllabic. You're jealous of the fact that we're even more curious about him now because he didn't give us answers. There must be a term for that." She looked at her female coworkers. "You know. Like the opposite of bromance, with jealousy."

Callie thought for a moment then shrugged. "I've got nothing."

"Hello," Jon said. "Standing right here and not jealous. I'm just wondering why no one wanted to know if I was married or seeing anyone."

"That's because we already know you're not. Doesn't

mean we don't love you, Doctor," Callie said. "I'm going in the kitchen to organize food and stuff."

"I'll help you," Brandy offered and headed after the other woman.

"Me, too." Dawn brought up the rear of the procession and was still close enough to hear what the new nurse said to Jon.

"You know," Lorajean started. "I can't speak to what happened before I started working at the clinic, but it's really quite obvious to me."

"What's that?" he asked.

"Why no one questioned you about dating. They know you're not because you only have eyes for Dawn."

Whoa, she thought. If it was that obvious, why hadn't she noticed? Holy moley, it was a good thing she didn't have to make conversation after overhearing *that.* She was as speechless as Dr. Shepard.

"I have to meet a patient at the clinic." Emmet broke the news after a short conversation on his cell phone. "It sounds like Mary Brady has pneumonia again. She's eighty-four and this can't wait until Monday."

There was a collective groan from the staff. After eating they'd been sitting outside on the patio, having a good time. Jon included. It was a beautiful night and, although getting late, he got the feeling that no one wanted to be the first to leave. If the guy in charge of the party left, so would everyone else.

Maybe Jon could take one for the team. "Emmet, let me go to the clinic. You're the host."

"Thanks, but you're not on call. And Mary would ask to see your driver's license to make sure you're not still a frat boy in college. If the patient was a baby, I'd send you with my blessing. But, alas…" He stood and looked around the wooden picnic table where they were gathered. "You all stay."

"I have to go anyway," Callie said, a soft smile on her face. "Nate is waiting."

Must be nice, Jon thought, *to have someone at home who cared where you were.* He had Rerun but it really wasn't the same.

"It's past my bedtime," Lorajean said. "I'm overdue for my beauty sleep."

"You don't need it," Emmet commented.

"Aren't you sweet." The older woman gave him a grateful smile.

Brandy stood up and stretched. "Lorajean might not need beauty sleep, but I do."

"Oh, pooh," Dawn protested. "You're just a baby and so beautiful. It will be a long time before you have to worry about that."

The two women happened to be next to each other on the far side of the table so Brandy leaned down to hug her coworker. "You are my queen. But I do have to go."

"Me, too," Steve said. Apparently he'd had his fill of bonding.

"Don't leave on my account," Emmet said. "Use the house. I really don't mind. If anything is missing I know where you live."

"It's like this. You're the glue that holds us together," Dawn teased. "If you go, we go. At least I will after I clean up the place for you."

The others offered to stay and help but Dawn assured them it wouldn't take long and they should head out.

"You're just trying to get brownie points from the boss," Callie joked.

"Of course I am. So don't get in my way." Dawn laughed.

Jon decided that was the most beautiful sound he'd ever

heard. Or maybe the way she looked in the moonlight just made it seem that way. Before thinking it through he said, "I'll stay and help you."

The whole staff stared at him for a beat. No one else had heard, but he couldn't forget Lorajean saying he only had eyes for Dawn. He was pretty sure that wasn't true. At least he hoped so because it was a bad idea. Staying was just about having a coworker's back and that's what this evening had been about.

Lorajean nodded. "Good. Now I don't have to feel guilty about leaving her here all alone. I see this bonding strategy really worked for you, Jon."

"Don't feel guilty," Dawn said, but there was something in her voice. A tension that hadn't been there before he volunteered to stay.

Emmet looked at the two of them. "Just so we're clear, no one is getting a raise."

Everyone laughed, then grabbed the containers with what remained of the food they'd brought. Emmet left and the rest of the staff lingered for a few moments at the front door, saying their goodbyes. Then Jon was alone with Dawn.

They stared at each other for several moments before she said, "Okay, then. I'll start in the kitchen."

He nodded and looked around the living room. "This needs straightening up, then I'll help you in there."

"Okay."

He grabbed a trash bag and went to work. When the room was done, he stopped before heading for the kitchen where Dawn was working.

He was really alone with her.

Had he volunteered *because* they would be alone? Had his subconscious taken over? Because his subconscious had been pretty active lately if his dreams were any indication. She'd been the star of most of them ever since he'd taken her to his place.

A little while ago he'd wanted to kiss her senseless when she'd laughed in the moonlight. That wasn't a very good idea.

"Jon? Do you have anything that needs to be washed?" she called from the other room.

"Quit stalling, Clifton," he muttered to himself. "Yeah. Coming."

There was no moonlight in the kitchen. That should be a safe zone.

He walked into the room where Dawn was standing in front of a sink filled with soapy water. She had on jeans and a lacy cream-colored tank top with matching sweater. Instantly he got an image of her in his house—relaxed, barefoot, smiling. Waiting for him.

He shook the image away and moved beside her, setting the dirty dishes on the counter. There was a dish towel next to the sink where clean glasses and plates were air-drying.

"I can finish this up," he said. "Why don't you take off?"

"Because I promised." She washed a knife and set it in the other side of the divided sink for rinsing. "It will go faster if we do this together. I don't mind hanging around."

"Okay." He found a clean dish towel in a drawer and started drying.

"Tonight was fun," she commented, making small talk. "Do you think everyone bonded?"

"Hard to say." He dried a wineglass, then found where it belonged in the cupboard. "Everyone seemed to get along. We'll know the answer to your question at work on Monday."

She nodded absently and washed a bowl that had held

baked beans. "We have one more day off before that. What do you do with your free time on the weekend?"

"Nothing much." He thought about it. "Cleaning up the cabin. Grocery shopping. Laundry."

"Seriously?" She looked surprised. "Is that why you were so put out when no one asked about your social life?"

"Tell me what that is again," he teased.

"Oh, please. Surely you haven't forgotten."

"I don't have one now and, honestly, it's been a while since I did."

She rested her wet hands against the edge of the sink, letting them drip inside as she studied him. "That can't be true."

"Sadly, it is." He wasn't looking for pity points, just being honest.

"Really? A guy who looks like you?" She stopped, a blush creeping up her neck as pink settled in her cheeks.

"You think I wouldn't have to sneak up on a glass of water?"

"I would say don't let it go to your head, but obviously it's too late for that." Her tone was teasing but the look on her face said she hadn't wanted to reveal her impression of him. "What I meant was that it doesn't say much for the single ladies of Rust Creek Falls. There was a time when women relocated to our fair town in hopes of meeting a handsome bachelor. And here you are. Completely eligible and not one of the girls has grabbed you up."

"It's my fault," he said, pleased more than he should be that she'd noticed. "No reflection on the lovely ladies who live here. I work all the time."

"It's just wrong that you're alone."

He didn't want her to think he was socially pathetic. That was his only excuse for saying what he did next. "I wasn't always alone."

"Oh?" She took the plug from the bottom of the sink and let the soapy water run out.

"I lived with a woman while finishing my residency. We met at a party. One of the other residents talked me into going because I needed to have some fun."

"Did you?" Dawn asked.

"Probably." Jon shrugged. "We really hit it off and pretty soon we moved in together. I was planning to propose after passing my boards. I had a job offer from the hospital and life seemed to have fallen into place according to my plan."

"What happened?" She lifted one shoulder. "Obviously something did because you're still a bachelor."

"Everything changed. I lost a patient." The pain of the memory was familiar, a scar that would never disappear. "It was one of those things. She was getting better and I was sure she'd be going home within a day or two. Then there was a turn for the worse and she died."

"I'm sorry." There was an expression in Dawn's eyes that said she understood and had experienced the same thing. "I've seen it, too. Science and medicine can't explain why a patient suddenly goes downhill. They do studies about the will to survive but how do you bottle that and give it to someone?"

"It's not like I didn't know what I was getting into when I became a doctor. You lose patients. It goes with the territory. You always do your best and put the rest in God's hands. But this one got to me. She was eight. Funny. Quirky. Precocious. Still, it shouldn't have hit me so hard, but…" He met her gaze. "It did. I took the job at Thunder Canyon Resort to figure out my next career move."

"That's understandable. Anyone who works with life and death should be all in. Soul-searching is healthy—for you but also for the patients you see. If your heart isn't in it and you hold back…it's not fair to the people who put their lives in your hands."

"The woman in my life didn't see it that way." He thought of that woman, the one he'd planned to get down on one knee for. Black hair, green eyes, beautiful Beth. An accountant. Numbers were her thing, not people. "When I told her about the job, she told me that moving to the backwoods of Montana wasn't what she'd signed up for."

"Witch," Dawn muttered.

"She accused me of being a cowboy."

One corner of her mouth curved up. "When we first met, that day at the clinic, I thought you were a cowboy."

Incredibly, that made him smile, but it faded just as abruptly. "In Rust Creek Falls it's not unusual to see a cowboy. She didn't mean it as a compliment, more an indictment of my character. That I shoot first and ask questions later because I didn't discuss my decision with her first."

"Well, she has a point."

"I agree. And I admitted as much to her. After a little groveling, I suggested we talk about things."

"Obviously that didn't work."

"I'll never know. She refused to discuss anything and walked out."

Dawn stared at him for several moments, letting his words sink in. "You were going to propose to her?"

"I'd already bought the ring."

"Oh, boy. There's no easy way to say this. She did you a big favor, Jon." There was absolute conviction in her voice, but white-hot anger underlined every word she said.

"It didn't feel that way."

"She wasn't in love with you."

"How do you figure?" Jon was drawn to the compassion and kindness in her blue eyes.

"If you're in love with someone you don't leave at the

first bump in the road. Clearly getting out was her go-to move and she didn't have deep feelings for you, the kind that last forever. If not then, sooner or later she would have walked out when you hit a rough patch."

"She was the first one I let in." He met her gaze and from the expression in her eyes he could tell she was feeling sorry for him. Couldn't have that. "Oh, I dated from time to time, but there was no one special. I never lived with anyone else. When she was gone, it was more solitary than I expected. That's kind of where I was when I found Rerun. He was alone, too."

"Oh, Jon—" Her expression brimmed with sympathy and support when she put her hand on his arm.

Her fingers were still wet from washing dishes but he could feel the heat in them and the touch set off a fire inside him. He saw it on her face, too, the moment when sympathy turned to something else. *Awareness.*

Jon would never be sure who moved first, but suddenly she was pressed against him and he lowered his mouth to hers.

Chapter Eight

Dawn froze when Jon folded her into his arms, then almost immediately heat surrounded her. There was a very good chance she would go up in flames and that was just fine with her. The moment her fingers had touched the skin of his forearm she knew he'd felt the spark, too.

His lips were soft, searching and warm. She savored the feel of them against her own and couldn't suppress a sigh. He lifted a hand, then gently brushed his knuckles over her cheek before cupping it in his wide palm. Her insides danced with joy at the sweet, intimate contact. Her hormones bubbled up, letting her know they might be rusty, but were still in good working order even though she hadn't been kissed in a long time.

And what a kiss. Jon might be a workaholic, but he sure knew how to take over a kiss and hit the high notes. He curved his hand around her neck and slid his fingers into her hair. Dawn rested her palms on his chest and felt the rapid beat of his heart. Her own was hammering just as hard.

His kisses were easy and slow, not pushy or insistent, just the right amount of pressure. Tenderly he brushed the curtain of her hair aside before his mouth moved to the expanse of her neck. And that was more than okay with her. Dawn tilted her head, giving him all the access he could want. He took it without hesitation and nibbled his way to the pulse point. The soft attention to that tender spot made her shiver and she arched against him.

She heard the sound of their mingled breathing, rapid and harsh, just before the distinctive ring of her cell phone. It was coming from her purse which was on the kitchen counter across from them, right where she'd left it earlier that night.

Jon lifted his head and looked at her, his eyes dark and smoky. "That's your phone."

"Yeah. My mom's ring." She sounded breathless, probably because she was.

"You should probably get that." His voice was ragged.

"It's okay. I can call her back. She understands. I'll let it go to voice mail." It was times like this when voice mail came in especially handy.

"She might need something," he said, annoyingly sensible.

She also noted that a conscience coupled with a finely tuned sense of responsibility was a very inconvenient thing. Dawn nodded, then cleared her throat and moved away to the counter across from him. It was a narrow space but she could no longer feel the heat of his body and felt cold. She grabbed her black leather purse and the phone stashed in one of the outside pockets where she could easily find it.

She looked at the caller ID and saw her mother's name, then answered. "Hi, Mom."

"Oh—Dawn—?"

"You sound surprised. Did you butt dial?" And interrupt the best kiss she'd had in—maybe ever.

"No, sweetie. I was going to leave a message. Didn't expect you to pick up, what with the staff party going on."

She and Jon were staff and it was a party—for two. One that made her feel all warm and gooey inside and she wanted to get back to the action. "I just happened to hear my phone. Is everything okay?"

"Fine. I just wondered if you could swing by Crawford's store before you come home and pick up a couple of things for breakfast in the morning."

She sneaked a look at Jon but his back was to her. She couldn't swear to it, but she thought there was tension in his broad shoulders. "It might not be open."

"If it is would you get some English muffins and a couple of potatoes? And some eggs?"

"Okay." *This couldn't have waited until morning?* she thought.

"I just thought it would be easier to go now, since you're already out," Glory said.

It was a little scary that her mother could read her mind. And she shouldn't be so irritated. It wasn't as if the woman didn't frequently call Dawn to stop and get something before she came home. Mostly Dawn was happy to help. Right at this particular moment? Not so much. "Sure, Mom. I can do that."

"You sound funny. Is everything okay, Dawn?"

Duh, she thought. Who wouldn't sound funny when a man you didn't even think you liked not so long ago kissed the living daylights out of you?

She took a deep breath. "Fine, Mom."

"Did Jon make it to the party?"

"Yes. Everyone did."

"Good. I liked him. He seems to be a very nice young man."

He was more than that. *Hot* was the word that came to mind. "I have to go, Mom."

"Right. Sorry to bother you, sweetie."

"No problem. If Crawford's is still open I'll pick up the stuff."

"Thanks. See you later. Have fun."

That was Dawn's plan. To pick up where they'd left off. She put her phone back into the pocket of her purse, then turned to see Jon studying her. "That was my mom," she said lamely.

"So you said. And what with you calling her Mom…" One corner of his mouth curved up. His look had changed from the heated, slightly frustrated one he'd had when her phone rang. Now he simply looked guarded.

So she put up her guard, too, and stayed right where she was. "You look as if you've got something on your mind."

"Yeah." He dragged his fingers through his hair.

"Just a wild guess…" Keep it light, she warned herself. Don't let him see that what happened had mattered to her. "You're having second thoughts about that kiss."

"Very perceptive, Nurse Laramie." His intense expression didn't match the teasing words.

"Don't worry. I won't read anything into it."

His smile was rueful. "Just so you know, I didn't stay to help because I planned that."

So, it was spontaneous. That was both better and worse.

"It never crossed my mind." She sincerely meant that. She'd let go of her notion about him being the devious new doctor after the night they'd gone to the Ace in the Hole.

"This is ironic, really, when you think about it."

"What's that?" She leaned back against the counter, leaving the narrow center of the kitchen between them.

"We…got close at an employee bonding party." He folded his arms across his broad chest. "I'm pretty sure that wasn't the sort of bonding Emmet had in mind when he decided to have us all over."

"Probably not," she agreed.

Dawn hoped that comment had come out of her mouth as cool and collected as it had sounded in her head. Because she felt the exact opposite of cool and collected. Her state of mind could best be described as mortified. With a capital *M*.

She'd been ready and willing to let Jon Clifton—*Dr. Jon Clifton*—have his way with her. In their boss's house, no less. On top of that, she'd been prepared to love every minute of it. Neither of them had planned for that to happen and getting carried away was understandable. She'd have gone anywhere with him if that call hadn't interrupted them. It was a cooling off period, literally. Time to take a breather and let rational thought come back. But she'd been ready, even eager, to ignore rational thought and pick up right where they'd left off.

All of that was bad enough, but not completely humiliating. What bothered her most was that a single touch of his lips to hers could so easily make her forget how much she never again wanted to be the doctor/nurse affair cliché. She never again wanted to feel so disgraced and ashamed. And now she needed to do some serious damage control.

She met his gaze directly, letting him see she was on the same page. "Look, Jon, no one understands better than me why this is a very bad idea. Anything personal between us, or anyone else at the clinic for that matter, could potentially undermine the team Emmet is building. I have enormous respect for him and would never jeopardize the work he's doing here in Rust Creek Falls."

"I couldn't have said it better."

"Good. And the two of us have buried the hatchet. We're clicking at the clinic and it wouldn't be smart to start anything. We work too closely together. Everyone notices our interaction. There's a tone to set."

"Agreed."

She forced a smile. "So, still friends?"

"If that's what you want." There was an edge to his voice, a rough sound that didn't quite mesh with what he said. Did he want to be more than friends?

Dawn couldn't go there. "I do."

That was a half-truth. She didn't want to go back to the tension between them and probably couldn't even if she tried. He was a good guy. And he'd given her a taste, a glimpse, of what it might feel like to be more than friends. For a lot of reasons it was best not to go there. But she couldn't help being the tiniest bit disappointed that he didn't push back just a little.

"Then friends it is."

She put a cheerfulness she didn't feel into her words. "What a relief."

And that was a flat-out lie. She wasn't at all relieved. He'd said all the right words, but she was almost sure he hadn't stopped looking at her with a dark intensity that said he was lying, too.

But they'd decided to pretend it never happened. Good luck with that.

A while after leaving Emmet's, Dawn walked into her house and quietly tiptoed into the kitchen. Right away she noticed there were new lights installed underneath the cupboards and they were on, illuminating the shad-

owy corners. Hank had been here. The thought didn't sit
well, but there was nothing to be done. And the bright-
ness *was* very cool.

She set the grocery bags on the counter, trying to keep
them from rustling. The TV was on in the family room
and Glory was curled up on the couch, probably sleeping.
At least Dawn hoped so. Jon's kiss had thrown her off
balance and she hadn't steadied herself yet. She wasn't
ready to pretend to her mom that she hadn't experienced
something epic.

"Hi, sweetie." Glory sat up and stretched, then rolled
off the couch before padding into the kitchen. "You don't
have to be quiet."

"I didn't want to disturb you. How come you're not in
bed?"

"It's only nine o'clock. I know my life is boring, but
bedtime now would just be pathetic, even for me."

"You just work so hard. Sometimes six days a week.
It's a grind and…" Dawn shrugged.

"That busy schedule is exactly why I'm still up. Tomorrow is my carved-in-stone day off and it's Saturday night.
I decided to get wild and stay up till ten. Maybe later."

"Yeah." Dawn tsked. "It's so out of control here the
sheriff will be stopping by any minute to warn you to keep
the noise down because the neighbors are complaining."

"It could happen." Glory grinned. "But probably not
tonight."

"That's what I thought." She reached into one grocery
bag and pulled out the carton of eggs and package of English muffins. "I guess since you sent me to the store for
this stuff we're having the traditional big Sunday family
breakfast tomorrow."

"Yes. Marina is bringing baby Sydney over and the

Laramie women are going to hang out." She looked at the bags. "But this is more than I asked you to get."

"I thought we could make omelets. The mushrooms, spinach and tomatoes looked really good." Dawn pulled out plastic bags of vegetables. There was no need to explain that she'd walked up and down the aisles at Crawford's trying to shake off the memory of Jon's kiss.

"That sounds like a plan and they do look wonderful," Glory said, eyeing everything.

Together they washed the fresh produce, then dried and stored it in Ziploc bags that went into the refrigerator. After folding the brown bags Dawn stored them to the side under the kitchen sink.

"Okay, Mom, I'll see you in the morning. Good night." She started out of the kitchen and nearly made it, too.

"Wait, sweetie. You didn't tell me how the party was."

"Good. Fun." She forced a positive note into her voice that was the complete opposite of her real feelings.

"Details would be nice," her mom urged.

"Like I told you, the whole staff was there," she said, crossing her fingers behind her back. They'd all been there, but not when her mom had called. "Including the new doctor and nurse I told you about."

"Right. How did they get along with everyone?"

"Lorajean is going to fit in great. Steve Shepard…" She shrugged. "Don't know yet."

Glory leaned back against the counter and folded her arms over her chest. "Why?"

"He doesn't say much." Unlike Jon, who practically gave her his life story that first day at the clinic.

The man was an open book. She'd just been too scarred by another man's deceit to meet him halfway in the beginning.

Tonight Glory's call had actually saved her from herself. She and Jon had had no business getting personal and that kiss destroyed her common sense,. But not Jon's. If she was the only one swept away… Not good.

"Sweetie?"

"Hmm?" Dawn saw the puzzled expression on her mom's face. "What?"

"I asked if there's something wrong. You just disappeared there for a minute."

That wasn't the first time tonight. Being in Jon's arms had sent her to a place she'd never been before where she disappeared in the best possible way. She'd hold the memory close because it wasn't going to happen again. "I'm fine, Mom."

"Don't lie to me, Dawn Debra Laramie."

Uh-oh. It was never good when your mother used all three names in a particular tone that said she wasn't kidding. The problem was, Dawn had already lied to her. Not an out-and-out falsehood, just a lie of omission.

She'd never told Glory what happened with the doctor at the hospital and the real reason for quitting that job. The looks of judgment in her coworkers' eyes left no doubt they believed she'd deliberately slept with a man who was practically married. To them that made her a slut. Dawn trusted her mother would believe she hadn't known he was engaged, but Glory wouldn't be able to hide her disappointment. That was something Dawn couldn't bear.

"It's nothing, Mom."

"Like I believe that."

Apparently omission was different from being a good liar. But she'd give it another try. "Really, it's all good."

"Seriously? Just because you're a grown woman, that doesn't mean I've stopped seeing right through you." Glory shook her head. "You are the only other person on this earth who knows what my heart sounds like from the inside of my body."

"Are you going to remind me how many hours of labor you went through when I was born?"

"If I have to." But Glory smiled for a moment. "Although that works better on your sister now because she knows what labor feels like since Sydney was born."

Her mother didn't mean that to hurt, but it did. Dawn wanted more than anything to be a mother, but had serious doubts she ever would be. Trusting a man again was a real long shot and she wouldn't be a single mom. So, that was that.

Glory sighed. "You've always told me everything."

And there it was. The mother of all guilt trips, no pun intended. The shame of her only secret tipped the scales but the why didn't really matter. The result was that she had to come clean about tonight. And do it in a way that didn't require the context of the betrayal for Glory to understand her reaction to what happened earlier with Jon.

Dawn moved beside her mom and rested her back against the counter. "Okay. You asked for it. Jon kissed me tonight."

"In front of everyone?"

"No. We were alone."

"In the backyard?"

"The kitchen, actually." It was as if her mother had turned into a prosecuting attorney who was cross-examining her for the evidence to make her case. The tenacity and attention to detail were astounding. "Why does that matter?"

"So," Glory said without answering the question, "exactly how did that happen? What with the party being at Emmet's house."

This was not going well, Dawn thought. But there was

no turning back now. "Emmet got a call from the answering service and had to meet a patient at the clinic."

"So the rest of the staff was in the living room playing charades while Dr. Clifton was having his way with you in the kitchen?"

How the mighty have fallen, Dawn thought. He'd gone from that nice Jon to Dr. Clifton the rat dog kitchen kisser.

"No. When Emmet was called in, everyone else decided to leave, too. I volunteered to clean up."

"And Jon stayed to help." There was an edge of suspicion in her voice.

"He did. But there was no ulterior motive if that's what you're implying."

Glory huffed out a breath. "And you know this how?"

"He told me."

Her mother had an acute maternal expression on her face, the one that said "hurt my baby and I'll rip your throat out." "And a man has never lied to you before?"

Dawn knew this was an opening to come clean about what happened at her old job. But she couldn't do it. The truth wouldn't change anything. Still, she hesitated and her mother didn't miss it.

"That was a yes or no question, Dawn."

"I believe Jon. I just do. He's a good guy." *Because he rescued a three-legged dog.* She kept that to herself since the information didn't prove anything. And probably you had to see him with Rerun to get it. And how great he was with the sick kids at the clinic.

Glory nodded thoughtfully. "Assuming you're right about him, that doesn't explain why you're spooked about a kiss."

"We work together. We talked about it and decided being just friends is the best way to go. Neither of us wants it to get weird."

"I hate to rain on your parade, but—" Glory shrugged. "Too late for that."

Dawn was afraid she was right but would argue until hell wouldn't have it. "No. It's all good."

"Did you kiss him back?"

"No." She hadn't squirmed this much since she was fourteen and had sneaked out of the house to meet her friends after being grounded. Someone had ratted her out and Glory had caught her, then looked at her a lot like she was now. "Okay, yes. Sort of."

Her mother nodded. "I'll admit I was born a million years ago. But I'll go out on a limb and say that probably not much has changed when it comes to chemistry between a man and a woman. He kissed you and you responded which means there's an attraction between the two of you."

"Okay, but—"

"I'm not finished. Where there's attraction you'll find hormones. Calling it friendship isn't necessarily going to keep them under control." Glory met her gaze. "Just saying."

"Mom, you're reading too much into it."

"If I'm doing anything, it's worrying about you, sweetie. I just don't want you to get hurt."

"That's not going to happen," Dawn assured her. "It's all good. We're just friends."

Glory slid her arm across Dawn's shoulders and squeezed. "I just love you, sweetie. I want only good things in your life."

"I know, Mom. I love you, too. Please don't worry about me."

"Yeah, that'll happen. Now it's almost ten o'clock." She smiled. "I'm going to bed."

"Sleep well."

"Good night."

When Dawn was by herself the bravado disappeared and all the doubts she'd held back swamped her. She truly believed Jon hadn't stayed to help her tonight in order to hit on her. That meant he wasn't a weasel dog toad boy. It would be better if he was. That would make resisting him easy. But in her heart she knew it wasn't going to be.

Chapter Nine

Jon turned off his computer, then stacked the completed patient charts in the outgoing box on his desk. Brandy would file them in the morning. And now he was finished. Finally. He was tired to the bone. He hadn't been this worn out since working all-night shifts during his internship and residency. This time, though, he couldn't blame fatigue on long hours with patients. It was Dawn's fault.

Thoughts of her were responsible for keeping him awake, and when he finally did manage to nod off, she invaded his dreams. A full-on sensuous assault that was a direct result of kissing her. He woke up to twisted sheets and an ache in his gut the size of Montana. At least things here at work were fine between them. She was cordial to him. Just friends. As agreed.

And yet…

He'd swear Dawn sometimes looked at him as if she wished things between them could be more. But maybe that's just what he wanted to see.

Whether it was there or not didn't matter. Both of them were committed to not complicating the work dynamic out of respect for Emmet. A line had been drawn in the sand last Saturday night and the days since then had proven neither of them were going to cross it. He'd agreed to that line, however reluctantly, and wouldn't be another man in her life who lied to her.

It was way past time to go home and try to get some rest. The cleaning service was here. He'd heard the guy working and would say good-night before letting him know to lock the place up.

"Knock, knock."

Jon looked up and saw Glory Laramie in the doorway. "Hi."

"You're working late."

"So are you." Jon was here late almost every night and had gotten to know the young guy who came in to clean.

Glory was wearing khaki pants and a T-shirt that said Laramie Cleaning Services on it. She was an attractive woman and Dawn would look a lot like her when she got older. But Jon probably wouldn't be around to see her grow more beautiful with age and the thought made him a little wistful.

"Where's Charlie?" he asked.

"College classes are starting up soon and he asked for the night off to hang out with his friends. I'm filling in for him."

"A lot of bosses would have sent someone else," he observed.

"I'm not other bosses."

"Obviously. That inspires a lot of loyalty in an employee."

"Before you nominate me for sainthood," she said wryly, "you should know that I had an ulterior motive for coming here myself."

"Oh?" This was about Dawn. It wasn't his remarkable intuition bringing him to that conclusion. There simply wasn't anything else.

"Charlie mentioned in passing that you're usually here doing paperwork when he comes in. When he asked for the night off I told him it wouldn't be a problem. Since I wanted to talk to you anyway." She shrugged. "Two birds, one stone."

"So you came to hit me with a rock?"

"No." She smiled, Dawn's smile. "But I have some things to say."

"Okay." He held out his hand toward the chairs in front of his desk. "Have a seat."

"Thanks." She moved farther into the room and set down her caddy filled with cleaning supplies. After sitting, she let out a sigh. "Long day."

"I know what you mean." He nodded toward the tall stack of patient charts he'd been working on. Should he make small talk or insist she just get straight to the point? Since he was in no hurry he opted for small talk. "How's business?"

"Good. Rust Creek Falls is growing and I'm picking up a lot of new clients. In fact I'm thinking of adding another part-time employee. I started out part-time when my girls were in school and I can attest that young moms who are looking to make some extra money without having the added expense of child care are the most conscientious workers."

"Something tells me you would be accommodating if one of them had a sick child or a school holiday."

Glory nodded. "Been there, done that. I know how complicated it can be so I do my best to find ways to help."

"That's great." So that topic was exhausted. "How are the house renovations coming along?"

"Also good. Hank and I have painted the kitchen, family room and entry."

"That's fast."

"Doesn't feel that way. We're both busy with businesses to run." She crossed one leg over the other, settling in. "But he is committed to getting it done."

"I guess he's a man on a mission."

"More than one." Her mouth pulled tight for a moment. "He's trying to make up for lost time with his daughters."

"I see." What could he say? That her daughter had told him her father was a weasel dog toad boy? Jon thought not.

"He has a lot to make up for. No question about that. But he's determined to be there for his girls." Glory's blue eyes lasered in on him in what looked a lot like a warning.

"It just takes time. Showing up over and over, keeping his word. Eventually those actions build trust."

"That's what I told Hank. Actions speak louder than words. They show a man's true intentions."

Here we go, he thought. She's narrowing her focus. But he was going to let her play out the hand in her own way. "Hank seems like a good guy."

"He is now, but he wasn't always. When the girls were little he wasn't there for us. I was a single mom and raised them alone. I helped with homework, nursed them when they were sick and held them when some guy broke their hearts."

"I can't even imagine how hard that was for you." Jon leaned forward in his chair and rested his forearms on the desk.

"Really hard when they were little." There was steely determination in her eyes. "But their grown-up problems are worse because you can't fix them. All you can do is watch."

"Oh?"

"Dawn had to leave her job at the hospital because of a man."

"You know about that?" He distinctly remembered her saying that the whole thing was so humiliating she didn't want her mother to know.

"Her sister told me. Dawn doesn't know I know." Anger and pain tightened her face into hard lines. "I thought holding them when they cried over a boy was awful, but not being able to hold them at all is worse. In front of me she pretended to be okay but I knew she wasn't. Even if I hadn't known the truth I would have known something wasn't right. That was hell."

"I imagine it was."

"Unless you've been a parent you have no idea. But I'm sure you can imagine that I would do whatever I could to keep her from being hurt like that again."

"I understand."

"Good. Because Dawn's been different since you came to work here at the clinic. And I noticed something between the two of you that night you came to dinner."

"I just brought her phone over," he said.

"I'm not accusing you of anything." She smiled. "Exactly."

"Really?" Good God, this felt like junior high, and he wished he didn't care one way or the other, but he did. "Because I sure feel as if I've been called into the principal's office. The thing is that Dawn and I are just coworkers."

"Are you in the habit of kissing your nurses? If so, that's going to be a problem."

Jon shifted in his chair and did his best not to show that he was squirming. "Dawn and I talked. It won't happen again. Neither of us wants to complicate the working environment here at the clinic. Emmet has put a lot of effort into getting it up and running and we both respect that. We're nothing more than friends."

"I'm going to tell you what I told my daughter." Glory's tone was textbook mother lion. "Calling attraction friendship isn't going to keep your hormones under control. I saw for myself that she was interested in you, Jon. If she knew I was here she would be angry, but I can't help it. I don't want to see her hurt again."

Jon linked his fingers together and rested his hands on the desk. "When I became a doctor I took an oath to do no harm and I take those words very seriously. And before you say it, I know that doesn't track for emotional stuff. But believe me when I say that I would never deliberately do anything to hurt Dawn. I wouldn't lie to her."

Glory studied him for several moments, then nodded. "Don't ask me why, but I believe you."

"Maybe it's my honest face?"

"No, your eyes are too close together." But she smiled with genuine amusement. "Dawn told me you're a good guy."

"It means a lot to me that she thinks so." That was so much more true than he wanted it to be.

"Thanks for listening, Jon. I hope I didn't scare you."

"Not much."

She laughed. "I'll stop harassing you now and go home. I'm done for the night."

"Let me walk you out," he offered.

"That would be nice."

He stood and moved around the desk to pick up the cleaning caddy for her. For Charlie he wouldn't have done that, but Glory was a woman and his mom would have something to say if he didn't. He opened the back door for her, then locked it behind them before accompanying her to her car.

"Good night," he said.

"Have a good evening."

Jon watched her little compact pull out of the parking lot and stood there until the red taillights disappeared. He'd made a solemn promise not to hurt her daughter and hoped it didn't bite him in the ass. The truth was that it had taken every last ounce of his willpower to push Dawn away and he was pretty sure there wasn't any left. If he kissed her again, he was all but certain he didn't have the resolve to stop there.

If only a treatment existed for what ailed him. Some pill, injection or immunization to stop him from thinking about kissing her again.

Or wanting her.

If he couldn't get these feelings under control, he was going to hell for telling her mother a big fat lie.

"I don't mind doing the grocery shopping by myself, Mom. Honest," Dawn said into her cell phone. They'd planned to go to Crawford's together when Glory got home from the new job she'd taken on.

"I know, sweetie. But you work hard all week and—"

"Seriously?" she interrupted. "This is Saturday and you're working. I'm not. So don't go there with me."

"Okay. Point taken. That's not the only reason for this call. I wanted to warn you."

"What?"

"Your father is coming over to paint. Some finishing touches."

"When?" Dawn asked.

"He should be there any minute. This job at the Dalton Law Office will only be a few hours, so when I get home I'm going to help him."

Great, Dawn thought. Grocery shopping was sounding better and better. "Do I need to let him in?"

"He has a key."

Super swell. "Okay."

"And before you say anything, I don't want you to help. No offense, sweetie, but you're not a very good painter. More of it goes on you than the walls."

For once incompetence worked in her favor. "Don't hold back, Mom. Tell me how you really feel."

Glory laughed, then there was a long silence.

"Mom? Are you still there?"

"Yes. I was just trying to decide whether or not to confess something to you."

"Well, now I'm curious. You can't drop that then clam up." Dawn straightened away from the kitchen counter. "What?"

"Has Dr. Clifton—Jon—said anything to you?"

"He says a lot." Dawn couldn't imagine where this was going. "After all, we work together."

"Did he mention that we talked the other night when I cleaned the clinic?"

Dawn's stomach knotted. The fact that their paths crossed wasn't a big deal. Everyone at the clinic knew he stayed after hours to catch up with paperwork. Glory had filled in for one of her employees, so of course they would exchange words. It was the *confess* part that gave her pause.

"What did you talk to him about, Mom?"

"Oh, this and that. Then I warned him that he better not hurt you."

"No." Dawn felt heat creep into her cheeks.

"It's been a couple days. I thought he might have said something."

"Actually we've been really busy. Hardly exchanged two

words that weren't about work." She was certainly at a loss for words now. This was embarrassing on so many levels.

"Hmm," Glory said. "Then I probably should have kept it to myself."

"Why didn't you?"

"I figured it would be best if you found out from me."

Dawn knew her mother had her reasons. "But why right now? Come on, out with it."

"Now seemed good because we're not in the same room. And you don't have to see Jon until Monday. That gives you two days to get over it."

"I can't believe you did that, Mom."

"The kiss shook you up. You're my child and I was concerned," Glory defended herself. "You can be mad at me if you want, but I would do it again."

"Oh, Mom—"

"It's no big deal. He said the same thing you did. Just friends and I believe him. No harm, no foul. Unless you have deeper feelings for him than you're admitting."

"Of course not."

That was probably true. Although she had to admit, if only to herself, that being off this weekend didn't inspire the usual elation, because work was so much more appealing with Jon there. She looked forward to seeing him every day. Except not so much now, after what her mom had done, no matter how well-intentioned.

"Okay, sweetie. I have to go. I'm sorry I interfered. Try not to stay mad at me for too long. Love you."

"Love you, too."

Dawn let out a long breath after ending the call. Remembering Hank was coming any minute, she grabbed her keys and purse, then headed to her car. From the house, she drove north on Main Street to Crawford's General Store. Her mother's declaration of guilt kept playing through her mind. And she was right about one thing. If she didn't care what Jon thought of her outside work it wouldn't matter that Glory butted in. With that in mind, Dawn tried not to be upset, but she couldn't quite manage it. How in the world was she going to face Jon on Monday morning?

She turned right on Cedar Street and into the store parking lot, then exited her car. Still preoccupied with the mother-daughter conversation she rounded the corner and headed for the store entrance. And that's when it happened.

She came face-to-face with Jon Clifton.

His face was as handsome as always but she could feel hers turning red.

"Hi." He was wearing his Stetson, aviator sunglasses, snap-front shirt, jeans and boots. Nothing about him screamed pediatrician. Anyone who didn't know him would figure he was a cowboy.

"Hi, yourself." Dawn had stopped just in front of him, close enough to feel the heat from his body.

"What are you doing here?"

"Grocery shopping." She forced herself to meet his gaze. "You?"

"Same. What are the odds of meeting like this?"

"Apparently one hundred percent."

He grinned, a look designed by God to make female hearts skip a beat. "What a coincidence."

To her it felt more like a force pulling them together. An ironic force, she thought. One that decided it would be amusing for her to see him within half an hour of learning her mom had warned him off.

"I'm so sorry, Jon," she blurted, twisting her fingers together.

"For grocery shopping? Why?" He took her elbow and steered her back a couple of steps away from the entrance in order not to block it. "This store isn't big enough for the both of us?"

"No. Of course not." She caught the corner of her lip between her teeth for a moment. "I found out that my mother talked to you. About me."

"Yes. The kiss," he confirmed. Damn sunglasses hid the expression in his eyes.

"Right. I didn't put her up to it." She held up her hand as if taking an oath in court.

"It never occurred to me that you did."

"That night—after the staff party—when I got home—"

"Yeah, she told me." He didn't look upset. "It's okay, Dawn. She's your mom. You're lucky to have her on your side."

"I know. It's just—well, you and I had a rocky start and we worked it out. Things are going well." And she cared what he thought of her outside of work. That pushed her feelings into the personal. "I just don't want to go back to the bad place."

"Not a chance. We're both reasonable people. If disagreements arise—and I'm sure they will—we know how to handle them. I'm truly not offended by what your mother said. I can sign something in blood if that would convince you I'm telling the truth."

"No. That won't be necessary." But she couldn't help laughing.

Jon studied her for a moment, hesitating, then said, "Do you want to grab a cup of coffee at Daisy's Donut Shop? I haven't eaten yet this morning because there was no food in the house. And you know what they say about shopping on an empty stomach."

"I do." A weight lifted from her. She was so relieved that he didn't seem upset about her mother's interference. "And I'm going to rationalize that a doughnut is the lesser of two evils. In five minutes I could shove enough junk food in my shopping basket to put on five pounds. Two and a half on each thigh. Not pretty."

He glanced down at her legs in her favorite worn jeans and there was a look of pure male appreciation on his face. "I disagree. Vehemently."

Dawn felt warmth in her cheeks again but this time in a good way. To take the heat off, she made a show of checking out his legs, looking awfully masculine in his own jeans. "Yours aren't so bad, either."

"Thank you."

This was definitely tipping into personal territory and she felt obligated to make at least a token attempt at a protest. "Since you grew up in Thunder Canyon you probably already know this, but if we are seen getting doughnuts together people will talk."

"True." Jon didn't look especially concerned. "Hmm. To the best of my knowledge I've never been the subject of town gossip. Might be fun to give everyone something to talk about," he suggested. "What do you think?"

"Has anyone ever told you that you're diabolical?"

"Are you flirting with me, Nurse Laramie?"

"Absolutely not, Dr. Clifton," she answered, in the spirit of teasing. "Just asking a question."

"Well, I'm turning over a new leaf. You should come along and watch. It could be very exciting." He tipped his sunglasses down to reveal a deliciously wicked look in his eyes that suddenly darkened to a sexy shade of bad boy blue.

"Be still my heart," she said. She fanned her face with a hand and was only half teasing. "How can a girl resist a temptation like that?"

"Excellent. Might as well walk. It's just a short way to Cedar Street and a half block down on Broomtail Road."

"Good idea. Work off that doughnut." Dawn fell into step beside him. "Not only do I love Daisy's buttermilk doughnuts, but the longer I'm out of the house, the better."

"Why?"

"Hank's coming over to paint."

"And you're trying to get out of baseboard duty?"

"Well, no. Actually I've been informed that my services aren't required."

"Why is that?" He had a long stride and it was a challenge to keep up.

"Probably because my mom wants the walls to actually look good." Dawn tripped on an uneven spot in the sidewalk because she'd been distracted by his grin.

He took her arm to steady her, then dropped his hand as if he'd touched a hot stove. "Your painting skills are substandard?"

"That's what I'm told. Apparently I have many fine qualities but painting isn't one of them."

"I sense there's another reason that you're grateful for a doughnut run giving you a reason to procrastinate."

"Besides being diabolical, you're very intuitive, Doctor." She met his gaze. "I don't particularly want to hang out with Hank. Mom gave him a key to the house."

They passed Bee's Beauty Parlor and Wings To Go, then stopped in front of the door to Daisy's and he grabbed the handle. "I'm also sensing hostility."

"Congratulations on your diagnosis."

When he opened the door, she preceded him inside where they got in line. The place was crowded and the tables filled with people talking. No one paid any attention to the newcomers.

"You know, Dawn, I have no business giving advice. I know anatomy and physiology. I'm a science guy and the intricacies of relationships confuse the hell out of me."

"But?" she prompted when he hesitated.

"But—" His observation had to wait as it was their turn to order.

They did and the service was quick. He ordered a lemon doughnut to her buttermilk, and neither wanted a fancy latte, just basic black coffee. Since it was a beautiful day they opted to sit at one of the outside tables by themselves.

Dawn broke off a piece of doughnut and ate it, then met his gaze. "So, relationships scare the hell out of you. That's because of your ex?"

"I take part of the responsibility because, like I said, relationships confuse the hell out of me. But we were talking about your father."

"Hank."

"Yes." He nodded. "It would appear he's trying to make amends."

"He's going to let my mother down again."

"Maybe." Jon blew on his hot coffee, then took a sip. "Maybe not. But it might be better if you let him screw up before punishing him."

"He's already screwed up. More times than I can count," she protested.

"Recently?" His voice was calm, an island of reason in a sea of chaos.

She thought about that and reluctantly admitted, "No."

"Could be he's turning over a new leaf. It's going around."

Impossibly, that made her smile. "Taking a page from the diabolical doctor's book?"

"Stranger things have happened." He shrugged. "Why not just meet him halfway?"

"You mean give him enough rope to hang himself?" she said.

"I'm glad to see you're so open-minded," he teased.

"Nice of you to notice."

"I aim to please."

He certainly pleased her, in a lot of ways. For one, he'd managed to get her to relax for the first time since the phone conversation with her mother and finding out Hank had a house key. Jon had given her a different perspective and she would think about what he'd said.

What didn't please her was how pathetically easy it had been for him to convince her to spend time with him. It was all kinds of dangerous, what with her hyperactive hormones that refused to behave. There must be a way to sedate them because nothing had changed. She still worked with him and the pesky attraction just wouldn't go away.

The bottom line was she didn't want to get hurt again and there were a lot of ways to get hurt when you crossed the line from friends to lovers.

Chapter Ten

On Monday Dawn managed to pull off a minor miracle and actually get home from the clinic a little early. Her sister and niece were coming over for dinner and she always looked forward to seeing them. After rounding the corner she saw that Glory hadn't arrived yet but Marina's car was in front of the house. Like Hank, she also had a key.

After hurrying up the sidewalk she let herself inside and immediately smelled the delicious aroma of the roast she'd put in the Crock-Pot before going to work that morning. She called out, "I'm home."

"In the family room."

Dawn saw her sister sitting on the floor with baby Sydney on an animal print blanket in front of her. "How's my favorite girl?"

"Great!" Marina said wryly.

"I was talking to my niece."

"I'm crushed." There was an amused expression on her sister's freckled face. "FYI, when you have a baby no one is interested in you anymore. The mother disappears. It's all about the child. Consider this a public service announcement so you'll be prepared."

"Duly noted." Dawn dropped her purse on the couch, then sat down on the floor beside her sister. "But your warning is wasted on me. I don't believe I will ever have a child."

"How can you be so sure?" Marina asked.

"You should understand better than anyone. I don't want a man."

"You don't need one." Marina thought about that statement for a moment. "Well, technically you do, but his presence isn't required in raising the child."

"We are proof of that," Dawn agreed. "And now that we don't need Hank around he keeps turning up. What's that about?"

"Beats me." Marina tenderly took her baby's bare foot and brushed her thumb over the bottom.

"Hank was here for dinner recently and he said something about Syd. Implied he'd seen her." The last time she'd seen her sister was Sunday breakfast, but her mom was there. She couldn't bring this up in front of Glory.

"Yeah. He brought a baby gift. A little stuffed pink unicorn." Her sister hesitated for a moment, then added, "And he put the crib together."

"No way." Dawn was surprised.

"Yeah. Syd's been sleeping in the cradle since she was born, but she's four months old now and is getting too big for it. The crib was still in the box and he offered to set it up." She tucked a long, straight strand of red hair behind her ear. "I let him."

Dawn had to admit the man was doing all the right things. He'd been there for Glory every time he said he would be. The faint smell of paint still lingered in the back bedrooms and was proof of his presence. Just a couple of days ago Jon had suggested she let him make a mistake before punishing him. But Jon hadn't experienced years of unmet expectations and broken promises. He didn't know the bitter disappointment, the soul-deep sadness of a little girl let down over and over again.

"How do you feel about him, Marina? Hank, I mean."

"I honestly don't know. It doesn't hurt me anymore but I worry about Mom. And now Syd. Protecting her is my top priority. A little girl without a father is especially vulnerable to the potential heartbreak of letting a man into her life who doesn't stick around."

"I never thought about it like that. You not only have to worry about yourself, but your baby girl." Affectionately she nudged her sister's shoulder with her own. She smiled at the little girl who was alternately waving her arms and legs and gnawing on her fist. "She's so beautiful. And you are an outstanding mom."

"I appreciate that and have to say I learned from the best." Marina nudged her back. "You'll be a terrific mother, too."

"Like I said, it's unlikely that I'll ever trust a man enough to let him into my life."

Her sister's blue eyes narrowed. "That's not what I heard."

"What did you hear?"

"Someone saw you and Jon Clifton chatting outside Crawford's General Store on Saturday morning. For a long time, I might add."

This was Monday, so it hadn't taken long for the two of them to be the subject of town gossip and for that gossip to reach her sister. "It's true. We did run into each other."

"And?"

"And what?" Dawn planned to make Marina work for

this. After all, what was the point of being the subject of gossip if you couldn't torture your sister with it?

"And then you went to Daisy's for coffee."

"Don't forget the buttermilk doughnut. And he had a lemon filled." She snapped her fingers. "We both take our coffee black."

"It's a sign." Marina was completely undaunted by the sarcasm and lack of cooperation in extracting information. "Of?"

"Compatibility."

"Don't be a romantic, sis."

"I'm not. But remember I said it first. I told you that you were wildly attracted to the new doctor. You were so passionate in putting him down that it was clear to me you were a little bit smitten."

At the time Dawn had wished her sister was wrong, but the reality was that she did like Jon. If he was a rancher, businessman or something other than a doctor at the clinic she would buy into the signs pointing to something serious brewing between them other than coffee. But that wasn't the case.

"He's a good guy but we work together. So, it's a bad idea." Dawn didn't dare tell Marina about the kiss. She was beginning to think her sister had turned the tables and was torturing her now. "Let's talk about something else."

"Like what?"

"It won't be long until school starts. Are you looking forward to going back? Filling those fertile minds with knowledge?"

Marina thought for a moment and shook her head. "I'd rather talk about Jon kissing you."

"Darn it. Can't tell Mom anything."

"She needed someone to talk to because she was worried."

"Why would she be? As far as she's concerned I haven't dated anyone for a while. She doesn't know about the weasel dog toad boy at the hospital—" Dawn stopped when she caught a glimpse of the guilt on her sister's face. A knot tightened in her stomach. "You told Mom."

"I'm sorry. She knew something was wrong and couldn't get any information from you so she came to me."

"And you bent like a palm tree in a hurricane."

"She's relentless." Marina's expression was filled with remorse. "We're talking about *Mom*. Have you ever tried to resist when she's determined to get something out of you?"

"Yes."

"Okay. Let me rephrase. Did you ever *successfully* resist?"

"No."

"I rest my case." Her sister's tone was triumphant.

"So that's why she went to Jon and warned him not to hurt me."

"Go, Mom!"

"Wait, I'm not finished being mad about you telling her why I left the hospital. I didn't want her to know how stupid I was. Or be disappointed in me."

Marina smiled down at her cooing little girl. "You don't have the market cornered on being foolish about a man. And I didn't have the luxury of hiding my stupidity. Do you think Mom is disappointed in me?"

"Of course not."

"Then why would she be disappointed in you?" Marina's look challenged her. "For that matter, she married our father. People who live in glass houses shouldn't throw stones."

Dawn let that sink in. "It's in our DNA. The curse of the Laramie women. You and I have not been wildly successful with relationships."

Surbiton Library

Items that you have borrowed

Title: An unlikely bride for the billionaire
ID: 39219849964
Due: 08 September 2022

Title: Safe in the rancher's arms
ID: 39219851146
Due: 08 September 2022

Title: Second chance summer
ID: 39217735468
Due: 08 September 2022

Total items: 3
Account balance: £0.00
Borrowed: 3
Overdue: 0
Hold requests: 0
Ready for collection: 0
18/08/2022 10:44

Tel: 0208 547 5006

"Not true. I get along with you, and Mom and other teachers at work. I have friends—"

Dawn put up a hand to stop her. "Let me rephrase. We are a disaster with men."

Just then the front door opened and closed. Their mother called out, "I'm home."

"It's Mom," Marina whispered. "Don't tell her I told you that I told her about—"

Glory walked into the room and dropped her purse on the couch next to Dawn's. She smiled at the baby, then the two of them. "My girls."

"Hi, Mom. Your granddaughter said to tell you thanks for the dinner invitation."

"I'm glad you could make it." She bent over and cooed to the baby who smiled back. "Hi, sweet girl. You're even more beautiful than the last time I saw you."

"It was just a couple days ago," Marina said wryly.

"That's too long." Then she looked at each of her daughters. "There's something I want to talk to you girls about."

"Should we be worried?" Dawn asked.

"No. It's a good thing." Glory brushed her hands over her worn jeans. "I'm going to change clothes and wash up so I can hold that baby girl and spoil her rotten. Be back in a couple minutes."

Marina watched their mother until she disappeared down the hall, then met Dawn's gaze. "You live here. Do you know what this is about?"

"Not a clue. She just asked me to put the roast in the Crock-Pot and that it was big enough to invite you over. Then she called you."

"Is she feeling all right?"

"As far as I know," Dawn answered. "Between her business and painting the house she's tired, but—"

"Isn't Hank helping?" her sister demanded.

"Yes, but it's still more work for her. And I don't trust him."

"Me, either." When the baby started to fuss Marina scooped her up. "But he came through on this project. It looks great."

"Yeah. Mom picked out the colors—"

The woman in question joined them again. She'd put on a pair of black sweatpants and a clean T-shirt. It was obvious she'd heard what they'd been discussing when she said, "What do you think of the new paint?"

"It looks beautiful, Mom. The soft gold walls with that bold olive green accent behind the fireplace is supercool." Marina glanced around the room, admiring the new look.

"I love it," Glory said. "It would have taken me forever without Hank's help."

With their shoulders brushing, Dawn felt her sister tense at the mention of their father. Neither of them said a word and the silence went from longer than normal to awkward. Then the baby started to cry.

"Can I hold her?" Their mother put out her arms and Marina handed Syd to her. She snuggled the little girl close and paced the family room to quiet her. "Part of the reason I wanted you both here was to show off the new paint. The other part is to tell you that I've forgiven your father for what happened when we were married."

The two sisters exchanged a glance. Dawn wasn't surprised but she didn't know what Marina was thinking.

"I understand that Hank wasn't there when you girls were growing up and I can't tell you how to feel about him. I can only explain where I'm coming from. Hank and I were too young to be parents but it happened anyway." She tenderly rubbed her palm over the baby's back to soothe her. "He was trying to do the right thing when he proposed and I was pregnant and scared so I said yes.

The odds were stacked against us, what with all the pressure. And we didn't handle it well."

"You didn't abandon us, Mom," Marina quietly pointed out.

Glory nodded. "Over time maturity set in and Hank realized he didn't accept the responsibility well, but he's older and wiser now. He's trying to make up for what he did. He's doing his best to be a stand-up guy. And he doesn't expect you to forgive or believe him but I've done both."

"Mom—" Dawn got a look and closed her mouth.

"He wants to be friends and I'm in favor of that. I don't expect you to agree with me, but I do expect that when he's a guest in my home you'll be polite to him."

Glory gave each of her daughters a look that clearly said she wouldn't tolerate rebellion in the ranks. Dawn knew when her mother made up her mind there was no changing it. Determination was both a blessing and curse.

"Understood, Mom," was all Marina said. After the words were out of her mouth Sydney let out a screeching howl. "She's hungry."

"She's not the only one," Glory said. "Let's get her fed and then we'll eat."

Glory and Marina took care of the baby while Dawn set the table and put the finishing touches on dinner. Her mind was spinning from what just happened. Her mother was choosing to put her trust in a man who had let her down too many times to count. That concerned her but it also made her think of Jon.

Dawn couldn't help comparing him to her father. Wasn't that why a girl needed a strong male role model when she was growing up? When she started to like boys that role model would help her to separate a heel from a hero. So where did that leave Dawn? All she'd learned was to be wary of men in general.

The only other man who'd tempted her had reinforced everything she believed. But now there was Jon and she had no evidence that he was anything other than the wonderful man he seemed to be. Marina had pointed out that Dawn was focusing on his faults. She realized that was true. It was a strategy to neutralize her reaction to him, like an antidote to poison.

Most people just avoided toxic substances entirely because they were bad for you. But Dawn couldn't avoid Jon. In fact she would see him in the morning. And, God help her, she was looking forward to it.

"There are a lot of sick kids coming in today and it's becoming a pattern. One I don't like."

Jon was standing in the clinic hallway talking to Steve Shepard. It was late afternoon and they'd been slammed with walk-ins all day. Most were children exhibiting cold and flu symptoms.

"What are you thinking?" Steve asked.

"RSV—respiratory syncytial virus."

"Yeah. It's not my sphere of expertise, but I know it can be dangerous."

"That's right." He leaned a shoulder against the wall. "And we seem to have an unusual number of cases. The waiting room is still full. And I've already got one really sick baby that I'm keeping here for observation."

"How can I help?" Steve asked.

Jon had to admit the guy was a team player, and in situations like this that was important. He thought for a moment. "Triage everyone who's waiting to see a doctor. If they can reschedule, have them check with Brandy to make another appointment. For the rest, the ones with the most severe symptoms need to be seen first. We need to get them out of here. Healthy people shouldn't be exposed and sick ones don't need to be sitting out there for hours while feeling like crap."

"Will do." Steve turned and headed for the waiting area.

"Wait."

The other doctor turned. "Yeah?"

"As best you can, isolate the sick kids from everyone else. Emmet and I are working on plans for a separate waiting room for kids but that won't help us today. Just put all the pediatric patients and their parents in a corner of the room and the adult patients as far away as possible."

"Got it." Steve nodded and hurried off.

Jon straightened away from the wall and prepared to go into an exam room, but hesitated when Dawn rounded the corner. She was like a breath of fresh air and he couldn't remember the last time he'd needed that as much as he did now.

"Hi," she said, stopping in front of him. There was a chart in her hands. "You don't look happy."

"What was your first clue?"

She studied him. "Your eyes. And you're not smiling."

"Do I smile so much that today is noteworthy?"

"Yes."

"Okay. I'll do my best to fix that," he said.

"I never said it was a problem." She was looking stressed, too, but managed a spirited, sassy tone.

It was amazing. They were slammed with patients but a little bit of her particular teasing took the edge off. And he really needed the edge off. "I'm not smiling because our resources are stretched to the limit and this concerns me."

"Yeah. I've worked here less than a year, but the clinic has never been this busy before."

"Then it would appear Emmet got reinforcements just in the nick of time."

"You'll get no argument from me." She handed over a chart for the patient in the exam room beside them. "Four-month-old Michael Sherman presents with fever, runny nose, productive cough and lethargy. His mother's name is Emily."

"Let's go take a look," he said.

"Okay."

He glanced through the chart, then opened the exam room door and walked in. The baby was in his mother's arms, listless and quiet. Jon much preferred loud crying. That was normal; this was not.

He recognized the fear in the young mother's brown eyes and smiled reassuringly. "Hi, Emily, I'm Jon Clifton."

"Nice to meet you, Doctor."

"What's going on with Michael?"

The young mother listed the baby's symptoms and responded to all of Jon's pointed questions. He didn't like the picture that was forming.

"When the runny nose started he didn't seem to be sick so I dropped him off at Just Us Kids."

Jon knew that was the new day care center in Rust Creek Falls. "By itself it's not indicative of anything serious."

The worried mother caught her bottom lip between her teeth, clearly upset and conflicted. It was the challenge of all working moms. "I have a baby book that says not to be too overprotective. That if their disposition is normal... I should have kept him home."

Dawn cleared her throat. "Don't go there, Emily. Let's not borrow trouble."

Way to go, Nurse Laramie. Give support to a frightened mother, calm her down.

"I'll try." She put the baby on the paper-covered exam table and removed his one-piece lightweight sleeper.

Jon listened and didn't like what he heard. For the second time that day he delivered the same message. "He's a very sick little boy. I want to start an IV to get medicine and hydration going. I also want to get moisture into his lungs."

"How? Why?" There was a hint of panic in Emily's voice.

"The technical name is an infant aerosol mask. We call it a face tent that fits over his nose and mouth. It's a nebulizer that will distribute cool, moist air for him to breathe. It should break up the mucous plugs."

"Will it hurt him? I'm not sure—"

"Some infants tolerate it fine." Jon suspected Michael would because of his sluggishness. "But if he has a problem with it, we can set up a tent that will do the same thing without making him feel so confined. This is medically necessary to prevent pneumonia and bronchiolitis, an inflammation of the small airways around the lungs."

Emily nodded. "Will it help?"

"Yes." It *would* help, but if she'd asked whether or not her son would be cured, Jon would have been more evasive. He'd learned the hard way never to commit unequivocally and tell a parent their child would be fine. Most of the time that was the case. But sometimes a patient's condition deteriorated for no apparent reason.

"All right, then."

"Dawn will be back in a few minutes so you two sit tight." He figured they would be here for a while. "You can get him dressed."

Emily nodded and he opened the door, letting Dawn precede him into the hall.

"There's something going on with the babies in this town." He was worried.

"Yeah." A serious look settled in Dawn's eyes. "You should know that Michael isn't the first child we've seen today from Just Us Kids. Almost every one of our patients today goes to that day care center."

"That's good information." And she was an excellent nurse to pick up that crucial detail and bring it to his attention. He knew that in close quarters viruses could easily spread and quickly. "I'll call the day care center and alert them that there could be a problem. Right after we start treatment on that little guy." He glanced through the boy's chart. "I don't see anything unusual in his medical history that would cause dangerous complications from RSV, so, for now, I'd like to avoid putting him through the trauma of a hospital. We'll keep him here and see if he responds to the standard treatment protocols. But—"

Dawn met his gaze. "What?"

"That means more work for you. The waiting room is packed. I have to see patients, so the burden of this is going to fall to you."

"Callie will help. And I'm sure I can count on Lorajean."

"I know. But with your pediatric hospital experience, you're the point on this. And he's the second baby you'll be looking after."

"Don't worry about me. I can handle it."

"Okay. I'll check in and if you need me holler."

"Will do. If you'll write up the treatment orders, I'll get the supplies."

"Right. And, Dawn?"

"Hmm?"

"Can you move Michael next to the room where the little Marshall girl is set up? I'd prefer to keep them isolated from each other, but it will be easier for you to go between them that way."

"No problem." She nodded and hurried away.

Jon let out a long breath, taking just a moment. It would probably be the last break for a while. Dawn was a remarkable woman and a damn fine nurse. Vital to making this medical facility run smoothly was her positive, team-centered attitude. And that could change if he didn't keep his personal feelings to himself. But not touching her was killing him. Especially after he'd kissed her and she'd kissed him back. It had been potent.

Right now selective amnesia would be good—just to erase memories of having her in his arms. Since that wasn't going to happen, he figured the next best thing was burying himself in work. And he had more of that than he wanted. At this rate he wasn't sure when he would get out of the clinic.

Of course that meant Dawn would be here, too.

Chapter Eleven

It was long after closing time before the clinic's two little patients finally went home. Dawn was beyond tired when she stopped in the break room to retrieve her purse and car keys. But the effort to actually pick them up seemed more than she could manage, so she sat in one of the chairs. Just for a minute, she told herself. That's where Jon found her.

"Are you okay?" His voice was deep, concerned.

"Hmm?" Her eyes snapped open and she saw him just inside the door.

"You were sleeping."

"Not quite." She stretched her arms over her head to loosen up the tight, cramped muscles. "What a day."

Jon sat down in the other chair. "That's an understatement."

"It's going to be a rough night for those parents."

"Yeah." His mouth pulled tight for a moment. "The babies aren't out of the woods, but I was satisfied that their temps were under control and their breathing was better."

"The attention of a loving mother, one-on-one, is probably the best medicine given the circumstances."

"There was nothing else we could do for them here," he agreed. "I gave them detailed instructions on care and my cell phone number. They have orders to call with any questions or concerns. And I told them what to watch for that could be trouble."

"Yeah. Like you said. It's either the hospital or home—" A yawn sneaked out before she could finish her thought.

"Speaking of home, I'm giving you strict instructions to get out of here."

"Sir, yes, sir." Dawn saluted. "There's only one problem with that."

"What?"

"To follow your orders I have to get up," she said. "I hate that part."

He stood and held out his hand. "Allow me."

"Thanks." She put her fingers in his palm and let him pull her up. Then the room began to spin and she started to go down.

Jon caught her, wrapped her in strong arms before gently settling her into the chair again. Then he went down on one knee in front of her, concern darkening his gaze as he checked her out. "You're white as a sheet. I'm guessing that's about being tired or hungry. Or both."

She touched a shaky hand to her forehead. "Now that I think about it, I don't remember eating lunch today."

"I should have paid more attention. Damn it." He looked angry, but it seemed directed at himself. "We're no good to the patients if we don't take care of ourselves. From now on there will be mandatory lunch breaks. We'll cover for each other, no matter how busy it is. Next time say something."

"Excellent idea, Doctor." She slapped her hands on her

thighs and prepared to stand. "Right now I think I'll go home, have a bowl of cereal and crawl into bed."

"You call that taking care of yourself?" If possible he looked even angrier. "Cereal is not a well-balanced meal."

"I don't have the energy for more than that. And there's no place in Rust Creek Falls that is open for takeout at this hour."

"Not even the Ace in the Hole?"

"They stop serving food at nine," she confirmed.

"Okay." He stood and settled his hands on his hips. "Plan B."

"And that is?"

"My place. Steak. I have one defrosted in the refrigerator and planned to throw it on the grill when I got home. Just didn't think it would be this late. I can throw together a salad and microwave a couple of potatoes for us."

"Oh, no. I can't let you—"

"I insist. After letting you starve all day, it's my duty to feed you."

She sighed then and nodded wearily. "But only because I'm too weak and tired to argue."

She wasn't so weak that her insides weren't all quivery, though. The prospect of spending time with him outside of work sent a shot of adrenaline through her that chased away exhaustion. She wanted to be alarmed about what could happen if they were alone, but quite frankly, she didn't have the energy to give a damn. Surely they could hang out as friends. Coworkers did it all the time.

He held out his hand again to help her up. "Slowly this time."

She did as instructed, half hoping he would have to catch her again. Because now her senses were wide-awake and cranking up the heat and awareness.

Jon refused to let her drive herself and insisted he didn't

mind bringing her back for her car. In a short time they pulled up in front of his house and Rerun enthusiastically greeted them at the door. Yipping and whining he danced around them until Jon ordered him to stop. Instantly he rolled on his back to get tummy rubs.

Dawn was delighted to oblige and swore the dog was smiling when she gave in. "It must be nice to come home to unconditional love like this."

"If you weren't here, I'd be on scratch-the-dog shift and dinner would have to wait." He went straight to the kitchen and washed his hands, then started assembling dinner. "But on long days—like today—I feel guilty because he's here by himself. I'm glad my brother and his wife are close by."

She scratched Rerun under his chin, then looked up when the back door opened and Jon went outside to deal with the barbecue. "Do you need any help?"

"No. Just relax."

Already done, she thought, brushing a hand over the three-legged animal's back. It was amazing how the day's tension just drained away. But the guilt of sitting there and doing nothing was too much so she pushed to her feet with a groan and walked into the kitchen, where Jon was opening a bottle of red wine.

He met her gaze. "Would you like some?"

"Do doctors and nurses make the worst patients?" She made a scoffing sound. "Of course I want some."

"Do you care whether or not it breathes before I pour?"

"You could put it in a plastic cup with a straw and I wouldn't judge at all."

"A girl after my own heart." There was just the slightest ragged edge to his voice but he covered it with a grin. "I may be a bachelor but I'm a bachelor with standards."

He opened a top cupboard, took out two stemless wine-glasses and poured some of the dark red liquid into each.

The kitchen was set off from the living room by a bar and she stood on the other side of it. He handed her a glass, then said, "Let's drink to healthy children."

"Amen." She tapped her glass to his and took a sip. And another. "You really like kids, don't you?"

"Yes." He took an already washed container of spring greens from the refrigerator and made two individual salads. "Oil and vinegar dressing okay?"

"Fine."

While the microwave hummed with nuking potatoes, he put plates and silverware on the table. Rerun looked up at him with longing and he said, "Later, buddy. Gotta put the steak on. Be good and you can have some."

Dawn followed him outside and watched him set the meat on the grill. With a sigh she glanced up at the sky. "It's beautiful out here."

"Yeah. Beautiful." He was looking over his shoulder and light from inside illuminated an exciting intensity in his eyes. "How do you like your steak cooked?"

"Medium rare."

"Me, too."

Another sign, she thought hazily. The wine was really hitting her on an empty stomach. But the coolest thing about rocking a buzz was that she didn't care about the filter between her brain and mouth being put out of commission.

"So why do you like kids?" she asked.

Those broad shoulders on full display lifted in a casual shrug. He turned the steak and there was a burst of flames before he shut the top of the barbecue and turned to her. "They're cute. Funny. Honest. What's not to like?"

"Is that why you became a pediatrician?"

"Yeah."

"Do you want kids of your own?"

His gaze narrowed on her. "Do you?"

"Fair enough. You don't want to talk about it." She didn't, either.

"Complicated subject."

"I know what you mean." A catch-22 situation for her. She wouldn't have kids without a man in her life and she didn't trust men enough to let one in. They had already agreed not to go there, so discussing it was pointless.

"The steaks look done," he finally said.

The smoky smell drifted to her and made her mouth water. "And not a moment too soon. It's official. I'm seriously starving."

Inside they sat across from each other at the small table and filled their plates. Rerun settled beside Jon and promptly fell asleep. For several minutes the only sound in the room was utensils cutting meat and forks scraping plates.

Dawn finished first. "That was quite possibly the best meal I've ever had in my entire life."

"I would take that as a compliment if you weren't in starvation mode when you ate." He left a small amount of steak on his plate, probably because he'd promised Rerun. "I feel much better now."

"Ditto."

She really expected him to say just leave the dishes and he would take her home. It would be for the best that she agree and say she needed to get her car at the clinic and call it a night. But she wasn't ready to leave yet and go back to just seeing him at work. Dragging out this moment with him suddenly seemed vitally important.

So instead of the right thing she said, "You cooked. Let me do the dishes."

"No way. I don't have a dishwasher and letting you do the grunt work just isn't going to happen. But you can help."

"Okay," she said happily.

Normally the mundane chore was annoying but necessary. With Jon, soaping up their dishes, then rinsing and handing them to him for drying was like a roller coaster ride at the state fair. Fortunately the buzz still making her glow from the inside out didn't let her consider how many ways that feeling was trouble.

"Done," he announced five minutes later after everything was cleaned, dried and put away.

"Would you mind if we sat outside for a few minutes? After being cooped up in the clinic all day the fresh air would feel so wonderful."

"You're reading my mind." He turned off the overhead kitchen lights and turned on a living room lamp for a more serene atmosphere.

Or maybe he was going for romantic?

Her heart skipped as she preceded him out the door into the cool night air. Just outside there was a wooden bench built for two where they sat down side by side and leaned against the cabin's back wall. Their shoulders brushed and she could almost see sparks floating in the darkness, as if someone had tossed a log on the embers of a fire to rekindle it. Every nerve ending in her body was tingling and aware. Her skin was sensitized, aching to be touched. And there was an ache in her chest, too, because she wanted to kiss him and didn't dare.

Dawn let out a big sigh. "Food and relaxation. You really know how to keep a promise, Doctor. I don't appreciate enough how beautiful it is here. The stars are like gold dust in the sky."

"Well said."

She started to say more but couldn't hold back a yawn. "Sorry. It's not the company. No offense."

"None taken."

"There's something about having a full stomach that makes a person sleepy. I'm sure there's a physiological reason for that."

"Would you like to hear it?" There was a smile in his voice.

"Maybe some other time. It would probably put me to sleep." She heard the way that sounded. "Not that you're boring."

"Way to slice and dice a guy's ego."

She laughed and then a companionable silence settled over them. She sat there quietly while the wine and Jon's warm body beside her combined to make her drowsy. Her head was so heavy and the most natural thing in the world was to rest it against his strong shoulder. And that's the last thing she remembered.

Dawn opened her eyes and was startled to be alone in a bed that wasn't hers and still wearing her scrubs from work. Then it all came rushing back. Jon had brought her to his place. After dinner they sat outside where she must have fallen asleep. The room was dim, but through the open door she could see light. "Jon…" she whispered.

She sat up and swung her legs to the side of the bed and slid to the floor. Her sneakers were there and she figured he must have taken them off, without waking her no less. How sweet and considerate was that?

After bending over to grab them, she went into the other room. Jon was sitting on the couch, his back to her. There was a bottle of water on the end table beside him and a lamp casting soft light.

"Jon?" She walked around and sat at the other end of the seen-better-days sofa and set her shoes on the floor.

"You're awake." He looked at her for a moment, tenderness sliding into his eyes just before they turned dark and smoky.

The expression was unguarded, involuntary, and her whole body responded. Heat turned up on hormones already simmering.

"What time is it?" she asked.

"Late."

"Why didn't you wake me?"

"You were sleeping."

That was the second time he'd said that to her today. Or maybe it was tomorrow. She didn't really want to know. "Sorry, I didn't mean to nod off. How rude is that."

"You were tired."

"The last thing I remember is going outside. How did I get into your bedroom?"

"I carried you."

Well, she was very sorry to have missed that but the thought sent a shivery feeling through her. "If I'd known that was going to happen, I wouldn't have eaten so much for dinner."

One corner of his mouth turned up. "Is this where I grunt like a caveman?"

"Did you throw me over your shoulder?"

"No."

"Then no grunt required," she assured him. "Too bad Rust Creek Falls doesn't have a chiropractor. You're probably going to need one to adjust your back."

"You're pretty light."

"And you're quite gallant." They smiled at each other for a moment too long and she needed to break the spell.

"However, at the risk of pushing the gallant thing too far, I really should get home."

"Right."

Dawn watched him drag his fingers through his hair, the gesture somehow highlighting his own fatigue.

"I should have brought my own car. You're just as tired as I am. Probably more. I had a nap. I really hate for you to drive me to Rust Creek Falls, then have to come all the way back here. Maybe I could take your truck and—"

"No. I'm not letting you go alone this time of night. I'll take you."

"I'm sorry, Jon. It's so late—"

"Just stay."

She was pretty sure he hadn't meant to say that. And it was probably her imagination or just exhaustion-induced hallucinations, but his voice sounded ragged, needy. As if he *wanted* her.

"What?" she asked. "You mean here?"

He nodded, then said again, "Stay."

How could a single word steal the breath right out of her lungs? It wasn't as if he'd said he wanted to take her to bed. Come to think of it he'd already done that and left her there alone. He hadn't even tried to take advantage of her, darn it.

"Dawn?"

"I don't know." If he was her sister or a girlfriend she wouldn't even hesitate. But he was *Jon* and she was trying to resist a stubborn attraction that threatened a nicely budding friendship. "But, you and me— How is this—"

"I'll sleep here on the couch."

"It's pretty lumpy and uncomfortable. No offense," she added.

"It's an old one that Will and Jordyn Leigh put in here when they remodeled the main house." He shrugged. "It's not much worse than the cot in the on-call room where I crashed at the hospital during my residency."

"It doesn't feel right to put you out of your bed. I'll take the couch."

He shook his head. "No you won't. It's impossible to sleep on this thing."

"So you lied." At his questioning look she added, "When you said you'd *sleep* here."

"You're splitting hairs," he said.

"Be that as it may…"

"I'm used to it."

"So you often spend the night on this thing?" She folded her arms over her chest.

He sighed as frustration and something else swirled in his eyes. "Has anyone ever told you that you're incredibly stubborn?"

"It's one of my best qualities." She stared at him for several moments, locked in a stalemate. His face was drawn and his eyes dull. She was concerned about him getting some rest and that made it an easy call. She was going to stay. "Look, let's just share the bed."

"Dawn, that's not—"

"We're adults. It's not a problem. And, quite frankly, this debate is seriously cutting into my beauty sleep." She thought he muttered something like "You don't need it," but couldn't be sure. "What?"

"Nothing."

"So, we're sharing the bed, right?" She stood up and met his gaze.

"Whatever you say."

Without further ado, Dawn went into the bedroom first. There was a bathroom off to the right and she ducked in to wash her face as best she could, then appropriated the toothpaste sitting on the small shelf beside the sink and brushed her teeth with her index finger. She thought about calling her mom to explain why she wouldn't be home but decided it was too late to wake her.

When she came out Jon took his turn. It was dark in the bedroom, the only illumination coming from the moonlight streaming through the window and around the closed bathroom door. Still wearing her scrubs, which she figured would be relatively comfortable to sleep in, she slid into the far side of the bed, as close to the edge as possible without falling off. Just as she settled on her back he opened the bathroom door and turned out the light.

She was pretty sure he'd taken off his shirt. It was just a glimpse before the darkness closed in, but a really good glimpse. Except that she wanted a better—and by better she meant longer—look. Maybe a touch.

Oh, dear God, it was going to be a long night. She rolled on her side with her back to him. As ideas went, this was not one of the best and unfortunately it had been hers. On a scale of one to ten, with ten being the worst, the reality of sharing a bed with Jon was a fifteen. It pushed twenty when she felt the mattress dip from his weight. And the masculine scent of his skin drifted to her, firing up her hormones even more.

"Good night."

"Night." His voice was ragged, rough.

And, instead of standing down, it made her nerves start to hum.

Eyes wide-open, she stared at the shadowy ceiling, waiting to hear the slow, deep breathing that meant he'd fallen asleep. Then she could sleep. There was no way to tell how long this went on, and although there was no movement from his side of the bed, she was almost certain he was still awake.

Dawn couldn't speak for him, but she was tense as a bowstring and ready to snap. "Jon, I—"

He threw back the covers. "This isn't going to work."

She rolled over to face him. "What's wrong?"

"I want you." There was no mistaking the need in his voice this time. It was honest and raw. "I can't help it. I can't make it stop. If I touch you—" He swore under his breath. "I'm going in the other room."

This time he didn't say anything about sleeping. And there was no mistaking the way her heart soared in response to his declaration. *He wanted her.*

Before he could get out of bed she moved closer and reached for him. It was automatic, instinctive. Her hand touched his arm, the warm skin. And this time she said the word. *"Stay."*

He covered her hand with his own. And there was intensity bordering on desperation in his voice when he asked, "Are you sure?"

"Yes."

He turned toward her and settled his mouth on hers. The kiss was frantic, reckless, dangerous and intoxicating. He reached for the hem of her scrub top and pulled it over her head, then tossed it into the darkness. Then he unhooked her bra and sent it wherever her top had gone. They were skin to skin from the waist up and it felt like heaven after doing an eternity of penance in purgatory. Her only regret was that he was in shadow and she couldn't see the muscular contours of his chest as the dusting of hair teased the tips of her breasts.

The sound of their uneven breathing filled the room as he slid off her pants and then his own. They were naked and the tension coiled inside her strained, clawed for release.

"Jon, please—"

"I know." He let her go and rolled away.

"What? I don't—"

"Condom," he rasped.

Oh, God! She was so far gone she hadn't even considered that. Beside the bed a drawer opened and he fumbled around before making a triumphant sound.

He tore open the packet and put it on, then pulled her back into his arms and settled her beneath him. With his knee he nudged her legs apart and slowly entered her. She could feel all of his concentration focused on her and holding back. But she wanted more and she wanted it now. Tilting her hips up, she let him know this was a stat request.

With exquisite restraint he continued to move slowly and deliberately, nudging her toward what she wanted. And suddenly her body tensed as a burst of pleasure roared through her. Tremors rocked her and Jon held her close until they stopped, keeping her from shattering.

Then he rested his forearms on either side of her, taking his weight on them before thrusting deeply. Once. Twice. The third time he cried out and buried his face in her neck until his breathing slowed and returned to normal.

He kissed her softly on the lips, then said, "I'll be right back. Don't go anywhere."

Dawn felt the mattress dip as he left the bed. Her muscles were like Jell-O and there was a better than even chance she couldn't move even if she wanted to. Vaguely she was aware that the bathroom light went on. She must have dozed off, because the next thing she knew he slipped back in beside her then tugged the sheet over their naked bodies.

He pulled her against him and she sighed with contentment. Before she fell asleep, she thought about how nice it was not being alone.

Chapter Twelve

When he felt his fingers being licked, Jon opened one eye and saw Rerun standing beside him prancing expectantly. Then something moved in the bed beside him and a smooth, decidedly female leg brushed his. Everything that happened came back in a rush. He looked at Dawn and smiled at the way her blond hair spilled over the pillow like gold silk.

Thank God it wasn't another dream.

Easing out of bed he quickly let the dog out, then returned. She was still asleep, either from complete exhaustion or because she was a very deep sleeper. He slid in beside her again and she rolled over, rubbing her leg against his. The slight touch sent heat blasting through him and blood heading to points south.

He wanted her again, if possible even more than he had last night. And last night he'd really wanted her bad.

According to the clock on his side of the bed, they

needed to get up soon if he was going to drop her at her car with enough time to go home and get ready for work. But he could give her a few more minutes.

Rerun came back and whined, this time for food. And that's when Dawn opened her eyes. She blinked once and he knew exactly when she remembered where she was and what they'd done. Her expression looked a little like buyer's remorse.

Jon wasn't sorry and would give almost anything for a repeat. This time with long, slow kisses that would start at the top of her head and end at the tips of her toes.

But the look in her eyes was telling him she had second thoughts about the first time which made another go-round out of the question.

"Good morning." He said it as if he wasn't sure if it was a statement or a question.

"I have to go. My car—"

"We've got time." He realized how that sounded and that it made things more awkward. Not what he'd meant to do. "I mean there's time for you to get to work."

"No. You don't understand. I just really have to go home. Now."

"Okay. I can do that."

She looked at him expectantly. "Well?"

"What?"

"You have to get up first," she said firmly.

The way she was holding the sheet to her breasts should have been a clue. But apparently he was really out of practice in reading a woman's body language. And he wished he could say he'd already seen every square inch of her but he hadn't because the room was dark when they'd ripped off each other's clothes. But his hands on her soft curves painted a really vivid picture in his head.

"I'll take a quick shower." A cold one since he wasn't

dumb enough to invite her to join him. He threw back the sheet and tried to think of something to lighten the mood. "Don't peek."

"If I got up first would you peek?"

"I have to be honest. Of course."

He was almost sure she stifled a laugh as he got up and walked to the bathroom. Just before closing the door he looked at Dawn. She was still clutching the sheet and her eyes were tightly shut. She was so cute and the power of the feelings crashing through him threatened to pull him under. That was bad. He closed the door and stepped in the shower, doing his best to wash away what he'd felt without much success.

In ten minutes he was ready. Dawn was in the living room, pacing nervously. Her purse was slung over her shoulder and yesterday's scrubs were a little wrinkled, having spent the night in a pile on the floor. And she looked guilty, like a teenager caught sneaking out.

He was pretty sure she didn't want coffee. "Are you ready to go?"

"Yes."

"Okay. Let's roll." He opened the door and she preceded him outside.

Just up a slight rise he saw his brother come out of the barn. Will waved and Jon acknowledged it. Dawn groaned and looked as if she'd just seen red flashing lights in her rearview mirror.

"Don't worry about Will," he said, but she didn't answer.

Jon opened the passenger door of his truck and, when she pulled herself into the cab, he resisted the urge to touch her. He wasn't sure she wouldn't shatter if he did. He just got in and headed for Rust Creek Falls.

Dawn didn't seem inclined to break the silence so he did.

"We need to talk about what happened."

"You're right." She sighed as if a great weight lifted from her shoulders. "I wanted to talk, but didn't know how to start."

"Why don't you tell me how you feel." A guy couldn't go wrong bringing that up, right? He couldn't study her face and gauge her reaction because he had to watch the road.

"I'm not sure how I feel. We agreed that we'd just be friends. That anything else could get complicated and affect our work relationship. Potentially creating a hostile environment at the clinic."

He didn't need a recap but figured she needed to say it. "We did."

"But last night we crossed the line."

"Did we?" He'd just admitted as much but wasn't sure what to say.

"Look, I know men are from Mars, women are from Venus. We process the same situation differently. I get that. But all the reasons we agreed not to get personal haven't changed."

"You're right." He wanted to keep her talking and his responses were designed to do that.

"Last night was really wonderful. I want you to know that. Dinner, relaxation and…everything else."

"I had a good time, too." Jon glanced over. She was twisting her fingers together, obviously nervous.

"The thing is—I want you to know that I know it didn't mean anything."

The hell it didn't.

But there was a note in her voice that he couldn't identify. Expectation? Was she looking for a specific response from him? He wasn't sure. This was delicate and he didn't want to say the wrong thing.

"Go on," was the best neutral response he could come up with.

"We can chalk it up to a little wine. The release of tension after a long, stressful day."

"I'm sure that's true."

It was certainly part of the reason it happened. But to be honest, they'd been headed in that direction almost from the moment they met. And especially after their kiss at Emmet's. She'd said then she wouldn't read anything into it. But he had news for her. Things had changed now. Sleeping together was *something* and he wasn't sure whether or not it was bad.

His almost-engagement had fallen through partly because he'd picked a woman who was too selfish to understand a doctor's life. But he had to take part of the blame. He tended to bury himself in work and hadn't seen the signs of trouble. That work had included losing a kid he'd grown close to and he hadn't seen that coming, either. It was something he didn't think his ex could understand and hadn't even tried to share with her. All of that baggage made him lousy relationship material.

In spite of that, the breakup had been hard. He'd wanted someone to grow old with, a marriage like his parents had. He'd finally let someone in and liked it. He'd been lonely when she left, but now he was used to being alone, and rocking the relationship boat again didn't seem the smartest move. It was probably better that Dawn believed sleeping together was just a casual hookup.

She didn't say anything else for the rest of the drive and Jon was deep into his own thoughts. So it was almost as if he was on automatic pilot when he turned left onto Commercial Street then left again on South Lodgepole Lane and into the clinic parking lot. He stopped the truck beside Dawn's small compact car.

After turning off the engine he looked at her. "Should I say I'm sorry?"

Big sunglasses hid the expression in her eyes. "Are you?"

Yes and no, he thought. Wasn't that the classic definition of conflict?

When he didn't answer right away her mouth pulled tight. "You know, it would probably be best if we put last night in the end-of-a-crazy-day file. We'll just go back to the way things were."

Without waiting for a response she got out of the truck and into her car. She drove away, never once looking at him.

Jon sat there. This was where he really felt the difference between book smart and street smart.

In the practice of medicine he had most of the answers. With women, not so much. But he'd learned to trust his gut. And when Dawn stated with absolute certainty that they could go back to the way things were, his gut had an answer.

When pigs fly.

After a long, tense day Dawn was tired and crabby. Her disposition didn't improve when she drove home and saw Hank's truck parked in front of the house. Wasn't that just the perfect end to a lousy day? Maybe it was time to make alternate living arrangements. The man who'd fathered her might not be the very last person she wanted to see right now, but he was darn close to the top of the list.

When she went inside, she heard voices coming from the kitchen.

"I'm home," she called out.

Talking stopped but there were no welcoming words from her mother as usual. That was not a good sign. She went into the kitchen and found her mother and Hank standing in front of the sink where, if she didn't miss her guess, he'd just installed a new faucet. The packaging and tools were spread out on the counter and the old, sad one was beside the sink.

"Hi." Her mom had been gone when she got home to shower and change this morning. This wasn't a good time to remember that note she'd planned to leave and didn't. Too many things on her mind and all of them were about Jon.

"Where have you been, Dawn Debra?" Glory glared at her.

It was a look Dawn hadn't seen for a very long time. And combined with her middle name, it meant she was in deep doo-doo.

She had an idea what this was about but preferred not to discuss it in front of her mother's ex-husband. She decided to answer exactly what she'd been asked.

"I've been at work."

"You know I don't mean today. Where were you last night?"

"There were some very sick babies at the clinic yesterday." Dawn knew that wasn't what her mother meant but plowed ahead with a diversionary response. Fingers crossed it would work. "The doctor kept them for observation. I was there late." That was absolutely true.

Glory put her hands on her hips, and the expression on her face said she was fully prepared to play this game. "Did you sleep at the clinic?"

If only, Dawn thought. She wouldn't have given in to the temptation to sleep with Jon. It was the best night of her life and the worst because of the talk they'd had afterward. But to answer her mother's question… "No."

"So where did you sleep? Because I know for a fact that it wasn't here in your own bed—"

"Now, Glory—" Hank's voice was deep and designed to soothe. The rose between two thorns. She recalled the phrase that Jon had used. In her father's case, it was ironic, since he'd always been the one to draw blood.

"No, I want to know where she was," her mother persisted.

"I'm not a teenager, Mom. I don't need your permission to stay out after curfew."

"That's true. You don't. But I didn't raise you to be disrespectful and discourteous. A text to let me know you were okay would have been nice." She paused before adding, "I had to call the clinic today to make sure you were all right."

Dawn winced. There was no defense for that and guilt squeezed her hard. It had crossed her mind to call but, if she was being honest, not picking up the phone was more than just the fact that it was late. There would have been a reality check from Glory, and Dawn hadn't wanted to hear it. She didn't want to talk about it now, either. Her gaze slid to Hank and she resented the fact that he was here at this awkward moment and not when she'd been a little girl who desperately needed her father.

She looked at the two of them standing side by side, presenting what parents liked to call a united front. "I had dinner with Dr. Clifton."

"All night?" her mother snapped.

"You know, Mom, I don't really have the reserves to get into this with you right now. I'm pretty tired and—"

"That's what happens when you're up all night doing God knows what. Funny how there just wasn't time to let your mother know you weren't lying in a ditch somewhere or trapped in the trunk of a serial killer's car trying to break the taillights and signal for help."

"Glory—" Hank put an arm across her shoulders, obviously sensing she was going over the edge. "You were worried and now you're venting to Dawn."

Dawn hated to be grateful to the man, but right this minute she was. "I'm sorry, Mom. I should have called. The thing is, if I didn't live under your roof, you wouldn't expect me home. Hence there would be no reason to be concerned about me. Do you want me to get my own place?"

"That's not what I'm saying. And for your information, you never stop worrying about your children, whether they live with you or not. I just wanted to know you were safe—" Glory started to cry.

Dawn felt like the lowest, slimiest life-form on the planet. She took a step forward to comfort her mother, but Hank was there.

He put his big arms around Glory and pulled her against his chest. "There, there. Don't cry, honey."

"C-can't help it—"

She felt as useless as a bump on a pickle. *She* should be the one patting her mother's back but there was Hank doing it. More often than not in the past he'd been the one making Glory cry but that dubious honor went to Dawn this time.

"I'm sorry, Mom," she said again. "If I were you, I'd take away my cell phone and ground me for a month."

As intended, Glory laughed. It was half sob, half snort, but Dawn would take what she could get. "I'm the world's worst daughter."

"No, you're not." Her mother gave Hank a grateful look, then sighed and stepped away. "Thoughtless, maybe. But your father's right. All the worry built up and I took it out on you. Not my finest hour, either."

"It's okay. I deserve whatever you can dish out and more. I thought about calling—"

"I see." The angry mom look was back. "And you didn't... Why?"

"That's a good question." Dawn wished she could have those words back. But that wasn't going to happen. "I should have called. It's just I didn't want to wake you and—"

"You were with Jon. Everything and everyone else just wasn't as important as what you were feeling for him at that moment."

In spite of the conflict ripping her apart, Dawn smiled. "Clearly you've experienced the phenomenon, too."

"I have." Her mother glanced at Hank. "And was Jon a gentleman?"

"Yes." Dawn had been right about not having the reserves for this conversation. That was the only explanation for why the next words came out of her mouth. "It got late and I didn't want him to take me to my car then drive all the way back to the ranch. We decided I would sleep there."

"I'm guessing you didn't do much sleeping." Glory's voice was dripping with sarcasm.

Hank didn't say anything but he looked mad enough to twist Jon's head off as easily as he did the cap on a beer bottle.

"We're not teenagers." Hadn't she already said that? Right, about herself. "We should have been able to share the bed without—" Her cheeks burned and she felt like the teenager she repeatedly denied being. But, for the rest of her life she would never forget the grinding need in his voice when he'd said he wanted her. Dawn was tired of resisting and had wanted him, too. But she thought he'd meant for more than a one-night stand and the pain of being wrong was profound. "He was going to sleep on the couch. I was the one who stopped him."

"You must really like that man," her mother said.

"I do. But he doesn't feel the same—" The pain of that realization grew bigger until it choked off her words. A sob escaped and she couldn't hold back the tears. She put her hands over her face and cried.

A pair of strong arms enveloped her, clearly not her mother's. At that moment the warmth and comfort felt better than the bitterness she'd carried around for her father. She couldn't bring herself to reject him.

"It's okay, honey," Hank said. "There, there. Please don't cry. If you want, I'll beat him up for you."

Dawn laughed and knew she sounded the same as Glory had. Like mother, like daughter. But she had this man's DNA, too. Maybe her instinct to rescue a situation with humor came from her father. Who knew she would ever find common ground with him?

"I appreciate the thought," she said.

"I'm not joking. If you want, I'll take him apart with my bare hands." There was no mistaking the sincerity in Hank's voice.

Funny how the threat of physical violence could warm a daughter's heart. She brushed away the tears on her cheeks and looked up at him, but didn't move away. "As appealing as that sounds, it's probably not a good idea. We finally have a pediatrician in Rust Creek Falls and hurting him wouldn't be good for the kids."

"She's right, Hank." Glory's eyes were full of motherly concern and just a little bit of teasing. "Think about our granddaughter's welfare before you do anything rash."

"Thinking about Sydney would be the rational thing to do but I'm not feeling it right now." He shrugged. "It's a guy thing."

More of a father thing, Dawn thought, grateful for the fact that he was respecting the boundaries she'd put up. But the lines were blurring now and she wasn't sure how she felt about it.

"Thanks for wanting to," she said. "But no promises were made on either side. There's nothing to punish him for. You can't force someone to feel the same way you do."

Hank nodded, then gave her a gentle hug before reluctantly letting her go. "Okay. But if you change your mind—"

"I'll be sure and let you know," she assured him.

Her mother moved in front of Dawn and took her face in her hands, then kissed her forehead. "I love you, sweetie. I was afraid this would happen. But you should know that anyone who hurts you has to deal with me."

"Thanks, Mom. I'm okay, just tired. This thing with Jon isn't serious." She was pretty sure about that, but not completely. "I'll be fine."

Glory nodded. "Are you and I fine? Or do you still want to move out?"

"We are fine. And I'm not sure about the moving out part. There are pros and cons."

"Okay. Table that for now," her mother said. "Speaking of tables, there will be an extra plate at ours tonight. Hank is having dinner with us. A thank-you for changing the faucet and all the painting and everything—"

"It's okay, Mom." She knew Glory expected her to push back, but she wasn't feeling the hostility anymore. She looked at Hank. "I'm glad you're staying."

"I'm glad you're glad," he said.

So there was some gladness going around as they worked together to get food on the table. But when Dawn thought about tomorrow, she wasn't feeling the joy. Tomorrow she would have to go back to her job and pretend that nothing had happened between her and Jon. It was going to take a lot of energy to live that lie in front of everyone. She had no idea how she was going to pull it off.

Chapter Thirteen

Working with Jon the day after her father offered to beat him up turned out to be just as uncomfortable as Dawn had expected. But she was soldiering on as best she could. And then the day got worse when her sister came into the clinic. It was Sydney's first sick visit. Dawn could see the worry on Marina's face. With a redhead's pale skin, the dark smudges of exhaustion beneath her blue eyes were really noticeable.

She showed them into an exam room and said, "So, what's going on with our baby girl?"

As if knowing she was being discussed, the whimpering child burrowed her face into her mother's neck. "She's got a fever. And I've never seen her so fussy. She keeps crying and pulling at her ear. I was in the glider chair with her all night. That was the only way I could get her to rest."

"Poor baby. Poor mom."

Dawn made notes in the chart for Jon to see, then put it in the holder outside the room with a color-coded clip that told Jon to come into this room next. Technically Syd wasn't an emergency, but it sure felt that way. She loved this baby so much and hated that she wasn't feeling well.

She braced herself for the coolly polite, hideously awkward experience of being in the same room with the man who was her one-night stand. So far today bracing herself hadn't worked very well and there was no reason to think that would change just because her family was here.

The rest of the staff knew about her sister and were picking up the slack so that Dawn could stay with her and lend moral support. And when Marina sat down and the baby shrieked, it was clear her sister needed all the support she could get.

"I can't sit unless it's to rock her. When that doesn't work I walk the floor—" Emotions choked off her words.

"Will she come to me?"

"It's worth a try."

"Can Auntie Dawn hold you, sweet girl?" She held out her arms and the baby came to her. She cuddled the small, warm body close. Her heart ached because this child she loved so much was miserable.

At that moment the door opened and Jon came in holding the chart. He saw her with the baby and stopped, staring at her with the strangest expression on his face. Then he noticed Marina who stood up and moved beside Dawn.

"Hi. I'm Dr. Clifton—Jon." He held out his hand.

Marina took it. "I've heard a lot about you. All of it good."

"That's nice to hear. Tell me what's going on with Sydney." He nodded thoughtfully when her sister ticked off the symptoms. After setting the chart on the counter he said, "Let's have a look at her."

Dawn knew that meant putting her on the exam table, but when she tried the baby started crying really hard. "Oh, baby girl, we just want to help you feel better."

"It's all right. I can get what I need if you hold her."
With the stethoscope he listened to her back. "Now if you
could turn her around, I'll listen to her chest and look in
her ears."

"Right." Dawn was able to put the baby's back to her
front without a major meltdown and Marina held one of
her tiny hands.

Jon moved close and she could feel the warmth of his
body, the masculine scent of his skin. Her heart was going
a mile a minute and if he had that stethoscope to her chest,
he would know exactly how his nearness affected her. But
this was about Sydney and she watched for his reactions
as he looked and listened. She knew him now, whether or
not he was concerned about something serious.

When he took the otoscope and checked both her ears,
he nodded slightly in a way that meant the mystery was
solved. He straightened and looked at Marina. "No wonder
she's an unhappy little girl. It's a bilateral ear infection."

"What does that mean?" Her sister looked anxious. "I
get the infection part, but—"

"Bilateral just means it's in both ears," he explained.

She didn't look any less worried. "What do I do?"

Apparently Jon heard the note of panic in her voice because he smiled his most reassuring smile. Dawn didn't
know if it worked on her sister, but it sure did on her. It
made her weak in the knees.

"This is common and very treatable," he said. "I'll write
a prescription for a liquid antibiotic which will fix her right
up. And I'll check her again in two weeks."

The worry in Marina's eyes was a little less intense.

"I'll make an appointment before I leave," she assured him.

He nodded. "I'll leave the prescription with her chart at
the front desk. Pick it up when you check out."

"I will."

"You have a beautiful little girl," he said, smiling at the baby who was studying him with wide blue eyes.

"Thank you. I think so, too."

"It was nice to meet you, Marina." He shook her hand again, then left the room.

Her sister looked puzzled. "That's weird."

"Not really. Ear infections are common in kids."

"Not that." The baby started to fuss and Marina took her. "He examined my daughter, who was in your arms, and managed not to look at you even once. What's that about?"

That was about sex and the fact that they shouldn't have done it. "Oh, I think your imagination is working overtime."

"I've had practically no sleep. Trust me, nothing in my body is working overtime." Marina thought for a moment. "Nope, you could cut the tension in this room with a butter knife. Again I ask—what's up, sis?"

Dawn sighed and leaned back against the exam table. "I don't know why I thought you wouldn't pick up on it. People here at work have noticed the change in the air."

"How do you know?" Marina swayed back and forth as the baby dozed off in her arms.

"Callie and Lorajean said something."

"Who?"

"Lorajean Quinn, the new nurse. She said the two of us were acting as if we'd unfriended each other on Facebook."

"What happened? I thought things were fine after you two cleared the air."

"Have you talked to Mom today?"

Marina shook her head. "Why?"

"Because she gave me the third degree last night. Dad was there and—"

"Since when did you start calling him *Dad*?" The baby started at the sharp tone and her sister made apologetic shushing sounds. "You said hell would freeze over before that happened."

"Well, don't look now, but it's getting a little cold." Dawn wouldn't have thought it possible that her attitude toward Hank would change but he'd kept every promise he made to Glory. And talking to him about Jon had helped.

"How? Why?"

As much as she didn't want to talk about this, she knew her sister wouldn't drop the subject until a satisfactory response was provided. She was a teacher and a stubborn redhead. So here it was. "I slept with Jon and Dad offered to beat him up for me."

Marina blinked, then shook her head. "For sure I'm sleep deprived and not firing on all cylinders, but I fail to see why Hank would offer to beat up the doctor for you. Did Jon not do it right?"

"No, he was fairly awesome." She felt heat creeping up her neck and into her cheeks. "It's about what happened after."

With the baby sound asleep in her arms, Marina wearily lowered herself into the chair. "I'm not following."

"The clinic was crazy and I didn't eat lunch. He insisted on feeding me."

"Well, that explains everything. By all means let's string him up by his thumbs."

"You don't understand."

"Not for lack of trying. More details would help. You sound like the one who's been up all night."

That wasn't far from the truth, Dawn thought. Jon had been on her mind, making sleep difficult to come by. And when she finally managed to nod off, dreams with him as the star were not very restful.

"Okay. From the top," she said. "After he kissed me we came to an agreement."

"And that was?"

"We decided it would be best if we just stayed friends."

"Even though the attraction is mutual?" Marina asked.

"Yes."

"You're my sister and you know I love you, right? But I think maybe you need therapy." Marina rubbed the baby's back. "He's a doctor so probably brighter than the average guy. He's nice. Likes kids, obviously. And—I just met him so I can verify this information personally—he's gorgeous. What is wrong with this picture?"

"He's a coworker. We work closely together and if things got weird—" Dawn lifted one shoulder in a shrug.

"Don't look now, but things are weird. You've got nothing to lose now by exploring a relationship."

Dawn took a breath. "He's leaving in a year."

"That's a long time. A lot can happen."

A lot had happened in the last couple of weeks and she'd ended up in his bed after swearing she wouldn't. Maybe they could ride out the weirdness, although judging by today a year might not be long enough.

"The thing is," she said, "we talked about it after."

"Oh, no. The dreaded postsex conversation. That's never good."

"Wish I could be the exception to that, but sadly I'm not." Dawn folded her arms across her waist. "I told him not to be concerned. That I knew it didn't mean anything."

"Please tell me he said you were wrong," Marina begged.

She shook her head. "So, I said we should just go back to the way things were."

"Oh, sweetie, that would be like trying to get glue back into the bottle."

"Tell me about it. You saw for yourself how strained things are."

"Give it time," her sister advised. "Things were uncomfortable between you in the beginning, too, and you worked through it. Follow your heart."

Her heart wanted him, so doing that could send her straight back into his arms. "I'm not going to chase him. I can't."

A move like that would only lead to rejection and another one from Jon could destroy not just her heart but her career.

Jon gathered plates and helped clear the table in Will's kitchen. "Dinner was really good, Jordyn Leigh."

She was a pretty blue-eyed blonde and completely unaware of her looks which was a big part of her charm. "Thank you, Jon. I appreciate that you want to help clean up, but please just sit and enjoy hanging out with your brothers."

Craig and Rob were visiting from Thunder Canyon and their sister-in-law had cooked for all of them. Jon realized he hadn't had a meal cooked by someone besides himself since the night he'd brought Dawn her cell phone and ended up invited to dinner with her parents. The memory made him acutely miss her playful teasing, the way she used to smile at him. The way it was before they slept together.

"Earth to Jon." That was Will's voice.

"Hmm?"

"Hey, Professor, you have a weird look on your face." Craig was studying him.

"I do?" Of course he did. Because it felt as if his life was screwed up. And by that he meant work, since he had no personal life. There was a brief glimpse of one with Dawn but now…not so much.

"There's that look again. What's up?" asked Rob, the youngest.

"You guys are full of it." Jon had to stop thinking about Dawn. These guys knew him too well. He glared around the table and gave each one a look that said back off.

"Does this brooding have anything to do with Dawn Laramie spending the night?" Will asked.

"What?" Jordyn Leigh stopped scrubbing the roasting pan and half turned toward them. "Dawn was here overnight?"

Jon squirmed. "Well, she—"

"Not you. That question was actually for my husband." She sounded a little put out. "You knew about this and didn't say anything to me? Your loving and supportive wife?"

Now Will was squirming. "Sweetheart—"

"Don't sweetheart me. I didn't think we kept secrets from each other."

"We don't," Will agreed. "But this wasn't my secret to share. It was Jon's."

"You're absolutely right." Jordyn Leigh smiled. "Okay, now you can call me sweetheart."

"And I'll be calling you butthead." Jon glared at her husband. "What the heck? You keep my private information to yourself, then drop it in casual conversation with Craig and Rob?"

"Don't forget Jordyn Leigh," Craig reminded him.

How could he forget? If this got out and the rumor mill spread it all over Rust Creek Falls, Dawn might think he'd told someone. She would never understand or forgive him. And that's when he realized just how important she'd become to him.

"Jon?" Jordyn Leigh had a sweet, sympathetic expression on her face. "I want you to know that I won't say anything to anyone about this."

"Thanks." What was it about women that they could read minds?

"Well," Rob piped up, "I'm not making any promises."

"If you breathe a word," Jon vowed, "I'll get even. You won't know when, where or how but there will be retribution."

"I'm scared," his youngest brother taunted.

"Don't worry." Jordyn Leigh dried her hands on a dish towel, then folded it and calmly set it beside the stainless steel sink. Then she gave them all a warning look. "He won't say anything."

"How can you be so sure?" Jon asked.

"Because Cliftons were raised to be gentlemen and would never deliberately do anything to humiliate or embarrass a woman." She met Rob's gaze and he squirmed. "Would you?"

"Not now." For a moment he looked properly chastised, and then he grinned. It was his patented smile, the one that charmed women and practically had them throwing their panties at him. "Don't worry, Professor, she's right. I would embarrass you in a hot minute, but never a lady."

"All right, then." Jon gave his sister-in-law a grateful look, and asked her, "Want to share the secret of how you got my little brother to surrender?"

"I work at Country Kids Day Care." She glanced at each of them, one by one. "You all were acting like children so I treated you the same way I would squabbling three-year-olds. You're a pediatrician, Jon. I should think you would know that."

"It's a different skill set." He shrugged.

"Right." She nodded, then raised one eyebrow, a look guaranteed to intimidate a roomful of unruly toddlers and grown men. "Now, I'm going to leave you guys alone to catch up. Behave yourselves."

"Yes, ma'am," Craig, Rob and Jon said together.

"Don't worry about us, sweetheart." But there was a twinkle in Will's eyes to let her know when she left the room all bets were off.

"I love you." She bent and kissed him. "Rob, Craig, I'll see you in the morning. Jon, don't let them get to you."

"I think you took care of that. Good night, Jordyn Leigh. And thanks again for dinner."

"You're welcome."

"Who wants another beer?" Will asked when they were alone. He got three affirmatives and pulled four longnecks out of the refrigerator, then sat down again. "So, do you want to talk about the pretty nurse?"

Since Jon was the only one of them with a passing acquaintance to a pretty nurse, he was fairly sure that question was directed to him. "If I say no?"

Craig twisted off the cap on his beer. "Seriously? Have you met us? We will hound you without mercy until you crack."

"Because that's how you roll." Jon knew his brothers had his back always. They would do anything for family. Behind that joking around and the relentless ribbing was a deep and protective love. Not one of them would hurt him or stand by if someone else did.

Where Dawn was concerned, he had tried to prevent a situation and his rational plan hadn't worked out so well. These three would go to the grave with whatever he told them and he really could use someone to talk to about this.

"I like Dawn." Three pairs of identical blue eyes stared

expectantly at him, waiting for more. "There's a mutual attraction between us."

"Come on, Professor." Rob rested his forearms on the table and turned the beer bottle in his hands. "Why can't you just say it like a normal guy? You're hot for her and she's hot for you."

"That's what I just said." Jon took a sip of his beer.

"Not exactly, but let's move on." Craig used his I'm-the-oldest-so-I'll-take-charge tone. "She spent the night with you and I'm going to go out on a limb here and guess that you didn't play cards."

"Not unless it was strip poker," Rob chimed in.

"Like your sister-in-law said, raised to be a gentleman." What happened with Dawn was personal and Jon intended to keep it that way. Besides, the point of talking to them was to figure out what was going on now. Each of them had more experience with women than him and he could use their perspective. "I neither confirm nor deny."

"Okay, we'll go with a yes on that," Rob said. "And yet there's still that weird look on your face. Why is that?"

Jon stared at his little brother. "Since when did you get so insightful?"

"I have my moments."

"Not many," Craig said, "so we should mark this day on the calendar and organize a parade in his honor."

Jon knew the remark was meant to cut the tension, lighten the moment with humor. He appreciated the effort.

"Since she spent the night, shall we say, she's been acting strangely. I thought we were on the same page as far as not getting serious, and everything was fine. But she's—" He didn't quite know how to phrase it.

"She's got her scrubs in a twist?" Craig finished for him.

"Yes. But I don't know what's going on." He looked at Rob. "Apparently you're the insightful one. What should I do?"

"Stop trying."

"Not possible. We work together," Jon persisted.

"All the more reason." Craig's voice had a "duh" qual-ity to it. "Back off. Be professional. She'll work through it and everything will go back to normal."

"He's right." Rob pretended to look surprised that those words had come out of his mouth. "Where Craig is con-cerned, I don't believe I've ever said that before. Another parade."

"What he's trying to say," Craig interrupted, "is keep it fun. Women shouldn't have to be so much trouble."

But that's the thing. Jon didn't think of Dawn as trouble. She was smart, funny, easy to be with. They'd had some-thing special. And now they didn't. And he missed her.

He looked at Will. "What do you think?"

"In my humble opinion you should disregard everything these two said. I used to think just like them. Then Jordyn Leigh and I got married."

Jon remembered Dawn's disapproval at the way he'd carelessly talked about his brother's sudden marriage. How someone doesn't do anything they don't really want to. "Was it an accident?"

"At first we thought so, then we realized we were in love." He glared at the mocking sounds his other brothers made and dared them to contradict him. "You two haven't met the right women yet. We'll talk when you do. Trust me, it's pretty awesome."

"Whatever." Rob waved his hand dismissively. "I'm telling you Dawn will get over it."

Will shook his head. "And I say leave yourself open to possibilities."

"Okay. Good talk," Jon said.

Honestly, he was more confused than ever. He and Dawn had determined there was no possibility for something serious between them and yet they couldn't keep their hands off each other. But what if she got over it and moved on? It was amazing how much he hated the thought of that.

Chapter Fourteen

It was Saturday and Dawn should have been relieved at the prospect of a time-out from the awkwardness of seeing Jon. But the truth was that she missed him. Two days without a guaranteed sighting of the hunky doctor depressed her. He was like that guy in high school you had a crush on. The one who made you want to get out of bed and go to class. There was no hope that he'd notice you in a special way, but the adrenaline rush of seeing him filled your heart and was enough. The truth was she looked forward to even a passing glance, a hurried conversation. Being in the same room. Since that feeling showed no sign of waning any time soon, she hoped her sister was right and they would get past their differences again.

Not only was it Saturday, this was also designated grocery shopping day and she pulled into the parking lot at Crawford's. After getting out of her compact she walked to the store's automatic doors. They opened up and not because she'd triggered the censor. Jon came through them. Déjà vu all over again.

The two of them stared at each other for a moment, and then both started talking at once.

"You first," Jon said, ever the gentleman.

"So, you're grocery shopping."

"I wish." His face was drawn and full of tension.

"What's wrong?" she asked. Then she noticed the stack of papers in his hands. "What's going on?"

"Rerun is missing. These are flyers with information in case anyone spots him."

"How did he get out?" She'd seen for herself that Jon was a conscientious pet parent and very protective of his dog.

"Will came by this morning and apparently didn't shut the front door all the way when he left. My guess is the little scoundrel managed to nudge it open. I don't even know when he got out or how long he's been gone. I looked all over the ranch and couldn't find him." His mouth pulled tight for a moment, and then he held up the papers. "I'm going to distribute these around town. It was all I could think of to do."

Dawn could see how worried he was. The normally cool-under-pressure doc was upset and her heart went out to him. She had to do something. "I'll help you look."

His face brightened for a second, but the expression disappeared and he shook his head. "You're here for groceries. I can't ask you to give up your Saturday for me."

She would give up a lot more than that for him.

The thought was suddenly just there and worse, it was completely true. If she was baring her soul to a shrink she'd put money on the fact that her feelings were way more than she wanted them to be. But this wasn't the time to analyze.

"Look, two pairs of eyes are better than one," she said

practically. "And even if I couldn't help with the looking, you could use the moral support."

"No question, but—"

"No buts. I may not have the same emotional investment in Rerun that you do, but I care about him, too." She gave him a look that dared him to tell her no. "I'm going to look for him—with or without you."

Gratitude brimmed in his eyes just before he impulsively pulled her into his arms. "Thanks."

"Don't mention it."

Did that response come out as breathless as she thought? Didn't much matter since she couldn't take it back. And, darn it, his arms felt so good. Being held, even for a moment, was wonderful. And a moment was all it was because he seemed to come to his senses and remember that this was forbidden.

He stepped away and again they stared into each other's eyes before he cleared his throat. "So, we need to get going." He held up the flyers.

"Should I follow you in my car?"

"It's probably better to go together."

"Okay."

Dawn fell into step beside him, then climbed into the passenger side of his truck. "Actually, having me along will save you time."

"How do you figure?"

"We'll do a drive-by and I can jump out and run a flyer into the building for you."

"Actually I'd prefer to stop the truck long enough for you to safely step out and do that," he said wryly.

"I thought that was implied. You're very literal."

"Yeah. It's a flaw."

"You could have worse," she pointed out. "Like being a slob."

"How do you know I'm not?"

"Are you?" She didn't think so. Both times she'd unexpectedly been to his house the place had been neat as a pin.

"Does leaving my coffee cup in the sink count?" he asked.

"I think that's a forgivable flaw." At least they were talking and teasing. It felt good. Returning to a state of frigid politeness wasn't an appealing thought. If friendship was all he could give, it would have to be enough. She'd rather have that than nothing.

Jon turned right out of the store parking lot onto North Main, then left on Sawmill Street. He stopped in front of the Dalton Law Office. "Might be closed on Saturday, but—"

"I'll check it out."

She slid out of the truck and went to try the front door. It was open and the attached bell sounded, but there was no one at the reception desk.

Lindsay Dalton walked through the doorway leading to the back offices. A former classmate of Dawn's, she was an attorney now, like her father, Ben. She was a pretty, blue-eyed brunette with her hair pulled into a sassy ponytail. The look suited her personality. In her jeans and T-shirt she looked more like a first-year college student than a high-powered legal eagle.

"Hi, Lindsay. Didn't think anyone would be here on the weekend."

"Work to catch up on." She slid her fingertips into the pockets of her worn jeans. "Do you have a legal problem I can help with?"

"I have problems, but not legal, thank goodness." She held out a flyer with Rerun's picture on it and the number to call if he was spotted. "I'm helping Jon—Dr. Clifton— look for his dog."

Lindsay took the paper and scanned it. "Aw, he has three legs."

"Yeah. He's spunky, sweet and adorable."

"You've met him." Lindsay wasn't asking and her look was speculative. "That's right. You work at the clinic. I've heard that your doctor is not hard on the eyes."

"He's not *my* doctor. But you're right. Women would not recoil in horror if they saw him on Main Street."

"So, for once, the rumor is true." The other woman laughed. "I'll put this in the front window. Anything else I can do for you?"

"Like you don't already have enough to do."

"Workaholic, I guess." Lindsay shrugged.

"I don't have anything now, but if I decide to sue someone, you'll be my first phone call." She smiled. "Gotta run. Jon's waiting."

"Good to see you, Dawn."

"Same here." She lifted her hand in a wave, then exited the office and hurried back to the truck idling at the curb. Climbing inside she said, "Lindsay Dalton is going to post it in the window."

"Good." He looked to make sure it was safe before pulling into the two-lane road. "I've been calculating our route. We'll cut down Broomtail Road to the sheriff's office and fire station. Then to Strickland's Boarding House on Cedar Street. Up Buckskin to Rust Creek Garage and Gas Station, then down Sawmill to the Ace in the Hole."

"That about covers it. Good plan."

Jon drove to all the places he'd mentioned and Dawn delivered the flyers. Everyone promised to post the paper and keep an eye out for the dog. Their last stop was the Ace in the Hole and he pulled the truck into the parking lot.

This was where they'd gone to resolve their initial differences and pave the way for a smooth working relationship. It was where he'd first told her about Rerun, where she'd seen glimpses of the caring man he was and gave him the benefit of the doubt. Where she'd confessed that she'd sworn off men, if not officially, then in spirit. This place would always have memories of him and that wasn't necessarily a good thing.

Side by side they walked into the place. It wasn't quite lunchtime so there was no crowd yet. Rosey Traven was filling napkin dispensers in the booths around the room, clearly getting ready for the Saturday rush.

When the squeaky screen door opened, then closed behind them she stopped, looked up and smiled. "Hey, if it isn't Rust Creek Fall's own medical A team."

"Hi, Rosey." Dawn hugged the older woman. "How are you?"

"Can't complain." She thought for a moment. "Well, I could, but no one wants to hear that."

"I do," Jon said. "It's sort of in my job description."

"I'm a little north of the age demographic you specialize in, Doc." Her voice was wry.

"Even so, I'm happy to listen."

"I'll keep that in mind." She looked from one to the other. "You two here for lunch?"

"No," he said, holding out a small stack of flyers. "My dog is missing."

"Sorry to hear that." She glanced at the information. "Poodle–Shih Tzu mix. Poor little thing is missing a leg."

"Yeah. He doesn't exactly blend into the pack." Jon smiled grimly.

"He's probably wandering around Will Clifton's ranch where Jon is staying," Dawn explained. "But just in case he gets this far and someone in town sees him…"

Rosey nodded. "I'll put the word out."

"Thanks," Jon said.

"Glad to help." The other woman looked from one of them to the other. "Can I get you something to eat? On the house?"

"Appreciate the offer," he said. "But I think I'll head back to the ranch and keep looking for him there."

"Okay." She nodded. "If I hear anything I'll let you know. Good luck."

"Thanks."

Dawn really felt for him. She knew Jon and Rerun had a strong bond and if anything happened to the little guy he would be devastated. "I'll go back to the ranch with you and help. If you want."

He looked down at her and there was something in his face, a dark intensity that she sensed wasn't entirely about his missing pet. "I'd like that very much."

"Okay, then."

As they reached the truck his cell phone rang. Maybe someone had seen Rerun, she thought hopefully.

"Dr. Clifton," he said after hitting the talk icon.

Dawn was standing on the other side of the truck but could see his face over the hood. His expression turned grim. The last time she'd seen him look this way was when the clinic had been slammed with sick babies.

"I'm in Rust Creek Falls. I'll meet you at the clinic," he said, his voice professional but serious. "Get her there as quickly as you can."

"What is it?" Dawn asked.

"That was Heather Marshall. The baby is not good." He unlocked the truck and got in.

"I'll go with you," she offered after climbing inside.

"I was going to ask," he admitted. "Since you're here."

This was not the way Dawn had expected her day off to go. Seeing Jon, putting their office awkwardness on hold had been a nice surprise. But a lost dog and a seriously ill baby were not the way she would have wanted it to happen.

At least he hadn't shut her out. That was something, right?

The Marshalls were waiting outside the clinic when Jon and Dawn drove into the parking lot. He turned off the ignition and looked over at her.

"I'm glad you're here."

"I'll do whatever I can to help," she said.

"That's why I'm glad you're here."

She could read the body language of the worried parents and her heart went out to them. "Let's go."

Quickly they walked to the clinic door where the young couple stood. Pete Marshall had a white-knuckle grip on the infant carrier. "Thank you for coming, Doctor."

"Of course." Jon unlocked the door and they all went inside. "Follow me."

Dawn flipped on the lights. "I'll get Georgina's chart."

"Thanks. This way," he said to the Marshalls. "We'll be in exam room one."

"Okay." She found the chart, then met everyone in the room.

Heather lifted the baby out of the infant carrier. "Should I take off her shirt?"

"Yes. I'll be right back." He walked out of the room.

"She just can't shake this cold," Heather put the child on the exam table. "We've been doing everything the doctor said. And then this morning—" Her voice caught and she put a hand over her mouth to hold back a sob.

"She'll be okay, honey. We have to believe that." Pete put a comforting arm across her shoulders. "She's going to be fine. Dr. Clifton is going to help her."

"I know." Her voice was shaky but she managed a nod and put the tears on hold.

Jon came back into the room with his stethoscope and read the notes from her recent visit to the clinic. He looked at Heather then listened to the baby's chest. As he did she described the symptoms. There was a worried look in his eyes and Dawn knew why. During her time in the hospital she'd seen and cared for babies who looked like this. The child's breathing was too rapid and there was a tinge of blue to her lips. Her lungs were compromised and she was having difficulty taking in enough oxygen.

He straightened and looked at the parents. "This is RSV."

"I thought she had a cold," Pete said.

"It has the same symptoms," Jon explained.

Heather had one hand on her baby and with the other gripped her husband's fingers. "You can give her a different prescription, right?"

"She needs to be transported to the closest medical facility with a Level I pediatric trauma center and ICU."

"That would be Mountain's Edge Hospital," Dawn said. "It's excellent. I used to work there."

"Okay." Pete was doing his best to stay calm but he was clearly on the edge. "We'll drive her—"

"It's an hour away." Jon's voice was firm but calm, not wanting to alarm the already scared parents. "I'm going to call for a care flight helicopter."

"Is she going to be okay? Please tell me she'll be all right," Heather begged.

There was a dark, troubled expression in his eyes. He wanted to say yes, but Dawn knew he couldn't tell them something he didn't know. "Everything possible will be done for your baby."

Jon left to make the arrangements and Dawn did what

she could to reassure the parents. But the doctor needed her, too.

She found Jon in his office talking on the phone. He stood with his back to her and she looked at his wide shoulders and listened to his deep, calm voice. He was such a good man, the kind who would be there for the people he loved. What a concept, she thought. A man who stayed.

"Okay," he said. "We'll be waiting." He put the phone down and turned, then leaned a hip on his desk. "The chopper is on the way."

"Good." She moved closer, stopping by the visitor chairs on the other side of the desk. "Heather and Pete are really scared."

"I know. Who can blame them?" He dragged his fingers through his hair. "I almost intubated her."

"Yeah, I could tell you were thinking about that. She's a very sick little girl. Why did you decide not to?"

"Because she should be in a hospital for a procedure like that where there's a ventilator to take the stress off her breathing and respiratory therapists to monitor it. It would help her rest and gather the reserves to fight this. I want a CAT scan. And sophisticated equipment that's not available here." Anger crept into his voice. "Damn it. This town needs more. You know as well as I do that with any trauma there's a golden hour, sixty minutes when medical intervention can save a life. We just don't have what we need here in the clinic."

"I know. But we're getting there." She badly wanted to touch him, somehow transfuse him with her own hope. "But until we have a hospital and more sophisticated equipment, it's all the more reason to have a dedicated, knowledgeable, caring staff like we're building right now."

He straightened away from the desk and looked down for a moment. When he met her gaze again his eyes were blazing with the fire of frustration. "Sometimes you can't do anything to stop a kid from dying. Call it God's will, fate, whatever helps you sleep at night."

"Jon—"

"Other times, with the right machine, the perfect diagnostic test, even medication administered quickly, you can spare parents the heartbreak of losing their child." He shook his head. "Those are the ones that keep me awake. The ones who could have been helped with the right stuff."

"You're thinking about the child who died unexpectedly," she guessed.

He nodded. "And you're going to remind me that it happened in a hospital with all the bells and whistles a health care facility can provide."

She had been, but didn't confirm that. This was his crisis of conscience, so to speak. It had been eating away at him and he needed to get everything out.

"I don't blame myself, if that's what you're thinking. But it affected me in a deep, profound way. Medical school teaches you anatomy and how to treat sick people but there are no courses or strategies for not becoming attached to your patients. I took a job that didn't allow me to form attachments or a long-term doctor-patient bond. But I became a doctor to help people and that's what I'm going to do."

Little Georgina Marshall had pushed all his hero buttons and snapped him back from a place where he'd been healing himself. This was a good thing; he was a gifted doctor. But Dawn couldn't help feeling as if she was the one losing out.

The distant sound of mechanical rotors drifted closer. Jon looked up and stated the obvious. "Chopper's almost here."

"Yeah. I'll go get the Marshalls ready."

He nodded. "I'm going with Georgina. Just in case she takes a bad turn and needs to be intubated before we can get her to the hospital."

"I figured you would." *Because that's what a good, caring, dedicated doctor would do*, Dawn thought. "I'll let Emmet know to take the calls until you're available."

"Thanks."

They were outside when the helicopter set down on the helipad in the clinic parking lot. Dawn stood a safe distance away and watched as Heather and the baby stepped in, followed by Jon. Due to space limitations Pete would drive to the hospital.

When everyone was onboard the door closed and the blades of the chopper picked up speed, stirring the wind. It blew the hair around Dawn's face and scattered the shattered pieces of her heart all to hell.

She was glad that Jon had reconciled what had happened in the past with his lifelong calling to be a healer. But she was pretty sure the message he was taking away from his time at the clinic in Rust Creek Falls was not the best one for her. He was going to leave this town behind in favor of a state-of-the-art hospital where he believed he could help more kids get better and make a bigger difference.

There was no way to make him see that he'd already made a tremendous difference in Rust Creek Falls.

And to her.

Because she was in love with him.

Too bad she figured that out at the same time she realized he wouldn't stay for her.

Chapter Fifteen

Dawn locked up the clinic after the chopper was gone with Jon and the baby. It was difficult to be left behind when one was so accustomed to helping. She could only wait for Jon's call when he had news about baby Georgina's condition. Now she should get back to her routine, even though she had the sinking feeling that nothing about her life would ever be routine again.

Having left her car in Crawford's parking lot, she walked back to the store on foot to complete her grocery shopping. A benefit of living in a small town.

She grabbed a basket out front and took it inside. That's when she realized a lot had happened in a few short hours. The awkwardness between her and Jon had dissipated after joining forces to look for his dog. And Dawn had realized she was in love with him.

"Dawn? Hi."

She looked up at the familiar voice. And this was the

downside of small town living, not being able to go to the store without running into someone you knew. "Lorajean. Hi."

The older woman looked at her closely and frowned. "Are you okay?"

"Of course. Why?"

"Seemed as if you were somewhere else and would have walked right on by me without saying a word."

"Sorry. It's been a weird morning."

"Speaking of that... Do you happen to know anything about that helicopter that flew in and out of here a little while ago?" Her sharp brown eyes could be warm and welcoming, or sometimes wary. But always perceptive. This woman did not miss much.

"I guess the whole town heard it," Dawn hedged.

"Pretty hard to miss, what with all that racket." The other woman leaned a forearm on the handle of her basket, settling in for a response.

Dawn thought about her answer, acutely aware of patient privacy. "Jon called care flight to transport a patient to Mountain's Edge Hospital."

"Georgina Marshall." Lorajean nodded. "I ran into Wendy Crane, a friend of Heather's, and she told me the baby wasn't getting better. That Pete and Heather were going to call Jon."

"Whoever came up with those privacy laws did not live in Rust Creek Falls." Dawn sighed. "And by that statement I neither confirm nor deny what you just said."

"Fair enough." The other woman met her gaze. "Did Jon go with Georgina?"

"He accompanied the patient, yes."

"So you were at the clinic with him."

"His dog is missing and I helped him hand out flyers

around town. I was there when he got the call and went to the clinic with him."

And he'd told her he was glad she was there. Because he knew she would do everything she could to help. That was professional, not personal, no matter how much she might wish it could be.

"What's wrong, Dawn?" Lorajean was studying her. "Before you try to tell me nothing, you should know I have keen powers of observation. Something is going on with you and unless I miss my guess, which almost never happens, it's about Jon."

They were standing in the canned food aisle blocking both lanes and someone was behind Lorajean. Dawn moved her basket, partly to be polite, but mostly to stall for time. She could dodge the direct question but didn't think the other woman would take no for an answer. She could come up with something.

"You're right. It is about Jon. I'm afraid he's going to leave Rust Creek Falls."

"What makes you say that?"

"He was pretty upset about the clinic's lack of sophisticated equipment and resources, not to mention the hospital being so far away."

"All the more reason to have good, competent medical staff on-site," Lorajean pointed out.

"That's what I told him, but it didn't seem to make a difference."

The other woman nodded thoughtfully. "Don't jump to conclusions."

"You didn't see how angry and concerned he was."

"No, but I see the way he looks at you." The expression in Lorajean's eyes was daring her to deny it.

"I don't know what that means. Could be he wants to choke me because I annoy him and test his patience. Or..."

Dawn was afraid to say it out loud. It wouldn't take much for false hope to dig in and that would make his leaving a lot harder to get over.

"Or he's lusting after you." Lorajean nodded for emphasis.

"The choking me because he's annoyed one is easier to believe."

"It is if you're planning to keep trying to hide what you feel. Take it from someone who knows, Dawn, you'll be sorry if you don't fight for what you want." The woman's smile was meant to ease tension, but there was some regret in it, too. "Now that I've stuck my nose in where I shouldn't, it's time for me to get my shopping done. My gray roots have a standing appointment at Bee's Beauty Parlor."

"Okay." The other woman started to turn away, but Dawn said, "Lorajean?"

"What?"

"Thanks for talking to me. And you didn't stick your nose in. Well, maybe a little but that's what friends do."

"You're sweet to say that. See you Monday."

"Bright and early," Dawn confirmed.

Her mind buzzed with what Lorajean had said, but Dawn managed to finish the shopping. She was certain that after taking the groceries home she would think of something important that she forgot.

But after getting home and putting everything away all she could think about was why Jon hadn't called with an update on Georgina Marshall. Dawn paced for a while, then noticed a piece of paper sticking out of her purse on the kitchen counter. It was one of the flyers Jon had made up about his lost dog.

She couldn't do anything for the sick baby but she could help by continuing the search for Rerun.

It was late afternoon when she got to the ranch and drove through the open gate with an arch over it that said Flying C. The main compound consisted of Will and Jordyn Leigh's house, the foreman's cottage which was where Will lived, the bunkhouse, barn and corrals. There was a series of fenced pastures close by.

She parked in front of the little house and got out of her car. There was no welcoming bark from inside and she could picture the worried look that would be on Jon's face if he was here.

His brother's truck was parked up at the house and before she beat the bushes, literally, it might be a good idea to check with Will and Jordyn Leigh, to see if the dog had returned. She walked up the hill, admiring the white-sided farmhouse with the blue shutters bracketing the upstairs windows. She stepped onto the wraparound porch and knocked on the front door.

Seconds later Will opened it. He didn't seem surprised to see her. "Dawn. Hi."

She lifted a hand in greeting. "Hey, Will. I ran into Jon in town and he said Rerun is missing—"

Just then she heard a high-pitched yipping coming from inside. She smiled at Jon's brother. "Is that who I think it is?"

"If you're thinking it's that rebellious rat dog, you'd be right."

The scoundrel in question appeared in the doorway, then danced over to her and put its one front paw up on her leg. Dawn dropped to one knee and scooped the disheveled creature into her arms, laughing when he licked her face.

"You little stinker. Do you have any idea how worried we were about you?" She looked up at Will. "Did he come home?"

"That would have been too easy." The man who looked

so much like Jon grinned down at her. "This little mutt doesn't work that way. I was out riding fences and found him wandering around. Either he lost his way or wasn't ready to stop chasing rabbits yet."

Dawn rubbed Rerun's back. The hair was matted and had stuff stuck in it. She scratched his chin. "Your dad is going to be very happy to know you're okay."

"Speaking of Jon… Where is he? I texted him about Rerun turning up."

"Good. He'll be glad to know that." She met his brother's gaze. "There was an emergency. He's with a patient at the hospital."

Will nodded. "Kid couldn't be in better hands."

"No question." She stood and grinned at the dog who was whining for more of her attention. "This guy seems okay."

"Yeah. He was thirsty and dirty, but I couldn't find anything wrong with him." Will shook his head. "I hate to leave him here alone, but Jordyn Leigh and I are meeting friends at the Ace in the Hole."

Without thinking it through Dawn said, "I'll clean him up and feed him."

Will's mouth curved up in a knowing smile. "Jon will be glad to see you when he gets home."

Lorajean's words came to mind as Dawn carried the dog back to the guesthouse. Maybe this was her fighting for what she wanted.

It was late when Jon was nearing the ranch. There was an almost full moon in the sky, bathing the landscape in a warm silver glow. But he wasn't feeling the usual wonder of the Montana scenery. All he could think about was Dawn and the hurt and disappointment on her face when he'd taken out his frustration on her. If he could delete what he'd said, he would do it in a heartbeat. That had been hours ago and he had no idea what she'd been thinking since then but it couldn't be good.

The truck's dashboard clock said it was midnight when he finally saw the Flying C arch and passed beneath it. Home at last. Sleep should have been his top priority but all he could think about was calling Dawn to explain and apologize. But it was too late to bother her.

He got closer to the guesthouse and saw a little compact car there. Exhaustion must be making him hallucinate because that couldn't be her car. It was a manifestation of how badly he wanted to see her. But when he stopped and parked, the vehicle hadn't disappeared.

Dawn was here.

He got out and heard a familiar welcoming bark that told him Rerun was here, too. Suddenly the door opened and the two of them stood there. Then the dog ran to him and Jon dropped to one knee on the porch for the rub and scratch ritual. This time the animal got a few extra rubs and scratches because when Jon had left here earlier he hadn't been sure he would ever see his dog again. He'd gotten Will's message, but it was a relief to see for himself that Rerun was okay.

"Hey, buddy. You gave me quite a scare. I'd appreciate it if you never do that again." He laughed when Rerun rolled onto his back, a clear request for a belly rub. Of course he obliged. What better way to teach his pet a lesson than by rewarding bad behavior?

Then the animal rolled back onto his three legs and ran to Dawn, as if to say, "Look who's here."

Jon stood and met her gaze, profoundly moved by the sight of her. She was, hands down, the most beautiful woman he'd ever seen. And all he could think to say to her was, "Hi."

She smiled a greeting. "I got your text that Georgina was going to be okay."

"Yeah. She's responding to treatment protocols and breathing easier. She's resting comfortably now and is in the excellent hands of the pediatric pulmonologist who says she will be just fine."

"Thank goodness." She blew out a long breath, then bent down to pick up the dog who was looking up at her expectantly. Instantly he relaxed in her arms.

Lucky dog, Jon thought. "Yeah. The Marshalls are understandably relieved."

"I can imagine." Absently she brushed her hand over Rerun's head. "The last I saw of you was your back as you climbed into a helicopter. Your truck was at the clinic. How did you get home?"

"Pete Marshall. When his daughter stabilized, he and Heather decided that she would sleep in the baby's hospital room and he'd drive to Rust Creek Falls to get her a few things. They'll probably be there for a day or two and he'll go back first thing in the morning. I hitched a ride back with him. He dropped me at the clinic to get my truck."

"Good."

"Yeah. Otherwise I'd have had to call Will for a ride home."

"Or me." Her voice was soft and there was something in her eyes. Something exciting that he hadn't dared hope to see again.

"I don't want to talk about carpooling."

"No?"

He shook his head. "I'd rather talk about why you're here." Then it sank in how that sounded and he wished words were his thing. "Not that I'm complaining about you being here. Because I'm not. It's just... I was wondering about you being in the house."

"For one thing, the door was unlocked."

"Yeah, we don't have many break-ins this far out." He took a step closer and could almost feel the softness of her skin. The scent of her drifted to him and settled around his heart, making it even harder to put his thoughts into the right words and form a coherent sentence. "What I meant was, why did you come out here and wait for me?"

"I was looking after Rerun. Why do you think?" She tilted her head to the side, a challenge in her eyes.

Okay. She wasn't going to make this easy on him. "The truth is that I'm not very good with the personal stuff. Which you may have already realized. But if I don't tell you how I feel my head just might explode."

Sympathy and amusement swirled together in her expression and she tsked. "Can't have that. So, spit it out, Doctor. How do you feel?"

He took a deep breath. "It's been a rough day."

"No kidding."

"First my dog ran away and then seeing that baby so sick…" He hesitated. "You'd think being a doctor I would instinctively get this, but—"

"What?" she encouraged.

"I've been avoiding feeling anything for so long that I forgot something pretty basic. Today I was reminded how short life can be. We waste too much time making excuses to keep people at a distance to protect ourselves because of what might happen."

"Go on," she urged.

"Look, Dawn, I know you've seen too many examples of men who are selfish and unsupportive. Men who use others to get what they want. I don't expect you to trust me, but—"

She shook her head. "Hold it right there. Because I have

known those men, one who isn't that way stands out like a fly in milk."

He knew she meant that in a good way but couldn't resist. "So, I'm a fly? Should I be offended?"

"It's late. That's the best figure of speech I could come up with. Trust me, Jon, you've shown me in every way that you're the kind of man a woman can count on."

"I'm glad you know that."

When the dog started squirming she put him down. "You can count on me, too."

"Not a doubt in my mind." He reached for her but she moved back.

"We're dancing around this," she said. "Before anything more happens or something is said that can't be taken back, I have to state the obvious. Our circumstances haven't changed. We still work together. Taking this—you and me—" she motioned to him, then herself "—to the next level could impact things if what we have goes south."

He moved close again and took her hands to keep her from backing away. "I have two things to say about that. First, we're professionals and the fact that we're so aware of what could happen to the clinic's work environment and care enough to put it before our own personal happiness means that we would never jeopardize it."

"Well said, Doctor." She smiled. "And what's the second thing?"

He raised her left hand and kissed her knuckles. "Nothing bad is going to happen with us."

"You can't know—"

"I can." He squeezed her fingers reassuringly. "You're a special woman. And I'm completely certain that neither of us would let anything get in the way of caring for the people of Rust Creek Falls."

Hope sparkled in her eyes. "Does that mean you're staying?"

"About that…"

Jon remembered what she'd said about being in love. That if you were, there was no leaving at the first bump in the road. The fact that she was here gave him hope, too.

He looked down for a moment, choosing his words carefully. "I was angry because that little girl was sick and I had to wait to help her."

"If not for you and your skill, the intervention she needed could have been delayed too long. Equipment is good, but instinct and decisive action make a difference."

He knew she was right and that wasn't ego. Just a fact. He was trained to know. "Still, what I said… It wasn't my finest hour. The thing is, I was frustrated and I couldn't show it in front of a very worried mom and dad." He met her gaze and willed her to believe him. "But I knew it was safe for you to see what I was feeling. And to understand it."

"That's true. You were safe with me and I do understand." But she still looked uncertain. "I also took it a step further. It seemed as if you wanted to leave, for a better equipped hospital to make a bigger difference."

"I was venting. That's all."

"So, you're going to stay in Rust Creek Falls?" she asked hesitantly.

"Try and get rid of me." He cupped her face in his hands and kissed her, letting his lips say everything he'd held back since the first time he'd seen her. And wanted her. "I love you, Dawn Laramie."

"Very smooth," she said breathlessly against his mouth. "And you're in luck. I love you, too, Dr. Clifton."

They held each other, smiling and savoring this moment. Then Dawn said, "I made a casserole. Are you hungry?"

"Only for you." He didn't wonder how she'd managed to find the ingredients for a casserole because all he could think about was how much he wanted her. He scooped her into his arms and carried her to his bed. "Whatever you made, can we eat it for breakfast? Because it might take all night to have my way with you."

"That works for me."

Everything about Dawn worked for him. He loved coming home to find her waiting. He loved that she cared about his dog as much as he did. He loved the beautiful, caring woman that she was.

And he especially loved loving her, then falling asleep holding her. Rerun curled at the foot of their bed. A contentment he'd never known settled over him, a feeling of how right this was. He'd never truly believed he could have a family until Dawn came along.

He believed it now.

Epilogue

Rust Creek Falls Park—Back-to-school picnic

"That isn't your baby." Homer Gilmore was staring.

Dawn held Sydney a little closer because she wasn't quite sure about this man. After the infamous spiked wedding punch incident it had been determined that he was harmless. Just wanted to play cupid. But that didn't stop her from being glad that Jon was sitting right next to her. When she slid a little closer to him, his arm automatically came around her.

"This is my sister's little girl," she said. "I'm taking care of her while Marina is bonding with her new students and meeting their parents."

The park was crowded with families and it seemed strange that the peculiar loner who'd spiked that punch would be here. But playing cupid when you were older than dirt was pretty strange, so go figure. No one knew his age, but his eccentricity was legendary.

"What's her name?" Homer asked.

"Sydney. This is Homer Gilmore," she said to Jon.

The man pointed a gnarled finger at him. "Who are you?"

"Jon Clifton. I'm a pediatrician." He didn't appear to be the least bit nervous around the man who was, in part, responsible for the town's escalated birth rate. In fact one could argue that Homer had created the need for his services. Job security.

"You're not from around here," the elderly man observed.

"I'm from Thunder Canyon."

Homer nodded as if that made sense. His eyes turned dark as a chunk of coal. "I know that place. DJ's Rib Shack is there."

"It is. Good food, too." Jon sent her a questioning look.

"I plan to put DJ's on the map. Everyone is going to know about it soon." Homer grinned. "I'm gonna sell my moonshine there."

Dawn glanced at Jon and knew he was thinking the same thing she was. It was common knowledge in Rust Creek Falls that Carson Drake had refused to market Homer Gilmore's moonshine through his liquor distribution company. "Oh?"

"Yup. I'll be famous." He looked at the cooing baby again and there was a soft expression in his eyes. "She's a pretty little girl."

"Yes, she is." Dawn glanced at her niece, then back up. But as suddenly as he'd shown up, Homer Gilmore was gone, disappearing into the crowd. "Amazing how a man of his advanced age can move that fast."

"Maybe it's the moonshine," Jon teased.

She kissed the baby's chubby, soft cheek and settled her hands on Sydney's waist as she stood on Dawn's thighs, happily bouncing. "You know, that concoction he cooked up might be a factor in Syd's birth. And I love her very much. Can't imagine life without her. But putting that stuff on the open market seems problematic to me."

"Let me count the ways," Jon said wryly.

"I'm sure there are rules against it," she continued. When he didn't answer right away she glanced at him. He had a weird look on his face. "What?"

"I'm all for rules," he said.

She smiled. "Me, too. Although we nearly missed out on something really special because of trying to follow the rules."

Fortunately they'd come to their senses. She'd moved into the cabin with him until they could find a bigger place. Going to work and coming home together made life practically perfect. Trusting a man and finding happiness with him had always seemed impossible, but she'd been wrong. She couldn't imagine things any better than they already were.

But Jon still had that funny look on his face as he stared at her. "We almost blew it and I don't ever want to lose you."

"You won't," she assured him, but he was still staring at her. "What's wrong?"

"Not a thing. In fact all is right. Everything is clear."

"You sound like the message in a fortune cookie. And I have to ask—why are you looking at me like that?"

He shrugged. "It's just that seeing you hold the baby triggered a realization for me. I just got it—"

"What?" she demanded.

"I want to have a family with you. I want to see you holding *our* child." He stood, then dropped to one knee. "I honestly didn't plan this but it feels exactly right. And in the spirit of not wasting time…"

Dawn was staring at him, but on some level she was aware that all conversation around them had stopped and you could hear a pin drop. The clinic crew was there along with Jon's brother and his wife. She knew her mom and dad were close by and from the corner of her eye saw Marina walk over and stand with them.

She sat Sydney on her lap, looked at Jon and said, "Yes."

"I haven't asked you anything yet." But the corners of his mouth curved up.

"Do you want to marry me or not?" she demanded.

"Yes."

"Okay, then. My answer is yes. Twice."

"I love you, Dawn." He leaned in for a kiss. "I can't wait to make you Mrs. Clifton."

"And I can't wait to be Mrs. Dr. Clifton."

Spontaneous applause broke out around them and even little Sydney clapped her chubby hands, probably imitating what everyone else was doing. Apparently the whole town approved.

But no one could approve more than Dawn. She planned to make this bachelor the happiest married maverick ever.

* * * * *

Don't miss the next installment of the new
Cherish continuity

MONTANA MAVERICKS:
THE BABY BONANZA

When rancher Anderson Dalton suddenly finds
himself daddy to the ten-year-old son he never knew,
a marriage of convenience gives him custody—
and the heart of a local teacher with a baby of her own!

Look for
A MAVERICK AND A HALF
by
USA TODAY *bestselling author*
Marie Ferrarella

On sale September 2016,
wherever Mills & Boon books and ebooks are sold.

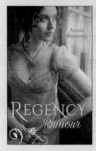

MILLS & BOON®

The Sara Craven Collection!